THE ROOM VANISHED

He was suddenly kneeling on a carpeted floor
that still felt strangely like the padded plastics
of the cell. The lights were dim, the walls expanded into an immense dark chamber of
carven screens and panels of alien design. A
woman in black and diaphanous violet stood
before him, a woman of the Orithain, of the
indigo-skinned iduve race. Her hair was black:
it hung like fine silk, thick and even at the level
of her shapely jaw. Her brows were dark, her
eyes amethyst-hued, without whites, and rimmed
with dark along the edge of the lid. Her nose
was arched but delicate, her mouth sensuous,
frosted with lavender, the whole of her face
framed within the absolute darkness of her hair.

He rose and gave her a proper bow for meeting despite their races. "Who was it who had me
brought here?" he demanded, anger springing
out of his voice to cover his fear. "And why
did you ask for *me*?"

"A matter of honor. You are of birth such
that your loss will be noticed: that has a certain
incidental value. And I have use for such as
you: world-born, but experienced of other
worlds."

He hated her. He said, "You'll regret that
choice."

Her eyes darkened perceptibly. "At the moment you are no more than sentient raw material, and it is useless to attempt rational conversation with you."

And with blinding swiftness the white light
of the cell was about him again.

UNIVERSITY OF WINNIPEG
PORTAGE & BALMORAL
WINNIPEG, MAN.   R3B 2E9
CANADA

Hunter of WORLDS

C. J. Cherryh

DAW BOOKS, INC.
DONALD A. WOLLHEIM, PUBLISHER

1301 Avenue of the Americas
New York, N. Y.   10019

Published by
THE NEW AMERICAN LIBRARY
OF CANADA LIMITED

To my mother, to my
father, and to David.

First DAW printing, August 1977

1 2 3 4 5 6 7 8 9

PRINTED IN CANADA
COVER PRINTED IN U.S.A.

1

HALFWAY THROUGH the second watch the ship put into Kartos Station—the largest thing ever seen in the zone, a gleaming silver agglomeration of vanes cradling an immense saucer body. It was an Orithain craft, with no markings of nationality or identification: the Orithain disdained such conventions.

It nestled in belly-on, larger than the station itself, positioned beside an amaut freighter off Isthe II that was completely dwarfed by its bulk. The umbilical of the tube, the conveyor-connection, went out to it, scarcely long enough to reach, although the Orithain's grapples had drawn herself and the Station into relative proximity.

As soon as that connection was secure, five members of the crew disembarked, four men and a woman. They were kallia, like many of the Station personnel—a race that belonged to Qao V, a tall graceful folk, azure-skinned and silver-haired; but these had never seen the surface of Aus Qao: each bore on the right wrist the platinum bracelet that marked a nas kame, a servant of the Orithain.

The visitors moved at will through the market, where amaut and kalliran commerce linked the civilized worlds, the *metrosi*, with the Esliph stars. They spoke not at all to each other, but paused together and occasionally designated purchases—lots that depleted whole sections of the market, to be delivered immediately.

The moment the Orithain had entered the zone, the Station office had moved into frantic activity. Station security personnel, both kallia and amaut, were scattered among the regular dock crews in diverse uniforms—not to stop the starlords; that was impossible. They were instead to restrain the Station folk from any unintended offense against them, for the whole of Kartos Station was in jeopardy as long as that silver dread-

5

naught was anywhere in the zone; an Orithain-lord minutely displeased was a bad enemy for a planet, let alone a man-made bubble like Kartos.

And the commanders of Kartos kept otherwise still, and sent no messages of alarm, either inside or outside the Station. There was a hush everywhere. Those that must move, moved quietly.

Ages ago the Orithain had first contacted the kallia, wrenching the folk of Aus Qao out of feudalism and abruptly into star-spanning civilization. Eight thousand years ago the Orithain had reached out to Kesuat, the home star of the amaut—podgy little gray-skinned farmers, broad-bellied and large-eyed, unlikely starfarers; but amaut were scattered now from Kesuat to the Esliph. The *metrosi* itself was an Orithain creation, modern technology an Orithain gift—but one that came at fearful price, a tyranny unimaginably cruel and irrational.

Then for five hundred years, as inexplicably as they did everything, the Orithain had vanished, even from their home star Kej. Ship-dwellers that they were, they began to voyage outward and elsewhere, and ceased to be seen in the range of kalliran ships or amaut. Some even dared to hope them dead—until seven years ago.

Suddenly Orithain were massing again near Kej. Ship by ship, they were reported coming in, gathering like great birds to the smell of death. The outmost worlds knew it, though the *metrosi* refused to admit it for fact. There was no defense possible: kallia knew this; no weapon would avail against Orithain ships, and the pride that the Orithain took in inventive cruelty was legendary. It was more comfortable not to acknowledge their existence.

But at Kartos, bordering the Esliph, the Orithain made their return to the *metrosi* clear beyond doubt.

At the end of the new-station docks the noi kame separated. Two, one carrying a small gray case, went up toward the Station office. The other three descended toward the old docks, that place notorious as the Blind Market, where berths and facilities were cheap and crowded, where goods were often traded unobserved by the overworked Station authorities: little freighters, small cargoes, often shoddy goods, damaged lots, pirated merchandise. Most of the ships docked here came from the Esliph, bearing raw materials and buying up necessities and a few civilized vices for the poorer, outermost worlds.

The security personnel who maintained their discreet watch were alarmed when the noi kame unexpectedly entered that tangle of small berths, and they were perplexed when the noi kame immediately sought the *Konut,* an ancient freighter from the Esliph fringe. Fat little amaut ran about in its open hold in an agony of panic at their coming, and the captain came waddling up on his short legs, working his wide mouth in an expression of extreme unease.

At the noi kame's order the amaut produced the manifest, which the noi kame scanned as they walked with the captain deep into the hold. Incredibly filthy compartments lined this aisle, a stench of unwashed amaut bodies heavy in the air, for the *Konut* trafficked in indentured labor, ignorant laborers contracted to the purchasing company for the usual ten years on a colonial world in exchange for land there—land, which they desired more than they feared the rigors of the journey. Amaut were at heart farmers and diggers in the earth, and the hope of these forlorn, untidy little folk was a small parcel of land somewhere—anywhere. Most would never achieve it: debt to the company would keep them forever tenant farmers.

And to the rear of the *Konut's* second hold was a matter which the captain neglected to report to Station customs: a wire enclosure where humans were transported. Kalliran law forbade traffic in human labor: the creatures were wild and illiterate, unable to make any valid contract—the dregs of the stubborn population left behind when the humans abandoned the Esliph stars and retreated to home space. Their ancestors might have been capable of starflight, but these were not even capable of coherent speech. They were sectioned off from the other hold because the amaut would not abide proximity to them: humans were notorious carriers of disease. One of them at the moment lay stiff and unnatural on the wire mesh flooring, dead perhaps from chill, perhaps from something imported from whatever Esliph world had sent him. Another sat staring, eyes dark and mad.

This was the place that interested the noi kame. They stopped, consulted the manifest, conferred with the captain. The one human still stared, crouched up very small as if he sought obscurity; but when the others suddenly rushed to the far corner, shrieking and clawing and climbing over one another in their witless panic, this one sat still, eyes following every movement outside the cage.

When at last the amaut captain turned and pointed at him, that human froze into absolute immobility, resisting the captain's beckoning.

The sweating captain beckoned at the other humans then, spoke one word several times: *chaju*—liquor. Suddenly the humans were listening, faces eager; and when the amaut pointed at the human that crouched at the center of the cage, the others shrieked in excitement and descended on the unfortunate creature, dragging him to the side of the cage despite his struggling and his cries of rage. They pressed him against the mesh until an attendant could administer an injection: his nails raked the attendant, who hit his arm and spat a curse, but already the human was sinking: the curiously alert eyes glazed, and he slumped down to the mesh flooring.

With no further difficulty the attendant entered the cage and dragged the unconscious human out, rewarding the others with a large flask of *chaju* that was instantly the cause of a fight.

The noi kame distastefully ignored these proceedings. They paid the price of the indenture in silver-weight, named a time for delivery, and walked back the way they had come.

The remaining noi kame, a man and a woman, had entered Station control without a glance at the frightened security personnel or a gesture of courtesy toward the Master. They went to the records center, dislodged the technician from his post, and connected the apparatus in the gray case to the machine.

"It will be necessary," said the woman to the Master, who hovered uncertainly in the background, "for this technician to follow our instructions."

The Master nodded to the operator, who resumed his post reluctantly and did as he was told. The Station's records, the log and the personnel files in their entirety, the centuries of accumulated knowledge of Esliph exploration, the patterns of treaties, of lane regulation and zonal government, bled swiftly into the Orithain's ken.

When the process was complete, the apparatus was discon-

nected, the case was closed, and the noi kame turned as one,
facing the Master.

"There is a man on this station named Aiela Lyailleue,"
said the man. "Deliver his records to us."

"The Master made a helpless gesture. "I have no authority
to do that," he said.

"We do not operate on your authority," said the nas kame.

The Master gave the order. A section of tape fed out of
the machine.

"Dispose of the original record," said the woman, winding
the tape about her first finger. "This person Aiela will report
to our dock for boarding at 0230 Station Time."

Kallia tended to a look of innocence. Their hair was the
same whatever their age, pale and silvery, individual strands
as translucent as spun glass. The pale azure of their skin in-
tensified to sapphire in the eyes, which, unlike the eyes of
amaut, could look left or right without turning the whole
head: it gave them a whole range of communication without
words, and made it difficult for them to conceal their feelings.
They were an emotional folk—not loud, like amaut, who
liked disputes and noisy entertainments, but fond of social
gatherings. One kallia proverbially never decided anything: it
took at least three to reach a decision on the most trivial of
matters. To be otherwise was *ikas*—presumptuous, and a
kalliran gentleman was never that.

Security agent Muishiph was amaut, but he had been long
enough on Kartos to know the kallia quite well, both the
good and the bad in them. He watched the young officer
Aiela Lyailleue react to the news—he stood at the door of
the kallia's onstation apartment—and expected some outcry
of grief or anger at the order. Muishiph had already nerved
himself to resist such appeals—even to defend himself; his
own long arms could crush the slender limbs of a kallia, although he certainly did not want to do that.

"I?" asked the young officer, and again: *"I?"* as though he
still could not believe it. He looked appallingly young to be a
ship's captain. The records confirmed it: twenty-six years old,
son of Deian of the Lyailleue house, aristocrat. Deian was
parome of Xolun *arethme,* and the third councilor in the
High Council of Aus Qao, a great weight of power and
wealth—probably the means by which young Lyailleue had

achieved his premature rank. Aiela's hands trembled. He jammed them into the pockets of his short jacket to conceal the fact and shook his head rather blankly.

"But do you have any idea why they singled me out?"

"The Master said he thought you might know," said Muishiph, "but I doubt he wants to be told, in any case."

The young man gazed at him with eyes so distant Muishiph knew he hardly saw him; and then intelligence returned, a troubled sadness. "May I pack?" he asked. "I suppose I may need some things. I hope that I will."

"They did not forbid it." Muishiph thrust his shoulder within the doorframe, for Aiela had begun to lift his hand toward the switch. "But I would not dare leave you unobserved, sir. I am sorry."

Aiela's eyes raked Muishiph up and down with a curiously regretful expression. At least, Muishiph thought uncomfortably, the Master might have sent a kallia to break the news and to be with him; he braced himself for argument. But Aiela backed away and cleared the doorway to let him enter. Muishiph stopped just inside the door, hands locked behind his thighs, swaying; amaut did that when they were ill at ease.

"Please sit down," Aiela invited him, and Muishiph accepted, accepted again when Aiela poured them each a glass of pinkish *marithe*. Muishiph downed it all, and took his handkerchief from his belly-pocket to mop at his face. Amaut perspired a great deal and needed prodigious quantities of liquid. It was the first time Muishiph had been in a kalliran residence, and the warm, dry air was unkind to his sensitive skin, the bright light hurt his eyes. He thrust the handkerchief back into his pocket and watched Aiela. The kallia, his own drink ignored, had taken a battered spaceman's case from the locker and was starting to pack, nervously meticulous.

Muishiph knew the records from the Master, who had sent him. The young kallia captained a small geological survey vessel named *Alitaesa*, just returned from the moons of Pri, far back on the Esliph fringe. That was amaut territory, but some kallia explored there, seeking mining rights with the permission of the great trading *karshatu* that ruled amaut commerce. Amaut, natural burrowers, would work as miners;

kallia, strongly industrial, would receive the ore and turn it back again in trade—an arrangement old as the *metrosi*.

But it was a rare kallia who ventured deep into the Esliph. It was a wild place and wide, with a great gulf beyond. Odd things happened there, strange ships came and went, and law was a matter of local option and available firepower. The amaut *karshatu* took care of their own, and brooked no intrusion on *karsh* lanes or *karsh* worlds: the kallia they tolerated, reckoning them harmless, for they were above all law-loving folk, their major vice merely a desire of wealth, not land, but monetary and imaginary. Kallia worshipped order: their universe was ordered in such a way that one could not determine his own worth save in terms of the respect paid him by others—and money was somehow a measure of this, as primogeniture was among amaut in a *karsh*. Mui?ship looked on the young man and wondered: as he reckoned kallia, they were shallow folk, never seeking power for its own sake. They had no ambitions: they hated responsibility, feeling that there was something sinister and *ikas* in tampering with destiny. An amaut might dream of having land, of founding a *karsh*, producing offspring in the dozens; but for a kallia the greatest joy seemed to be to retire into a quiet community, giving genteel parties for small gatherings of all the most honorable people, and being a man to whom others resorted for advice and influence—a safe life, and quiet, and never, never involving solitary decisions.

If Aiela Lyailleue was a curiosity to the Orithain, he was no less a puzzle to Muiship: an untypical kallia, a wealthy *parome's* son who chose the hazardous life of the military, exploring the Esliph's backside. It was the hardest and loneliest command any officer, amaut or kallia, could have, out where there was no one to consult and no law to rely on. This was not a kalliran life at all.

Aiela had packed several changes of clothing, everything from the drawers. "Some things are on my ship," he said. "Surely they will send my other belongings home to my family."

"Surely," Muiship agreed, miserable in the lie. When a *karsh* outgrew its territory, the next-born were cast out to fend for themselves. Some founded *karshatu* of their own, some became bondservants to other *karshatu* or sought employment by the kallia, and some simply died of grief. What

amaut literature there was sang mournfully of the misery of
such outcasts, who were cut off and forgotten quickly by
their own kind. The kallia talked of his house as if it still existed for him. Muishiph rolled his lips inward and refused to
argue with the childish faith.

Aiela gathered his pictures off the desk last of all: an
adult-children group that must be his kin, a young girl with
flowers in her silver hair—*ko shenellis,* the coming-of-age:
Muishiph had heard of the ceremony and recognized it, wondering if the girl were kinswoman or intended mate. Aiela
himself was in the third picture, a younger Aiela in civilian
clothes, standing by a smiling youth his own age, the crumbling walls of some ancient kalliran building fluttering with
flags in the background. They were perplexing bits and pieces
of a life Muishiph could not even imagine, things and persons
that had given joy to the kallia, reminders that he once had
had roots—things that were important to him even lost as he
was. The pictures were turned, one by one, face down on the
clothing in the case. With them went a small box of tape cas-
settes. Aiela closed and locked the case, turned with a gesture
of entreaty.

"Do you suppose," he asked, "that there is time to write a
letter?"

Muishiph doubtfully consulted his watch. "If you do, you
must hurry about it."

Aiela bowed his gratitude, a courtesy Muishiph returned on
reflex; and he waited on his feet while Aiela opened the desk
and sat down, using some of the Station's paper.

After a time Muishiph consulted his watch again and
coughed delicately. Aiela hastened his writing, working feverishly until a second apologetic cough advised him of
Muishiph's impatience. Then he arose and unfastened his collar, drawing over his head a metal seal on a chain: its em-
bossed impression sealed the message—a house crest. Kalliran
aristocrats clung to such symbols, prized relics of the feudal
culture that had been theirs before the starlords found them.

And before Muishiph realized his intention, Aiela had
thrust the seal into the disposal chute. It would end floating
in space, disassociated atoms of precious metals. Muishiph
gaped in shock; kalliran matters, those seals, but they were
ancient, and the destruction of something so old and familial
struck Muishiph's heart with a physical sickness.

"Sir," he objected, and met sudden coldness in the kallia's eyes.

"If I had sent it home," said Aiela, "and it had been lost, it would have been a shame on my family; and it is not right to take it as a prisoner either."

"Yes, sir," Muishiph agreed, embarrassed, uneasy at knowing Aiela doubted Kartos' intentions of his property. There was more sense to the kallia than he had reckoned. He became the more perturbed when Aiela thrust the letter into his hands.

"Send it," said Aiela. "Private mails. I know it costs——" He took out his wallet and pressed that too into Muishiph's hand. "There's more than enough. Please. Keep the rest. You'll have earned it."

Muishiph stared from the wallet and the letter to Aiela's anxious face. "Sir, I protest I am an officer of——"

"I know. Break the seal, read it—copy it, I don't care. Only get it to Aus Qao. My family can reward you. I want them to know what happened to me."

Muishiph considered a moment, his mouth working in distress. Then he slipped the letter into his belly-pocket and patted it flat. But he kept only two of the larger bills from the wallet and cast the wallet down on the table.

"Take it all," said Aiela. "Someone else will, that's certain."

"I don't dare, sir," said Muishiph, looking at it a second time regretfully. He put it from his mind once for all with a glance at his watch. "Come, bring your baggage. We have orders to anticipate that deadline. The Station is taking no chances of offending them."

"I am sure they would not." For a moment his odd kalliran eyes fixed painfully on Muishiph, asking something; but Muishiph hurriedly shrugged and showed Aiela out the door, walking beside him as soon as they were in the broad hall. Another security guard, a kallia, met them at the turning: he carried a sheaf of documents and a tape-case.

"My records?" Aiela surmised, at which the kalliran guard looked embarrassed.

"Yes, sir," he admitted. "They are being turned over. Everything is."

Aiela kept his eyes forward and did not look at that man after that, nor the man at him.

Muishiph fingered the outline of the letter in his belly-pocket, and carefully extracted his handkerchief and mopped at his face. It was too much to ask. To deceive the lords of *karshatu* and to cross the Qao High Council were both perilous undertakings, but the starlords were an ancient terror and their reach was long and their knowledge thorough beyond belief. The letter burned like guilt against Muishiph's belly. Already he began to imagine his position should anyone guess what he had agreed to do.

And then it occurred to him to wonder if Aiela had told the truth of what it contained.

The Orithain vessel itself was not visible from the dock. There was only the entry tube and its conveyor, disappearing constantly upward as the supplies flooded toward the unseen maw of the ship. Aiela stopped with his escort and set his case beside him on the tiled flooring, the three of them conspicuous in an area where no spectators would dare to be. Aiela shivered; his knees felt loose. He hoped it was not evident to those with him. Courage to cross that small area without faltering: that was all he begged of himself.

He was not, he had assured his family in the letter, expecting to die; execution could be accomplished with far more effect in public. He did not know what had drawn the Orithain's attention to him: he had touched nothing and done nothing that could have accounted for it, to his own knowledge, and what they intended with him he only surmised. He would not return. No one had ever been appropriated by the Orithain and walked out again free; but it would please him if his family would think of him as alive and well. He had saved five thousand lives on Kartos by his compliance with orders: he was well sure of this; there was cause for pride in that fact.

Empty canisters clanged on the dock, the horrid crash rumbling through his senses, dislodging him from his privacy. He looked and saw a frightened amaut crew trying to stop machinery. An amaut had been injured. The minute tragedy occupied him for the moment. None of the bystanders would help. They only stared. Finally the amaut was allowed to lie alone. The others worked feverishly with the lading of canisters, trying to make their deadline. The machinery started again.

His father would understand, between the lines of what he had written. *Parome* Deian was on the High Council, and knew the reports that never went to earthsiders. There was an understanding as old as the kallia's first meeting with the Orithain: their eccentricities were not for comment and their names were not to be uttered; the Orithain homeworld at Kej still lay deserted, legendary cities full of supposed treasure—but *metrosi* ships avoided that star; for nine thousand years the Orithain had been the central fact of *metrosi* civilization, but no research delved into their origins, few books so much as mentioned them save in oblique reference to the Domination, and nothing but legend reported their appearance. But they were remembered. In the independence of space the old tales continued to be told, and legends were amplified now with new horrors of Orithain cruelty. Deian was one of nine men on all Aus Qao who received across his desk all the statistics and the rumors.

And if the statistics preceded his letter, Aiela reflected sorrowfully, his father would receive that cold message first. It would be the final cruelty of so many that had passed between them.

If that were to go first, witnesses would at least say that he had gone with dignity.

At the end, he could give nothing else to his family.

The lefthand ramp had been clear of traffic for several moments. Now it reversed, and one of the noi kame descended. Aiela bent and picked up his case when the man came toward them; and when they met, the kalliran agent gave into the nas kame's hands the documents and the tape case—the sum of all records in the zone regarding Aiela and his existence. It was terrible to believe so, but even Qao might follow suit, erasing all records even to his certificate of birth, forbidding mention of him even by his family. Fear of the Orithain was that powerful. Aiela was suddenly bitterly ashamed for his people, for what the starlords had made them be and do. He began to be angry, when before he had felt only grief.

"Come," said the nas kame, accepting the sheaf of documents and the case under his arm. But he looked down in some surprise as the amaut agent suddenly pushed forward, proffering a letter in his trembling hand.

"His too, lord, his too," said the amaut.

The nas kame took the letter and put it among the

documents; and Aiela looked toward the amaut reproach-fully, but the amaut bowed his head and stood rocking back and forth, refusing to look up at him.

Aiela turned his face instead toward the nas kame, ap-palled that there was no shame there—eyes as kalliran as his that held no recognition of him and cared nothing for his misery.

The nas kame brought him to the moving ramp and preceded him up, looking back once casually at the scene below, ignoring Aiela. Then the belt set them both into the ship's hold.

Aiela's eyes were drawn up by the sheer echoing immensity of the place. This hold, as was usual with supply holds, was filled with frames and canisters of goods, row on row, dated, stamped to be listed in the computer's memory. But it could have contained an entire ship the size of the one Aiela had lately commanded—without the frames and the clutter. No doubt there were other holds that did hold such things as transfer ships and shuttles available at need. It staggered the mind.

The nas kame took his case from him and handed it to an amaut, who waddled ahead of them to a counter and had it stamped and listed and thrust up a conveyor to disappear. Aiela looked after it with a sinking heart, for among his folded clothing he had put his service pistol—nonlethal, like all the weapons of the kalliran service. He had debated it; he had done it, terrified in the act and terrified to go defenseless, without it. But there were no defenses. Standing where he was now, with all Kartos so small and fragile a place beneath them, he realized it for a selfish and cowardly thing to do.

"There was a weapon in that," he said to the nas kame.

The nas kame took notice of him directly for the first time, regarding him with mild surprise. He had just put the documents and the tape case on the counter to be similarly stamped and sent up the conveyor. Then he shrugged. "Se-curity will deal with it," he said, and took Aiela's arm and held his hand on the counter, compelling him to accept a stamp on the back of his hand, like the other baggage.

Aiela received it with so deep a confusion that he failed to protest; but afterward, with the nas kame holding his arm and guiding him rapidly through the echoing hold, a wave of such shame and outrage came over him that he was almost shaking. He should have said something; he should have done something. He worked his fingers, staring at the purple symbols that rippled across the bones of his hand, and was only gathering the words to object to the indignity when the nas kame roughly turned him and thrust him toward a personnel lift. He went, turned once inside, and expected the nas kame to step in too; but the door slid shut and he was hurtled elsewhere on his own. The controls resisted his attempt to regain the loading deck.

In an instant the lift came to a cushioned halt and opened on a cargo area adapted to the reception of live goods; there were a score or more individual cells and animal pens, some with bare flooring and some padded on all surfaces. Gray-smocked noi kame and amaut in green were waiting for him, took charge of him as he stepped out. One noted the number from his hand onto a slate, then gestured him to move.

As he walked the aisle of compartments he saw one lighted, its facing wall transparent; and his flesh crawled at the sight of the naked pink-brown tangle of limbs that crouched at the rear of it. It looked moribund, whatever it had been—the Orithain ranged far: perhaps it was only one of the forgotten humans of the Esliph; perhaps it was some more dangerous and exotic specimen from the other end of the galaxy, where no *metrosi* ship had ever gone. He delayed, looked more closely; a nas kame pushed him between the shoulders and moved him on, and by now he was completely overwhelmed, dazed and beyond any understanding of what to do. He walked. No one spoke to him. He might have been a nonsentient they were handling.

Physicians took him—at least so he reckoned them—kallia and amaut, who ordered him to strip, and examined him until he was exhausted by their thoroughness, the cold, and the endless waiting. He was beyond shame. When at last they thrust his wadded clothing at him and put him into one of the padded cells to wait, he stood there blankly for some few moments before the cold finally urged him to dress.

He shivered convulsively afterward, walking to lean against one and another of the walls. Finally he knelt down on the floor to rest, limbs tucked up for warmth, his muscles still racked with shivers. There was no view, only white walls and a blank, padded door—cold, white light. He heard nothing to tell him what passed outside until the gentle shock of uncoupling threw him off-balance: they were moving, Kartos would be dropping astern at ever-increasing speed.

It was irrevocable.

He was dead, so far as his own species was concerned, so far as anything he had known was concerned. There were no more familiar reference points.

He was only beginning to come to grips with that, when the room vanished.

He was suddenly kneeling on a carpeted floor that still felt strangely like the padded plastics of the cell. The lights were dim, the walls expanded into an immense dark chamber of carven screens and panels of alien design. A woman in black and diaphanous violet stood before him, a woman of the Orithain, of the indigo-skinned iduve race. Her hair was black: it hung like fine silk, thick and even at the level of her shapely jaw. Her brows were dark, her eyes amethyst-hued, without whites, and rimmed with dark along the edge of the lid. Her nose was arched but delicate, her mouth sensuous, frosted with lavender, the whole of her face framed with the absolute darkness of her hair. The draperies hinted at a slim and female body; her complexion, though dusky from the kalliran view, had a lustrous sheen, as though dust of violet glistened there, as if she walked in another light than ordinary mortals, a universe where suns were violet and skies were of shadowy hue.

He rose and, because it was *elethia*, he gave her a proper bow for meeting despite their races: she was female, though she was an enemy. She smiled and gave a nod of her graceful head.

"Be welcome, *m'metane*," she said.

"Who was it who had me brought here?" he demanded, anger springing out of his voice to cover his fear. "And why did you ask for *me*?"

"*Vaikka*," she said, and when he did not understand, she shrugged and seemed amused. "*Au, m'metane*, you are ignorant and *anoikhte*, two conditions impossible to maintain aboard *Ashanome*. We carry no passengers. You will be in my service."

"No." The answer burst out of him before he even reckoned the consequences, but she shrugged again and smiled.

"We might return to Kartos," she said. "You might be set off there to advise them of your objections."

"And what then?"

"I would prefer otherwise."

He drew a long breath, let it go again. "I see. So why do you come offering me choices? Noi kame can't make any, can they?"

"I have scanned your records. I find your decision expected. And as for your assumption of noi kame—no: kamethi have considerable initiative; they would be useless otherwise."

"Would you have destroyed Kartos?"

His angry question seemed for the first time to perplex the Orithain, whose gentle manner persisted. "When we threaten, *m'metane*, we do so because of another's weakness, never of our own. It was highly likely that you would choose to come: *elethia* forbids you should refuse. If you would not, surely fear would compel them to bring you. Likewise it is certain that I would have destroyed Kartos had it refused. Any other basis for making the statement would have been highly unreasonable."

"Was it you?" he asked. "Why did you choose me?"

"*Vaikka*—a matter of honor. You are of birth such that your loss will be noticed among kallia: that has a certain incidental value. And I have use for such as you: world-born, but experienced of outer worlds."

He hated her, hated her quiet voice and her evident delight in his misery. "Well," he said, "you'll regret that particular choice."

Her amethyst eyes darkened perceptibly. There was no longer a smile on her face. "*Kutikkase-metane*," she said. "At the moment you are no more than sentient raw material, and it is useless to attempt rational conversation with you."

And with blinding swiftness the white light of the cell was about him again, yielding white plastic on all sides, narrow walls, white glare. He flinched and covered his eyes, and fell to his knees again in the loneliness of that cubicle.

Then, not for the first time in the recent hour, he thought of self-destruction; but he had no convenient means, and he had still to fear her retaliation against Kartos. He slowly realized how ridiculous he had made himself with his threat against her, and was ashamed. His entire species was powerless against the likes of her, powerless because, like Kartos, like him, they would always find the alternative unthinkably costly.

He came docilely enough when they brought him out into the laboratory, expecting that they would simply lock about his wrist the *idoikkhe,* such as they themselves wore—that ornate platinum band that observers long ago theorized provided the Orithain their means of control over the noi kame.

Such was not the case. They had him dress in a white wrap about his waist and lie down again on the table, after which they forcibly administered a drug that made his senses swim, dispersing his panic to a vague, all-encompassing uneasiness.

He realized by now that becoming nas kame involved more than accepting that piece of jewelry—that he was going under and that he would not wake the same man. In his drugged despair he begged, he invoked deity, he pleaded with them as fellow kallia to consider what they were doing to him.

But they ignored his raving and with an economy of effort, slipped him to a movable table and put him under restraint. From that point his perceptions underwent a rapid deterioration. He was conscious, but he could not tell what he was seeing or hearing, and eventually passed over the brink.

2

THE DAZED STATE gave way to consciousness in the same tentative manner. Aiela was aware of the limits of his own body, of a pain localized in the roof of his mouth and behind his eyes. There was a bitter chemical taste and his brow itched. He could not raise his hand to scratch it. The itch spread to his nose and was utter misery. When he grimaced to relieve it, the effort hurt his head.

He slept again, and wakened a second time enough to try to move, remembering the bracelet that ought to be locked about his wrist. There was none. He lifted his hand—free now—and saw the numbers still stamped there, but faded. His head hurt. He touched his temple and felt a thin rough seam. There was the salt of blood in his mouth toward the back of his palate; his throat was raw. He felt along the length of the incision at his temple and panic began to spread through him like ice.

He hated them. He could still hate; but the concentration it took was tiring—even fear was tiring. He wept, great tears rolling from his eyes, and even then he was fading. Drugs, he thought dimly. He shut his eyes.

A raw soreness persisted, not of the body, but of the mind, a perception, a part of him that could not sleep, like an inner eye that had no power to blink. It burned like a white light at the edge of his awareness, an unfocused field of vision where shadows and colors moved undefined. Then he knew what they had done to him, although he did not know the name of it.

"No!" he screamed, and screamed again and again until his voice was gone. No one came. His senses slipped from him again.

21

At the third waking he was stronger, breathing normally, and aware of his surroundings. The sore spot was there; when he worried at it the place grew wider and brighter, but when he forced himself to move and think of other things, the color of the wall, anything at all, it ebbed down to a memory, an imagination of presence. He could control it. Whatever had been done to his brain, he remembered, he knew himself. He tested the place nervously, like probing a sore tooth; it reacted predictably, grew and diminished. It had depth, a void that drew at his senses. He pulled his mind from it, crawled from bed and leaned against a chair, fighting to clear his senses.

The room had the look of a comfortable hotel suite, all in blue tones, the lighted white doorway of a tiled bath at the rear—luxury indeed for a starship. His disreputable serviceman's case rested on the bureau. A bench near the bed had clothing—beige—laid out across it.

His first move was for the case. He leaned on the bureau and opened it. Everything was there but the gun. In its place was a small card: *We regret we cannot permit personal arms without special clearance. It is in storage. For convenience in claiming your property at some later date, please retain this card, 509-3899-345.*

He read it several times, numb to what he felt must be a certain grim humor. He wiped at his blurring vision with his fingers and leaned there, absently beginning to unpack, one-handed at first, then with both. His beloved pictures went there, so, facing the chair which he thought he would prefer. He put things in the drawer, arranged clothing, going through motions familiar to a hundred unfamiliar places, years of small outstations, hardrock worlds—occupying his mind and keeping it from horrid reality. He was alive. He could remember. He could resent his situation. And this place, this room, was known, already measured, momentarily safe: it was *his,* so long as he opened no doors.

When he felt steady on his feet he bathed, dressed in the clothes provided him, paused at the mirror in the bath to look a second time at his reflection, when earlier he had not been able to face it. His silver hair was cropped short; his own face shocked him, marred with the finger-length scar at his temple, but the incision was sealed with plasm and would go away in a few days, traceless. He touched it, wondered, ripped his thoughts back in terror; light flashed in his mind, pain. He stumbled, and came to himself with his face pressed to the cold glass of the mirror and his hands spread on its surface to hold him up.

"Attention please." The silken voice of the intercom startled him, "Attention. Aiela Lyailleue, you are wanted in the *paredre*. Kindly wait for one of the staff to guide you."

He remembered an intercom screen in the main room, and he pushed himself square on his feet and went to it, pressed what he judged was the call button, several times, in increasing anger. A glowing dot raced from one side of the screen to the other, but there was no response.

He struck the plate to open the door, not expecting that to work for him either, but it did; and instead of an ordinary corridor, he faced a concourse as wide as a station dock.

At the far side, stars spun past a wide viewport in the stately procession of the saucer's rotation. Kallia in beige and other colors came and went here, and but for the luxury of that incredible viewport and the alien design of the shining metal pillars that spread ornate flanged arches across the entire overhead, it might have been an immaculately modern port on Aus Qao. Amaut technicians waddled along at their rolling pace, looking prosperous and happy; a young kalliran couple walked hand in hand; children played. A man of the iduve crossed the concourse, eliciting not a ripple of notice among the noi kame—a tall slim man in black, he demanded and received no special homage. Only one amaut struggling along under the weight of several massive coils of hose brought up short and ducked his head apologetically rather than contest right of way.

At the other end of the concourse an abstract artwork of metal over metal, the pieces of which were many times the size of a man, closed off the columned expanse in high walls. At their inner base and on an upper level, corridors led off into distance so great that the inner curvature of the ship played visual havoc with the senses, door after door of what Aiela judged to be other apartments stretching away into brightly lit sameness.

The iduve was coming toward him.

Panic constricted his heart. He looked to one side and the other, finding no other cause for the iduve's interest. And then a resolution wholly reckless settled into him. He turned and began at first simply to walk away; but when he looked back, panic won: he gathered his strength and started to run.

Noi kame stared, shocked at the disorder. He shouldered past and broke into a corridor, not knowing where it led—the ship, vast beyond belief, tempted him to believe he could lose himself, find its inward parts, at least understand the sense of things before they found him again and forced their purposes upon him.

Then the section doors sealed, at either end of the hall.

Noi kame stared at him, dismayed.

"Stand still," one said to him.

Aiela glanced that way: hands took his arms and he twisted out and ran, but they closed and held him. The first man rash enough to come at him from the front flew backward under the impact of his thin-soled boot; but he could not free himself. An amaut took his arms, a grip he could not break, struggle as he would; and then the doors parted and the iduve arrived with a companion, frowning and businesslike. When Aiela attempted to kick at them, that iduve's backhand exploded across his face with force enough to black him out: a hypospray against his arm finished his resistance.

He was not entirely unconscious. He tried to walk because the grip on his arms hurt less when he carried his own weight, but it was some little distance before he even cared where they were taking him. For a dizzying moment they rode a lift, and stepped off into another corridor, and then came into a hall. On the left a screen of translucent blue stone carved in scenes of reeds and birds separated a vast dim hall from this narrower chamber.

Then he remembered this place, this hall like a museum, with its beautiful fretted panels and lacquered ceiling, its cases for display, its ornate and alien furnishings. He had stood here once before from the vantage point of his cell, but this was reality. The carpets he walked gave under his boots, and the woman that awaited them was not projection, but flesh and blood.

"Aiela," she said in her accented voice, "Aiela Lyailleue: I am Chimele, Orithain of *Ashanome*. And such action is hardly an auspicious introduction, nor at all wise. *Takkh-ar-rhei, nasithi.*"

Aiela found himself free—dizzied, bruised, thoroughly dispossessed of the recklessness to chance another chastisement at their hands. He moved a step—the iduve behind him moved him back precisely where he had stood.

She spoke to her people, frowning: they answered. Aiela waited, with such a physical terror mounting in him as he had never felt in any circumstances. He could not even shape it in his thoughts. He felt disconnected, smothered, wished at once to run and feared the least movement.

And now Chimele turned from him and returned with the wide band of an *idoikkhe* open in her indigo fingers—a band of three fingers' width, with a patchwork of many colors of metal on its inner surface, a thread of black weaving through it all. She held it out for him, expecting him to offer his wrist for it, and now, now was the time if ever he would refuse anything again. He could not breathe, and he felt strongly the threat of violence at his back; his battered nerves refused to carry the right impulses. He saw himself raise an arm that seemed part of another body, heard a sharp click as the cold band locked, felt a weight that was more than he had expected as she took her hands away.

A jewel of milk and fire shone on its face. The asymmetry of iduve artistry flashed in metal worth a man's life in the darker places of the Esliph. He stared at it, realizing beyond doubt that he had accepted its limits, that no foreign thing in his skull had compelled the lifting of his arm; there was a weakness in Aiela Lyailleue that he had never found before, a shameful, unmanning terror.

It was as if something essential in him had torn away, left behind in Kartos. He feared. For the first time he knew himself less than other beings. Without dignity he tore at the band, but of the closure no trace remained save a faint diffraction of light—no clasp and no yielding.

"No," she said, "you cannot remove it."

And with a gesture she dismissed the others, so that they stood alone in the hall. He was tempted then to murder, the first time he had ever felt a hate so *ikas*—and then he knew that it was out of fear, female that she was. He gained control of himself with that thought, gathered enough courage to plainly defy her: he spun on his heel to stalk out, to make them use force if they would. That much resolve he still possessed.

The *idoikkhe* stung him, a dart of pain from his fingertips to his ribs. At the next step it hurt; and he paused, measuring the long distance to the door against the pain that lanced in rising pulses up his arm. A greater shock hit him, waves enough to jolt his heart and shorten his breath.

He jerked about and faced her—not to attack: if he had any thought then it was to stand absolutely still, anything, anything to stop it. The pulse vanished as he did what she wanted, and the ache faded slowly.

"Do not fear the *idoikkhe*," said Chimele. "We use it primarily for coded communication, and it will not greatly inconvenience you."

He was shamed; he jerked aside, hurt at once as the *idoikkhe* activated, faced her and felt it fade again.

"I do not often resort to that," said Chimele, who had not yet appeared to do anything. "But there is a fine line between humor and impertinence with us which few *m'metanei* can safely tread. Come, *m'metane-toj*, use your intelligence."

She allowed him time, at least: he recovered his composure and caught his breath, rebuilding the courage it took to anger her.

"So what is the law here?" he asked.

"Do not play the game of *vaikka* with an iduve." He tried to outface her with his anger, but Chimele's whiteless eyes locked on his with an invading directness he did not like. "You are bound to find the wager higher than you are willing to pay. You have not been much harmed, and I have extended you an extraordinary courtesy."

"I don't think so," he said, and knew what to expect for it, knew and waited until his nerves were drawn taut. But Chimele broke from his eyes with a shrug, gestured toward a chair.

"Sit and listen, kameth. Sit and listen. I do not notice your attitude. You are only ignorant. We are using valuable time."

He hesitated, weighed matters; but the change in her manner was as complete as it was abrupt, almost as if she regretted her anger. He still thought of going for the door; then common sense reasserted itself, and he settled on the chair opposite the one she chose.

Pain hit him, excruciating, lancing through his eyes and the back of his skull at once. He bent over, holding his face, unable to breathe. That sensation passed quickly, leaving a throbbing ache behind his eyes.

"Be quiet," she said. "Anger is the worst possible response."

And she brought him a tiny glass of clear liquid. He drank, too shaken to argue, set the empty crystal vessel on the table. He missed the edge with his distorted vision: it toppled off and she imperturbably picked it up off the costly rug and set it securely on the table.

"I am not responsible," she said when he looked hate at her.

There was something at the edge of his mind, the void now full of something dark that reached up at him, and he fought to shut it out, losing the battle as long as he panicked. Then it ceased, firmly, outside his will.

"What was done to me?" he cried. "What was it?"

"The *chiabres*, the implant: I would surmise, though I do not do so from experience, that you reacted on a subconscious level and triggered defenses, contacting what was not prepared to receive you. This *chiabres* of yours has two contacts, mind-links to your asuthi—your companions. One is probably in the process of waking, and I assure you that fighting an asuthe is not profitable."

"I had rather be dead," he said. "I would rather die."

"*Tekasuphre*. Do not try my patience. I called you here precisely to explain matters to you. I have great personal regard for your asuthe. Do I make myself clear?"

"Am I joined to one of you?"

"No," she said, suddenly laughing—a merry, gentle sound, but her teeth were white and sharp. "Nature provided for us in our own fashion, *m'metane*. Kallia and even amaut find *asuthithekkhe* pleasant, but we would not."

And the walls closed about them. Aiela sprang to his feet in alarm, while Chimele arose more gracefully. The light had brightened, and beside them was a bed whereon lay a kalliran woman of great beauty. She stirred in her sleep, silvery head turning on the pillow, one azure hand coming to her breast. There was the faint seam of a new scar at her temple.

"She is Isande," said Chimele. "Your asuthe."

"Is it—usual—that different sexes—"

Chimele shrugged. "We have not found it of concern."

"Was she the one I felt a moment ago?"

"It is not reasonable to ask me to venture an opinion on

something I have never experienced. But it seems quite possible."

He looked from Chimele to the sweet-faced being who lay on the bed, the worst of his fears leaving him at once. He felt even an urge to be sorry for Isande, no less than for himself; he wondered if she had consented to this unhappy situation, and was about to ask Chimele that question.

The walls blinked smaller still, and they stood in a room of padded white, a cell. At their left, leaning against the transparent face of the cell, was that same naked pink-brown creature Aiela remembered lying inert in the corner on his entry into the lab. Now it turned in the rapid dawning of terror: one of the humans of the Esliph, beyond doubt, and as stunned as he had been that day—how long ago?—that Chimele had appeared in his cell. The human stumbled back, hit the wall where there was no wall in his illusion, and pressed himself there because there was no further retreat.

"He is *Daniel*," said Chimele. "We think this is a name. That is all we have been able to obtain from him."

Aiela looked at the hair-matted face in revulsion, heart beating in panic as the human stretched out his hands. The human's dark eyes stared, white around the edges, but when his hands could not grasp them he collapsed into a knot, arms clenched, sobbing with a very manlike sound.

"This," said Chimele, "is your other asuthe."

Aiela had seen it coming. When he looked at Chimele it was without the shock that would have pleased her. He hardened his face against her.

"And you know now," she continued, unmoved, "how it feels to experience the *chiabres* without understanding what it is. This will be of use to you with him."

"I thought," he recalled, "that you had regard for Isande."

"Precisely. *Asuthithekkhe* between species has always failed. I am not willing to risk the honor of *Ashanome* by endangering one of my most valued kamethi. You are presently expendable. Surgery will be performed on this being in two days. You had that interval to learn to handle the *chiabres*. Try to approach the human. Perhaps he will respond to you. Amaut are best able to quiet him, but I do not think he finds pleasure in their company or they in his. Those two species demonstrate a strong mutual aversion."

Aiela nerved himself to take a step toward the being, and another. He went down on one knee and extended his hand.

The creature gave a shuddering sob and scrambled back from any contact, wild eyes locked on his. Of a sudden it sprang for his throat.

The cell vanished, and Aiela had sprung erect in the safety of the Orithain's own shadowed hall. He still trembled, in his mind unconvinced that the hands that had reached for his throat were insubstantial.

"You are dismissed," said Chimele.

The nas kame who escorted him simply abandoned him on the concourse and advised him to ask someone if he lost his way again. There was no mention of any threat, as if they judged a man who wore the *idoikkhe* incapable of any further trouble to anyone.

In effect, he knew, they were right.

He walked away to stand by the immense viewport, watching the stars sweep past, now and again the awesome view of the afterstructure of the ship as the rotation of the saucer carried them under the holding arm, alternate oblivion and rebirth from the dark, rotation after slow rotation, the blaze of *Ashanome's* running lights, the dark beneath, the lights, the star-scattered fabric of infinity, a ceaseless rhythm.

Likely none of the thousands of kallia that came and went on the concourse knew much of Aus Qao. They had been born on the ship, would live their lives, bear their children, and die on the ship. Possibly they were even happy. Children came, their bright faces and shrill voices and the rhymes of the games they played the same as generations before had sung, the same as kalliran children everywhere. They flitted off again, their glad voices trailing away into the echoing immensities of the pillared hall. Aiela kept his face toward the viewport, struggling with the tightness in his throat.

Kartos Station would be about business as usual by now, and its people would have cleansed him from their thoughts and their conscience. Aus Qao would do the same; even his family must pick up the threads of their lives, as they would do if he were dead. His reflection stared back out of starry space, beige-clad, slender, crop-headed—indistinguishable from a thousand others that had been born to serve the ship.

He could not blame Kartos. It was a fact as old as civiliza-

tion in the *metrosi*, a deep knowledge of helplessness. It was
that which had compelled him to take the *idoikkhe*. Kallia
were above all peaceful, patiently stubborn, and knew better
how to outwait an enemy that how to fight.

To wait.

There was an Order of things, and it was reasonable and
productive. For one nas kame to defy the Orithain and die
would accomplish nothing. An unproductive action was not a
reasonable action, and an unreasonable action was not virtue,
was not *kastien*.

Should he have died for nothing?

But all reasonable action on *Ashanome* operated in favor
of the Orithain, who understood nothing of *kastien*.

Until the *idoikkhe* had locked upon his wrist, he had been
a person of some *elethia*. He had been a man able to walk
calmly through Kartos Station under the witness of others.
He had even imagined the moment he had just passed, in a
hundred different manners. But he had expected oblivion, a
canceling of self—a state in which he was innocent.

He had accepted it. He would continue to accept it, every
day of his life, and by its weight, that metal now warmed to
the temperature of his own body, he would remember what it
cost to say no.

He had despised the noi kame. But doubtless their ancestors had resolved the same as he, to live, to wait their chance,
which only hid their fear; waiting, they had served the Orithain, and they died, and their children's children knew nothing else.

Something stabbed at him behind his eyes. He caught at
his face and reached for the support of the viewport. Waking.
Conscious.

Isande.

It stopped. His vision cleared.

But it was coming. He stood still, waiting—impulses to
flight, even to suicide beat along his nerves; but these things
were futile, *ikas*. It was possible—he thought blas-
phemously—that *kastien* demanded this patience of kallia because they *were* otherwise defenseless.

Slowly, slowly, something touched him, became pressure in
that zone of his mind that had been opened. He shut his eyes
tightly, feeling more secure as long as outside stimuli were
limited. This was a being of his own kind, he reminded him-

self, a being who surely was in no happier state than himself.

It built in strength.

Different: that was the overwhelming impression, a force that ran over his nerves without his willing it, callous and unfamiliar. It invaded the various centers of his brain, probing one and another with painful rapidity. Light blazed and faded, equilibrium wavered, sounds roared in his ears, hot and cold affected his skin.

Then it invaded his thoughts, his memories, his inmost privacy.

O God! he thought he cried, like a man dying. There was a silence so dark and sudden it was like falling. He was leaning against the viewport, chilled by it. People were staring at him. Some even looked concerned. He straightened and shifted his eyes from the reflection to the stars beyond, to the dark.

"I am Isande." There grew a voice in his mind that had tone without sound, as a man could imagine the sound of his own voice when it was silent. A flawed dim image of the concourse filled his eyes. He saw the viewport at a distance, marked a slender man who seemed tiny against it—all this overlaid upon his own view of space. He recognized the man for himself, and turned, seeing things from two sides at once. Imposed on his own self now was a distant figure he knew for Isande: he felt her exhaustion, her impatience.

"I'll meet you in your quarters," she sent.

Her turning shifted his vision, causing him to stagger off-balance; reflex stopped the image, screened her out. He suddenly realized he had that defense, tried it again—he could not cope with the double vision while either of them was moving. He shut it down, an irregular flutter of on-off. It was hard to will a thing that decisively, that strongly, but it could be done.

And he began to suspect Chimele had been honest when she told him that kamethi found the *chiabres* no terror. It was a power, a compensation for the *idoikkhe*, a door one could fling wide or close at will.

Only what territory lay beyond depended entirely on the conscience of another being—on two asuthi, one of whom might be little removed from madness.

He did not touch her mind again until he had opened the door of his quarters: she was seated in his preferred chair in

a relaxed attitude as if she had a perfect right to his things.
When he realized she was speculating on the pictures on the
bureau she pirated the knowledge of his family from his
mind, ripped forth a flood of memories that in his disorgani-
zation he could not prevent. He reacted with fury, felt her retreat.

"I'm sorry," she said smoothly, shielding her own thoughts
with an expertise his most concentrated effort could not penetrate. She gestured toward the other chair and wished him
seated.

"These are my quarters," he said, still standing. "Or do
they move you in with me? Do they assume that too?"

Her mind closed utterly when she felt that, and he could
not reach her. He had thought her beautiful when he first saw
her asleep; but now that her body moved, now that those blue
eyes met his, it was with an arrogance that disturbed him
even through the turmoil of his other thoughts. There was a
mind behind that pretty façade, strong-willed and powerful,
and that was not an impression beautiful women usually
chose to send him. He was not sure he liked it.

He was less sure he liked her, despite her physical attrac-
tions.

"I have my own quarters," she said aloud. "And don't be
self-centered. Your choices are limited, and *I* am not one of
them."

She ruffled through his thoughts with skill against which he
had no defense, and met his temper with contempt. He thrust
her out, but the least wavering of his determination let her
slip through again; it was a continuing battle. He took the
other chair, exhausted, beginning to panic, feeling that he was
going to lose everything. He would even have struck her—he
would have been shamed by that.

And she received that, and mentally backed off in great
haste. "Well," she conceded then, "I am sorry. I am rude. I
admit that."

"You resent me." He spoke aloud. He was not comfortable
with the *chiabres*. And what she radiated confirmed his impression: she tried to suppress it, succeeded after a moment.

"I wanted what you are assigned to do," she said, "very
badly."

"I'll yield you the honor."

Her mind slammed shut, her lips set. But something escaped her barriers, some deep and private grief that touched him and damped his anger.

"Neither you nor I have that choice," she said. "Chimele decides. There is no appeal."

Chimele. He recalled the Orithain's image with hate in his mind, expected sympathy from Isande's, and did not receive it. Other images took shape, sendings from Isande, different feelings: he flinched from them.

For nine thousand years Isande's ancestors had served the Orithain. She took pride in that.

Iduve, she sent, correcting him. *Chimele is the Orithain; the people are iduve.*

The words were toneless this time, but different from his own knowledge. He tried to push them out.

The ship is Ashanome, she continued, ignoring his awkward attempt to cast her back. *WE are* Ashanome: *five thousand iduve, seven thousand noi kame, and fifteen hundred amaut. The iduve call it a nasul, a clan. The nasul Ashanome is above twelve thousand years old; the ship Ashanome is nine thousand years from her launching, seven thousand years old in this present form. Chimele rules here. That is the law in this world of ours.*

He flung himself to his feet, finding in movement, in any distraction, the power to push back Isande's insistent thoughts. He began to panic: Isande retreated.

"You do not believe," she said aloud, "that you can stop me. You could, if you believed you could."

She *pitied* him. It was a mortification as great as any the iduve had set upon him. He rounded on her with anger ready to pour forth, met a frightened, defensive flutter of her hand, a sealing of her mind he could not penetrate.

"No," she said. "Aiela—no. You will hurt us both."

"I have had enough," he said, "from the iduve—from noi kame in general. They are doing this to me—"

"—to us."

"Why?"

"Sit down. Please."

He leaned a moment against the bureau, stubborn and intractable; but she was prepared to wait. Eventually he yielded and settled on the arm of his chair, knowing well enough that she could perceive the distress that burned along his nerves, that threatened the remnant of his self control.

You fear the iduve, she observed. *Sensible. But they do not hate; they do not love. I am Chimele's friend. But Chimele's language hasn't a single word for any of those things. Don't attribute to them motives they can't have. There is something you must do in Chimele's service: when you have done it, you will be let alone. Not thanked: let alone. That is the way of things.*

"Is it?" he asked bitterly. "Is that all you get from them— to be left alone?"

Memory, swift and involuntary: a dark hall, an iduve face, terror. Thought caught it up, unraveled, explained. *Khasif: Chimele's half-brother. Yes, they feel. But if you are wise, you avoid causing it.* Isande had escaped that hall; Chimele had intervened for her. It haunted her nightmares, that encounter, sent tremors over her whenever she must face that man.

To be let alone: Isande sought that diligently.

And something else had been implicit in that instant's memory, another being's outrage, another man's fear for her—as close and as real as his own.

Another asuthe.

Isande shut that off from him, firmly, grieving. "Reha," she said. "His name was Reha. You could not know me a moment without perceiving him."

"Where is he?"

"Dead." Screening fell, mind unfolding, willfully.

Dark, and cold, and pain: a mind dying and still sending, horrified, wide open. Instruments about him, blinding light. Isande had held to him until there was an end, hurting, refusing to let go until the incredible fact of his own death swallowed him up. Aiela felt it with her, her fierce loyalty, Reha's terror—knew vicariously what it was to die, and sat shivering and sane in his own person afterward.

It was a time before things were solid again, before his fingers found the texture of the chair, his eyes accepted the color of the room, the sober face of Isande. She had given him something so much of herself, so intensely self, that he found his own body strange to him.

Did they kill him? he asked her. He trembled with anger, sharing with her: it was his loss too. But she refused to assign the blame to Chimele. Her enemies were not the iduve of *Ashanome.* His were.

He drew back from her, knowing with fading panic that it was less and less possible for him to dislike her, to find evil in any woman that had loved with such a strength.

It was, perhaps, the impression she meant to project. But the very suspicion embarrassed him, and became quickly impossible. She unfolded further, admitting him to her most treasured privacy, to things that she and Reha had shared once upon a time: her asuthe from childhood, Reha. They had played, conspired, shared their loves and their griefs, their total selves, closer by far than the confusion of kinswomen and kinsmen that had little meaning to a nas kame. For Isande there was only Reha: they had been the same individual compartmentalized into two discrete personalities, and half of it still wakened at night reaching for the other. They had not been lovers. It was something far closer.

Something to which Aiela had been rudely, forcibly admitted.

And he was an outsider, who hated the things she and Reha had loved most deeply. *Bear with me,* she asked of him. *Bear with me. Do not attack me. I have not accepted this entirely, but I will. There is no choice. And you are not unlike him. You are honest, whatever else. You are stubborn. I think he would have liked you. I must begin to.*

"Isande," he began, unaccountably distressed for her. "Could I possibly be worse than the human? And you insist you wanted that."

I could shield myself from that—far more skillfully than you can possibly learn to do in two days. And then I would be rid of him. But you—

Rid? He tried to penetrate her meaning in that, shocked and alarmed at once; and encountered defenses, winced under her rejection, heart speeding, breath tight. She turned off her conscience where the human was concerned. He was nothing to her, this creature. Anger, revenge, Reha—the human was not the object of her intentions: he simply stood in the way, and he was alien—*alien!*—and therefore nothing. Aiela would not draw her into sympathy with that creature. She would not permit it. *NO!* She had died with one asuthe, and she was not willing to die with another.

Why is he here? Aiela insisted. *What do the iduve want with him?*

Her screening went up again, hard. The rebuff was almost physical in its strength.

He was not going to obtain that answer. He had to admit it finally. He rose from his place and walked to the bureau, came back and sprawled into the chair, shaking with anger.

There was something astir among iduve, something which he was well sure Isande knew: something that could well cost him his life, and which she chose to withhold from him. And as long as that was so there would be no peace between them, however close the bond.

In that event she would not win any help from him, nor would the iduve.

No, she urged him. *Do not be stubborn in this.*

"You are Chimele's servant. You say what you have to say. I still have a choice."

Liar, she judged sadly, which stung like a slap, the worse because it was true.

Images of Chimele: ancestry more ancient than civilization among iduve, founded in days of tower-holds and warriors; a companion, a child, playing at draughts, elbows-down upon an *izhkh* carpet, laughing at a *m'metane's* cleverness; Orithain—

—isolate, powerful: *Ashanome's* influence could move full half the *nasuli* of the induve species to Chimele's bidding— a power so vast there could be no occasion to invoke it.

Sole heir-descendant of a line more than twelve thousand years old. *Vaikka:* revenge; honor; dynasty.

Involving this human, Aiela gleaned on another level.

But that was all Isande gave him, and that by way of making peace with him. She was terrified, to have given him only that much.

"Aiela," she said, "you are involved too, because *he* is, and you were chosen for him. Even iduve die when they stand between an Orithain and necessity. So did Reha."

I thought they didn't kill him.

"Listen to me. I have lived closer to the iduve than most kamethi ever do. If Reha had been asuthe to anyone else but me, he might be alive now, and now you are here, you are Chimele's because of me; and I am warning you, you will need a great deal of good sense to survive that honor."

"And you *love* a being like that." He could not understand. He refused to understand. That in itself was a victory.

"Listen. Chimele doesn't ask that you love her. She couldn't understand it if you did. But she scanned your records and decided you have great *chanokhia*, great—fineness— for a *m'metane*. Being admired by any iduve is dangerous; but an Orithain does not make mistakes. Do you understand me, Aiela?"

Fear and love: noi kame lived by carefully prescribed rules and were never harmed—as long as they remembered their place, as long as they remained faceless and obscure to the iduve. The iduve did not insist they do so: on the contrary the iduve admired greatly a *m'metane* who tried to be more than *m'metane*.

And killed him.

"There is no reason to be afraid on that score," Isande assured him. "They do not harm us. That is the reason of the *idoikkhei*. You will learn what I mean."

His backlash of resentment was so strong she visibly winced. She simply could not understand his reaction, and though he offered her his thoughts on the matter, she drew back and would not take them. Her world was enough for her.

"I have things to teach *you*," he said, and felt her fear like a wall between them.

"You are welcome to your opinions," she said at last.

"Thank you," he said bitterly enough; but when she opened that wall for a moment he found behind it the sort of gentle being he had seen through Reha's thoughts, terribly, painfully alone.

Dismayed, she slammed her screening shut with a vengeance, assumed a cynical façade and kept her mind taut, more burning than an oath. "And I will maintain my own," she said.

3

TWO DAYS COULD not prepare him, not for this.

He looked on the sleeping human and still, despite the hours he had spent with Isande, observing this being by monitor, a feeling of revulsion went through him. The attendants had done their aesthetic best for the human, but the sheeted form on the bed still looked alien—pale coloring, earth-brown hair trimmed to the skull-fitting style of the noi kame, beard removed. He never shuddered at amaut: they were cheerful, comic fellows, whose peculiarities never mattered because they never competed with kallia; but this—*this*—was bound to his own mind.

And there was no Isande.

He had assumed—they had both assumed in their plans—that she would be with him. He had come to rely on her in a strange fashion that had nothing to do with duty: with her, he knew *Ashanome,* he knew the folk he met, and people deferred to his orders as if Isande had given them. She had been with him, a voice continually in his mind, a presence at his side; at times they had argued; at others they had even found reason to be awed by each other's worlds. With her, he had begun to believe that he could succeed, that he could afterward settle into obscurity among the kamethi and survive.

He had in two days almost forgotten the weight of the bracelet upon his wrist, had absorbed images enough of the iduve that they became for him individual, and less terrible. He knew his way, which iduve to avoid most zealously, and which were reckoned safe and almost gentle. He knew the places open to him, and those forbidden; and if he was a prisoner, at least he owned a fellow-being who cared very much for his comfort—it was her own.

They were two: *Ashanome* was vast: and it was true that kamethi were not troubled by iduve in their daily lives. He saw no cruelty, no evident fear—himself a curiosity among Isande's acquaintances because of his origins: and no one forbade him, whatever he wished to say. But sometimes he saw in others' eyes that they pitied him, as if some mark were on him that they could read.

It was the human.

As this went, he would live or die; and at the last moment, Chimele had recalled Isande, ordering her sedated for her own protection. *I value you,* Chimele had said. *No. The risk is considerable. I do not permit it.*

Isande had protested, furiously; and that in a kameth was great bravery and desperation. But Chimele had not used the *idoikkhe;* she had simply stared at Isande with that terrible fixed expression, until the wretched *nas kame* had gone, weeping, to surrender herself to the laboratory, there to sleep until it was clear whether he would survive. The iduve would destroy a kameth that was beyond help; she feared to wake to silence, such a silence as Reha had left. She tried to hide this from him, fearing that she would destroy him with her own fear; she feared the human, such that it would have taxed all her courage to have been in his place now—but she would have done it, for her own reasons. She would have stood by him too—that was the nature of Isande: honor impelled her to loyalty. It had touched him beyond anything she could say or do, that she had argued with Chimele for his sake; that she had lost was only expected: it was the law of her world.

"Take no chances," she had wished him as she sank into dark. "Touch the language centers only, until I am with you again. Do not let the iduve urge you otherwise. And do not sympathize with that creature. You trust too much; it's a disease with you. Feelings such as we understand do not reside in all sentient life. The iduve are proof enough of that. And who understands the amaut?"

What do they want of him? he had tried to ask. But she had left him then, and in that place that was hers there was quiet.

Now something else stirred.

He felt it beginning, harshly ordered medical attendants out: they obeyed. He closed the door. There was only the rush of air whispering in the ducts, all other sound muffled.

The darkness spotted across his vision, dimming senses.

The human stirred, and light hazed where the dark had been.
Then he discovered the restraints and panicked.

Aiela flung up barriers quickly. His heart was pounding
against his ribs from the mere touch of that communication.
He bent over the human, seized his straining shoulders and
held him.

"Be still! Daniel, Daniel—be still."

The human's gasps for breath ebbed down to a series of
panting sobs. The dark eyes cleared and focused on his. Because touch was the only safe communication he had, Aiela
relaxed his grip and patted the human's shoulder. The human
endured it: he reminded Aiela of an animal soothed against
its will, a wild thing that would kill, given the chance.

Aiela settled on the edge of the cot, feeling the human
flinch. He spoke softly, tried amautish and kalliran words
with him without success, and when he at last thought the human calm again, he ventured a mind-touch.

A miasma of undefined feeling came back: pain-panic-con-
fusion. The human whimpered in fright and moved, and
Aiela snatched his mind back. His own hands were trembling.
It was several moments before the human's breathing rate returned to normal.

He tried talking to him once more, for a long time nothing
more than that. The human's eyes continually locked on his,
animal and intense; at times emotion went through them visibly—a look of anxiety, of perplexity.

At last the being seemed calmer, closed his eyes for a few
moments and seemed to slip away, exhausted. Aiela let him.
In a little time more the brown eyes opened again, fixed upon
his: the human's face contracted a little in pain—his hand
tensed against the restraints. Then he grew quiet again,
breathing almost normally; he suffered the situation with a
tranquillity that tempted Aiela to try mind-touch again, but he
refrained, instead left the bedside and returned with a cup of
water.

The human lifted his head, trusted himself to Aiela's arm
for support while he drained the cup, and then sank back
with a shortness of breath that had no connection with the effort. He wanted something. His lips contracted to a white
line. He babbled something that had to do with amaut.

He did speak, then. Aiela set the cup down and looked
down on him with some relief. "Is there pain?" he asked in

the amautish tongue, as nearly as kalliran lips could shape
the sounds. There was no evidence of comprehension. He sat
down again on the edge.

The human stared at him, still breathing hard. Then a
glance flicked down to the restraints, up again, pleading—repeated the gesture. When Aiela did nothing, the human's eyes
slid away from him, toward the wall. That was clear enough
too.

It was madness to take such a chance. He knew that it
was. The human could injure himself and kill him, quite easily.

He grew like Isande, who hated the creature, who would
deal with him harshly; like the iduve, who created the
idoikkhei and maintained matters on their terms, who could
see something suffer and remain unmoved.

Better to die than yield to such logic. Better to admit that
there was little difference between this wretched creature that
at least tried to maintain its dignity, and a kalliran officer
who walked about carrying iduve ownership locked upon his
wrist.

"Come," he said, loosed one restraint and the others in
quick succession, dismissing iduve, dismissing Isande's distress
for his sake. *He* chose, *he* chose for himself what he would
do, and if he would die it was easier than carrying out iduve
orders, terrifying this unhappy being. He lifted the human to
sit, steadied him on the edge, found those pale strong hands
locked on his arms and the human staring into his face in
confusion.

Terror.

Daniel winced, grimaced and clutched at his head, discovered the incision and panicked. He hurled himself up,
sprawled on the tiles, and lay there clutching his head and
moaning, sobbing words of nonsense.

"Daniel." Aiela caught his own breath, screening heavily:
he knew well enough what the human was experiencing, that
first horrible realization of the *chiabres,* the knowledge that
his very self had been tampered with, that there was something else with him in his skull. Aiela felt pressure at his defenses, a dark force that clawed blindly at the edges of his
mind, helpless and monstrous and utterly vulnerable at this
moment, like something newborn.

He let the human explore that for himself, measure it, dis-

cover at last that it was partially responsive to his will. Aiela
sat still, tautly screened, sweat coursing over his ribs; he
would not admit it, he would not admit it—it was dangerous,
unformed as it was. It moved all about the walls of his mind,
sensing something, seeking, aggressive and frightened at once.
It acquired nightmare shape. Aiela snapped his vision back to
now and destroyed the image, refusing it admittance, saw the
human wince and collapse.

He was not unconscious. Aiela knew it as he knew his own
waking. He simply lay still, waiting, waiting—perhaps gathering his abused senses into some kind of order. Perhaps he
was wishing to die. Aiela understood such a reaction.

Several times more the ugliness activated itself to prowl the
edges of his mind. Each time it fled back, as if it had learned
caution.

"Are you all right?" Aiela asked aloud. He used the tone,
not the words. He put concern into it. "I will not touch you.
Are you all right?"

The human made a sound like a sob, rolled onto an arm,
and then, as if he suddenly realized his lack of *elethia* before
a man who was still calmly seated and waiting for him, he
made several awkward moves and dragged himself to a
seated posture, dropped his head onto his arms for a moment,
and then gathered himself to try to rise.

Aiela moved to help him. It was a mistake. The human
flinched and stumbled into the wall, into the corner, very like
the attitude he had maintained in the cell.

"I am sorry." Aiela bowed and retreated back to his seat
on the edge of the bed.

The human straightened then, stood upright, released a
shaken breath. He reached again for the scar on his temple:
Aiela felt the pressure at once, felt it stop as Daniel pulled
his mind back.

"Daniel," he said; and when Daniel looked at him curiously, suspiciously, he turned his head to the side and let
Daniel see the scar that faintly showed on his own temple.

Then he opened a contact from his own direction, intending the slightest touch.

Daniel's eyes widened. The ugliness reared up, terrible in
its shape, Vision went. He screamed, battered himself against
the door, then hurled himself at Aiela, mad with fear. Aiela
seized him by the wrists, pressing at his mind, trying to ig-

nore the terror that was feeding back into him. One of them knew how to control the *chiabres:* uncontrolled, it could do unthinkable harm. Aiela fought, losing contact with his own body: sweat poured over him, making his grip slide; his muscles began to shake, so that he could not maintain his hold at all; he knew himself in physical danger, but that inside was worse. He hurled sense after sense into play, seeking what he wanted, reading the result in pain that fed back into him, nightmare shapes.

And suddenly the necessary barrier crashed between them, so painful that he cried out: in instinctive reaction, the human had screened. There was separation. There was self-distinction.

He slowly disengaged himself from the human's grip; the human, capable of attack, did not move, only stared at him, as injured as he. Perhaps the outcry had shocked him. Aiela felt after the human's wrist, gripped it not threateningly, but as a gesture of comfort.

He forced a smile, a nod of satisfaction, and uncertainly Daniel's hand closed—of a sudden the human gave a puzzled look, a half-laugh, half-sob.

He understood.

"Yes," Aiela answered, almost laughed himself from sheer relief. It opened barriers, that sharing.

And he cried out in pain from what force the human sent. He caught at his head, signed that he was hurt.

Daniel tried to stop. The mental pressure came in spurts and silences, flashes of light and floods of emotion. The darkness sorted itself into less horrid form. It was not an attack. The human *wanted;* so long alone, so long helpless to tell—he *wanted.* He wept hysterically and held his hands back, trembling in dread and desire to touch, to lay hold on anyone who offered help.

Barriers tumbled.

Aiela ceased trying to resist. Exhaustion claimed him. Like a man rushing downhill against his will he dared not risk trying to stop; he concentrated only on preserving his balance, threading his way through half-explored contacts, unfamiliar patterns at too great a speed. Contacts multiplied, wove into pattern; sensations began to sort themselves into order, perceptions to arrange themselves into comprehensible form:

body-sense, touch, equilibrium, vision—the room writhed out of darkness and took form about them.

Suddenly deeper senses were seeking structure. Aiela surrendered himself to Daniel's frame of reference, where right was human-hued and wrong was different, where morality and normality took shapes he could hardly bear without a shudder. He reached desperately for the speech centers for wider patterns, establishing a contact desperately needed.

"I," he said silently in human speech. "Aiela—I. Stop. Stop. Think slowly. Think of now. Hold back your thoughts to the pace of your words. Think the words, Daniel: my language, yours, no difference."

"What—" the first response attempted. Apart from Aiela's mind the sound had no meaning for the human.

"Go on. You understand me. You can use my language as I use yours. Our symbolizing facility is merged."

"What—" Death was in his mind, gnawing doubt that almost forced them apart. "What is going to happen to me? What are you?"

His communication was a babble of kalliran and human language, amaut mixed in, voiced and thought, echoes upon echoes. He was sending on at least three levels at once and unaware which was dominant. *Home, help, home* kept running beneath everything.

"Be calm," Aiela said. "You're all right. You're not hurt."

"I have—come a long way, a very long way from home. I don't even know where I am or why. I know—" *No, no, not accusation; soft with him, soft, don't make him angry.* "I know that you are being kind, that I—am being treated well—" Cages were in his mind; he thought them only out of sight on the other side of the wall, shrieks and hideous noise and darkness. *At least he looks human,* the second level ran. *Looks. Looks. Seems. Isn't. God, help me.* "Aiela, I—understand. I am grateful, Aiela—"

Daniel tried desperately to screen in his fear. It was a terrible effort. Under it all, nonverbal, there was fear of a horrible kind, fear of oblivion, fear of losing his mind altogether; but he would yield, he would merge, anything, anything but lose this chance. It was dangerous. It pulled at both of them. Aiela screened briefly, stopping it.

"I don't know how to help you," Aiela told him gently.

"But I assure you I don't want to harm you. You are safe. Be calm."

*Information—they want—*home came to mind, far distant, a world of red stone and blue skies. The memory met Aiela's surmise, the burrows of amaut worlds, human laborers, and confused Daniel greatly. *Past or future,* Daniel wondered. *Mine? Is this mine? Is this what I'm going to?*

Aiela drew back, trying to sort the human thoughts from his own. Nausea assailed him. The human's terrors began to seem his, sinister things, alien; and the amaut were at the center of all the nightmares.

"How did you come here, then?" Aiela asked. "Where did you come from, if not from the amaut worlds?"

And where is here and what are you? the human responded inwardly; but in the lightning-sequencing of memory, answers came, random at first, then deliberate—remembrances of that little world that had been home: poverty, other humans, anger, a displaced folk yearning toward a green and beautiful home that had no resemblance to the red desolation in which they now lived: an urge toward ships, and voyaging, homecoming and revenge.

Years reeled backward and forward again: strange suns, worlds, service in many ships, machinery appallingly primitive, backbreaking labor—but among humans, human ships, human ports, scant resources, sordid pleasures. Above all a regret for that sandy homeland, and finally a homecoming—to a home dissolved, a farm gone to dust; more port cities, more misery, a life without ties and without purpose. The thoughts ran aimlessly into places so alien they were madness.

These were not the Esliph worlds. Amaut did not belong there. Human space, then, human worlds, where kalliran and amaut trade had never gone.

Amaut. Daniel's mind seized on the memory with hate. Horrible images of death, bodies twisted, stacked in heaps—prisoners—humans—gathered into camps, half-starved and dying, others hunted, slaughtered horribly and hung up for warnings, the hunters humankind too; but among them moved dark, large-eyed shapes with shambling gait and leering faces—amaut seen through human eyes. Events tumbled one over the other, and Aiela resisted, unknowing what terrible place he was being led next; but Daniel sent, forcefully,

no random images now—hate, hate of aliens, of him, who
was part of this.

Himself. A city's dark streets, a deserted way, night, fire
leaping up against the horizon, strange hulking shapes looming above the crumbling buildings—a game of hunter and
hunted, himself the quarry, and those same dread shapes
loping ungainly behind him.

Ambush—unconsciousness—death?—smothered and torn
by a press of bodies, alien smells, the cutting discomfort of
wire mesh under his naked body, echoing crashes of
machinery in great vastness, cold and glaring light. Others
like himself, humans, frightened, silent for days and nights of
cold and misery and sinister amaut moving saucer-eyed beyond the perimeter of the lights—cold and hunger, until in
increasing numbers the others ended as stiff corpses on the
mesh.

More crashes of machinery, panic, spurts of memory inter-
spersed with nightmare and strangely tranquil dreams of
childhood: drugs and pain, now gabbling faces thrust close to
his, shaggy, different humans incapable of speech as he knew
it, overwhelming stench, dirty-nailed fingers tearing at him.

Aiela jerked back from the contact and bowed his head
into his hands, nauseated; but worse seeped in after: cages,
transfer to another ship, being herded into yet filthier confinement, the horror of seeing fellow beings reduced to mouthing
animals, constant fear and frequent abuse—himself the victim almost always, because he was different, because he could
not speak, because he did not react as they did—the cunning
humor of the savages, who would wait until he slept and then
spring on him, who would goad him into a rage and then
press him into a corner of that cage, tormenting him for their
amusement until his screams brought the attendants running
to break it up.

At last, strangers, kallia; his transfer, drugged, to yet another wakening and another prison. Aiela saw himself and
Chimele as alien and shadowy beings invading the cell: Daniel's distorted memory did not even recognize him until he
met the answering memory in Aiela's mind.

Enemy. Enemy. Interrogator. Part of him, enemy. The terror boiled into the poor human's brain and created panic, violence echoing and re-echoing in their joined mind, division
that went suicidal, multiplying by the second.

Aiela broke contact, sick and trembling with reaction. Daniel was similarly affected, and for a moment neither of them moved.

No matter, no matter, came into Daniel's mind, remembrance of kindness, reception of Aiela's pity for him. *Any conditions, anything.* He realized that Aiela was receiving that thought, and hurt pride screened it in. "I am sorry," he concentrated the words. "I don't hate you. Aiela, help me. I want to go home."

"From what I have seen, Daniel, I much fear there is no home for you to return to."

Am I alone? Am I the only human here?

The thought terrified Daniel; and yet it promised no more of the human cages; held out other images, himself alone forever, victim to strangers—amaut, kallia, aliens muddled together in his mind.

"You are safe," Aiela assured him; and was immediately conscious it was a forgetful lie. In that instant memory escaped its confinement.

They. They—Daniel snatched a thought and an image of the iduve, darkly beautiful, ancient and evil, and all the fear that was bound up in kalliran legend. He associated it with the shadowy figure he had seen in the cell, doubly panicked as Aiela tried to screen. *No! What have you agreed to do for them? Aiela!*

"No." Aiela fought against the currents of terror. "No. Quiet. I'm going to have you sedated—*No!* Stop that!—so that your mind can rest. I'm tired. So are you. You will be safe, and I'll come back later when you've rested."

You're going to report to them—and to lie there—The human remembered other wakings, strangers' hands on him, his fellow humans' cruel humor. Nausea hit his stomach, fear so deep there was no reasoning. There were amaut on the ship: he dreaded them touching him while he was unconscious.

"You will be moved," Aiela persisted. "You'll wake in a comfortable place next to my rooms, and you'll be free when you wake, completely safe, I promise it. I'll have the amaut stay completely away from you if that will make you feel any better."

Daniel listened, wanting to believe, but he could not. Mercifully the attendant on duty was both kalliran and gentle of

manner, and soon the human was settled into bed again, slid-
ing down the mental brink of unconsciousness. He still
stretched out his thoughts to Aiela, wanting to trust him,
fearing he would wake in some more incredible nightmare.

"I will be close by," Aiela assured him, but he was not sure
the human received that, for the contact went dark and numb
like Isande's.

He felt strangely amputated then, utterly on his own
and—a thing he would never have credited—wishing for the
touch of his asuthe, her familiar, kalliran mind, her capacity
to make light of his worst fears. If he were severed from the
human this moment and never needed touch that mind again,
he knew that he would remember to the end of his days that
he had for a few moments *been* human.

He had harmed himself. He knew it, desperately wished it
undone, and feared not even Isande's experience could help
him. She had tried to warn him. In defiance of her advice he
had extended himself to the human, reckoning no dangers but
the obvious, doing things his own way, with *kastien* toward a
hurt and desolate creature.

He had chosen. He could no more bear harm to Isande
than he could prefer pain for himself: iduvish as she was, he
knew her to the depth of her stubborn heart, knew the *elethia*
of her and her loyalty, and she in no wise deserved harm
from anyone.

Neither did the human. Someone meant to use him, to
wring some use from him, and discard him or destroy him afterward—*be rid of him,* Isande had said, even she callous
toward him—and there was in that alien shell a being that
had not deserved either fate.

*It is not reasonable to ask me to venture an opinion on
something I have never experienced,* Chimele had told him at
the outset. She did not understand kalliran emotion and she
had never felt the *chiabres.* Of a sudden he feared not even
Chimele might have anticipated what she was creating of
them, and that she would deal ruthlessly with the result—a
kameth whose loyalty was half-human.

He was kallia, *kallia!*—and of a sudden he felt his hold on
that claim becoming tenuous. It was not right, what he had
done—even to the human.

Isande, he pleaded, hoping against all knowledge to the

contrary for a response from that other, that blessedly kalliran mind. *Isande, Isande.*

But his senses perceived only darkness from that quarter.

In the next moment he felt a mild pulse from the *idoikkhe*, the coded flutter that meant *paredre*.

Chimele was sending for him.

There was the matter of an accounting.

4

CHIMELE WAS PERTURBED. It was evident in her brooding expression and her attitude as she leaned in the corner of her chair; she was not pleased; and she was not alone for this audience: four other iduve were with her, and with that curious sense of *déjà vu* Isande's instruction imparted, Aiela knew them. They were Chimele's *nasithi-katasakke*, her half-brothers and -sister by common-mating.

The woman Chaikhe was youngest: an Artist, a singer of songs; by kalliran standards Chaikhe was too thin to be beautiful, but she was gentle and thoughtful toward the kamethi. She had also thought of him with interest: Isande had warned him of it; but Chimele had said no, and that ended it. Chaikhe was becoming interested in *katasakke*, in common-mating, the presumable cause of restlessness; but an iduve with that urge would rapidly lose all interest in *m'metanei*.

Beside Chaikhe, eyeing him fixedly, sat her full brother Ashakh, a long-faced man, exceedingly tall and thin. Ashakh was renowned for intelligence and coldness to emotion even among iduve. He was *Ashanome's* chief Navigator and master of much of the ship's actual operation, from its terrible armament to the computers that were the heart of the ship's machinery and memory. He did not impress one as a man who made mistakes, nor as one to be crossed with impunity. And next to Ashakh, leaning on one arm of the chair, sat Rakhi, the brother that Chimele most regarded. Rakhi was of no great beauty, and for an iduve he was a little plump. Also he had a shameful bent toward *kutikkase*—a taste for physical comfort too great to be honorable among iduve. But he was devoted to Chimele, and he was extraordinarily kind to the noi kame and even to the seldom-noticed amaut, who adored him as their personal patron. Besides, at the heart

50

of this soft, often-smiling fellow was a heart of greater
bravery than most suspected.

The third of the brothers was eldest: Khasif, a giant of a
man, strikingly handsome, sullen-eyed—older than Chimele,
but under her authority. He was of the order of Scientists, a
xenoarchaeologist. He had a keen *m'melakhia*—an impelling
hunger for new experience—and noi kame made themselves
scarce when he was about, for he had killed on two occasions. This was the man Isande so feared, although—she had
admitted—she did not think he was consciously cruel. Khasif
was impatient and energetic in his solutions, a trait much
honored among iduve, as long as it was tempered with re-
finement, with *chanokhia*. He had the reputation of being a
very dangerous man, but in Isande's memory he had never
been a petty one.

"How fares Daniel?" asked Chimele. "Why did you ask
sedation so early? Who gave you leave for this?"

"We were tiring," said Aiela. "You gave me leave to order
what I thought best, and we were tired, we—"

"Aiela-kameth," Chaikhe intervened gently. "Is there
progress?"

"Yes."

"Will complete *asuthithekkhe* be possible with this being?
Can you reach that state with him, that you can be one with
him?"

"I don't—I don't think it is safe. No. I don't want that."

"Is this yours to decide?" Ashakh's tones were like icewater
on the silken voice of Chaikhe. "Kameth—you were instructed."

He wanted to tell them. The memory of that contact was
still vivid in his mind, such that he still shuddered. But there
was no patience in Ashakh's thin-lipped face, neither patience
nor mercy nor understanding of weakness. "We are
different," he found himself saying, to fill the silence. Ashakh
only stared. "Give me time," he said again.

"We are on a schedule," Ashakh said. "This should have
been made clear to you."

"Yes, sir."

"Specify the points of difference."

"Ethics, experience. He isn't hostile, not yet. He mistrusts—he mistrusts me, this place, all things alien."

"Is it not your burden to reconcile these differences?"

"Sir." Aiela's hands sweated and he folded his arms, pressing his palms against his sides. He did not like to look Ashakh in the face, but the iduve stared at him unblinkingly. "Sir, we are able to communicate. But he is not gullible, and I'm running out of answers that will satisfy him. That was why I resorted to the sedative. He's beginning to ask questions. I had no more easy answers. What am I supposed to tell him?"

"Aiela." Khasif drew his attention to the left. "What is your personal reaction to the being?"

"I don't know." His mouth was dry. He looked into Khasif's face, that was the substance of Isande's nightmares, perfect and cold. "I try—I try to avoid offending him—"

"What is the ethical pattern, the social structure? Does he recognize kalliran patterns?"

"Close to kallia. But not the same. I can't tell you: not the same at all."

"Be more precise."

"Am I supposed to have learned something in particular?" Aiela burst out, harried and regretting his tone at once. The *idoikkhe* pulsed painlessly, once, twice: he looked from one to the other of them, not knowing who had done it, knowing it for a warning. "I'm sorry, but I don't understand. I was primed to study this man, but no one will tell me just what I was looking for. Now you've taken Isande away from me too. How am I to know what questions to start with?"

His answer caused a little ruffling among the iduve, and merry Rakhi laughed outright and looked sidelong at Chimele. "*Au,* this one has a sting, Chimele." He looked back at Aiela. "And what have you learned, thus ignorant of your purpose, *o m'metane?*"

"That the amaut have intruded into human space, which they swore in a treaty with the *Halliran Idai* they would never do. This man came from human space. They lost most of his shipment because these humans weren't acclimated to the kind of abuse they received. Is that what you want to hear? Until you tell me what you mean to do with him, I'm afraid I can't do much more."

Chimele had not been amused. She frowned and stirred in her chair, placing her hands on its arms. "Can you, Aiela, prepare this human for our own examination by tomorrow?"

"That's impossible. No. And what kind of—?"

"By tomorrow evening."

"If you want something, then make it clear what it is and maybe I can learn it. But he wants answers. He has questions, and I can't keep putting him off, not without creating you an enemy—or do you care?"

"You will have to—put him off, as you express it."

"I'm not going to lie to him, even by omission. What are you going to do with him?"

"I prefer that this human not be admitted to our presence with the promise of anything. Do you understand me, Aiela? If you promise this being anything, it will be the burden of your honor to pay for it; make sure your resources are adequate. I will not consider myself or the *nasul* bound by your ignorant and unauthorized generosity. Go back to your quarters."

"I will not lie to him for you."

"Go back to your quarters. You are not noticed." This time there was no softness at all in her tone, and he knew he dared not dispute with her further. Even Rakhi took the smile from his face and straightened in his chair. Aiela omitted the bow of courtesy, turned on his heel and walked out.

He had ruined matters. When he was stressed his voice rose, and he had let it happen, had lost his case for it. He had felt when he walked in that Chimele was not in a mood for patience; and he realized in hindsight that the *nasithi* had tried to avert disaster: Rakhi, he thought, Rakhi, who had always been kind to Isande, had wished to stop him.

He returned to the kamethi level in utmost dejection, realized the late hour and considered returning to the lab and requesting to have a sedative for himself. His nerves could bear no more. But he had never liked such things, liked less to deal with Ghiavre, the iduve first Surgeon; and it occurred to him that Daniel might wake prematurely and need him. He decided against it.

He went to his quarters and prepared for bed, settled in with notebook and pen and diverted his thoughts to record-keeping on Daniel, then, upon the sudden cold thought that the iduve might not respect the sanctity of his belongings, he tore up everything and threw it into the disposal. The suspicion distressed him. As a kallia he had never thought of such things; he had never needed to suspect such *ikastien* on the part of his superiors.

Daniel had learned such suspicion. It was human.

With that distressing thought he turned out the lights and lay still until his muddled thoughts drifted into sleep.

The *idoikkhe* jolted him, brutally, so that he woke with an outcry and clawed his way up to the nearest chair.

Isande, he had cast, the reflex of two days of dependency; and to his surprised relief there was a response, albeit a muzzy one.

Aiela, she responded, remembered Daniel, instantly tried to learn his health and began to pick up the immediate present: Chimele, summoning him, angry; and Daniel—*What have you done?* she sent back, shivering with fear; but he prodded her toward the moment, thrusting through the flutter of her drug-hazed thoughts.

"This is Chimele's sleep cycle too," he sent. "Does she always exercise her tempers in the middle of the night?"

The *idoikkhe* stung him again, momentarily disrupting their communication. Aiela reached for his clothes and pulled them on, while Isande's thoughts threaded back into his mind. She scanned enough to blame him for matters, and she was distressed enough to let it seep through; but she had the grace to keep that feeling down. Now was important. He was important. He had to take her advice now; he could be hurt, badly.

"Chimele's hours are seldom predictable," she informed him, her outermost thoughts calm and ordered. But what lay under it was a peculiar physical fear that unstrung his nerves.

He looked at the time: it was well past midnight, and Chimele, like Ashakh, did not impress him as one who took the leisure for whimsy. He pulled his sweater over his head, started for the door, but he paused to hurl at Isande the demand that she drop her screening, guide him. He felt her reticence; when it melted, he almost wished otherwise.

Fear came, nightmares of Khasif, chilling and sexual at once. Few things could cause an iduve to act irrationally, but there was one outstanding exception, and iduve when irritated with kamethi were prone to it.

He stopped square in the doorway, blood leaving his face and returning in a hot rush. Her urgency prodded him into motion again, her anger and her terror like ice in his belly. *No,* he insisted again and again. Isande had been terrified once and long ago: she was scarred by the experience and dwelled on it excessively—it embarrassed him, that he had to express that thought: he knew it for truth. He wished her still.

"It happens," Isande insisted, with such firmness that it shook his conviction. "It is *katasukke*—pleasure-mating." And quickly, without preface, apology, or overmuch delicacy, she fed across what she knew or guessed of the iduve's intimate habits—alienness only remotely communicated in *katasukke* with noi kame, a union between iduve in *katasakke* that was fraught with violence and shielded in ritual and secrecy. *Katasukke* was gentler: sensible noi kame were treated with casual indulgence or casual negligence according to the mood of the iduve in question; but cruelty was *e-chanokhia*, highly improper, whatever unknown and violent things they did among themselves. But both *katasakke* and *katasukke* triggered dangerous emotions in the ordinarily dispassionate iduve. *Vaikka* was somehow involved in mating, and it was not uncommon that someone was killed. In Isande's mind any irrationality in the iduve emanated from that one urge: it was the one thing that could undo their common sense, and when it was undone, it was a madness as alien as their normal calm.

He shook off these things, hurried through the corridors while Isande's anxious presence thrust into his mind behaviors and apologies, fawning kameth graces meant to appease Chimele. *Vaikka* with a nas kame had this for an expected result, and if he provoked her further now he would be lucky to escape with his life.

He rejected Isande and her opinions, prideful and offended, and knew that Isande was crying, and frustrated with him and furious. Her anger grew so desperate that he had to screen against her, and bade her leave him alone. He was ashamed enough at this disgraceful situation without having her lodged as resident observer in his mind. He knew her hysterical upon the subject, and even so could not help fearing he was walking into something he did not want to contemplate.

With Isande aware, mind-bound to him.
Leave me alone! he raged at her.
She went; and then he was sorry for the silence.

Chimele was waiting for him, seated in her accustomed
chair as a tape unreeled on the wall screen with dizzying rapidity: the day's reports, quite probably. She cut it off, using
a manual control instead of the mental ones of which the
iduve were capable—a choice, he had learned, which betokened an iduve with mind already occupied.

"You took an unseemly amount of time responding," she
said.

"I was asleep." Fear added, shaming him: "I'm sorry."

"You did not expect, then, to be called?"

"No," he said: and doubled over as the *idoikkhe* hit him
with overwhelming pain. He was surprised into an outcry, but
bit it off and straightened, furious.

"Well, consider it settled, then," she said, "and cheaply so.
Be wiser in the future. Return to your quarters."

"All of you are demented," he cried, and it struck, this
time enough to gray the senses, and the pain quite washed his
mind of everything. When it stopped he was on his face on
the floor, and to his horror he felt Isande's hurt presence in
him, holding to him, trying to absorb the pain and reason
with him to stay down.

"Aiela," said Chimele, "you clearly fail to understand me."

"I don't want—" the *idoikkhe* stung him again, a gentle
reproof compared with what had touched him a moment before. It jolted raw nerves and made him cringe physically in
dread: the cowardice it instilled made him both ashamed and
angry; and there was Isande's anxious intrusion again. The
two-sided assault was too much. He clutched his head and
begged his asuthe to leave him, even while he stumbled to his
feet, unwilling to be treated so.

She can destroy you, Isande sent him hysterically. *She has
her honor to think of.* Vaikka, *Aiela,* vaikka!

"Is it Isande?" asked Chimele. "Is it she that troubles you?"

"She's being hurt. She won't go away. Please stop it."

And then he knew that Isande's *idoikkhe* had pained her,
once, twice, with increasing severity, and the mournful and
loyal presence fled.

"Aiela," said Chimele, "all my life I have dealt gently with my kamethi. Why will you persist in provoking me? Is it ignorance or is it design?"

"It's my nature," he said, which further offended her; but this time she only scowled and regarded him with deep dissatisfaction.

"Your ignorance of us has not been noticed: the nearest equivalent is 'forgiven.' It will be a serious error on your part to assume this will continue without limit."

"I honestly," he insisted, "do not understand you."

"We are not in the habit of patience with *metane-tekasuphre*. Nor do we make evident our discomforts. *Au, m'metane*, I should have the hide from you." There was self-control; and under it there was a rage that made his skin cold: run now, he thought, and become like the others—no. She would deal with him, explaining matters; he would stand there until she did so.

For a long moment he stood still, expected the touch of the *idoikkhe* for it; she did not move either.

"Aiela," she said then, in a greatly controlled voice, "I was disadvantaged before my *nasithi-katasakke*." And when he only stared at her, helplessly unenlightened: "For three thousand years *Ashanome* has taken no outsider-*m'metane* aboard," she said. "I have never dealt with the likes of you."

"What am I supposed to say?"

"You disputed with my *nasithi*. Then you turned the same discourtesy on me. Had you no perception?"

"I had cause," he declared in temper too deep-running to reckon of her anger, and his hand went to the *idoikkhe* on reflex. "*This* doesn't turn off my mind or my conscience, and I still want to know what you intend with the man Daniel."

Chimele literally trembled with rage. He had never seen so dangerous a look on any sane and sentient face, but the pain he expected did not come. She stilled her anger with an evident effort.

"*Nas-suphres*," she said in a tone of cosmic contempt. "You are hopeless, *m'metane*."

"How so?" he responded. "How so—*ignorant*?"

"Because you provoke me and trust my forbearance. This is the act of a stupid or an ignorant being. And did I truly believe you capable of *vaikka*, you would find yourself woefully outmatched. You are not irreplaceable, *m'metane*, and you are perilously close to extinction at this moment."

"I have no confidence at all in your forbearance, and I well know you mean your threats."

"The clumsiness of your language makes rational conversation impossible. You are nothing, and I could wipe you out with a thought. I should think the reputedly ordered processes of the kalliran mind would dictate caution. I fail to perceive why you attack me."

Mad, he thought in panic, remembering at the same time that she had mental control of the *idoikkhe*. He wanted to leave. He could not think how. "I have not attacked you," he said in a quiet, reasoning voice, as one would talk to the insane. "I know better."

She arose and moved away from him in great vexation, then looked back with some semblance of control restored. "I warned you once, Aiela, do not play at *vaikka* with us. You are incredibly ignorant, but you have a courage which I respect above all *metane*-traits. Do you not understand I must maintain *sorithias*—that I have the dignity of my office to consider?"

"I'm afraid I don't understand."

"*Au*, this is impossible. Perhaps Isande can make it clear."

"*No!* No, let her alone. I want none of her explanations. I have my mind clear enough without need of her rationalizations."

"You are incredible," Chimele exclaimed indignantly, and returned to him, seized both his hands, and made him sit down opposite her, a contact he hated, and she seemed to realize it. "Aiela. Do not press me. I *must* retaliate. We delight to be generous to our kamethi, but we will not have gifts demanded of us. We will not be pressed and not retaliate, we will not be affronted and do nothing. It is physically impossible. Can you not comprehend that?"

Her hands trembled. He felt it and remembered Isande's warning of iduve violence, the irrational and uncontrollable rages of which these cold beings were capable. But Chimele seemed yet in control, and her amethyst eyes locked with his in deep earnest, so plain a look it was almost like the touch of his asuthi. She let him go.

"I cannot protect you, poor *m'metane*, if you will persist in playing games of anger with us, if you persist in incurring punishment and fighting back when you receive the consequences of your impudence. You do not want to live under our law; you are not capable of it. And if you were wise, you would have left when I told you to go."

"I do not understand," he said. "I simply do not understand."

"Aiela—" Her indigo face showed stress. His hand still rested across his knee as he leaned forward, too tense to move. Now she took it back into hers, her slim fingers moving lightly across the back of it as if she found its color or the texture of his skin something remarkably fascinating. Pride and anger notwithstanding, he sensed nothing insulting in that touch, rather that Chimele drew a certain calm from that contact, that her mood shifted back to reason, and that it would be a perilous move if he jerked his hand away. He sweated with fear, not of iduve science or power—his rational faculty feared that; but something else worked in him, something subconscious that recognized Chimele and shuddered instinctively. He wished himself out that door with many doors between them; but her hand still moved over his, and her violet eyes stared into him.

"If you had been born among the kamethi," said Chimele softly, "you would never have run afoul of me, for no nas kame would ever have provoked me so far. He would have had the sense to run away and wait until I had called him again. You are different, and I have allowed for that—this far. And so that you will understand, ignorant kameth: you were impertinent with others and impertinent exceedingly with me—and being Orithain, I dispense judgments to the *nasithi*. How then shall I descend to publicly chastise a nas kame? They wished to persuade me to be patient; and I chose to be patient, remembering what you are; but then, *au*, after trading words with my *nasithi*, you must ignore my direct order and debate me what disposition I am to make of this human." She drew breath: when she went on it was in a calmer voice. "Rakhi could not reprimand my kameth in my presence; I could not do so in theirs. And there you stood, gambling with five of us in the mistaken confidence that your life was too valuable for me to waste. Were you iduve, I should say that were an extremely hazardous form of *vaikka*. Were you iduve, you would have lost that game. But because you

are *m'metane*, you were allowed to do what an iduve would
have died for doing."

"And is iduve pride that vulnerable, then?"

"Stop challenging me!"

It was a cry of anguish. Chimele herself looked terrified,
reminding him for all the world of an essentially friendly animal being provoked beyond endurance, a creature teased to
the point of madness by some child it loved, shivering with
taut nerves and repressed instincts. She could not help it, as
an animal could not resist a move from its prey.

Vaikka.

He grasped it then—a game that was indeed for iduve
only, a name that shielded a most terrifying instinct, one that
the iduve themselves must fear, for it tore apart all their careful rationality. The compulsion must indeed be involved in
their matings—intricate, unkalliran instinct. It was reasonable
that the noi kame feared above all the iduve's affections,
feared closeness. A kallia quite literally did not have a nervous system attuned to that kind of contest. A kallia would
want to play the game part of the way and then quit before
someone was hurt; but there was a point past which the iduve
could not quit.

"It is possible," he said carefully, "that I did not use good
judgment."

She grew perceptibly calmer at that slight retreat, slowed
her breathing, patted his arm with the thoughtless affection
one might show a pet, and then drew back her hand as if
mindful of his inward shudder. "Surely then," she said, "understanding your nature and ours, you need not stand so
straight or stare so insolently when that irrepressible tongue
of yours brings you afoul of our tempers."

"I was not educated as kameth."

"I perceive your difficulty. But do not seek to live by our
law. You cannot. And it is not reasonable for you to expect
us to bear all the burden of self-restraint. I thrust you into
close contact with us, a contact most kameth-born scarcely
know. It cannot be remedied. I trusted your common sense
and forgot kalliran—I know not whether to say obstinacy or
elethia, an admirable trait—but that and our aggressiveness,
our *m'melakhia*, is a very volatile combination."

"I begin to see that."

"Go back to your quarters this night, for your safety's

sake. I will respect your *m'melakhia*, your—protection—of your human asuthe as much as I can, and I will not remember this conversation to your hurt. You are wiser than you were. I advise you to make it apparent to my *nasithi-katasakke* that *vaikka* has been settled."

"How?"

"By your amended attitude and increased discretion in our presence."

"I understand," he said, hesitated awkwardly until an impatient gesture made clear his dismissal. Almost he delayed to thank her, but looking again into her eyes chilled the impulse into silence: he bowed, turned, felt her eyes on his back the whole long distance to the door.

The safety of the hall, the sealing of the door behind him, brought a physical relief. He lowered his eyes and flinched past an iduve who was passing, secured the lift alone, and was glad to find the kamethi level, where kallia thronged the concourse—the alternate day-cycle, whose waking was his night.

He knew the iduve finally.

Predators.

Outsiders had never understood the end of the Domination, the Sundering of the iduve empire. He began to.

They were hunters from their very origins—a species for whom all else that moved was prey, for whom others of their own kind were intolerable. They had hunted the *metrosi* to exhaustion and drifted elsewhere. Now they were back. The enormity of the surmise grew in him like a sickly chill.

The *nasul*—jealously controlling its territory.

Perhaps even the iduve themselves had forgotten what they were; the pride of ritual and ceremony shielded their instincts, civilized them, as civilization had dealt with the instincts of kallia, who had been the natural prey of other hunters in packs, on the plains of prehistoric Aus Qao. Subtle reactions, a tensing of muscles, an interchange of movements, the steadiness of the eyes—these defined hunter and hunted. That was the thing he had looked in the face when he had stared into Chimele's at close range. He had wished to run and had instinctively known better—that if he stayed very, very still, it might pad softly away.

He shivered, the hair rising at the nape of his neck as if she still watched him. When he felt Isande's frightened

presence beginning to creep back into his mind, he screened
heavily, for he still was shaken, and he was ashamed for her
to know the extent of it.

You nearly killed yourself, she accused him. *I warned you,
I warned you—*

"Not well enough," he returned. "You have a blind spot.
Or you do not understand them."

"I have lived my whole life among them," she retorted,
"and I have never seen what you saw tonight—not even from
Khasif."

He accepted that for truth. Likely kamethi had been taught
never to draw such responses. But he was world-born; he
himself had sat by fires at night in the wilds of Lelle, with a
ring of light to guard his sleep, and he knew Chimele in all
the atavistic fears of his species.

A predator who had assumed civilization.

Who had touched him gently and refrained, despite his
best attempt to provoke her—*ignorant,* she had called him,
and justly.

"Chimele is iduve." Isande hurled against the warmth of
that thought, forcefully, for she hated worse than anything to
have her advice ignored. "And you will live longer if you
remember that we are only kamethi, and avoid provoking her
and avoid attracting her notice to yourself."

This from Isande, Isande who loved Chimele, who willingly
served the iduve: who trembled in her heart each time she
dealt with Chimele's temper. It was a sorrowful life she had
accepted: he let that slip and was sorry, for Isande flared, hot
and unshielded.

Am I nothing, she fired at him, *because I was born kameth? My world-born friend, I have been places you have
not dreamed of, and seen things you cannot understand. And
as it regards the iduve, my friend, I have lived among them,
and what of their language you know, you lifted from my
mind, what of their customs you understand you have
learned from me, and what consideration you had from
Chimele you have because of me, so do not lecture me as an
expert on the iduve. If you were not so ikas, you would not
have had so dangerous an experience.*

Well, he returned, *I hardly seem to have a monopoly on
vanity or selfishness or arrogance, do I?*

And the resentments that echoed back and forth, too much truth, sent both personalities reeling apart, hurt.

Isande was first to touch again, grieving. "Aiela," she pleaded, "Asuthi must not quarrel. Please, Aiela."

"I am vain and arrogant," he admitted, "and I have had almost all the damage my sanity can stand tonight, Isande. I'm tired. Go away."

Daniel, she remembered, dismay and regret sharp in her; she remembered other things she had gleaned of his mind, and riffled through all the memory he left unscreened, gathering this and that with a rising feeling of distress, of outrage. He felt her, poised to blame him for everything, to accuse him of things the worse because they were just.

And she did not. He was so tired his legs shook under him, and he felt himself very lonely, even in her presence: he had disregarded everything she had meant to protect them both, and now that she had utmost cause to rage against him she pitied him too much to accuse him. She knew his nature and his incapacity, and she pitied him.

Leave me alone, he wished her. And then furiously: *Leave me alone, will you?*

She fled.

He undressed, washed, went through all the ritual of preparing for bed, and tried to sleep. It was impossible. Reaction still had his muscles in knots. When he closed his eyes he saw the *paredre,* Chimele—cages.

He arose and walked the floor, tried listening to his old tapes, that he had brought from Kartos. It was worse than the silence. He cut off the sound, idly cut in on the monitor that was preset for Daniel's next-door apartment. The human was still blissfully unconscious.

And the memory returned, how it had felt to live in that envelope of alien flesh. He broke the connection, dizzied and disoriented, wandered back to the bath, drifting as he had a dozen times, to the full-length mirror. It contained all in *Ashanome* that was familiar, that was known.

His image stared back at him, naked of everything but the *idoikkhe* that circled his wrist like some bizarre barbaric ornament. His silver hair was beginning a slow recovery from the surgeons' unimaginative barbering, and he had grown accustomed to the change. His features among kallia were con-

sidered proper: straight silver brows, a straight nose with a
little flare to the nostrils, a mouth wide enough to show generosity, a chin prominent as with all the Lyailleues. He fingered the high prominence of his cheekbone and the hollow
beneath, staring into his own eyes closely in the mirror, wondering how much of the iduve eye was iris. Was it all? And
could they see color as kallia could? Humans did. He knew
that. He considered the rest of himself, 7.8 *meis* in stature, a
little taller than the average, broad-shouldered and slim at the
hips, with the slender, well-muscled limbs of an athlete, the
flat belly and muscular girdle of a runner, a hard-trained
body that had no particular faults. He had never known serious illness, had suffered no wounds, had never known priva-
tion that was not his own choice. He was *parome* Deian's
only son; if he had had any faults at birth, no money would
have been spared to mend them. If he had lacked any in wit,
parome Deian's money would have purchased every known
aid to teach him and improve his mind. When he grew bored,
there had instantly been toys and games and hunts and athletics, and when he became a young man, there had been all the
loveliest and most proper girls, the most exclusive parties.
There were private instructors, the most proper and demanding schools; and there had been family despair when he insisted on pursuing athletics to the detriment of his studies, on
risking his life in hunts, on turning down a career in district
politics that was calculated to lead to the highest levels of
government—a lack of family and filial *giyre* that his father
refused to understand ("*Ikas,*" Deian had said, "and ungrate-
ful." "Am I *ikas,*" he had answered, eighteen and all-know-
ing, "because it is not my pattern to be like you?" "There
have been Lyailleues on the High Council for two hundred
years, honoring Xolun and this house. My son will not take it
on himself to end that tradition.")

Once that year he had thought of hurling his plane (a luxury model) in a pyrotechnic finish at Mount Ryi, in full view
of all the fashionable estates and the Xolun zone capitol. The
news services would be buzzing with wonder for days: Son of
Deian, Suicide; and people would be shaking their heads and
making small noises of despair and secretly hating him, thinking if only they had had his advantages they would not have
thrown them away. When he was nineteen he had quit school
so that his father Deian would disinherit him and his mother

and sister would give him up; but he also saw it broke their hearts, and his few passages with the pleasures of the *metrosi's* darker side left him disgusted and embarrassed, for these things were also available in the estates in the shadow of Ryi—without the filth and the fear. In the end he had surrendered and returned home to the respectability planned for him, to learn the business of government.

("Son, it is always necessary to compromise. That's how things are done." "Even when one is right, sir?" "Right— right; you always assume you know exactly where that is, don't you? I'm sure I don't. If you go on like that, no one could ever agree. Compromise. Sometimes you have to yield a little to win a little later on.")

He had tried.

A year later he had sought the anonymity of the service, and even that had proved no refuge secure from Deian's money and influence. Perhaps, he thought, it was his father's way of setting him free; or perhaps Deian still believed he would have come home, older, wiser. He would have come home, sooner or later. He had spent his life pursuing the elusive hope of adequacy, a constant struggle for breath in the rarified atmosphere of his father's ambitions and the *giyre* of his ancient family.

("I would have come home someday," he had written in that final letter. "I have gained the good sense to honor your wisdom and experience, Father, and I have gained enough wisdom of my own to have kept on in my own path. What *giyre* I had of my crew, I earned; and that is important to me. What *giyre* I gave, I chose to give, and that was important too. I honor you, very much; but I would not have left the service.")

It was irony. He closed his hand about the *idoikkhe* and reminded himself what he was worth at the end of all his father's planning and his resisting: a being scantly adequate to serve the iduve, equal to a gracious (if vain) young woman and a battered bit of human freight off an amaut transport. He had lived with the sky overhead to be reached, whether or not he chose to try, and whether or not he had realized it before, he had been an arrogant and a stubborn man. Now he had been shown where the sky stopped, and it was a shattering experience.

He imagined Daniel's image in the glass. The skin went

shades of brown and pink, the silver hair turned dark, the eyes shadowed and hunted, his body slight with hunger, crossed with red and purple scars from untreated wounds, feet lacerated by the cruel mesh. His mind held memories of absolute horror, cages, brutality unimagined in the *Halliran Idai*. Even before those, there were memories of hunger, a childhood in a dark, cement-walled house beside a trickling canal, summers of sandstorms that blasted crops, dunes that year by year encroached upon fields, advanced upon the house, threatened the life-giving canal. At some time—Aiela had inherited the memories in bits and snatches—Daniel had left that world for the military, and he had served as a technician of limited skills. He had known a great many primitive human ports, until the life sickened him and he went home again, only to find his father dead, his mother remarried, his brothers gone offworld, the farm buried under dunes.

War. Shipping lanes closed, merchantmen commandeered for military service. Daniel—senior now over inexperienced recruits, wearing the crisp blue of a technician on a decent ship, well fed, with money promised to his account. That had lasted seven days, until two stunning defeats had driven the human forces into retreat and then into rout, and men were required by martial law to seek their home ports and keep order there as the panic spread.

That was the way fortune operated for Daniel. His hands had been emptied every time he had them full; but being Daniel, he would shrug perplexedly, get down on his knees and begin picking up the pieces. He was uneducated, but he had a keen intuition, an intelligence that sucked in information like a vacuum drawing air, omnivorously, taking scrap and debris along with the pure, sorting, analyzing. He had never been anyone, he had never had anything; but he was not going to stop living until he was sure there was nothing to be had. That was Daniel—a man who had always been hungry. *M'melakhia*, Chimele would call it.

And Daniel's desire was the fevered dream of his half-sensible interludes in the cage, when the fields were green and the canal pure and full and orchards bloomed beside a white-walled house. He asked nothing more nor less than that—except the company of others of his kind. He had never deserved to be appropriated to *Ashanome*, swallowed whole by the pride of a Lyailleue and linked to a kalliran woman who had never learned to be kallia, who was more than a little iduve.

Aiela, Isande's thought reproved him, sorrowing.

How long have you been with me? He flushed with anger, for he had been deep in his own concerns and Isande's skill was such that he did not always perceive her touch. It was not the visual sense that embarrassed him: she knew his body as he knew hers, for that was a part of self-concept. It was his mind's privacy that he did not like thus exposed, and he knew at once from the backspill that she had caught rather more than she thought he would like.

"Dear Aiela," her silent voice came echoing. "No, don't screen me out. I am sorry for quarreling. I know I offend you."

"I am sorry," he sent, the merest surface of his thoughts, "for a great many things."

"You are not sure you can handle me," she said. "That troubles you. You are not accustomed to that. You are not half so cruel or fierce as I am, I know it; but you are twice as brave—too much so, sometimes, when that terrible pride of yours is touched."

"I have no pride," he said. "Not since Kartos."

She was amused, which stung. "No. No. It is there; but you have had it bruised—" the amusement faded, regretting his offense, and yet she knew herself right by his very reaction: right, and self-confident. "Chimele—the iduve in general—have touched it. You are just now realizing that this is forever, and it frightens you terribly."

Her words stung, and a feeling wholly *ikas* rose up in him. "I don't need to live on your terms. I will not."

She was silent for a time, sifting matters. "You do not understand *Ashanome.* Tonight you saw the *chanokhia* of Chimele, and I am afraid you have begun to love her. No—no, I know: not in that way. It is something worse. It is *m'melakhia*-love. It is *arastiethe* you want from her—iduve honor; and no *m'metane* can ever have that."

"You can't even think like a kallia, can you?"

"Aiela, Aiela, you are dealing with an iduve. Realize it. You are reacting to her as she *is.* You are thinking *giyre,* but Chimele cannot give you what she cannot even understand. For her there is only *arastiethe,* and the honor of an iduve demands too much of us. It costs too much, Aiela."

"She might be capable of understanding. Isande, she tried—"

"Avoid her!"

Screens dropped. Loneliness, a dead asuthe, years of silence. There was still loneliness, an asuthe who rejected her advice, who blindly, obstinately sought what had killed the other. Was the fault in her? Was it she that killed? She loved Chimele, and gave and gave, and the iduve knew only how to take. Reha had loved Chimele: asuthe to herself, how could he have helped it? He would be alive now, but that he had learned to love Chimele. She would not teach another.

Darkness. Cold. Screens tumbled. Aiela flinched and she snatched the memory away, recovering herself, smothering it as she had learned to do.

You denied, he reminded her gently, *That* Ashanome *killed him. Was Chimele responsible, after all?*

The screens stayed in place. Only the words came through, carefully controlled. "She was not responsible. Honor is all she can give. To the *nasithi,* that is everything. But what is it worth to a *m'metane?*"

Yet you do love her, Aiela sent, and sad laughter bubbled back.

"Listen—she tried with all her iduvish heart to make me happy. Three times she asked me to take another asuthe. 'He is like you,' she said this time. 'He is intelligent, he is of great *chanokhia* for a *m'metane.* Can you work with this one?' I consented. She risked a great deal to offer me that choice. You would have to know the iduve to realize how difficult that was for her—to try a thing when she has only reason to help her. She does feel—something. I am not sure what. After all these years, I am not sure what. Maybe we *m'metanei* try to read into them what we wish were there. Perhaps that is why we keep giving, when we know better."

"Let me alone," he wished her. "If I'm to make a mistake, then let it be my mistake."

"And when you make it," she said, "we will both pay for it. That is the way this arrangement works, Aiela."

It was truth; he recognized it—resented her being female. It was an unfair obligation. "I am sorry," he said after a moment. "Then it will happen. I will not be held by you."

"I disturb you."

"In several senses."

She snatched a thought half-born from his mind, the suspicion that the iduve knew enough of kalliran emotion to use it, to manipulate it at will. Isande was beautiful: he had eyes to notice that. He kept noticing it, again and again. That she constantly knew it, embarrassed him; he knew that she was not willing to think of him in that way. But, he sent her, if she were in the ungraceful position of having to share a man's inmost thoughts, she might receive things even more direct from time to time. Or had Reha been immune to such things?

The screen closed tightly on those memories, as it always had: the privacy she had shared with Reha was not for him. "He and I began so young we were like one mind; there could never be that between us. Asuthi ought never to share that part of their lives: some illusions have to be maintained. I am not for games, not for your amusement, nor are you for mine, dear friend. There is an end of it. You came too close to that being, you refuse my warnings about the iduve, and I see I can't help you: you resent being advised by a woman. But I can at least exercise the good sense to keep my distance from you when it happens."

Hurt feelings. Bitterly hurt feelings.

"Don't," he said, reaching out to her retreating mind. And when she lingered, questioning, he searched for something to say. "If you're not going to sleep, stay awhile. It's miserably quiet here."

Softness touched his mind. He had pleased her by asking. Her spirits brightened and amusement rippled from her, to think that he found in her the power to deal with the nightmares that troubled him: human ghosts and iduve went flitting into retreat at her kalliran presence.

"Go to bed," she told him. "You need your rest. I'll stay awhile if it pleases you."

She hovered about his thoughts for a long time thereafter, half-asleep herself at the last and warm in her own bed, lending him the comforting trivia of pleasant memories, the distant voyagings of *Ashanome*, strange worlds and different suns; and she stole from his memories, filching little details of his past and embroidering them with questions until he grew too tired to answer. She, never having walked upon the face of a world, delighted in the memories of wind and rain and sunsets, the scent of green grass after a shower, and the drifting wonder of snow. There were no ill dreams. She held onto his senses and finally, mischievously, she sent him a few drowsy impressions that were less than sisterly.

He fired back indignation. "Games," he reminded her.

Vaikka, she whispered into his consciousness. *And you do not want to tell me to go away, do you?*

He did not, but he screened, and headed himself deliberately toward the darkness of sleep.

5

ISANDE WAS THERE in the morning. Her cheerful presence burst in enthusiastically while Aiela was putting his boots on, and it was as if a door had opened and someone were standing behind him—where there was neither door nor body.

"Must you be so sudden?" he asked her, and her joy plummeted. He was sorry. Isande had never been so vulnerable before. He was concerned about last night and out of sorts about time wasted and a tight schedule with Daniel.

"I would try to help," she offered.

His screens tightened; he knew her opinion of the human, her dislike of the creature. If it were not unlike her, he would have suspected her of wishing to harm Daniel: her feelings were that strong.

What do you expect of me? she asked, offended.

Answers. What do they want with him?

And a strange uneasiness was growing in him now that Daniel was on his mind; Isande's thoughts grew hard to unravel. Daniel was waking; Aiela's own heart began to speed, his breathing grew constricted in sympathetic reaction.

"Calm!" he cast him. "Calm! It's Aiela. It's all right."

Isande—who is Isande?

Daniel perceived her through him. Aiela's impulse was to interrupt that link, protecting both of them; but he sensed no harm from either direction, and he hesitated, suffering a strange double-passage of investigation as they probed each other. Then he received quite an unpleasant impression as the human realized Isande was female: curiosity reached for body-sense, to know.

Violently he snapped that connection, at once prey to the outrage of them both.

"I can fend for myself," Isande voiced to him, seething

with offended pride. "He is not of our species, and I'm sure his curiosity means nothing to me."

But Daniel was too angry to voice. He was embarrassed and furious, and for a moment his temper obscured the fact that he was not equal to a quarrel either with Aiela or with his situation.

Aiela fired back his own feelings upon the instant: frustration with the ungovernable Isande, revulsion at having been made the channel for an alien male's obscene curiosity—male, not man, not fit to touch a kalliran woman.

Barriers went up against him, fell again. Aiela felt the human's despair like a plunge into darkness, a hurt mingled with his own guilt. He was too disoriented to prevent its flow to Isande. Her anguish struck him from the other side, coldly doused as she flung up a screen.

"Aiela! The echo—stop it."

He understood: mind-linked as they were, each brain reacted to the other's emotions. It was a deadly self-accelerating process. His reaction to Daniel's offended masculinity had lowered a screen on an ugliness he had not suspected existed in himself.

"Daniel," he sent, and persisted until the unhappy being acknowledged his presence. It was a terrible flood he received. All screens went, *asuthithekkhe*, mind-link, defense abandoned. The images came so strongly they washed out vision: amaut, cages, dead faces, grief upon grief. Daniel's mind was the last citadel and he hurled it wide open, willing to die, at the end of his resistance.

I am sorry, Aiela hurled into that churning confusion like a voice into a gale. *Daniel! I was hurt too. Stop this. Please. Listen.*

Gradually, gradually, sanity gathered up the pieces again, the broken screens rebuilt themselves into separate silence; and Aiela rested his head in his hands, struggling against a very physical nausea that swelled in his throat. His instincts screamed *wrong*, his hands were cold and sweating at the proximity of a being unutterably twisted, who rejected *giyre* and *kastien*, who loathed the things most kalliran.

Aiela. Daniel reached the smallest tendril of thought toward him. He did not understand, but he would seal the memory behind a screen and not let it out again. Dying was not worse than being alone. Whatever the rules Aiela set, he would conform.

I'm sorry, Aiela replied gently. *But your perceptions of us are not exactly without prejudice; and you were rude with Isande.*

Isande is yours? Daniel snatched at that possibility. It touched something human as well as kalliran. He was anxious to believe he was not hated, that he had only made a mistake.

It was like that, Aiela admitted, embarrassed. He had never expected to have to share such intimate thoughts with the creature. It disturbed him, made him feel unclean; he screened those emotions in, knowing he must dispose of them.

"This arrangement," Daniel said, scanning the situation to the limit Aiela allowed, "with a woman and the two of us—is not the best possible, is it?"

That was sent with wistful humor. The human foresaw for himself a lifetime of being different, of being alone. Aiela was sorry for him then, deeply sorry, for there was in the being an *elethia* worth respect.

"We are at the mercy of the iduve," Aiela said, "who perceive our feelings only at a distance."

"There are so many things I don't understand here that I can hardly keep my thoughts collected. There are moments when I think I'm going to—"

"Please. Keep your questions a little longer. I will find it easier to explain when you have seen a little of the ship. Come, get dressed. Food comes before other things. We'll go out to the mess hall and you can have a look about."

Daniel was afraid. He had caught an impression of the way they would walk, crowds of kalliran strangers; and when Aiela let him know that there would be amaut too, he looked forward to breakfast with no appetite at all.

"Trust me," said Aiela. "If the iduve wished you harm, no place would be safe, and if they wish you none, then you are safe anywhere on this ship. They rule all that happens here."

Daniel acquiesced unhappily to that logic. In a little time they were out on the concourse together, Daniel looking remarkably civilized in his brown clothing—Aiela let that thought slip inadvertently and winced, but Daniel accepted the judgment with wry amusement and little bitterness. He was not a vain man, and the amaut had removed whatever vanity he had had.

It was the mess-hall company he could not abide. As they were eating, two amaut chanced to stand near their table talking, popping and hissing in the odd rhythms of their native tongue. Daniel's hand began to shake in the midst of carrying a bite to his mouth, and he laid the utensil aside a moment and covered the action by reaching for his cup. When Aiela picked up the thought in his mind, the memory of that cage and his voyage, he nearly lost his own appetite.

"These are decent folk," Aiela assured him, silently so the amaut would not realize the exchange.

"See how people look at me when they think I am looking away. I had as soon be an exhibit in a zoo. And I know the amaut. I know them; don't try to tell me otherwise. It doesn't help my confidence in you."

Is the human species then without its bandits, its criminals and deviates?

Aiela caught a disturbing flash of human history as Daniel pondered that question; and with a deliberate effort Daniel put the memory of the freighter from his mind. But he still would not look at the amaut.

Aiela. That was Isande, near them. She queried Aiela, did he mind, and when he extended her the invitation, she came into the mess hall, took a hot drink from the dispenser, and joined them. Through Aiela she reached for Daniel's mind and touched, introducing herself.

Her bright smile (it was a weapon she used consciously) elicited a shy response from Daniel, who was still nervous about Aiela's reactions; but when Aiela had approved, the human opened up and smiled indeed, the first time Aiela had known any moment of unblighted happiness in the being. Isande's presence with them was like a sunshine that drowned all the shadows, an assurance to Daniel that here was a healthy, whole world, a normality he had almost forgotten.

"I," said Daniel aloud, struggling with the unfamiliar sounds of the kalliran language, "I am really very sorry for offending you."

"You are a kind man," said Isande, and patted his hand— Aiela was glad he had his own screens up during that moment. He had foreseen this, and knew Isande well enough to know that she would purposely defy him in some way. Poor Daniel looked quite overcome by her, not knowing what to do then; and Aiela dropped his screen on Isande's contact, letting her know what he thought of her petty *vaikka*.

Stop it, Isande. Be kallia for once. Feel something.

She had not realized about Daniel, not known him so utterly vulnerable and frightened of them. Now she saw him through Aiela's eyes.

"Please," said Daniel, who had not been privy to that small exchange, but was painfully aware of the silence that excluded him. "I am an inconvenience to you both—but save us all embarrassment. Tell me why I have been brought here, why I have been—unwelcomely attached—to you both."

Isande was dismayed and ashamed; but Aiela looked on the human with as much respect at that moment as he had felt for any man.

"Yes," said Aiela, "I think it is time we went aside together, the three of us, and did that."

It would have been merciful, Aiela reflected, if Chimele had elected to talk to the human with as little distraction about him as possible. Instead, when he and his two asuthi entered the *paredre*, there were not only the *nasithi-katasakke*, but what Isande flashed them in dismay was the entire *Melakhis*. The blue screen was thrust back, opening up the audience hall, and nearly fifty iduve were there to observe them. *Kamethi*, Isande sent, *are not normally involved before the Melakhis. Iduve together are dangerous. Their tempers can become violent with no apparent reason. Be very careful, Daniel; be extremely careful and respectful.*

Chimele met them graciously, gave Aiela a nod of particular courtesy. Then she looked full at Daniel, whose heart was beating as if he feared murder.

Be calm, Aiela advised him. *Be calm. Isande and I are here to advise you if you grow confused.*

"Please sit," said Chimele, including them all. She resumed the central chair in the *paredre*—a ceremonial thing, perhaps of great age, ornate with serpents and alien or mythical beasts worked in wood and gold and amber. "Daniel. Do you understand where you are?"

"Yes," he answered. "They have explained to me who you are and that I must be honest with you."

Some of the elder iduve frowned at that; but Chimele heard that naive reply and inclined her head in courtesy.

"Indeed. You are well advised to be so. Where is your home, Daniel, and how did you come into the hands of the amaut of *Konut?*"

Suspicion ran through Daniel's mind: attack, plunder—these the agents of it, seeking information. Isande had threshed out the matter with him repeatedly, assuring him of *Ashanome's* indifference to the petty matter of his world. Suddenly Daniel was not believing it. Fight-flight-escape ran through his mind, but he did not move from his chair. Aiela seized his arm to be sure that he did not.

"Pardon," Aiela said to Chimele softly, for he knew her extreme displeasure when Daniel failed to respond. She had shown courtesy to this being before her people; and Daniel for his part looked into those whiteless eyes and met something against which the alienness of the amaut was slight in comparison. They had shown Daniel iduve in his mind; he had even seen Chimele—shadowy and indistinct in his cell; but the living presence of them, the subtle communication of arrogance and their lack of response to emotion, he hated, loathed, feared. *Their pattern is different,* Aiela sent him. *It is affecting you. Don't let it overcome you. Instinct is not always positive for survival when you are offworld. You are the stranger here.*

"*M'metane,*" Chimele said, labored patience in her voice, "*m'metane,* what is the difficulty?"

"I—" Daniel shared a moment into Chimele's violet eyes and tore his glance away, fixing it unfocused on the panel just beyond her shoulder. "I have no way to know that we are not still in human space, or that this is not the upper part of the ship where I was a prisoner. I have seen amaut on my world. I don't know who sent them. Perhaps they brought themselves, but on this ship they take your orders."

There was a great shifting of bodies among the iduve, a dangerous and unpredictable tension; but Chimele leaned her chin on her hand and studied Daniel with heightened interest. Of a sudden she smiled, showing her teeth. "Indeed. I hope you have not seen much similarity between the decks of *Ashanome* and that pestiferous freighter, *m'metane.* Yet your caution I find admirable. Amaut on your world? And where is your world, Daniel? Surely not in the Esliph."

"Why?" Daniel asked, though Isande tried to prevent him. "What exactly do you want to know?"

"*M'metane,* I am informed, perhaps correctly, perhaps not, that your people have been attacked. If this is so, we did not order it. We pursue our own business, and your asuthi will advise you that I am being extraordinarily courteous. Now as you hope for the survival of your species, I advise you not to insult that courtesy by being slow in your answers."

Does she mean that against all humanity—a threat? Daniel asked them, shaken. *Would they declare war? Have they?*

In the name of reason don't try to bargain with her, Aiela flung back. *Iduve don't bluff.*

Daniel folded, sick inside, a simple man out of his depth and fearing both alternatives. He took the one advised and began to tell them the things they wanted to know, his origin on a world named Konig, beyond the Esliph, his life there, his brief service in the military, his world's fall to the amaut. The iduve listened with unnerving patience, even interrupting him to ask more detail of the history of his people, particularly as it regarded the Esliph frontier.

"We never consented, sir," he told Rakhi, who had asked about the human retreat from the Esliph worlds. "Those were our farms, our cities. The amaut drove us out with better weapons and we went back to safe worlds across the Belt."

Rakhi frowned. "Most unfortunate, this human problem," he said to his *nasithi.* "Our departure from the *metrosi* seems to have thrown the amaut and kalliran powers into considerable turmoil. We appear to have served some economic purpose for them. When we withdrew, the amaut seem to have found themselves in particular difficulty. They drew back and abandoned the Esliph. Then the humans discovered it. And, under renewed population pressures, the amaut return, reclaim the Esliph—it is altogether logical for them to use force to take land they already considered theirs, or to use force in meeting competitors. But *m'metane,* were there not agreements, accommodations?"

"Only that we were let off with our lives," said Daniel. Of iduve that questioned him, Rakhi drew the most honest responses; and upon this question, centuries ago as the event was, Daniel allowed anger to move him. Amaut, iduve, even kallia blurred into one polity in his image of the forced evacuation of his people, for the invaders had been faceless beings in ships, giving orders; and to the human mind, all nonhumans tended to assume one character. "We were pushed off before we could be properly evacuated, crowded onto inadequate ships. Some refused to board and commit themselves to that; they stayed to fight, and I suppose I know what became of them. The ones that migrated and survived to reach the other side of the belt were about twenty out of a hundred. We landed without enough equipment, hardly with the means to survive the winter. The worlds were undeveloped, bypassed in our first colonization, undesirable. We scratched a living out of sand and rock and lost it to the weather more often than not. Now they've come after us there."

"Undoubtedly," said Khasif, "as the abandoned humans did not fit the amaut social pattern, indenture became the amaut's solution for the humans. Beings that cannot interbreed with amaut could not exit indenture by normal legal process, so the humans remain in this status perpetually."

"Yet," objected another of Khasif's order, "one wonders why the other humans did not eventually seek better territories, if the worlds in question were so entirely undesirable."

Answer, Isande flashed, for that was a question to Daniel, stated in the often oblique manner of iduve courtesy. "The Esliph was ours," Daniel replied, "and we always meant to come and take it back."

"Prha," said Chaikhe to that person, *"vaikka/ tomes-melakhia-sa, ekutikkase."*

"We did not so much want revenge," Daniel responded to the comment, for he had caught the gist of it through Isande, "as we wanted justice, our own land back. Now the amaut have come looking for us, even across the Belt. They're murdering my people."

"Why?" asked Chimele.

The sudden harshness of her tone panicked the human; his own murder flashed to mind—the easy, gentle manner of the others' questions some game they played with him. *No!* Isande sent him. *Stay absolutely still. Don't move. Answer her.*

"I don't know why. They came—they came. Unprovoked."

"Human ships had not crossed to the Esliph?"

"No," he said quickly, surprised by the accusation. "No."

"How do you know this?"

He did not. He was no one. He had no perfect knowledge of his people's actions. Aiela sent him an urging to keep still, for Chimele frowned.

"M'metane," said Chimele, "disputing another's experience is most difficult. Yet there remains the possibility that the amaut responded to a human intrusion into Esliph space. They are not prone to act recklessly where there is an absence of threat to their own territory, and they are not prone to aggression without the certainty of profit. When there is either motivation, then they move most suddenly and decisively. Our acquaintance with the amaut is long, but I am not satisfied that you know them as well as you believe. Consider every detail of your acquaintance with these uncommon amaut, from the beginning. Let Isande have these thoughts."

He did so, the image of a ship, of amaut faces, another ship, a city, fire—he flashed backward, seeking the origin, the first intimation of danger to human worlds. Merchant ship, military ship—vanished, only gaseous clouds to mark their passing. Ships grounded. Another vessel. Alien. A human war fleet, drawn from worlds to the interior of human space: this the real defense of their perimeters, large, ships technologically not far from par with the *metrosi*. Demolished, traceless. Mindless panic among human colonies, wild rumors of landings in the system. A second, local fleet gone, thirty ships at once.

Daniel still sent, but Isande had glanced sharply at Chimele, and Aiela did not need her interpretation to understand. Amaut *karshatu* maintained weapons on their merchantmen, but they were not capable of disposing of whole warfleets: the *karshatu* never combined. In that respect they were as solitary as the iduve.

Amaut, Daniel insisted, and there were amautish ships in his mind, such as he had seen onworld, great hulking transports, hardly capable of fighting: carriers of equipment and indentured personnel; smaller ships, trade ships that plied the high-speed supply runs, taking back the only export these raw new worlds would supply as yet, not to make an empty run on either direction: human cargo, profitably removed from a place where their numbers made them a threat to places where they were a commodity. But these amaut were not fighters either. Daniel, confused, searched into dimmer memories.

Darkness, images on a viewing screen, a silver shape in hazy resolution, lost to view almost instantly, pursued in vain. Isande caught at the memory eagerly, drawing more and

more detail from Daniel, making him hold the image,
concentrate upon it, focus it.

"He has seen an *akites*," Isande's soft voice translated.
"Distant, his ship pursued, lacked speed, lost it. He thinks it
was amaut, knows—this was what arrived—disorganized the
entire human defense. They resisted—mistook it for several
ships, not knowing its speed—perhaps—perhaps more than
one, I can't tell—they provoked—they provoked, not knowing what—Daniel, please!"

"Was it yours?" Daniel cried, on his feet, closing screens
with abrupt violence. Iduve moved, and Aiela, hardly slower,
sprang up to put himself between Daniel and Chimele.

"Sit down," Aiela exclaimed. "Sit down, Daniel."

Contempt came across: it was in Daniel's eyes and burning
in his mind. *Theirs. Not your kind either, but you crawl at
their feet. You come apart inside when they look at you—I'm
sorry—* He felt Aiela's pain, and tears came to his eyes.
What are you doing to us? Not human. Aiela!"

Aiela seized, held to him, shamed by the emotion, shamed
to feel when their observers could not. Isande—she, apart,
despising, angry. He gained control of himself and forced the
dazed human into a chair, stood over him, his fingers
clenched into the man's shoulder.

Calm, be calm, he kept sending. After a moment Daniel's
muscles relaxed and his mind assumed a quieter level, questioning, terrified.

Why are they asking these things? he kept thinking. *Aiela,
Aiela, help me—tell me the truth if you know it.* And then at
the angry touch of Isande's mind: *Who is Tejef?*

Terror. She flung herself back, screened so violently Daniel
cried out.

And the iduve were utterly still, every eye upon them, the
nasithi gathered close about Chimele, with such a look of
menace that they seemed to have grown and the room to
have shrunk. Indeed more had come, dark faces frowning
with anger, unasking and unasked. Still they came, and the
concourse began to be crowded with them. None spoke.
There was only the sound of steps and the rustling of thousands of bodies.

"Is this aberrance under control?" Chimele wondered quietly, her eyes on Aiela.

It is not aberrance, he wanted to cry at her. *Can't you per-*

ceive it? But the iduve could not comprehend. He bowed deeply. "He was alarmed. He perceived a threat to his species."

Chimele considered that. Iduve faces, whose eyes were almost incapable of moving from side to side, had always a direct, invading stare, communicating little of what processes of thought went on behind them. At last she lifted her hand and the tension in the room ebbed perceptibly.

"This being is capable of a certain *elethia*," she said. "But he is not wise to think that *Ashanome* could not deal with his species more efficiently if their destruction were our purpose. How long ago, *o m'metane,* did your worlds realize the presence of such ships?"

"I've lost count," Daniel replied: truth. "A year, perhaps—maybe a little less. It seems forever."

"Do you reckon in human time?"

"Yes." An impulse rose in him, defiant, suicidal. "Who is Tejef?"

The effect was like a weapon drawn. But this time Chimele refused to be provoked. Interest was in her expression, and she held her *nasithi* motionless with a quick lift of her fingers.

"Chimele," said Isande miserably, "he took it from me, when I thought of ships."

"Are you sure it was only then?"

"I am sure," she said, but an iduve from the *Melakhis* stepped into the *paredre* area: a tall woman, handsome, in black as stark and close-fitting as iduve men usually affected.

"Chimele-Orithain," said that one. "I have questions I would ask him."

"Mejakh *sra*-Narach, *sra*-Khasif, you are out of order, though I understand your *m'melakhia* in this matter. *Hold, Mejakh!*" Chimele's voice, soft, snapped like a blow to the face in the stillness, and the woman stopped a second time, facing her.

"This human is not kameth," said Mejakh, "and I consider that he is out of order, Chimele, and probably in possession of more truth than he is telling."

"More than he knows how to tell, perhaps," said Chimele. "But he is mine, o mate of Chaxal. Honor to your *m'melakhia*. It is well known. Have patience. I am aware of you."

"Honor to you," said Khasif softly, drawing that woman to his side. "Honor always, *sra*-of-mine. But do not notice this ignorant being. He is harmless and only ignorant. Be still. Be still."

The room grew quiet again. Chimele looked at last upon Daniel and Aiela. "Estimate a human year in Kej-time. Ashakh, assist them."

It needed some small delay. Daniel inwardly recoiled from Ashakh's close presence, but with quiet, precise questions, the iduve obtained the comparisons he wanted. In a moment more the computer had the data from the *paredre* desk console and began to construct a projection. A considerable portion of the hall went to starry space, where moving colored dots haltingly coincided.

"From the records of Kartos Station," said Ashakh, "we have traced the recent movements of the ships in all zones of the Esliph. This new information seems to be in agreement. See, the movements of amaut commerce, the recent expansion of the lines of this *karsh*"—the image shifted, a wash of red light at the edge of the Esliph nearest human space—"by violent absorption of a minor *karsh* and its lanes; and the sudden shift of commerce here"—another flurry of lights— "indicate a probable direction of origin for that *akites* our instruments indicate over by Telshanu, directly out of human space. Now, if this being Daniel's memory is accurate, the time coincides admirably for the intrusion of that *akites;* again, it falls well into agreement with this person's account."

"In all points?" asked Chimele, and when Ashakh agreed: "Indeed." The image of Esliph space winked into the dimlighted normalcy of the *paredre*. "Then we are bound for Telshanu. Advise *Chaganokh* to await our coming.

"Chimele!" cried Mejakh. "Chimele, we cannot afford more time. This persistence of yours in—"

"It has thus far preserved *Ashanome* from disaster. You are not noticed, Mejakh. Ashakh, set our course. We are dismissed, my *nasithi*."

As silently as they had assembled, the *nasul* dispersed, the *Melakhis* and the *nasithi-katasakke* too; and Chimele leaned back in her chair and stared thoughtfully at Daniel.

"Your species," she said, "seems to have begun *vaikka* against one of the *nasuli*, most probably the *vra-nasul Chaganokh*. The amaut are a secondary problem, inconsequential by comparison. If you have been wholly truthful, I may perhaps remove the greater danger from human space.

But be advised, *m'metane,* you came near to great harm. You are indeed kameth to *Ashanome,* although not all the *nasithi* seem to acknowledge that fact. Yet for reasons of my own I shall not yet permit you the *idoikkhe*—and you must therefore govern your own behavior most carefully. I shall not again count you ignorant."

"You deny you're responsible for what is happening to Konig?"

"*Tekasuphre.*" Chimele arose and plainly ignored Daniel, looking instead at Isande. "I think it may be well if you make clear to this person and to Aiela my necessities—and theirs."

Isande's quarters, a suite of jewel-like colors and glittering light-panels, had been the place of Daniel's instruction before the interview; it was their refuge after, Isande curled into her favorite chair, Aiela in the other, Daniel sprawled disconsolate on the couch. Their minds touched. It was Daniel they tried to comfort, but he ignored them, solitary and suicidal in his depression. Regarding the impulse to self-destruction, Aiela was not greatly concerned: it was not consistent with the human's other attitudes. Daniel was more likely to turn his destructive urges on someone else, but it would not be his asuthi. That was part of his misery. He had no reachable enemies.

"You have done nothing wrong," said Isande. "You have not hurt your people."

Silence.

Daniel, Aiela sent, *I could not lie to you; you would know it.*

I hate the sight of you, Daniel's subconscious fired out at him; but his upper mind suppressed that behind a confused feeling of shame. "That is not really true," he said aloud, and again, forcefully: "That is not true. I'm sorry."

Aiela cast him a feeling of total sympathy, for proximity still triggered a scream of alarm over his nerves and unsettled his stomach; but the reaction was already becoming less and less. Someday he would shudder no longer, and they would have become one monstrous hybrid, neither kalliran nor human. And now it was Isande who recoiled, having caught that thought. She rejected it in horror.

"I don't blame you," Daniel answered: somehow it did not seem unnatural that he should respond instead, so deeply was he in link with Aiela. He dropped the contact then, grieving, knowing Isande's loathing for him.

"We have not used you," Isande protested.

Daniel touched Aiela's mind again, reading to a depth Aiela did not like. "And haven't we all done a little of that?" Daniel wondered bitterly. "And isn't it only natural, after all?" Was this the beaten, uneducated creature about whose sentience they had wondered? Aiela looked upon him in uncomfortable surmise, all three minds suddenly touching again. From Daniel came a bitter mirth.

You've taught me worlds of things I didn't know. I don't even remember learning most of it; I just touch your minds and I know. And I suppose you could pass for human if it weren't for your looks. But what use do they have for me on Ashanome? *Teach me that if you can.*

"Our life is a pleasant one," said Isande.

"With the iduve?" Daniel swung his legs off the couch to sit upright. "They aren't human, they aren't even as human as you are, and I believe you when you say that don't have feelings like we do. It agrees with what I saw in there tonight."

"They have feelings," said Isande, letting pass his remark about the humanity of kallia. "Daniel, Chimele wishes you no harm."

"Prove it."

She met his challenge with an opening of the mind from which he retreated in sudden apprehension. Strange, iduve things lay beyond that gate. She remained intent upon it even while she rose and poured them each a glass of *marithe*, pressing it at both of them. She was seated again, and stared at Daniel.

All right, Daniel sent finally. It was difficult for him, but to please Aiela, desperate to please someone in this strange place, he yielded down all his barriers.

Isande sent, with that rough impatience she knew how to use and Daniel did only by instinct, such a flood of images that for a time *here* and *now* did not exist. Even Aiela flinched from it, and then resolved to himself that he would let Isande have her way, trusting her nature if not her present mood.

There were things incredibly ancient, gleaned of tapes, of records inaccessible to outsiders. There was Kej IV under its

amber sun, its plains and sullen-hued rivers; tower-holds and
warriors of millennia ago, when each *nasul* had its *dhis*, its
nest-tower, and *ghiaka*-wielding defenders and attackers raged
in battles beyond number—*vaikka-dhis*, nest-raid, when an
invading *nasul* sought to capture young for its own *dhis*,
sought prisoners of either sex for *katasakke*, though prisoners
often suicided.

Red-robed *dhisaisei*, females-with-young, kept the inner
sanctity of the *dhis*. Most females gave birth and ignored
their offspring, but within the *nasul*, there were always certain
maternal females of enormous ferocity who claimed all the
young, and guarded and reared them until on a day their
dhisais-madness should pass and leave them ready to mate
again. Before them even the largest males gave way in terror.

The *dhis* was the heart and soul of the *nasul*, and within it
was a society no adult male ever saw again—a society rigid in
its ranks and privileges. Highest of rank were the *orithaikhti*,
her-children to the Orithain; and lowest in the order, the off-
spring-without-a-name: no male could claim parentage without the female's confirmation, and should she declare of her
offspring: *Taphrek nasiqh*—*"I do not know this child"*—it
went nameless to the lowest rank of the *dhis*. Such usually
perished, either in the *dhis*, or more cruelly, in adulthood.

It was the object of all conflict, the motive of all existence,
the *dhis*—and yet forbidden to all that had once passed its
doors, save for the Guardians, for the *dhisaisei*, and for the
green-robed *katasathei*—pregnant ones, whose time was near.
The *katasathei* were for the rest of the *nasul* the most visible
symbol of the adored *dhis*: males full-*sra* to a *katasathe* drove
her recent mate and all other males from her presence; females of the *nasul* gave her gifts, and forlorn non-*sra* males
would often leave them where she could find them. Her only
possible danger came from a female Orithain who also
chanced to be *katasathe*. Then it was possible that she could
be driven out, forbidden the *dhis* altogether, and her protective *sra* endangered: the ferocity of an Orithain was terrible
where it regarded rival offspring, and even other *nasuli* gave
way before a *nasul* whose Orithain was *katasathe*, knowing
madness ruled there.

That was the ancient way. Then Cheltaris began to rise,
city of the many towers, city of paradox. There had never
been government or law; *nasuli* clustered, co-existed by

means of ritual, stabilized, progressed. It was dimly remembered—Cheltaris: empty now, deserted *nasul* by *nasul* as the *akitomei* launched forth; and what curious logic had convinced the *nasuli* their survival lay starward was something doubtless reasonable to iduve, though to no one else.

Where each *dhis* was, there was home; and yet, shielded as the *dhis* had become within each powerful, star-wandering *akites,* without *vaikka-dhis* and the captures, inbreeding threatened the *nasuli.* So there developed the custom of *akkhres-nasuli,* a union of two *akitomei* for the sharing of *katasakke.*

It was, for the two *nasuli* involved, potentially the most hazardous of all ventures, civilized by oaths, by elaborate ritual, by most strict formalities—and when all else proved vain, by the power and good sense of the two *orithainei.*

Chaxal.

Dead now.

Father to Chimele.

In his time, far the other side of the *metrosi,* by a star called Niloqhatas, there had been *akkhres-nasuli.*

Such a union was rare for *Ashanome;* it was occasioned by something rarer still—a ceremony of *kataberihe.* The Orithain Sogdrieni of *nasul Tashavodh* had chosen Mejakh *sra-*Narach of *Ashanome* to become his heir-mate and bear him a child to inherit *Tashavodh.* The bond between *Tashavodh* and *Ashanome* disturbed the iduve, for these were two of the oldest and most fearsome of the *nasuli* and the exchange they contemplated would make profound changes in status and balance of power among the iduve. Tensions ran abnormally high.

And trouble began with a kameth of *Tashavodh* who chanced to cross the well-known temper of Mejakh *sra-*Narach. She killed him.

Mejakh was already aboard *Tashavodh* in the long purifications before *kataberihe.* But in rage over the matter Sogdrieni burst into her chambers, drove out her own kamethi, and assaulted her. Perhaps when tempers cooled he would have allowed her to begin purifications again, *vaikka* having been settled; but it was a tangled situation: Mejakh was almost certainly now with child, conception being almost infallible with a mating. But he misjudged the *arastiethe* of Mejakh: she killed him and fled the ship.

In confusion, *Ashanome* and *Tashavodh* broke apart, *Tashavodh* stunned by the death of their Orithain, *Ashanome* satisfied that they had come off to the better in the matter of *vaikka*. It was in effect a *vaikka-dhis*, the stealing of young; and to add *chanokhia* to the *vaikka*, in the very hour that Mejakh returned to *Ashanome* she entered *katasakke* with an iduve of nameless birth.

So she violated purification of her own accord this time, and so blotted out the certainty of her child's parentage. With the condemnation—*taphrek nasiqh*—she sent him nameless to the incubators of the *dhis* of *Ashanome*—the dishonored heir of Sogdrieni-Orithain.

Of Mejakh's great *vaikka* she gained such *arastiethe* that she met in *katasakke* with Chaxal-Orithain of *Ashanome*, and of that mating came Khasif, firstborn of *Ashanome's* present ruling *sra*, but not his heir. Chaxal took for his heir-mate Tusaivre of *Iqhanofre*, who bore him Chimele before she returned to her own *nasul*. Other *katasakke*-mates produced Rakhi, and Ashakh and Chaikhe.

But the nameless child survived within the *dhis*, and when he emerged he chose to be called Tejef.

Isande's mind limned him shadowlike, much resembling Khasif, his younger half-brother, but a quiet, frightened man despite his physical strength, who suffered wretchedly the violence of Mejakh and the contempt of Chaxal. Only Chimele, who emerged two years later, treated him with honor, for she saw that it vexed Mejakh—and Mejakh still aspired to a *kataberihe* with Chaxal, an heir-mating which threatened Chimele.

Until Chaxal died.

New loyalties sorted themselves out; a younger *sra* came into power with Chimele. There were changes outside the *nasul* too—all relations with the *orith-nasuli*, the great clans, must be redefined by new oaths. There must be two years of ceremony at the least, before the accession of Chimele could be fully accomplished.

Death.

The dark of space.

Reha.

Screens went up. Isande flinched from that. Aiela tore back. *No*, he sent, shielding Daniel. *Don't do that to him.*

Isande reached for her glass of *marithe* and trembled only

slightly carrying it to her lips. But what seeped through the
screens was ugly, and Daniel would gladly have fled the
room, if distance and walls could have separated him from
Isande.

"An Orithain cannot assume office fully until all *vaikka* of
the previous Orithain is cleared," Isande said in a quiet, precise voice, maintaining her screens. "*Tashavodh's* Orithain—
Kharxanen, full brother to Sogdrieni—had been at great
niseth—great disadvantage—for twenty years because Chaxal
had eluded all his attempts to settle. But now that *Ashanome's* new Orithain was needing to assume office, settlement
became possible. Chimele needed it as badly as Kharxanen.

"So *Tashavodh* and *Ashanome* met. Something had to be
yielded on *Ashanome's* side. Kharxanen demanded Mejakh
and Tejef; Chimele refused—Mejakh being *bhan-sra* to her
own *nas-katasakke* Khasif, it struck too closely at her own
honor. Even *Tashavodh* had to recognize that.

"But she gave them Tejef.

"Tejef was stunned. Of course it was the logical solution;
but Chimele had always treated him as if he were one of her
own *nasithi*, and he had been devoted to her. Now all those
favors were only the preparation of a terrible *vaikka* on
him—worse than anything that had ever been done to him, I
imagine. When he heard, he went to Chimele alone and unasked. There was a terrible fight.

"Usually the iduve do not intervene in male-female fights,
even if someone is being maimed or killed: mating is usually
violent, and violating privacy is *e-chanokhia*, very improper.
But Chimele is no ordinary woman; all the *sra* of an Orithain
have an honorable name, and *taphrek-nasiqh* is applicable
only to paternity: the thing Tejef intended would give his offspring the name he lacked; and if he died in the attempt, it
would still spite Chimele, robbing her of her accommodation
with *Tashavodh*.

"But Chimele's *nasithi-katasakke* broke into the *paredre*.
What happened then, only they know, but probably there was
no mating—there never was a child. Tejef escaped, and when
Mejakh put herself in his way trying to keep him from the
lift, he overpowered her and took him down to the flight deck.
The *okkitani-as* on duty there knew something terrible was
wrong—alarms were sounding, the whole ship on battle alert,
for the Orithain was threatened and we sat only a few

leagues from *Tashavodh*. But the amaut are not fighters, and they could do little enough to stop an iduve. They simply cowered on the floor until he had gone and then the bravest of them used the intercom to call for help.

"My asuthe Reha was already on his way to the flight deck by the time I reached Chimele in the *paredre*. He seized a second shuttlecraft and followed. A kameth has immunity among iduve, even on an alien deck, and he thought if he could attach himself to the situation before *Tashavodh* could actually claim Mejakh, he could possibly help Chimele recover her and save the *arastiethe* of *Ashanome*.

"But they killed him." Screens held, altogether firm. She sipped at the *marithe*, furiously barring a human from that privacy of hers; and Daniel earnestly did not want to invade it. "They swore later they didn't know he was only kameth. It did not occur to them that a kameth would be so rash. When he knew he was dying he fired one short at Tejef, but Tejef was within their shields already and it had no more effect than if he had attacked *Tashavodh* with a handgun.

"The iduve—when the stakes are very high—are sensible; it is illogical to them to do anything that endangers *nasul* survival. And this was highly dangerous. *Vaikka* had gotten out of hand. *Tashavodh* was well satisfied with their acquisition of Mejakh and Tejef, but in the death of a kameth of *Ashanome*, Chimele had a serious claim against them. There is a higher authority: the Orithanhe; and she convoked it for the first time in five hundred years. It meets only in Cheltaris, and the ships were four years gathering.

"When the Orithanhe reached its decision, neither Chimele nor Kharxanen had fully what they had demanded. Mejakh had been forced into *katasakke* with a kinsman of Kharxanen; and by the Orithanhe's decision, *Tashavodh's dhis* obtained her unborn child for its incubators and *Ashanome* obtained Mejakh—no great prize. She has never been quite right since. Chimele demanded Tejef back; but the Orithanhe instead declared him out-kindred, outlaw—*e-nasuli*.

"So by those terms, by very ancient custom, Tejef was due his chance: a Kej year and three days to run. Now *Ashanome* has its own: two years and six days to hunt him down—or lose rights to him forever."

"And they have found him?" asked Daniel.

"You—may have found him." Isande paused to pour her-

self more *marithe*. She scarcely drank, ordinarily, but her
shaken nerves communicated to such an extent that they all
breathed uneasily and struggled with her to push back the
thoughts of Reha. *Revenge* ran cold and sickly through all
her thoughts; and grief was there too. Aiela tried to reach her
on his own, but at the moment she thought of Reha and did
not want even him.

"There is the *vra-nasul Chaganokh*," said Isande. "Vassal-
clan, a six-hundred-year-old splinter of *Tashavodh*, nearby
and highly suspect. We have sixty-three days left. But you
see, Chimele can't just accuse *Chaganokh* of having aided
Tejef with nothing to support the claim. It's not a matter of
law, but of *harachia*—seeing. *Chaganokh* will look to see if
she has come merely to secure a small *vaikka* and annoy
them, or if she is in deadly earnest. No Orithain would ever
harm them without absolute confidence in being right: *orithainei* do not make mistakes. *Chaganokh* will therefore base
its own behavior on what it sees: by that means they will determine how far *Ashanome* is prepared to go. If she shows
them truth, they will surely bend: it would be suicide for a
poor *vra-nasul* to enter *vaikka* with the most ancient of all
clans—which *Ashanome* is. They will not resist further."

"And what does she mean to show them?"

"You," she said; Aiela instinctively flung the *chiabres*-link
asunder, dismayed by that touch of willful cruelty in Isande:
she *enjoyed* distressing Daniel. The impulse he sent in her
direction carried anger, and Isande flinched, and felt shame.
"We searched to find you," she said then to Daniel. "Oh, not
you particularly, but it came to Chimele's attention that humans from beyond the Esliph were turning up—we have followed so many, many leads in recent months, through the
iduve, kallia, even the amaut, investigating every anomaly.
We traced one such shipment toward Kartos—economical:
Chimele knew she would at least find Kartos' records of
value in her search. You were available; and you have
pleased her enormously—hence her extraordinary patience
with you. Only hope you haven't misled her."

"I haven't led her at all," Daniel protested. "Amaut were
all I ever saw, the ugly little beasts, and I never heard of
iduve in my life." And hidden in his mind were images of what
might become of him if he were given to the iduve of *Chaga-*

nokh for cross-examination, or if thereafter he had no value to the iduve at all.

"You are kameth," said Isande. "You will not be discarded. But I will tell you something: as far as iduve ever bluff, Chimele is preparing to; and if she is wrong, she will have ruined herself. Three kamethi would hardly be adequate *serach*—funeral gift—for a dynasty as old and honorable as hers. We three would die; so would her *nasithi-katasakke*, *serach* to the fall of a dynasty. The induve could destroy worlds of *m'metanei* and not feel it as much as they would the passing of Chimele. So be guided by us, by Aiela and by me. If you do in that meeting what you did today—"

Now it was Daniel who screened, shutting off the images from Isande's mind. She ceased.

Do not be hard with him, Aiela asked of her. *There is no need of that, Isande.*

She did not respond for a moment; in her mind was hate, the thought of what she would do and how she would deal with the human if Aiela were not the intermediary, and yet in some part she was ashamed of her anger. Asuthi must not hate; with her own clear sense she knew it, and submitted to the fact that he was appended to them. *If you fail to restrain him,* she sent Aiela, *you will lose him. You have fallen into a trap; I had prepared myself to remain distinct from him, but you are caught, you are merging; and because I regard you, I am caught too. Restrain him. Restrain him. If he angers the iduve, three kamethi are the least expensive loss that will result.*

6

————⋊⋉—————

THE ORITHAIN OF *Chaganokh* was a lonely man in the *paredre* of *Ashanome*. He wore the close-fitting garment common to iduve, but of startling white and complicated by overgarments and robes and a massive silver belt from which hung a *ghiaka*. His name was Minakh, and he was a conspicuous gleam of white and silver among so much indigo and black, with the fair colors of kallia and human an unintentional counterpoint across the room. Chimele faced him, seated, similarly robed and bearing a *ghiaka* with a raptor's head, but her colors were dusky violet.

Tension was electric in the air. Daniel shivered at being thrust so prominently into the midst of them, and Aiela mentally held to him. Contact among the asuthi seemed uncertain, washed out by the miasma of terror and hostilities in the hall, which was filled with thousands of iduve. Bodies went rigid at the presence of Minakh, whiteless eyes dilated to black, breathing quickened. A dozen of the most powerful of *nasul Ashanome* were ranged about Chimele, behind, on either side of her: Khasif, Ashakh—great fearsome men, and two women, Tahjekh and Nophres, who were guardians of the *dhis* and terrible to offend.

Minakh's eyes shifted from this side to that of the gathering. While he was still distant from Chimele he went to his knees and raised both hands. Likewise Chimele lifted her hands to salute him, but she remained seated.

"I am Orithain of the *nasul Chaganokh*," said Minakh. "Increase to the *dhis* of *Ashanome*. We salute you."

"We are *Ashanome*. May your eye be sharp and your reach long. For what grace have you come?"

"We have come to ask the leave of the *orith-nasul Ashanome* to go our way. The field is yours. May your affairs prosper."

"Honor to the *vra-nasul Chaganokh* for its courtesy. We have heard that the zone of Kej is uncommonly pleasant of late. May your affairs prosper there."

Minakh inclined his body gracefully to the carpet at this order, although it must have rankled; and he sat back on his heels, hands at his thighs, elbows outward.

"We rejoice at *Ashanome's* notice," he said flatly, and again came the concentration of hostilities, scantly concealed.

"Happy are the circumstances when *nasuli* may pass without *vaikka*," said Chimele. "Honor to the wisdom of the Orithanhe which has made this possible."

"Long life to those who respect its decrees."

"Long life indeed, and may we remember this meeting with good pleasure. The *vra-nasul Chaganokh* has voyaged far and accrued honors; at its presence the Esliph shudders, and the untraveled space of the human folk has now been measured."

"The praise of *Ashanome*, hunter of worlds, is praise indeed." Minakh's face was utterly impassive, but his eyes flashed aside to Daniel, dark and terrible.

"Indeed *Chaganokh* is deserving of honor. So great is our admiration for its acquisition of wisdom that we lay at *Chaganokh's* feet the matter nearest our heart. We search for a man who was once of *Ashanome*. Perhaps this inconsequential person has crossed the affairs of *Chaganokh*. We should not be surprised to learn that he has attempted to shake us from his trail in the uncharted human zones. *Chaganokh's* recently acquired knowledge of this region seems to us an excellent source of precise knowledge. We are of course in great haste. Our time is slipping from us, and *Chaganokh* in its wisdom will surely accommodate our impatience in this regard."

There was a long and deadly silence. Minakh's eyes rested on Daniel with such hate that it was almost tangible, and every iduve in the room bristled. The silence persisted, broken ominously by a hiss from one of the *dhis*-guardians.

Minakh sweated. His belly heaved with his breathing. At last he prostrated himself and sat back again on his heels, looking dispirited.

"We delight to offer our assistance. This person attached himself to us at a distance. We ceased to notice him shortly after we entered the human zones, near a world known to those creatures as Priamos. Our own affairs occupied us thereafter."

"May your *dhis* ever be safe, o *Chaganokh*. Again let us trouble your gracious assistance. Are the humans wise to think that the amaut are the cause of their unhappy state?"

"When were the *m'metanei* ever wise, o *Ashanome*, hunter of worlds? The amaut are carrion-eaters who seek scraps where we have passed. When has it ever been otherwise?"

"The wisdom of *Chaganokh* is commendable. Prosperity to its affairs and grace to its offspring. Pass, o *Chaganokh*."

Now Minakh arose and backed away, backed entirely out of the *paredre* before he turned. No one of *Ashanome* stirred. No one seemed to breathe until at last the voice of Rakhi from the control station announced Minakh off the ship and the hatch sealed.

"Honor to the discretion of *Chaganokh*," Chimele laughed softly. "Go your ways, my *nasithi*. Ashakh—"

"Chimele."

"Set our course for the human zones as soon as you can make a proper determination from *Chaganokh's* records. You are clear to put us underway at maximum, priority signal. Secrecy no longer applies. Either I am right, or I am wrong."

Ashakh acknowledged the order with a nod, turned and left. Silently the iduve were dispersing, by ones and by twos, amiable now Minakh's *harachia* was removed; and Chimele leaned back in her chair and looked for the first time at her kamethi.

"And you, poor *m'metanei*—an uncomfortable moment. Did you follow what was said?"

"As far," said Aiela, "as *m'metanei* are wise."

Chimele laughed merrily and rose, a violet splendor in her robes. She put off the *ghiaka* and laid it aside. "The Orithain of *Chaganokh* will not soon forget this day: unhappy puppet. Doubtless *Tashavodh* thrust Tejef off upon him, so he was obliged to try, at least, although his chances were poor from the beginning."

Does she care nothing, Daniel thrust at his asuthi, *for the misery they have caused my people?*

Be still, Isande returned through Aiela. *You do not know Chimele.*

"You look troubled, Daniel."

"Where do my people fit in this?"

"They are not my concern."

She means it kindly, Isande protested against his outrage. *She means no harm to them.*

"What happened to them was your fault," Daniel said to Chimele. "And you owe us at least—"

Aiela saw it coming, caught his human asuthe by the arm to draw him back; but the *idoikkhe* pained him, a lancing hurt all the way to his side, and that arm was useless to him for the moment. He knew that Daniel felt it too, knew the human angered instead of restrained. He seized him with his other hand.

She has been in the presence of an enemy, Isande sent Daniel. *Her nerves are still at raw ends. Be still, be still, o for Aiela's sake, Daniel, be still.*

Daniel's anger flowed over them both, sorrowing at once. "I'm sorry," he told Chimele. "but you had no business to harm him for it."

Chimele gave a slight lift of the brows. "Indeed. But Aiela has a *m'melakhia* for you, *m'metane-toj,* and he chose. Consider that, and consider your asuthi the next time you presume upon my self-restraint. Aiela, I regret it."

The pain had vanished. Aiela bowed, for it was great courtesy that Chimele offered regret: iduve offended her, and received less. Chimele returned him a nod of her head, well pleased.

"Daniel," she said then, "do you know the world of Priamos?"

Hate was in his mind, fear; but so was fear for Aiela. He abandoned his pride. "Yes," he said, "I've been there several times."

"Excellent. You will be provided facilities and assistance. I want maps and names. Is their language yours?"

"It is the same." The impulse was overwhelming. "Why do you want these things? What are you about to do?"

Chimele ignored the question and turned on Aiela a direct and commanding look. "This is your problem," she said. "See to it."

They had come. Set on a grassy plain a hundred *lioi* from the river settlements, Tejef knew it, facing toward the east where the sun streamed into morning. *Chaganokh* had yielded and *Ashanome* had come.

It had been a long silence, unbearably long. Many times he had thought he would welcome any contact with his own kind, even to die. It was a loneliness no *m'metane* could understand, save one who had been *asuthithekkhe* and separated, a deep and terrible silence of the mind, a stillness where there were no brothers, no *nasithi*, nothing. No iduve could bear that easily, to be separated from *takkhenes*, the constant sense of brother-presence that never ceased, waking and sleeping, the pack-instinct that had been the driving force of his kind since the dawn of the race. From his birth he had it, seldom friendly in its messages, but there, a lodestar about which all life had its direction. It flowed through his consciousness like the blood through his veins, the unity of impulse through which he sensed every mood of his *nasithi,* their presence, their *m'melakhia,* his possession or lack of *arastiethe*.

Now *takkhenes* was back. He felt them, the *Ashanome*-pack, who had given him birth and decreed his death; and he knew that if they grew much closer they could sense him, weak in his own single *takkhenois* was. The fine hair at the nape of his neck bristled at that proximity; the life-instinct that had ebbed in him quickened into anger.

They were on the hunt, and he their game this time, he that had hunted with them. He could sort out two of the minds he knew best: Khasif, Ashakh, grim and deadly men. Chimele would not have descended with them to the surface of this wretched world: *Ashanome* would be circling in distant orbit, and Chimele would be scanning the filthy business in progress on its surface, directing the searchers. One day soon they would find him, and *vaikka* would be settled—their victory.

The logical faculty said that he might win something even now by surrendering, cringing at Chimele's feet like a *katasathe*. She would kick him aside and the *nasul* would close on him and maul him senseless, but they would not likely kill him. His life thereafter would be lived from that posture, a constant terror, being forever the recipient of everyone's temper and contempt. It would gradually take the heart from him: the *takkhenes* would overwhelm all his instinct to fight

back and he would exist until he was finally mauled to death
by some *nas* in *katasakke,* or starved, or was cast out during
akkhres-nasuli—because the *takkhenes* of neither *nasul* recognized him as theirs. Such were the things that awaited the
outcast, and a long shiver of rage ran up the muscles of his
belly, for he had his bearings again. *Arastiethe* forbade any
yielding. He would end under their hands, literally mauled to
death if they could get him within their reach, but they would
feel the damage he could do them. Ironically, Tejef, who until now had lacked the will to be drawn into a confrontation
with any of the wretched humans the amaut used for prey on
this forsaken world, began to lay plans to work harm on
Ashanome and to end his life with *chanokhia.*

His resources were few, a miserable and war-torn world
where earth-hungry amaut plundered a dying human population, a human species that had gone mad and that now fur-
nished mercenary troops to the brutish amaut for the final
pillage of their own world. Such madness, he reflected, would
have been understandable had it been a matter of *nasul*-loy-
alty among these humans, but it was not. They knew no loyalties, committed *arrhei-nasul* at the simple exchange of
goods or silver, engaged in *katasakke* and then slaughtered
the females, who were pathetic and ineffectual creatures.
They gathered no young in this fashion, and indeed slaughtered what young they did find—comprehensible, at least, if
there had been *nasithi-tak* in these human warbands. There
were not, and the ultimate result seemed to be suicide for the
entire species. Tejef had long since ceased to be amazed by
the final madness of this furious people: perhaps this savagery was an instinct no longer positive for survival—it was
one that the amaut had certainly turned to their own advantage. Now perhaps there was a way to turn it to the advantage of Tejef *sra*-Sogdrieni, a means to *vaikka* upon
Ashanome, one that would deserve their respect when they
killed him.

The night was warm. A slight breeze blew in through the
protective grille of the window and rippled through the drap-
ery behind the bed. The moonlight cast restless shadows of
branches on the wall.

One of the dogs began to bark, joined by the others, and
the child in the bed stirred, sat upright, eyes wide. She lis-

tened a moment, then turned on her knees so that she could lean against the headboard and the sill and look out into the dark. Now the dogs were off at the distance, perhaps chasing some night-wandering bounder through the fields. Their cries echoed among the rocks in which the house was set, secure behind its stone wall and steel gate, with the cliffs towering up on either side.

In Arle's estimation this house was an impenetrable fortress. It had not always needed to be so. The wall and the gate were new, and when she was nine the men had not gone with guns to work the fields, and there had been no guards on the heights. But the world had changed. She was ten now, and thought it settled that she would never again walk to the neighbors' house to play, or even go out the gates to the fields and the orchard without one of her brothers to attend her, rifle over his arm, checking with each of the sentry stations along the way. The family had not been to church in the valley in months, nor valley market, and no one mentioned school starting. This was the way the world had become. And they were fortunate—for there were rumors of burnings downland at the mouth of the Weiss, that very same sleepy river that rolled through their valley and made the crops grow, and made Upweiss the best and richest land on all Priamos.

Arle knew something of the outside, knew that they were from the Esliph, which was very far, and green and beautiful, but she was not sure in her mind whether that were real or not, or only one of the old stories her parents had told her, like faery princesses and heroes. She knew also that they were all once upon a time from a world called Earth, every human that breathed, but it was hard to imagine all the populations of all the worlds she knew of crowded onto one globe. This was too difficult a thought, and she was not sure which stories were about Earth and which were about the Esliph, or whether they were one and the same. She kept it stored up as one of those things she would understand when she was older, which was what her parents answered when her questions ran ahead of her understanding. She was content to let this be, although it seemed that there were many things of late which she was not old enough to know, while her parents talked in secret councils with her grown brothers and with the neighbors and the younger children were sent off to play with guns to guard them.

She was aware of terrible things happening not too far away. Sometimes she heard a thing the adults said and lay awake at night sick at her stomach and wondering if really they were all going to die before she had a chance to grow up and understand it all. But then she would imagine growing up, and that convinced her that the future was still there, all waiting to be experienced; and the grownups understood matters and still planned for next year, for planting crops, hoping for better rains from the mountains, hoping the winds would not come too late in the spring or the hail ruin the grain. These were familiar enemies, and they were forever. These awful gray people that were said to be burning towns and farms and shooting people—she was not sure that they were real. When she was little, her parents had not been able to persuade her not to climb the cliffs, so they had told her about a dog that had gone mad and lived up in those rocks waiting to kill children. It had stalked her nightmares for years and she would rather anything than go up into the dark crevices of those rocks. But now she was ten and knew sensibly that there was no dog, and that it had been all for the good purpose of keeping her from having a bad fall. *That* was the dog in the rocks, her own curiosity; but she was not sure if the downland monsters were not something similar, so that silly children would not ask unanswerable questions.

There had been smoke on the horizon two days ago. All the sentries had reported it, and the children had thronged the big dome rock in the throat of the pass to see it. But then her father had chased them all back into the yard and told them that the strangers would get them if they did not stay where they belonged. So Arle reasoned that it was like the dog, something for them tò be afraid of while the grownups understood what it really was and knew how to deal with it. They would take care of matters, and the crops would go in come fall, and be harvested next spring, and life would go on quite normally.

She curled up again in her bed and pulled the sheet up to her chin. It made it feel like bed, and protection. Soon she shut her eyes and drifted back to sleep.

Something boomed, shook the very floor and the bottles on

the dresser and lit the branches in red relief on the wall. Arle
scrambled for the view at the window, too sleepy and too
stunned to have cried out at that overwhelming noise. Men
were running everywhere. The gate was down with fire beyond and dark shapes against it, and people ran up and down
the hall outside her room. Her oldest brother came bursting
in with a flashlight, exclaimed that she should get out of the
window and seized her by the wrist, not even waiting for her
to get her feet under her. He pulled her with him at a run,
taking her, she knew, to the cellar, where the children had always been told to go in an emergency. She began to cry as
they hit the outside stairs, for she did not want to go down
into that dark place and wait.

Suddenly light broke about them, awful heat and noise,
stone chips and powder showering down upon them. Arle
sprawled, hurting her hands and ribs and knees upon the
steps, crawling back from the source of that light even before
her mind had awakened to the fact that something had exploded. Then she saw her brother's face, odd-tilted on the
steps, his eyes with the glazed look of a dead animal's. His
hand when she took it was loose. Light flashed. Stone show-
ered down again, choking with dust.

What she did then she only remembered later—tumbling
off the side of the steps, landing in the soft earth of the flower-
bed, running, lost among the dark shapes that hurtled this
way and that.

She found herself crouching in the rubble at the gate, while
dark bodies moved against the light a little beyond her. The
yard was like that cellar, a horrible dead-end place where one
could be trapped. She broke and ran away from the house,
trying to go down the pass a little way to that forbidden path
up the cliffs, to hide and wait above until she could come
back and find her family.

It was dark among the rocks for a moment, the light of the
fire cut off by the bending of the road; and then as she
rounded the bend toward the narrowing of the cliffs a dark
man-shape stood by the dome rock in the very narrowest
part of the pass, outlined against the moon and the downslope
of the road toward the valley fields. Arle saw him too late,
tried to scramble aside into the rocks, but the man seized her,
drew her against him with his arm, and silenced her with a

hand that covered her mouth and nose and threatened to break her neck as well.

He released her when her struggles grew weak, seized the collar of her thin gown, and raised his other hand to hit her, but she whimpered and flinched down as small as she could. Instead he raised her back by both arms and shook her until her head snapped back. His shadowed face stared into hers in the moonlight. She stood still and suffered him to cup her small face between his rough hands, to smooth her tangled hair, to use his thumbs to wipe the tears from her cheeks.

"Help us," she said then, thinking this was one of the neighbor men come to aid them. "Please come and help us."

His hands on her shoulders hurt her. He stood there for a moment, while she trembled on the verge of tears, and then he gripped her arm in one cruel hand and began to walk down the road away from the house, dragging her with him, making her legs keep his long strides.

She stumbled on the rocks as they descended from the road to the orchard and turned her ankle in the soft ground among the apple and peach trees; and there were thorns and cutting stubble on the slopes of the irrigation ditch. He strode across the water, hauling her up the other side by one arm as a careless child might handle a doll, and waited only an instant to let her gain her feet before he walked on, dragging her at a near run, until at last she did stumble and fell to her knees sobbing.

Then he drew her aside, into the shadow of the trees, set her against the low limb of an aged apple tree, and looked at her, still holding her by a firm grip on her arm. "Where were you going?" he asked her.

She did not want to tell him. The scant light there was filtering through the apple leaves showed the outline of boots, loose trousers, leather harness, clothing such as no farmer wore, and his lean, hard face was strange to her. But he shook her and repeated the question, and her lips trembled and clear sense left her.

"I was going to hide and come back."

"Is there any help you can get to?"

She jerked her head in the direction of the Berney farm, where Rachel Berney lived, and her brother Johann and the Sullivans, who had a daughter her age.

"You mean that house five kilometers west of here?" he asked. "Forget it. Is there anywhere else?"

"I don't know," she said. "I—could hide in the rocks."

He took her hand again, a dry, strong grip that frightened her, for he could crush the bones if he closed down harder. "And where would you go after? There's not going to be anything left back there."

"I want to go home."

"You can't. Think. Think of some place safe I could leave you."

"I don't know any."

"If I left you right here, could you walk down from the heights to the river? Could you walk that far?"

She looked at him in dismay. The river was visible from the heights, far, far down in the valley. When they went, it meant taking the truck and going a long distance down the road. She could not imagine how long it would take to walk it, and it was hot in the daytime—and there were men like him on the roads. She began to cry, not alone for that, for everything, and she cried so hard she was about to be sick. But he shook her roughly and slapped her face. The hurt was already so much inside that she hardly knew the pain, except that she was afraid of them and she was going to be sick at her stomach. Out of fear she swallowed down the tears and the sickness with them.

"You have to think of somewhere I can put you. Stop that sniffing and think."

"I want to go *home*," she cried, at which he looked at her strangely and his grip lessened on her arm. He smoothed her hair and touched her face.

"I know you do. I know. You can't."

"Let me go."

"They're dead back there, can't you understand that? If they catch either one of us now they'll skin us alive. I have to get rid of you."

"I don't know what to do. I don't know. I don't know."

Then she thought he would hit her. She screamed and flinched back. But instead he put his arms about her, picked her up, hugged her head down into his shoulder, rocking her in his arms as if she had been an infant. "All right," he said. "I'll see what I can do."

Aiela took the corridor to the *paredre,* his mind boiling with frustration and smothered kalliran and human obscenities, and raged at Isande's gentle presence in his thoughts until she let him alone. For fifteen precious days he had monitored Daniel's every movement. The human language began to come more readily than the kalliran: human filth and human images poured constantly through his senses, blurring his own perception of what passed about him, cannibalizing his own life, his own separate thoughts.

Now, confronted by an iduve at the door of the *paredre,* he could scarcely gather enough fluency to explain his presence in any civilized language. The iduve looked at him sharply, for his behavior showed a mental disorder that was suspect, but Chimele had given standing orders and the man relented.

"Aiela?" Chimele arose from her desk across the room, her brows lifted in the iduve approximation of alarm. Aiela bowed very low. Courtesy demanded it, considering the news he bore.

"Daniel has encountered a difficulty," he said.

"Be precise." Chimele took a chair with a mate opposite and gestured him to sit.

"The Upweiss raid," Aiela began hoarsely: Chimele insisted upon the chronological essentials of a thing. He forced his mind into order, screened against the random impulses that fed from Daniel's mind and the anxious sympathy from Isande's. "It went as scheduled. Anderson's unit hit the Mar estate. Daniel hung back—"

"He was not to do so," Chimele said.

"I warned him; I warned him strongly. He knows Anderson's suspicions of him. But Daniel can't do the things these men do. His conscience—his *honor,*" he amended, trying to choose words that had clear meaning for Chimele—"is offended over the killings. He had to kill a man in the last raid."

Chimele made a dismissing move of her hand. "He was attacked."

"I could explain the human ethical—"

"Explain what is at hand."

"There was a child—a girl. It was a crisis. I tried to reason with him. He shut me out and took her away. He is still going, deserting Anderson—and us."

There were no curses in the iduve language. Possibly that contributed to their fierceness. Chimele said nothing.

"I'm trying to reason with him," Aiela said. "He's exhausted—drained. He hasn't slept in twenty hours. He lay awake last night, sick over the prospect of this raid. He's going on little sleep, no water, no food. He can't expect to find water as he's heading, not until the river. They can't make it."

"This is not a rational human response." That was a question. Chimele's voice had an utter calm, not a good sign in an iduve.

"It is a human response, but it is not rational."

Chimele hissed and rose, hands on her hips. "Is it not your duty to anticipate such responses and deal with them?"

"I don't blame him," he said. Then, from his heart: "I'm only afraid I might have done otherwise." And that thought so depressed him he felt tears rise. Chimele looked down on him in incredulity.

"*Au*, by what am I served? Explain. I am patient. Is this a predictable response?"

Aiela could have screamed aloud. The *paredre* faded. He shivered in the cold of a Priamid night, the glory of spiraling ribbons of stars overhead, the fragile sweet warmth of another being in his arms. Tears filled his eyes; his breath caught.

"Aiela," Chimele said. The iduve could not cry; they lacked the reflex. The remembrance of that made him ashamed in her sight.

"The reaction," he said, "is probably instinct. I—have grown so much into him I—cannot tell. I cannot judge what he does any longer. It seems right to me."

"Is it *dhis*-instinct, a response to this child?"

"Something like that," he said, grateful for her attempt at equation. Chimele considered that for a moment, her eyes more perplexed now than angry.

"It is difficult to rely on such unknown quantities. I offer my regret for what you must be feeling, though I am not sure I can comprehend it. Other humans—like Anderson—are immune to this emotion where the young are concerned. Why does Daniel succumb?"

"I don't live inside Anderson. I don't know what goes on in his twisted mind. I only know Daniel—this night—could not have done otherwise."

"Kindly explain to Daniel that, we have approximately three days left, his time. That Priamos itself has scarcely that long to live, and that he and the child will be among a million beings perishing if we have to resort to massive attack on this world."

"I've tried. He knows these things. intellectually, but he shuts me out. He refuses to think of that."

"Then we have wasted fifteen valuable days."

"Is that all?"

There was hysteria in his voice; and it elicited from Chimele a curious look, the embarrassment of an observer who had no impulse to what he felt.

"You are exhausted," she judged. "You can be sedated for the rest of the world's night. You can do nothing more with this person and I know how long you have worked without true rest."

"No." He assumed a taut control of his voice and slowed his breathing. "I know Daniel. Good sense will come back to him after he has run awhile. That area is swarming with trouble in all forms. He will need me."

"I honor your persistence. Stay in the *paredre*. If you are going to attempt to advise him I should prefer to know how you are faring. If you change your mind about the sedation, tell me; if we are to lose Daniel, your own knowledge of humans becomes twice valuable. I do not want to risk your health. I leave matters in your hands; rest, if you can."

"Thank you." He drew himself to his feet, bowed, and moved away.

"Aiela."

He looked back.

"When you have found an explanation for his behavior, give it to me. I shall be interested."

He bowed once more, struggling between loathing and love for the iduve, and decided for the moment on love. She did try. She tried with her mind where her heart was inadequate, but she wanted to know.

In the shadows of the *paredre* a comfortable bowl chair, such as the iduve chose when they would relax, provided a retreat. He curled into its deep embrace and leaned his head back upon the edge, slipping again into the mental rhythms of Daniel's body, becoming human, feeling again what he felt.

In the small corner of his mind still himself, Aiela knew the answer. It had been likely from Daniel's first step onto the surface of Priamos.

Years and a world ago, when Aiela was a boy, the staff had brought into the lodge one of the hunting birds that nested in the cliffs of the mountains, wing-broken. He had nursed it, he had been proud of it, thought it his. But the first time it felt the winds of Ryi under its wings, it was gone.

7

AIELA WAS BACK. Daniel clamped down a silence against him, shifted the child's slight weight in his arms, and felt her arms tighten reflexively about his neck. Above them a star burned, a blaze of white brighter than any star that had ever shown in Priamid skies. When people saw it they thought *amaut* and shuddered at the presence, aware it was large, but yet having no concept what it was. They might never know. If it swung into tighter orbit it would be the final spectacle in Priamos' skies, that had of late seen so many comings and goings, the baleful red of amaut ships, the winking white of human craft deploying troops, mercenaries serving the amaut. When *Ashanome* came it would be one last great sunset over the world at once, the last option of the iduve in a petty quarrel that threatened the existence of his species, that counted one man or one minor civilization nothing against the games that occupied them.

You know better, Aiela sent him. Simultaneous with the words came rage, concern for them, fear of Chimele. Daniel seized wrathfully upon the latter, which Aiela vehemently denied.

Daniel. Think. You don't know where you're going or what you're going to do with that girl. All right. Defeat. Aiela recognized the loathing Daniel felt for what they had asked him to do. Human as he was, he had been able to cross the face of Priamos unremarked, one of the countless mercenaries that looted and killed in small bands at the amaut's bidding. He was a rough man, was Daniel: he could use that heavy-barreled primitive gun that hung from his belt. His slender frame could endure the marches, the tent-camps, the appallingly primitive conditions under which the human force operated. But he had no heart for this. He had been rackingly sick after the only killing he had done, and Ander-

son, the mercenary captain, had put him on the notice he
would be made an example if he failed in any order. This
threat was nothing. If Daniel could ignore the orders of
Chimele of *Ashanome*, nothing the brutish Anderson could
invent was enough; but Anderson fortunately had not realized
that.

I can't help you, Aiela said. *That child cried for home, and
you lost all your senses, every other bond. Now I suppose I'm
the enemy.*

No, Daniel thought, irritated by Aiele's analysis. *You
aren't.* And: *I wish you were*—for it was his humanity that
was pained.

*Listen to me, Daniel. Accept my advice and let me guide
you out of this incredible situation.*

The word choice might have been Chimele's. Daniel
recognized it. *"Kill the girl." Why don't you just come out
with the idea? "Kill her, one life for the many." Say it, Aiela.
Isn't that what Chimele wants of me?* He hugged the sleeping
child so tightly it wakened her, and she cried out in memory
and fought.

"Hush," he told her. "Do you want to walk awhile?"

"I'll try," she said, and he chose a smooth place on the dirt
road to set her down, she tugging in nervous modesty at the
hem of her tattered gown. Her feet were cut with stubble and
bruised with stones. She limped so it hurt to watch her, and
held out her hands to balance on the edges of her feet. He
swore and reached out to take her up again, but she resisted
and looked at him, her elfin face pale in the moonlight.

"No, I can walk. It's just sore at first."

"We're going to cut west when we reach the other road.
Maybe we'll find a refugee family—there's got to be some-
body left."

"Are you going to leave those men and not go back?"

The question disturbed him. Aiela pressed him with an
echo of the same, and Daniel screened. "They'll have my
hide if they find me now. Maybe I'll head northwest and pick
up with some other band." That for Aiela. *A night's delay, a
day at the most. I can manage it. I'll think of something.* "Or
maybe I'll go west too. I'll see you safe before I do anything."

A man alone can't make it across that country, Aiela insisted. *Get rid of her, let her go. No! listen, don't shut me out.*

I'll help you. Your terms. Give me information and I'll take your part with Chimele.

Daniel swore at him and closed down. Even suggesting harm to the girl tore at Aiela's heart; but he was afraid. His people had had awe of the iduve fed into them with their mothers' milk, and he was not human; Daniel knew the kallia so well, and yet there were still dark corners, reactions he could not predict, things that had to do with being kallia and being human. Aiela's people had no capacity to fight: it was not in the kalliran nature to produce a tyranny, not in a culture where there was no supreme executive, but a hierarchy of councils. One kallia simply lacked the feeling of adequacy to be either tyrant or rebel. *Giyre* was supposed to be mutual, and he had no idea how to react when trust was betrayed. Kallia were easy prey for the iduve: they always yielded to greater authority. In the kalliran mind it just did not occur that it could be morally wrong, or that the Order in which they believed did not exist off Aus Qao.

Daniel. The quiet touch was back in his mind, offended, as angry as Daniel had ever felt him. *The things you do not know about kallia are considerable. You lack any sense about giyre yourself, so I suppose it does not occur to you that I have it for all beings with whom I deal—even for you. I am not human. I do not lie to my friends, destroy what is useless, or break what is whole. I can also accept defeat when I meet it. Abandon the child there. I will get her to safety, I will be responsible, even if I must come to Priamos myself. Just get out of the area. You've already created enough trouble for yourself. Don't finish ruining your cover.*

No, Daniel sent. *One look at that kalliran face of yours and you would never catch her. Send your ship. But you'll do things on my terms.*

There was no answer. Daniel looked up again at the star that was *Ashanome.* A second brilliant light had appeared not far from it; and a third, unmoving to the eye. They were simply there, and they had not been.

Aiela, he flung out toward the first star.

But this time Aiela shut him out.

The *paredre* blazed with light. The farthest side of it, bare of furniture, was suddenly occupied by consoles and screens and panels rippling with color. In the midst of it stood Chimele with her *nas-katasakke* Rakhi, and they spoke urgently of the startling appearance of two of the *akitomei*. The image of them hung third-dimensional in the cube of darkness on the table, projection within projection, mirror into mirror.

Suddenly there was only Chimele and the darker reality of the *paredre*. Aiela met her quick glance uneasily, for kamethi were not admitted to control stations.

"Isande has been summoned," said Chimele. "Cast her the details of the situation here. Keep screening against Daniel. Are you strong enough to maintain that barrier?"

"Yes. Are we under attack?"

The thought seemed to surprise Chimele. "Attack? No. The *nasuli* are not prone to such inconsiderate action. This is *harathos*, the Observance. *Tashavodh* has come to see *vaikka* done, and *Mijanothe* is the neutral Observer, who will declare to all the *nasuli* that things were done rightly. This is expected, and unexpected. It might have been omitted. It would have pleased me if it had been."

In his mind, Isande had already started for the door of her apartment, pulled her tousled head through the sweater; the sweater was tugged to rights, her thin-soled boots pattering quickly down the corridor. He fired her what information he could, coherent, condensed, as he had learned to do.

And Daniel? she asked in return. *What has happened to him?*

Her question almost disrupted his screening. He clamped down against it, too incoherent to screen against Daniel and explain about him at once. Isande understood, and he was about to reply again when he was startled by a projection appearing not a pace from him.

Mejakh! He jerked back even as he flashed the warning to Isande. His dealings with the mother of Khasif and Tejef had been blessedly few, but she came into the *paredre* more frequently now that other duties had stripped Chimele of the aid of her *nasithi-katasakke*—for Chaikhe's pursuit of an iduve mate had rendered her *katasathe* and barred her from the *paredre*, Khasif and Ashakh were on Priamos, and poor Rakhi was on watch in the control room trying to manage all the duties of his missing *nasithi* to Chimele's demanding satisfaction. Mejakh accordingly asserted her rank as next closest, of an indirectly related *sra*, for Chimele had no other. Seeing that she had children now adult, she might be forty or more in age, but she had not the apologetic bearing of an aging female. She moved with the insolent grace of a much younger woman, for iduve lived long if they did not die by violence. She was slim and coldly handsome, commanding in her manner, although her attractiveness was spoiled by a rasping voice.

"Chimele," said Mejakh, "I heard."

Chimele might have acknowledged the offered support by some courtesy: iduve were normally full of compliments. All Mejakh received was a stare a presumptuous nas kame might have received, and that silence found ominous echo in the failure of Mejakh to lower her eyes. It was not an exchange an outsider would have noted; but Aiela had been long enough among iduve to feel the chill in the air.

"Chimele," Rakhi said by intercom, "projections incoming from *Tashavodh* and *Mijanothe*."

"Nine and ten clear, Rakhi."

The projections took instant shape, edges blurred together, red background warring against violet. On the left stood a tall, wide-shouldered man, square-faced with frowning brows and a sullen mouth: *Kharxanen,* Isande read him through Aiela's eyes, hate flooding with the name, memories of dead Reha, of Tejef, of Mejakh's dishonor; he was Sogdrieni's full brother, Tejef's presumed uncle. The other visitor was a woman seated in a wooden chair, an iduve so old her hair had silvered and her indigo skin had turned fair—a little woman whose high cheekbones, strong nose, and large, brilliant eyes gave her a look of ferocity and immense dignity. She was robed in black; a chromium staff lay across her lap. Somehow it did not seem incongruous that Chimele paid her deference in this her own ship.

"Thiane," Isande voiced him in a tone of awe. "O be careful not to be noticed, Aiela. This is the president of the Orithanhe."

"Hail *Ashanome*," said Thiane in a soft voice. "Forgive an old woman her suddenness, but I have too few years left to waste long moments in hailings and well-wishing. There is no *vaikka* between us."

"No," said Chimele, "no, there is not. Thiane, be welcome. And for Thiane's sake, welcome Kharxanen."

"Hail *Ashanome*," the big man said, bowing stiffly. "Honor

to the Orithanhe, whose decrees are to be obeyed. And hail Mejakh, once of *Tashavodh*, less honored."

Mejakh hissed delicately and Kharxanen smiled, directing himself back to Chimele.

"The infant the *sra* of Mejakh prospers," he said. "The honor of us both has benefited by our agreement. I give you farewell, *Ashanome*: the call was courtesy. Now you know that I am here."

"Hail *Tashavodh*," Chimele said flatly, while Mejakh also flicked out, vanished with a shriek of rage, leaving Chimele, and Thiane, and Aiela, who stood in the shadows.

"*Au*," said Thiane, evidently distressed by this display, and Chimele bowed very low.

"I am ashamed," said Chimele.

"So am I," said Thiane.

"You are of course most welcome. We are greatly honored that you have made the *harathos* in person."

"Chimele, Chimele—you and Kharxanen between you can bring three-quarters of the iduve species face to face in anger, and does that not merit my concern?"

"Eldest of us all, I am overwhelmed by the knowledge of our responsibility."

"It would be an incalculable disaster. Should something go amiss here, I could bear the dishonor of it for all time."

"Thiane," said Chimele, "can you believe I would violate the terms? If I had wished *vaikka* with *Tashavodh* to lead to catastrophe, would I have convoked the Orithanhe in the first place?"

"I see only this: that with less than three days remaining, I find you delaying further, I find you with this person Tejef within scan and untouched, and I suspect the presence of *Ashanome* personnel onworld. Am I incorrect, Chimele *sra*-Chaxal?"

"You are quite correct, Thiane."

"Indeed." Her brows drew down fiercely and her old voice shook with the words. "Simple *vaikka* will not do, then; and if you do miscalculate, Chimele, what then?"

"I shall take *vaikka* all the same," she answered, her face taut with restraint. "Even to the destruction of Priamos. The risk I run is to mine alone, and to do so is my choice, Thiane."

"*Au*, you are rash, Chimele. To destroy this world would

have sufficed, although it is a faceless *vaikka.* You have committed yourself too far this time. You will lose everything."

"That is mine to judge."

"It is," Thiane conceded, "until it comes to this point: that there be a day remaining, and you have not yet acted upon your necessities. Then I will blame you, that with *Tashavodh* standing by in *harathos,* you would seem deliberately to provoke them to the last, threatening the deadline. There will be no infringement upon that, Chimele, not even in appearance. Any and all of your interference on Priamos will have ceased well ahead of that last instant, so that *Tashavodh* will know that things were rightly done. I have responsibility to the Orithanhe, to see that this ends without further offense; and should offense occur, with great regret, Chimele, with great regret, I should have to declare that you had violated the decrees of the Orithanhe that forbade you *vaikka* upon *Tashavodh* itself. *Ashanome* would be compelled to surrender its Orithain into exile or be cast from the kindred into outlawry. You are without issue, Chimele. I need not tell you that if *Ashanome* loses you, a dynasty more than twelve thousand years old ceases; that *Ashanome* from being first among the kindred becomes nothing. Is *vaikka* upon this man Tejef of such importance to you, that you risk so much?"

"This matter has had *Ashanome* in turmoil from before I left the *dhis,* o Thiane; and if my methods hazard much, bear in mind that our primacy has been challenged. Does not great gain justify such risk?"

Thiane lowered her eyes and inclined her head respectfully. "Hail *Ashanome.* May your *dhis* increase with offspring of your spirit, and may your *sra* continue in honor. You have my admiration, Chimele. I hope that it may be so at our next meeting."

"Honor to *Mijanothe.* May your *dhis* increase forever."

The projection vanished, and Chimele surrounded herself with the control room a brief instant, eyes flashing though her face was calm.

"Rakhi. Summon Ashakh up to *Ashanome* and have him report to me the instant he arrives."

Rakhi was still in the midst of his acknowledgment when Chimele cut him out and stood once more in the *paredre.* Isande, who had waited outside rather than break in upon

Thiane, was timidly venturing into the room, and Chimele's sweeping glance included both the kamethi.

"Take over the desk to the rear of the *paredre.* Review the status and positions of every amaut and mercenary unit on Priamos relative to Tejef's estimated location. Daniel must be reassigned."

Had it been any other iduve, even Ashakh, that so ordered him, Aiela would have cried out a reminder that he had been almost a night and a day without sleep, that he could not possibly do anything requiring any wit at all; but it was Chimele and it was for Daniel's sake, and Aiela bowed respectfully and went off to do as he was told.

Isande touched his mind, sympathizing. "I can do most of it," she offered. "Only you sit by me and help a little."

He sat down at the desk and leaned his head against his hands. He thought again of Daniel, the anger, the hate of the being for him over that child. He could not persuade them apart; he had tried, and probably Daniel would not forgive him. Reason insisted, reason insisted: Daniel's company itself was supremely dangerous to the child. They were each safer apart. Priamos was safer for it, he and the child hopeless of survival otherwise; leaving her was a risk, but it was a productive one. It was the reasonable, the orderly thing to do; and the human called him murderer, and shut him out, mind locked obstinately into some human logic that sealed him out and hated. His senses blurred. He shivered in a cool wind, realized the slip too late.

Aiela. Isande's presence drew at him from the other side, worried. He struggled back toward it, felt the physical touch of her hand on his shoulder. The warmth of the *paredre* closed about him again. *Too long in contact,* she sent him. *Aiela, Aiela, think of here. Let go of him, let go.*

"I am all right," he insisted, pushing aside her fear. But she continued to look at him concernedly for a little time more before she accepted his word for it. Then she reached for the computer contact.

The *paredre* door shot open, startling them both, and Mejakh's angry presence stopped Isande's hand in midmove. The woman was brusque and rude and utterly tangible. Almost Isande called out to Chimele a frightened appeal, but Chimele looked up from her own desk a distance away and fixed Mejakh with a frown.

"You were not called," Chimele said.

Mejakh swept a wide gesture toward Aiela and Isande. "Get them out. I have a thing to say to you, Chimele-Orithain, and it is not for the ears of *m'metanei.*"

"They are aiding me," said Chimele, bending her head to resume her writing. "You are not. You may leave, Mejakh."

"You are offended because I quit the meeting. But you had no answer when Kharxanen baited me. You enjoyed it."

"Your incredible behavior left me little choice." Chimele looked up in extreme displeasure as Mejakh in her argument came to the front of the desk. Chimele laid aside her pen and came up from her chair with a slow, smooth motion. "You are not noticed, Mejakh. Your presence is ignored, your words forgotten. Go."

"*Ashanome* has no honor when it will not defend its own."

Chimele's head went back and her face was cold. "You are not of my *sra*, Mejakh. Once you had honor and Chaxal was compelled to notice you, but in his wisdom he did not take you for *kataberihe*. You are a troublemaker, Mejakh. You threw away your honor when you let yourself be taken into *Tashavodh* by Tejef. There was the beginning of our present troubles; and what it has cost us to recover you to the *nasul* was hardly worth it, o Mejakh, trouble-bringer."

"You would not say so if Khasif were here to hear it."

"For Khasif's sake I have tolerated you. I am done."

Mejakh struggled for breath. Could iduve have wept she might have done so. Instead she struck the desk top with a crash like an explosion. "Bring them all up! Bring up Khasif, yes, and this human nas kame, all of them! Wipe clean the surface of this world and be done! It is clear, Orithain, that you have more *m'melakhia* than *sorithias*. It is your own *vaikka* you pursue, a *vaikka* for the insult he did you personally, not for the honor of *Ashanome.*"

Chimele came around the side of the desk and Isande's thoughts went white with fear: *Rakhi, get Rakhi in here,* she flashed to Aiela, and reached for the desk intercom; Aiela launched himself toward the two iduve.

His knees went. Unbelievable pain shot up his arm to his chest and he was on his face on the floor, blood in his mouth, hearing Isande's sobs only a few feet away. The pain was a dull throb now, but he could not reach Isande. His limbs could not function; he could not summon the strength to move.

After a dark moment Chimele bent beside him and lifted his head, urging him to move. "Up," she said. "Up, kameth."

He made the effort, hauled himself up by the side of a chair and levered himself into it, searching desperately with his thoughts for Isande. Her contact was active, faint, stunned, but she was all right. He looked about when his vision had cleared and saw her sitting in a chair, head in her hands, and Rakhi standing behind her.

"Both of them seem all right," said Rakhi. "What instructions about Mejakh?"

"She is forbidden the *paredre*," Chimele said, and looked toward her kamethi. "Mejakh willed your death, but I overrode the impulse. It is a sadness; she had *arastiethe* once, but her loss of it at Tejef's hands has disturbed her reason and her sense of *chanokhia*."

"She has had misfortune with her young," said Rakhi. "Against one she seeks *vaikka*, and for his sake she lost her honor. Her third was taken from her by the Orithanhe. Only in Khasif has she honorable *sra*, and he is absent from her. Could it be, Chimele, that she is growing *dhisais?*"

"Make it clear to the *dhis*-guardians that she must not have access there. You are right. She may be conceiving an impulse in that direction, and with no child in the *dhis*, there is no predicting what she may do. Her temper is out of all normal bounds. She has been disturbed ever since the Orithanhe returned her to us without her child, and this long waiting with Priamos in view—*au*, it could happen. Isande, Aiela, I must consider that you are both in mortal danger. Your loss would disturb my plans; that would occur to her, and kamethi have no defense against her."

"If we were armed—" Aiela began.

"*Au*," Chimele exclaimed, "no, *m'metane*, your attitude is quite understandable, but you hardly appreciate your limitations. You almost died a moment ago, have you not realized that? The *idoikkhei* can kill. *Chanokhia* insists kamethi are exempt from such extreme *vaikka*, but Mejakh's sense of *chanokhia* seems regrettably lacking."

"But a *dhisais*," Aiela objected, "can be years recovering."

"Yes, and you see the difficulty your attempt to interfere

has created. Well, we will untangle the matter somehow, and, I hope, without further *vaikka.*"

"Chimele," said Rakhi, "the kameth has a valid point. Mejakh has proved an embarrassment many times in the matter of Tejef. Barring her from the *paredre* may not prove sufficient restraint."

"Nevertheless," said Chimele, "my decision stands."

"The Orithain cannot make mistakes."

"But even so," Chimele observed, "I prefer to proceed toward infallibility at my own unhurried pace, Rakhi. Have you heard from Ashakh yet?"

"He acknowledged. He has left Priamos by now, and he will be here with all possible speed."

"Good. Go back to your station. Aiela, Isande, if we are to salvage Daniel, you must find him a suitable unit and dispose of that child by some means. I trust you are still keeping your actions shielded from him. His mind is already burdened with too much knowledge. And when I do give you leave to contact him, you may tell him that I am ill pleased."

"I have already made that clear to him."

"She is not his," Chimele objected, still worrying at that thought.

"She attached herself to him for protection. She became his."

"There is no *nasith-tak,* no female, no *katasathe,* no *dhisais.* Is it reasonable that a male would do this, alone?"

"I am sure it is. An iduve would not?"

That was a presumptuous question. Isande reproved his asking, but Chimele lowered her eyes to show decent shame and then looked up at him.

"A female would be moved to do what he has done as if she were *katasathe* and near her time. A male could not, not without the presence of a female with whom he had recently mated. But is not this child-female close to adulthood? Perhaps it is the impulse to *katasakke* that has taken him."

"No," said Aiela, "no, when he thinks of her, it is as a child. That—unworthy thought did cross his mind; he drove it away. He was deeply ashamed."

He wished he had not said that private thing to Chimele. Had he not been so tired he would have withheld it. But it had given her much to ponder. Bewilderment sat in her eyes.

"She is *chanokhia* to him," Aiela said further. "To him she is the whole human race. You and I would not think so, but to him she is infinitely beautiful."

And he rejoined Isande at the desk, where with trembling hands she began to ply the keyboard again and to call forth the geography of Priamos on the viewer, marking it with the sites of occupied areas, receiving reports from the command center, updating the map. There were red zones for amaut occupation, green for human, and the white pinpricks that were iduve: one at Weissmouth in a red zone, that was Khasif; and one in the continental highlands a hundred *lioi* from Daniel, which was Tejef at best reckoning.

When Aiela chanced at last to notice Chimele again she was standing by her desk in the front of the *paredre,* which had expanded to a dizzying perspective of *Ashanome's* hangar deck, talking urgently with Ashakh.

It was fast coming up dawn in the Weiss valley. The divergent rhythms of ship and planetary daylight systems were not least among the things that had kept Aiela's mind off-balance for fifteen days. He thought surely that Daniel would have been compelled by exhaustion to lie down and sleep. He could not possibly have the strength to go much further. But even wondering about Daniel could let information through the screening. Aiela turned his mind away toward the task at hand, sealing against any further contact.

The light was beginning to rise, chasing Priamos' belt of stars from the sky, and by now Daniel's steps wandered. Oftentimes he would stop and stare down the long still-descending road, dazed. Aiela's thoughts were silent in him. He had felt one terrible pain, and then a long silence, so that he had forgotten the importance of his rebellion against Aiela and hurled anxious inquiry at him, whether he were well, what had happened. The silence continued, only an occasional communication of desperation seeping through. It was Chimele's doing, then, *vaikka* against Aiela, thoroughly iduve, but against him, against all Priamos, her retaliation would not be so slight.

In cold daylight Daniel knew what he had done, that a world might die because he had not had the stomach to commit one more murder; but he refused steadfastly to think that far ahead, or to believe that even Chimele could carry out a threat so brutally—that he and the little girl would become only two among a million corpses to litter the surface of a dead world.

His ankle turned. He caught himself and the child's thin arms tightened about his neck. "Please," she said. "Let me try to walk again."

His legs and shoulders and back were almost numb, and the absence of her weight was inexpressible relief. Now that the light had come she looked pitifully naked in her thin yellow gown, very small, very dislocated, walking this wilderness all dressed for bed, as if she were the victim of a nightmare that had failed to go away with the dawn. At times she looked as if she feared him most of all, and he could not blame her for that. That same dawn showed her a disreputable man, face stubbled with beard, a man who carried an ugly black gun and an assassin's gear that must be strange indeed to the eyes of the country child. If her parents had ever warned her of rough men, or men in general—was she old enough to understand such things?—he conformed to every description of what to avoid. He wished that he could assure her he was not to be feared, but he thought that he would stumble hopelessly over any assurances that he might try to give her, and perhaps might frighten her the more.

"What's your name?" she asked him for the first time.

"Daniel Fitzhugh," he said. "I come from Konig."

That was close enough she would have heard of it, and the mention of familiar places seemed to reassure her. "My name is Arle Mar," she said, and added tremulously: "That was my mother and father's farm."

"How old are you?" He wanted to guide the questioning away from recent memory. "Twelve?"

"Ten." Her nether lip quivered. "I don't want to go this way. Please take me back home."

"You know better than that."

"They might have gotten away." He thought she must have treasured that hope a long time before she brought it out into the daylight. "Maybe they hid like I did and they'll be looking for me to come back."

"No chance. I'm telling you—no."

She wiped back the tears. "Have you got an idea where we should go? We ought to call the Patrol, find a radio at some house—"

"There's no more law on Priamos—no soldiers, no police, nothing. We're all there is—men like me."

She looked as if she were about to be sick, as if finally all of it had caught up with her. Her face was white and she stood still in the middle of the road looking as if she might faint.

"I'll carry you," he offered, about to do so.

"No!" If her size had been equal to her anger she would have been fearsome. As it was she simply plumped down in the middle of the road and rested her elbows on her knees and her face in her hands. He did not press her further. He sat down crosslegged not far away and rested, fingers laced on the back of his neck, waiting, allowing her the dignity of gathering her courage again. He wanted to touch her, to hug her and let her cry and make her feel protected. He could not make the move. A human could touch, he thought; but he was no longer wholly human. Perhaps she could feel the strangeness in him; if that were so, he did not want to learn it.

Finally she wiped her eyes a last time, arose stiffly, and delicately lifted the hem of her tattered nightgown to examine her skinned knees.

"It looks sore," he offered. He gathered himself to his feet.

"It's all right." She let fall the hem and gave the choked end of a sob, wiping at her eyes as she surveyed the valley that lay before them in the sun, the gently winding Weiss, the black and burned fields. "All this used to be green," she said.

"Yes," he said, accepting the implied blame.

She looked up at him, squinting against the sun. "Why?" she asked with terrible simplicity. "Why did you need to do that?"

He shrugged. It was beyond his capacity to explain. The truth led worse places a lie. Instead he offered her his hand. "Come on. We've got a long ways to walk."

She ignored his hand and walked ahead of him. The road was soft and sandy with a grassy center, and she kept to the sand; but the sun heated the ground, and by the time they had descended to the Weiss plain the child was walking on the edges of her feet and wincing.

"Come on," he said, picking her up willing or not with a sweep of his arm behind her knees. "Maybe I—"

He stopped, hearing a sound very far away, a droning totally unlike the occasional hum of the insects. Arle heard it too and followed his gaze, scanning the blue-white sky for some sign of an aircraft. It passed, a high gleam of light, then circled at the end of the vast plain and came back.

"All right," he said, keeping his voice casual. *Aiela, Aiela, please hear me.* "That's trouble. If they land, Arle, I want you to dive for the high weeds and get down in that ditch." *Aiela! give me some help!*

"Who are they?" Arle asked.

"Probably friends of mine. Amaut, maybe. Remember, I worked for the other side. I may be picked up as a deserter. You may see some things you won't like." *O heaven, Aiela, Aiela, listen to me!* "I can lie my way out of my own troubles. You, I can't explain. They'll skin me alive if they see you, so do me a favor: take care of your own self, whatever you see happen, and stay absolutely still. You can't do a thing but make matters worse for me, and they have sensors that can find you in a minute if they choose to use them. Once they suspect I'm not alone, you haven't got a chance to hide from them. You understand me? Stay flat to the ground."

It was coming lower. Engines beating, it settled, a great silver elongate disc that was of no human make. A jet noise started as they whined to a landing athwart the road, and the sand kicked up in a blinding cloud. Under its cover Daniel set Arle down and trusted her to run, turned his face away and flung up his arms to shield his eyes from the sand until the engines had died away to a lazy throb. The ship shone blinding bright in the sun. A darkness broke its surface, a hatch opened and a ramp touched the ground.

Aiela! Daniel screamed inwardly; and this time there was an answer, a quick probe, an apology.

Amaut, Daniel answered, and cast him the whole picture in an eyeblink, the ship, the amaut on the ramp, the humans descending after. *Parker: Anderson's second in command.* Daniel cast in bursts and snatches, abjectly pleading with his asuthe, forgive his insubordination, tell Chimele, promise her anything, do something.

Aiela was doing that; Daniel realized it, was subconciously aware of the kallia's fright and Chimele's rage. It cut away at his courage. He sweated, his hand impelled toward the gun at his hip, his brain telling it no.

Parker stepped off the end of the ramp, joined by two

more of the ugly, waddling amaut, and by another mercenary, Quinn.

"Far afield, aren't you?" Parker asked of him. It was not
friendliness.

"I got separated last night, didn't have any supplies. I decided to hike back riverward, maybe pick up with some other
unit. I didn't think I rated that much excitement from the captain." It was the best and only lie he could think of under the
circumstances. Parker did not believe any of it, and spat ex-
pressively into the dust at his feet.

"Search the area," the amaut said to his fellows. "We had
a double reading. There's another one."

Daniel went for his pistol. *No!* Aiela ordered, throwing
him off-time, making the movement clumsy.

The amaut fired first. The shot took his left leg from under
him and pitched him onto his face in the sand. Arle's thin
scream sounded in his ears—the wrist of his right hand was
ground under a booted heel and he lost his gun, had it torn
from his fingers. Aiela, driven back by the pain, was trying to
hold onto him, babbling nonsense. Daniel could only see—
sideways—Arle, struggling in the grip of the other human,
kicking and crying. He was hurting her.

Daniel lurched for his feet, screamed hoarsely as a streak
of fire hit him in the other leg. When he collapsed writhing
on the sand Parker set his foot on his wrist and took deliberate aim at his right arm. The shot hit. Aiela left him, every
hope of help left him.

Methodically, as if it were some absorbing problem, Parker
took aim for the other arm. The amaut stood by in a group,
curiosity on their broad faces. Arle's shrill scream made
Parker's hand jerk.

"No!" Daniel cried to the amaut, and he had spoken the
kalliran word, broken cover. The shot hit.

But the amaut's interest was pricked. He pulled Parker's
arm down; and no loyalty to the ruthless iduve was worth
preserving cover all the way to a miserable death. Daniel
gathered his breath and poured forth a stream of oaths, native and kalliran, until he saw the mottled face darken in anger. Then he looked the amaut straight in his froggish eyes,
conscious of the fear and anger at war there.

"I am in the service of the iduve," he said, and repeated it
in the iduve language should the amaut have any doubt of it.

"You lay another hand on me or her and there will be cinders where your ship was, and you know it, you gray horror."

"Hhhunghh." It was a grunt no human throat could have made. And then he spoke to Parker and Quinn in human language. "No. We take thiss—thiss." He indicated first Daniel and then Arle. "You, you, walk, report Anderson. Go. Goodbye."

He was turning the two mercenaries out to walk to their camp. Daniel felt a satisfaction for that which warmed even through the pain: *Vaikka?* he thought, wondering if it were human to be pleased at that. A hazy bit of yellow hovered near him, and he felt Arle's small dusty hand on his cheek. The remembrance of her among the amaut brought a fresh effort from him. He tried to think.

Daniel. Aiela's voice was back, cold, efficient, comforting. *Convince them to take you to Weissmouth. Admit you serve the iduve there; that's all you can do now.* Chimele was furious. That leaked through, frightening in its implications. The screen went up again.

"That ship overhead," Daniel began, eyeing the amaut, drunk with pain, "there's no place on this world you can hide from that. They have their eye on you this instant."

The other amaut looked up as if they expected to see destruction raining down on them any second; but the captain rolled his thin lips inward, the amaut method of moistening them, like a human licking his lips.

"We are small folk," he said, mouth popping on all the explosive consonants, but he spoke the kalliran language with a fair fluency. "One iduve-lord we know. One only we serve. There is safety for us only in being consistent."

"Listen, you—listen! They'll destroy this world under you. Get me to the port at Weissmouth. That's your chance to live."

"No. And I have finished talking. See to him," he instructed his subordinates as he began to walk toward the ramp, speaking now in the harsh amaut language. "He must live until the lord in the high plains can question him. The female too."

"He had no choice," said Aiela.

Chimele kept her back turned, her arms folded before her. The *idoikkhe* tingled spasmodically. When she faced him

again the tingling had stopped and her whiteless eyes stared
at him with some degree of calm. Aiela hurt; even now he
hurt, muscles of his limbs sensitive with remembered pain,
stomach heaving with shock. Curiously the only thing clear in
his mind was that he must not be sick: Chimele would be
outraged. He had to sit down. He did so uninvited.

"Is he still unconscious?"

Chimele's breathing was rapid again, her lip trembling, not
the nether lip as a kalliran reaction would have it: *Attack!*
his subconscious read it; but this was Chimele, and she was
civilized and to the limit of her capacity she cared for her kamethi. He did not let himself flinch.

"We have a problem," she said by way of understatement,
and hissed softly and sank into the chair behind her desk. "Is
the pain leaving?"

"Yes." *Isande—Isande!*

His asuthe stood behind him, took his hand, seized upon
his mind as well, comforting, interfering between memory
and reality. *Be still*, she told him, *be still. I will not let go.*

"Could you not have prevented him talking?" Chimele
asked.

"He was beyond reason," Aiela insisted. "He only reacted.
He thought he was lost to us."

"And duty. Where was that?"

"He thought of the child, that she would be alone with
them. And he believed you would intervene for him if only
he could survive long enough."

"The *m'metane* has an extraordinary confidence in his own
value."

"It was not a conscious choice."

"Explain."

"Among his kind, life is valued above everything. I know, I
know your objections, but grant me for a moment that this is
so. It was a confidence so deep he didn't think it, that if he
served beings of *arastiethe*, they would consider saving his
life and the child's of more value than taking that of Tejef."

"He is demented," Chimele said.

Careful, Isande whispered into his mind. *Soft, be careful.*

"You gave me a human asuthe," Aiela persisted, "and told
me to learn his mind. I'm kallia. I believe *kastien* is more important than life—but Daniel served you to the limit of his
moral endurance."

"Then he is of no further use," said Chimele. "I shall have to take steps of my own."

His heart lurched. "You'll kill him."

Chimele sat back, lifted her brows at this protest from her kameth, but her hand paused at the console. "Do you care to stay *asuthithekkhe* with him while he is questioned by Tejef? Do not be distressed. It will be sudden; but those who harmed him and interfered with *Ashanome* will wish they had been stillborn."

"If you can intervene to kill him, you can intervene to save him."

"To what purpose?"

Aiela swallowed hard, screened against Isande's interference. He sweated; the *idoikkhe* had taught its lesson. "It is not *chanokhia* to destroy him, any more than it was to use him as you did."

The pain did not come. Chimele stared into the trembling heart of him. "Are you saying that I have erred?"

"Yes."

"To correctly assess his abilities was your burden. To assign him was mine. His misuse has no relevance to the fact that his destruction is proper now. Your misguided *giyre* will cost him needless pain and lessen the *arastiethe* of *Ashanome*. If he comes living into the hands of Tejef he may well ask you why you did not let him die; and every moment we delay, intervention becomes that much more difficult."

"He is kameth. He has that protection. It would not be honorable for Tejef to harm him."

"Tejef is *arrhei-nasuli*, an outcast. It would not be wise to assume he will be observant of *nasul-chanokhia*. He is not so bound, nor am I with him. He may well choose to harm him. We are wasting time."

"Then contact that amaut aircraft and demand Daniel and the child."

"To what purpose?"

The question disarmed him. He snatched at some logic the iduve might recognize. "He is not useless."

"How not? Secrecy is impossible now. Tejef will be alerted to the fact that I have a human *nas kame*; besides, the amaut in the aircraft would probably refuse my order. Tejef is their lord; they said so quite plainly, and amaut are nothing if not consistent. To demand and to be refused would mean that we had suffered *vaikka,* and I would still have to destroy a kameth of mine, having gained nothing. To risk this to save what I am bound to lose seems a pointless exercise; the odds are too high. I am not sure what you expect of me."

"Bring him back to *Ashanome.* Surely you have the power to do it."

"There is no longer time to consider that alternative. Shall I commit more personnel at Tejef's boundaries? The risk involved is not reasonable."

"No!" Aiela cried as she started to turn from him. He rose from his chair and leaned upon her desk, and Chimele looked up at him with that bland patience swiftly evaporating.

"What are you going to do with Priamos when you've destroyed him?" Aiela asked. "With three days left, what are you going to do? Blast it to cinders?"

"Contrary to myth, such actions are not pleasurable to us. I perceive you have suffered extreme stress in my service and I have extended you a great deal of patience, Aiela; I also realize you are trying to give me the benefit of our knowledge. But there will be a limit to my patience. Does your experience suggest a solution?"

"Call on Tejef to surrender."

Chimele gave a startled laugh. "Perhaps I shall. He would be outraged. But there is no time for a *m'metane's* humor. Give me something workable. Quickly."

"Let me keep working with Daniel. You wanted him within reach of Tejef. Now he is, and whatever else, Tejef has no hold over him with the *idoikkhe.*"

"You *m'metanei* are fragile people. I know that you have *giyre* to your asuthe, but to whose advantage is this? Surely not to his."

"Give me something to bargain with. Daniel will fight if he has something to fight for. Let me assure him you'll get the amaut off Priamos and give it back to his people. That's what he wants of you."

Chimele leaned back once more and hissed softly. "Am I at disadvantage, to need to bargain with this insolent creature?"

"He is human. Deal with him as he understands. Is that not reasonable? *Giyre* is nothing to him; he doesn't understand *arastiethe.* Only one thing makes a difference to him: convince him you care what—"

A probing touch found his consciousness and his stomach turned over at foreknowledge of the pain. He tried to screen against it, but his sympathy made him vulnerable.

"Daniel is conscious." Isande spoke, for at the moment he had not yet measured the extent of the pain and his mind was busy with that. "He is hearing the amaut talk. The child Arle is beside him. He is concerned for her."

"Dispense with his concern for her. Tell him you want a report."

Aiela tried. Tears welled in his eyes, an excess of misery and weariness; the pain of the wounds blurred his senses. Daniel was half-conscious, sending nonsense, babble mixed with vague impressions of his surroundings. He was back on the amaut freighter. There was wire all about. *Aiela, Aiela, Aiela,* the single thread of consciousness ran, begging help.

I'm here, he sent furiously. *So is Chimele. Report.*

"'I,'" Aiela heard and said aloud for Chimele, "'I'm afraid I have—penetrated Tejef's defenses—in a somewhat different way than she had planned. We're coming down, I think. Stay with me—please, stay with me, if you can stand it. I'll send you what I—what I can learn.'"

"And he will tell Tejef what Tejef asks, and promise him anything. A creature that so values his own life is dangerous." Chimele laced her fingers and stared at the backs of them as if she had forgotten the kamethi or dismissed the problem for another. Then she looked up. "*Vaikka.* Tejef has won a small victory. I have regarded your arguments. Now I cannot intervene without using *Ashanome's* heavy armament to pierce his defenses—a quick death to Tejef, ruin to Priamos, and damage to my honor. This is a bitterness to me."

"Daniel still has resources left," Aiela insisted. "I can advise him."

"You are not being reasonable. You are fatigued: your limbs shake, your voice is not natural. Your judgment is becoming highly suspect. I have indeed erred to listen to you." Chimele gathered the now-useless position report together and put it aside, pushed a button on the desk console, and frowned. "Ashakh: come to the *paredre* at once. Rakhi: contact Ghiavre in the lab and have him prepare to receive two kamethi for enforced rest."

Rakhi acknowledged instantly, to Aiela's intense dismay.

He leaned upon the desk, holding himself up. "No," he said, "no, I am not going to accept this."

Chimele pressed her lips together. "If you were rational, you would recognize that you are exceeding your limit in several regards. Since you are not—"

"Send me down to Priamos, if you're afraid I'll leak information to Daniel. Set me out down there. I'll take my chances with the deadline."

Chimele considered, looked him up and down, estimating. "Break contact with Daniel," she said. "Shut him out completely."

He did so. The effort it needed was a great one. Daniel screamed into the back of his mind, his distrust of Chimele finding echo in Aiela's own thoughts.

"Very well, you may have your chance," said Chimele. "But you will sleep first, and you will be transported to Priamos under sedation—both of you. Isande is likewise a risk now."

He opened his mouth again to protest: but Isande's strong will otherwise silenced him. She was afraid, but she was willing to do this for him. *No harm will come to us,* she insisted. *Chimele will not permit it. Kallia can hardly operate in secrecy on a human world, so we shall go under* Ashanome's *protection. Besides, you have already pressed her to the limit of her patience.*

He silently acknowledged the force of that argument, and to Chimele he bowed in respect. "Thank you," he said, meaning it.

Chimele waved a hand in dismissal. "I know this kalliran insanity of joy in being disadvantaged. But it would be improper to let you assume I do this solely to give you pleasure. Do not begin to act rashly or carelessly, as if I were freeing you of bond to *Ashanome* or responsibility to me. Be circumspect. Maintain our honor."

"Will we receive orders from you?"

"No." Again her violet nail touched the button, this time forcefully. "Ashakh! Wherever you are, acknowledge and report to the *paredre* at once." She was becoming annoyed; and for Ashakh to be dilatory in a response was not usual.

The door from the corridor opened and Ashakh joined them; he closed the door manually, and looked to have been running.

"There was a problem," he said, when Chimele's expression commanded an explanation. "Mejakh is in an argumentative mood."

"Indeed."

"Rakhi has now made it clear to her that she is also barred from the control center. What was it you wanted of me?"

"Take Aiela and Isande to their quarters and let them collect what they need for their comfort on Priamos. Then escort them to the lab; I will give Ghiavre his instructions while you are at that. Then arrange their transport down to Priamos; and it would not be amiss to provide them arms."

"I have my own weapon," said Aiela, "if I have your leave to collect it from storage."

"Armament can provide you one more effective, I am sure."

"I am kallia. I'm afraid if I had a lethal weapon in my hands I couldn't fire it. Give me my own. Otherwise I can't defend myself as I may need to."

"Your logic is peculiar to your people, I know, but I perceive your reasoning. Take it, then. And as for instruction, kamethi—I provide you none. I am sure your knowledge of Priamos and of Daniel is thorough, and I trust you to remember your responsibility to *Ashanome*. One thing I forbid you: do not go to Khasif and do not expect him to compromise himself to aid you. You are dismissed."

Aiela bowed a final thanks, waited for Isande, and walked as steadily as he could after Ashakh. Isande held his arm. Her mind tried to occupy his, washing it clean of the pain and the weakness. He forbade that furiously, for it hurt her as well.

In his other consciousness he was being handled roughly down a ramp, provided a dizzying view of a daylit sky: he dreaded to think what could happen to Daniel while he was helpless to advise him, and he imagined what Daniel must think, abandoned as he had been without explanation. *We'll be there,* Aiela sent, defying orders; *hold on, we're coming;* but Daniel was fainting. He stumbled, and Isande hauled up against him with all her strength.

"Ashakh!"

The tall iduve stopped abruptly at the corridor intersection a pace ahead of them and roughly shoved them back. Mejakh confronted them, disheveled and with a look of wildness in her eyes.

"They are killing me!" she cried hoarsely and lurched at Ashakh. "O *nas*, they are killing me—"

"Put yourself to order, *nasith*," said Ashakh coldly, thrusting off her hands. "There are witnesses."

Mejakh's violet eyes rolled aside to Aiela and back again, showing whites at the corners, her lips parted upon her serrate teeth. "What is Chimele up to?" she demanded. "What insanity is she plotting, that she keeps me from controls? Why will no one realize what she is doing to the *nasul? O nas*, do you not see why she has sent Khasif away? She has attacked me; Khasif is gone. And you have opposed her—do you not see? All that dispute her—all that protest against her intentions—die."

"Get back," Ashakh hissed, barring the corridor to her with his arm.

Aiela felt the *idoikkhe* and doubled; but Ashakh's will held that off too, and he shouted at the both of them to run for their lives.

Aiela stumbled aside, Isande's hand in his, Mejakh's harsh voice pursuing them. He saw only closed doors ahead, a monitor panel at the corner such as there was at every turning. He reached it and hit the emergency button.

"Security!" he cried, dispensing with location: the board told them that. "Mejakh—!"

Through Isande's backturned eyes he saw Ashakh recoil in surprise as Mejakh threatened him with a pistol. It burned the wall where Ashakh had been and had he not gone sprawling he would have been a dead man. His control of the *idoikkhei* faltered. Isande's scream was half Aiela's.

The weapon in Mejakh's hand swung left, drawn from Ashakh by the sound. *Down!* Aiela shrieked at Isande and they separated by mutual impulse, low. The smell of scorched plastics and ozone attended the shot that missed them.

Ashakh heaved upward, hit Mejakh with his shoulder, sending her into the back wall of the corridor with a thunderous crash; but she did not fall, and locked in a struggle with him, he seeking to wrest the gun from her hand, she seeking to use it. Aiela scrambled across the intervening distance, Isande's mind wailing terror into his, telling him it was suicide; but Ashakh maintained a tight hold on the *idoikkhei* now so that Mejakh could not send. Aiela seized Mejakh's other arm to keep her from using her hand on Ashakh's throat.

It was like grappling with a machine. Muscles like steel cables dragged irresistibly away from his grip, and when he persisted she struck at him, denting the wall instead and hurting her hand. She swung Ashakh into the way, trying to batter them both against the wall, and Aiela realized to his horror that Isande had thrown herself into the struggle too, trying vainly to distract Mejakh.

Suddenly Mejakh ceased fighting, and so did Ashakh. About them had gathered a number of iduve, male and female, a *dhisais* in her red robes, three *dhis*-guardians in their scarlet-bordered black and bearing their antique *ghiakai*. Mejakh disengaged, backed from them. Ashakh with offended dignity straightened his torn clothing and turned upon her a deliberate stare. It was all that any of them did.

The door of the *paredre* opened at the other end of the corridor and Chimele was with them. Mejakh had been going in that direction. Now she stopped. She seemed almost to shrink in stature. Her movements hesitated in one direction and the other.

Then with a hiss rising to a shriek she whirled upon Ashakh. The *ghiakai* of the *dhis*-guardians whispered from their sheaths, and Aiela seized Isande and pulled her as flat against the wall as they could get, for they were between Mejakh and the others. From the *dhisais* came a strange keening, a moan that stirred the hair at the napes of their necks.

"Mejakh," said Chimele, causing her to turn. For a moment there was absolute silence. Then Mejakh crumpled into a knot of limbs, her two arms locked across her face. She began to sway and to moan as if in pain.

The others started forward. Chimele hissed a strong negative, and they paused.

"You have chosen," said Chimele to Mejakh.

Mejakh twisted her body aside, gathered herself so that her back was to them, and began to retreat. The retreat became a sidling as she passed the others. Then she ran a few paces, bent over, pausing to look back. There was a terrible stillness in the ship, only Mejakh's footsteps hurrying more and more quickly, racing away into distant silence.

The others waited still in great solemnity. Ashakh took Aiela and Isande each by an arm and escorted them back to Chimele.

"Are you injured?" Chimele asked in a cold voice.

"No," said Aiela, finding it difficult to speak in all that silence. He could scarcely hear his own voice. Isande's contact was almost imperceptible.

"Then pass from this hall as quickly as you may. Do you not see the *dhisais?* You are in mortal danger. Keep by Ashakh's side and walk out of here very quietly."

8

IT WAS DONE at last. From his vantage point behind the glass Tejef watched the human grow still under the anesthetic and trusted him to the workmanlike mercies of the amaut physician—not an auspicious prospect if the wounds were much worse, if there were shattered joints or pieces missing. Then it would need the artistry of an iduve of the Physicians' order. Tejef himself had only a passing acquaintance with the apparatus that equipped his ship's surgery, a patch-and-hope adequacy that had been able to save a few human lives on Priamos. He had not sought them out, of course, but occasionally the *okkitani-as* brought them in, and a few rash humans had actually come begging asylum, desperate and thirsty in the grasslands that surrounded the ship. Most injured that Tejef had treated lived, and acknowledged themselves mortally disadvantaged, and, in the curious custom of their kind, bound themselves earnestly to serve him. He was proud of this. He had gathered twenty-three humans in this way. They were not kamethi in the usual sense, for he had no access to *chiabres* or *idoikkhei;* still he reasoned that their service gave him a certain *arastiethe,* and although it was improper to hold *m'metanei* by no honorable bond of loyalty, but only their own acknowledged disadvantage, that was the way of these beings, and he accepted the offering. He had also a hundred of the amaut attending him as *okkitani-as,* and had others dispersed into every center of amaut authority on Priamos. The amaut knew indeed that there was an iduve among them and they took him into account when they made their plans. In fact, he had directly applied pressure on their high command to give him this surgeon, for it was not proper that he practice publicly what was to him only an amateurish skill. He had been of the order of Science, and although it was his doom to perish world-bound, he still had some pride left in his order, not to soil his hands with work inexpertly done.

As his glance swept the small surgery his attention came again to the small yellow person who had defended the man so bravely. He remembered her hovering on this side and on that of the wounded man as he was borne across the field to the ship, darting one way and the other among the irritated amaut to keep sight of him while they brought him in, actually attacking one—a mottled, thick-necked fellow—who tried to keep her out of the surgery. She had gone for him with her teeth, that being all she had for weapons, and being batted aside, she darted under his reach and ensconced herself on a cabinet top in the corner, defying them all. Tejef had laughed to see it, although he laughed but seldom these days.

Now the wretched little creature sat watching the surgeon work, her face gone a sickly color even for a human. Her hand clutched her rag of a garment to her flat chest; her feet and knees were bloody and incredibly filthy—by no means proper for the surgery. She had not stopped fighting. She fairly bristled each time one of the amaut came near her in his ministrations, and then her eyes would dart again mistrustfully to see what the surgeon was doing with the man.

Tejef opened the door, signed the amaut not to notice him. Her eyes took him in too, seeming to debate whether he needed to be fought also.

"It's all right," he told her, exercising his scant command of her language. She looked at him doubtfully, then unwound her thin legs and came off the countertop, her lips trembling. When he beckoned her she ran to him, and to his dismay she flung her thin dirty arms about him and pressed her damp face against his ribs: he recoiled slightly, ashamed to be so treated before the amaut, who wisely pretended not to notice. The child poured at him a veritable flood of words, much more rapidly than he could comprehend, but she seemed by her actions to expect his protection.

"Much slower," he said. "I can't understand you."

"Will he be all right?" she asked of him. "Please, please help us."

Perhaps, he thought, it was because there was a certain physical similarity between iduve and human: perhaps to her desperate need he looked to be of her kind. He had schooled himself to a certain patience with humans. She was very young and it was doubtless a great shock to her to be hurled out of the security of the *dhis* into this frightening profusion of faces and events. Even young iduve had been known to behave with less *chanokhia*.

"Hush," he said, setting her back and making her straighten her shoulders. "They make him live. You—come with me."

"No. I don't want to."

His hand moved to strike; he would have done so had a youngish iduve been insubordinate. But the shock and incomprehension on her face stopped him, and he quickly disguised the gesture, twice embarrassed before the *okkitani-as*. Instead he seized her arm—carefully, for *m'metanei* were inclined to fragility and she was as insubstantial as a stem of grass. He marched her irresistibly from the infirmary and down the corridor.

A human attendant was just outside the section. The child looked up at the being of her own species in tearful appeal, but she made no attempt to flee to him.

"Call Margaret to the *dhis*," Tejef ordered the man, and continued on his way, slowing his step when he realized how the child was having to hurry to keep up with him.

"Where are we going?" she asked him.

"I will find proper—a proper—place for you. What is your name, *m'metane?*"

"Arle. Please let go my arm. I'll come."

He did so, giving her a little nod of approval. "Arle. I am Tejef. Who is your companion? Is he—a relative?"

"No." She shook her head violently. "But he's my friend. I want him to be all right—please—I don't want him to be alone with them."

"With the amaut? He is safe. *Friend:* I understand this idea. I have learned it."

"What are you?" she asked him plainly. "And what are the amaut and why did they treat Daniel like that?"

The questions were overwhelming. He struggled to think in her language and abandoned the effort. "I am iduve," he said. "Ask your kind. I don't know enough words." He paused at the entrance of the lift and set his hand on her shoulder, causing her to look up. It was a fine face, an impossibly delicate body. A creature of air and light, he thought in his own

136   *C. J. Cherryh*

language, and rejected it as an expression more appropriate to Chaikhe than to one of his order. As an *iduve* this little creature would scarcely have survived the *dhis*, where the strength to take meant the right to eat and a *nas* of small stature or nameless birth needed extraordinary wit and will to live. He had survived despite the active persecution of the *dhisaisei* and of Mejakh, and he had done so by a determination out of proportion to his origins. He prized such a trait wherever he found it.

"Are you going to help us?" she asked him.

He took her into the lift and started it moving downward.

"You are mine, you, your friend. You must obey and I must take care for you. You stand straight, have no fear for amaut or human. I take care for you." The door opened and let them out on the level of what had been the *dhis*, sealed and dark until now.

There was Margaret, whom he had not seen in two days. He did not smile at her, being put off by her instant attachment to the child, for she exclaimed aloud and opened her arms to the child, petting her and making much of her with all the protective tenderness of a *dhisais* toward young.

In some measure Tejef was relieved, for he had not been sure how Margaret would react. In another way he was troubled, for her accepting the child made her inappropriate as a mate and made final a parting he still was not sure he wanted. Margaret was the most handsome of the human females, with a glorious mane of fire-colored hair that made her at once the most alien and the most attractive. He had taken her many times in *katasukke*, but she troubled him by her insistence on touching him when they were not alone, and in her display of feelings when they were. She had wept when he admitted at last at great disadvantage that he did not understand the emotions of her kind in this regard, and did not know what she expected of him. He had been compelled to dismiss her from the *khara-dhis* after that, troubled by the heat and violence she evoked in him, by the emotions she expected of him. She certainly could not hold her own if he forgot himself and treated her as *nas*. He would surely kill her, and when he came to himself he would regret it bitterly, for her irritating concern was well-meant, and he had a deep regard for her, almost as if she were indeed one of his own kind. That was the closest he dared come to what she wanted of him.

"Margaret," he said with great dignity, "she is Arle."

"The poor child." She had her arms about the bedraggled girl and petted her solicitously. "How did she come here?"

"Ask her. I want to know. She is a child, yes? No?"

"Yes."

He looked upon the pair of them, women that had been his first mate and this immature being of her own species, and was deeply disturbed. He knew it was very wrong to have brought this pale creature to the *dhis* instead of assigning her among the kamethi, but now that it was done it was good to know that the *dhis* held at least one life, and that Margaret, whom he must put away, had the child he could not give her. It was an honorable solution for Margaret. It was hard to give her up. Desire still stirred in him when he looked at her, nor could she understand why he suddenly rejected her. Hurt pleaded with him out of her eyes.

"She is yours," he told her. "I give her. You will transfer your belongings here. She is your responsibility—yes?"

"All right," she said.

He turned away abruptly, not to be troubled more by the *harachia* of them. He knew that the door opened and closed, that the *dhis,* where no male and no nas kame or amaut might ever go, had been possessed by humans at his own bidding. He was ashamed of what he had done, but it was done now, and a strange furtive elation overrode the sense of shame. He had acquired a certain small *vaikka,* not alone in the disadvantaging of Chimele, but in the acquisition of the *arastiethe* she had decided to take from him. The *dhis* that had remained dark and desolate now held light, life, and *takei*—females; his little ship had a comfort for him now it had lacked before those lights went on and that door sealed.

The sensible part of him insisted that he had plumbed the depths of disgrace in letting this happen; but those who decreed the traditions of honor could not understand the loneliness of an *arrhei-nasuli* and the sweetness there was in knowing he had worth in the sight of his kamethi. It lightened his spirit, and he told himself knowingly a great lie: that he had *arastiethe* and a *takkhenois* adequate to all events. He clutched to himself what he knew was a greater lie: that he might yet outwit *Ashanome* and live. Like a gust

of wind he stepped from the lift, grinned cheerfully at some
of his startled kamethi and went on to the *paredre*. There
were plans to make, resources to inventory.

"My lord." Halph, assistant to the surgeon, came waddling
after, operating gown and all. He bobbed his head many
times in nervous respect.

"Report, Halph."

"The *chiabres* is indeed present, lord Tejef. The honorable
surgeon Dlechish will attempt to remove it if you wish, but
removing it intact is beyond his knowledge."

"No," he said, for the human prisoner would be irrepara-
bly damaged by amaut probing at the *chiabres* if he allowed
it. The human was a danger, but properly used, he could be
of advantage. Kameth though he was, Chimele had most
likely intended him as a spy or an assassin: against an *arrhei-
nasuli* the neutrality of kamethi did not apply, and Chimele
was not one to ignore an opportunity; the intricacy of the
attempt against him that had failed delighted him. "You have
not exposed it, have you?"

"No, no, my lord. We would not presume."

"Of course. You are always very conscientious to consult
me. Go back to Dlechish and tell him to leave the *chiabres*
alone, and to take special care of the human. Remember that
he can understand all that you say. If it can be done safely in
his weakened condition, hold him under sedation."

"Yes, sir."

The little amaut went away, and Tejef spied another of the
okkitani-as, a young female whom her kind honored as extraordinarily attractive. This was not apparent to iduve eyes,
but he trusted her for especial discretion and intelligence.

"Toshi, collect your belongings. You are going to perform
an errand for me in Weissmouth."

"The kamethi have now been sent to Priamos," said
Ashakh. "They will know nothing until they wake onworld.
The shuttle crew will deliver them to local authorities for
safekeeping."

"I did somewhat regret sending them." Chimele arose, acti-
vating as she did so the immense wall-screen that ran ten me-
ters down the wall behind her desk. It lit up with the blue
and green of Priamos, a sphere in the far view, with the pal-
lor of its outsized moon—the world's redeeming beauty—to

its left. She sighed seeing it, loving as she did the stark contrasts of the depths of space, lightless beauties unseen until a ship's questing beam illumined them, the dazzling splendors of stars, the uncompromising patterns of dark-light upon stone or machinery. Yet she had a curiosity, a *m'melakhia*, to set foot on this dusty place of unappealing grasslands and deserts, to know what lives *m'metanei* lived or why they chose such a place.

"What manner of people are they?" she asked of Ashakh. "You have seen them close at hand. Would we truly be destroying something unique?"

Ashakh shrugged. "Impossible to estimate what they were. That is a question for Khasif. I am of the order of Navigators."

"You have eyes, Ashakh."

"Then—inexpertly—I should say that it is what one might expect of a civilization in dying: victims and victimizers, pointless destruction, a sort of mass urge to *serach*. They know they have no future. They have no real idea what we are; and they fear the *amaut* out of all proportion, not knowing how to deal with them.'

"Tejef's *serach* will be great beyond his merits if he causes us to destroy this little world."

"It has already been great beyond his merits," said Ashakh. "*Chaganokh* ruined this small civilization by guiding Tejef among them. It is ironical. If these humans had only known to let them escort Tejef in and depart unopposed, they would not have lost fleets to *Chaganokh*, the amaut would not have been attracted, and they might have had a fleet left to maintain their territories against the amaut if the invasion occurred. Likely then it would have been impossible for us to have traced Tejef before the time expired, and they would not now be in danger from us."

"If the humans are wise, they will learn from this disaster; they will not fight us again, but let us pass where we will. Still, knowing what I do of Daniel, I wonder if they are that rational."

"They have a certain *elethia*," said Ashakh quietly.

"*Au*, then you have been studying them after all. What have you observed?"

"They are rather like *kallia*," said Ashakh, "and have no viable *nasul*-bond; consequently they find difficulty settling differences of opinion—rather more than kallia. Humans actually seem to consider divergence of opinion a positive value, but attach negative value to the taking of life. The combination poses interesting ethical problems. They also have a capacity to appreciate *arrhei-akita,* which amaut and kallia do not; and yet they have deep tendency toward permanent bond to person and place—hopelessly at odds with freedom such as we understand the word. Like world-born kallia, they ideally mate-bond for life; they also spend much of their energy in providing for the weaker members of their society, which activity has a very positive value in their culture. Surprisingly, it does not seem to have debilitated them; it seems to provide a *nasul*-substitute, binding them together. Their protective reaction toward weaker beings seems instinctive, extending even to lower life forms; but I am not sure what kind of feeling the *harachia* of weakness evokes in them. I tend to think this behavior was basic to the civilization, and that what we see now is the work of humans in whom this response has broken down. Their other behavior consequently lacks human rationality."

"In my own experience," Chimele said ruefully, "behavior with this protective reaction also seems highly irrational."

The door opened and there was Rakhi. A little behind him stood Chaikhe, the green robes of a *katasathe* proclaiming her condition to all about her; and when she saw Chimele she folded her hands and bowed her head very low, trembling visibly.

"Chaikhe," said Chimele; and Ashakh, who was of Chaikhe's *sra,* quickly moved between them; Rakhi did the same, facing Ashakh. This was proper: a protection for Chaikhe, a respect for Chimele.

"I am ashamed," said Chaikhe, "to be so when you need me most, I am ashamed."

This was ritual and truth at the same time, for it was proper for a *katasathe* to show shame before an *orithain-tak,* and Chimele had made clear to her a more than casual irritation. ("You are a person of *kutikkase,*" Chimele remembered saying to her: it had bitterly embarrassed the gentle Chaikhe, who prided herself on her *chanokhia,* but it was truly an unfortunate time for the *nas-katasakke* to go off on an emotional bent.)

"Later might have been more appropriate," said Chimele. "But come, Chaikhe. I did not call you here to harm you."

And while Chaikhe still maintained that posture of submission, Chimele came to her and took her by the hands. Then only did Chaikhe straighten and venture to look her in the eyes.

"We are *sra*," said Chimele to her and to the others, "and we have always been close." With a gesture she offered them to sit and herself assumed a plain chair among them. They looked confused; she did not find that surprising.

"Mejakh has been given a ship," she said softly. "You know that she wanted it so. She had honor once. I debated it much, considering the present situation, but it seemed right to do. She is *e-takkhe* and henceforth *arrhei-nasul*."

"Hail Mejakh," said Ashakh in a low voice, "for she truly meant to kill you, Chimele, and her *takkhenois* was almost strong enough to try it."

"I perceive your disapproval."

"I am *takkhe*. I agree to your decisions in this matter. At least there is no probability that she will seek union with either *Tashavodh* or *Tejef*."

"I hope that she will approach *Mijanothe* and that they will see fit to take her. I am relieved to be rid of her, and anxious at once that she may attempt some private *vaikka* on *Tejef*. But to destroy her without Khasif's consent would have provoked difficulty with him and weakened the *nasul*. My alternatives were limited. She made herself *e-takkhe*. What else could I have done?"

Of course there was nothing else. The *nasithi* were both uncomfortable and unhappy, but they put forward no opposition.

"*Mijanothe* and *Tashavodh* have been advised of Mejakh's irresponsible condition," Chimele continued, "and I have warned Khasif. Rakhi, I want her position constantly monitored. Apply what encouragement you may toward her joining *Mijanothe* or departing this star altogether."

"Be assured I shall," said Rakhi.

"We have bitter choices ahead in the matter of Tejef. You know that Daniel has been lost. Against the *arastiethe* of *Ashanome*, Khasif himself has now become expendable."

"Have you something in mind, Chimele," asked Ashakh, frowning, "or are you finally asking advice?"

"I have something in mind, but it is not a pleasant choice. You are all, like Khasif, expendable."

"And shall we die?" asked Rakhi somewhat wryly. "Chimele, I am a lazy fellow, I admit it. I have little *m'melakhia* and the pursuit of *vaikka* is too much excitement for my tastes—"

The *nasithi* smiled gently, for it was high exaggeration, and Rakhi was exceedingly *takkhe*.

"—so, well, but if we are doomed," Rakhi said, "need we be uncomfortable in the process? Perhaps a transfer earthward at the moment of oblivion would suffice. Or if not, perhaps Chimele will honor us with her confidence."

"No," said Chimele, "no, Rakhi, a warning is all you are due at the moment. But"—her face became quite earnest—"I regret it. What I must do, I will do, even to the last of you."

"Then I will go down first," said Ashakh, "because I know that Rakhi would indeed be miserable; and because I do not want Chaikhe to go at all. Omit her from your reckoning, Chimele. She is *katasathe* and carries a life; *Ashanome* has single lives enough for you to spend."

"Inconvenient as this condition is," said Chimele, "still Chaikhe will serve me when I require; but your request to go first I will gladly honor, and I will not treat Chaikhe recklessly."

"It is not my wish," said poor Chaikhe, "but I will give up my child to the *dhis* this day if it will advantage *Ashanome*."

Chimele leaned over to take the *nasith's* hand and pressed it gently. "Hail Chaikhe, brave Chaikhe. I am not of a disposition ever to become *dhisais*. I shall bear my children for *Ashanome's* sake as I do other things, of *sorithias*. Yet I know how strong must be your *m'melakhia* for the child: you are born for it, your nature yearns for it as mine does toward *Ashanome* itself. I am disadvantaged before the enormity of your gift, and I mean to refuse it. I think you may serve me best as you are."

"The sight of me is not abhorrent to you?"

"Chaikhe," said Chimele with gentle laughter, "you are a great artist and your perception of *chanokhia* is usually unerring; but I find nothing abhorrent in your happiness, nor in your person. Now it is a bittersweet honor I pay you," she added soberly, "but Tejef has always honored you greatly, and so, *katasathe*, once desired of him, you now become a weapon in my hands. How is your heart, Chaikhe? How far can you serve me?"

"Chimele," Ashakh began to protest, but her displeasure silenced him and Chaikhe's rejection of his defense finished the matter. He stretched his long legs out before him and studied the floor in grim silence.

"Once," said Chaikhe, "indeed I was drawn to Tejef, but I am *takkhe* with *Ashanome* and I would see him die by any means at all rather than see him take our *arastiethe* from us."

"Where Chaikhe is," murmured Chimele, "I trust that all *Ashanome's* affairs will be managed with *chanokhia.*"

9

"MY LORD nas kame."

Aiela came awake looking into the mottled gray face of an amaut, feeling the cold touch of broad fingertips on his face, and lurched backward with a shudder. There was the yielding surface of a bed under his back. He looked to one side and the other. Isande lay beside him. They were in a plaster-walled room with paned doors open on a balcony and the outside air.

He probed at Daniel's mind and found the contact dark. Fear clawed at him. He attempted to rise, falling on the amaut's arms and still fighting to find the floor with his feet.

"O sir," the amaut pleaded with him, and resorted at last to the strength of his long arms to force him back again. Aiela struggled blindly until the gentle touch of Isande's returning consciousness reminded him that he had another asuthe. She felt his panic, read his fear that Daniel was dead, and thrust a probe past him to the human.

Not dead, her incoherent consciousness judged. *Let go, Aiela.*

He obeyed, trusting her good sense, and blinked sanely up at the amaut.

"Are you all right now, my lord nas kame?"

"Yes," Aiela said. Released, he sat on the edge of the bed holding his head in his hands. "What time is it?"

"Why, about nine of the clock," said the amaut. That was near evening. The amaut used the iduve's ten-hour system, and day began at dawn.

That surprised him. It ought to be dark in Weissmouth, which was far to the east of Daniel and Tejef's ship. Aiela tried to calculate what should have happened, and uneasily asked the date.

144

"Why, the nineteenth of Dushaph, the hundred and twenty-first of our colony's—"

Aiela's explosive oath made the amaut gulp rapidly and blink his saucer eyes. A day lost, a precious day lost with Chimele's insistence on sedation; and Daniel's mind remained silent in daylight, when the world should be awake.

"And who are you?" Aiela demanded.

The amaut backed a pace and bowed several times in nervous politeness. "I, most honorable sir? I am Kleph son of Kesht son of Griyash son of Kleph son of Oushuph son of Melkuash of *karsh* Melkuash of the colony of the third of Suphrush, earnestly at your service, sir."

"Honored, Kleph son of Kesht," Aiela murmured, trying to stand. He looked about the room of peeling plaster and worn furniture. Kleph in nervous attendance, hands ready should he fall. On Kleph's shoulder was the insignia of high rank: Airela found it at odds with the amaut's manner, which was more appropriate to a backworld dockhand than a high colonial official. Part of the impression was conveyed by appearance, for Kleph was unhappily ugly even by amaut standards. Gray-green eyes stared up at him under a heavy brow ridge and the brow wrinkled into nothing beneath the dead-gray fringe of hair. Most amauts' hair was straight and neat, cut bowl-fashion; Kleph's flew out here and there in rebel tufts. The average amaut reached at least to the middle of Aiela's chest. Kleph's head came only scantly above Aiela's waist, but his arms had the growth of a larger man's and hung nearly past his knees. As for mottles, the most undesirable feature of amaut complexion, Kleph's face was a patchwork of varishaded gray.

"May I help you, sir?"

"No." Aiela shook off his hands and went out onto the balcony, Kleph hovering still at his elbow.

Weissmouth lay in ruins before them. Almost all the city had been reduced to burned-out shells, from just two streets beyond to the Weiss river, that rolled its green waters through the midst of the city to the salt waters of the landlocked sea. Only this sector preserved the human city as it had been, but there had never been beauty in the red clay brick and the squat square architecture, the concrete-and-glass buildings that crowded so closely on treeless streets. It had a sordid quaintness, alien in its concept, the sole city of an impoverished and failing world. Under amaut care the ravaged land might flourish again: they had skill with the most stubborn ground and their endurance in physical labor could irrigate the land and coax lush growth even upon rocky hillsides, hauling precious water by hand-powered machines as old as civilization in the zones of Kesuat, digging their settlements in under the earth with shovels and baskets where advanced machinery was economically ruinous, breeding until the settlement reached its limit and then launching forth new colonies until the world of Priamos could support no more. Then by instinct or by conscious design the birthrate would decline sharply, and those born in excess would be thrust offworld to find their own way. This was always the pattern.

But, Aiela remembered with a coldness at his belly, in less than two days neither human nor amautish skill would suffice to save the land: there would be only slag and cinders, and the green-flowing Weiss and the salt sea itself would have boiled into steam.

"What do you want here?" Aiela asked of Kleph. "Who sent you?"

Again a profusion of bows. "Lord *nas kame,* I am *bnesych* Gerlach's Master of Accounts. Also it is my great honor to serve the *bnesych* by communicating with the starlord in the port."

"Khasif, you mean."

Terror shone in the round face. Lips trembled. All at once Aiela realized himself as the object of that terror: found himself the stranger in the outside, and saw Kleph's eyes flinch from his. "Lord—they use no names with us. Please. To the ship in the port of Weissmouth, if that is the one you mean."

"And who assigned you here?"

"*Bnesych* Gerlach, honorable lord. To guard your sleep."

"Well, I give you permission to wait outside."

Kleph looked up and blinked several times, then comprehended the order and bowed and bobbed his way to the door. It closed after, and Aiela imagined the fellow would be close by it outside.

The sun was fast declining to the horizon. Aiela leaned upon the railing with his eyes unfocused on the golding clouds, reaching again for Daniel—not dead, not dead, Isande assured him. So inevitably Daniel would wake and he would be wrenched across dimensionless space to empathy with the human, in whatever condition his body survived. His screening felt increasingly unreliable. Sweat broke out upon him. He perceived himself drawn toward Daniel's private oblivion and fought back; the railing seemed insubstantial.

Isande perceived his trouble. She arose and hurried out to reach him. At her second step from the bed, mind-touch screamed panic. Her hurtling body fell through the door, her hands clutching for the rail. Aiela seized her, straining her stiff body to him. Her eyes stared upward into the sky, her mind hurtling up into the horrifying depth of heaven, a blue-gold chasm that yawned without limit.

He covered her eyes and hugged her face against him, diz-zied by the vertigo she felt, the utter terror of sky above that alternately gaped into infinity and constricted into a weight she could not bear. Proud Isande, so capable in the world of *Ashanome:* to lift her head again and confront the sky was an act of bravery that sent her senses reeling.

Nine thousand years of voyaging—and world-sense was no longer in her. "It is one thing to have seen the sky through your eyes," she said, "but I feel it, Aiela, I feel it. Oh, this is wretched. I think I am going to be sick."

He helped her walk inside and sat with her on the bed, holding her until the chill passed from her limbs. She was not sick; pride would not let her be, and with native stubbornness she tore herself free and staggered toward the balcony to do battle with her weakness. He caught her before she could fall, held her with the same gentle force she had lent him so often at need. Her arms were about him and for a brief moment she picked up his steadiness and was content just to breathe.

The feeling of wrongness persisted. Her world had been perceptibly concave, revolving in perceptible cycles, millen-nium upon millennium. The great convexity of Priamos seemed terrifyingly stationary, defying reason and gravity at once, and science and her senses warred.

"How can I be of use," she cried, "when all my mind can give yours is vertigo? O Aiela, Aiela, it happens to some of us, it happens—but oh, why me? Of all people, why me?"

"Hush." He brought her again to the bed and let her down upon it, propping her with pillows. He sat beside her, her small waist under the bridge of his arm. In deep tenderness he touched her face and wiped her angry tears and let his

hand trail to her shoulder, feeling again an old familiar long-
ing for this woman, muted by circumstances and their own
distress; but he would hurt with her pain ánd be glad of her
comfort for a reason in which the *chiabres* was only incidental.

My *selfishness*, he thought bitterly, *my cursed selfishness in
bringing you here;* and he felt her mind open as it had never
opened, reaching at him, terrified—she would not be put
away, would not be forgotten while she chased after human
phantoms, would not find him dying and unreachable again.

He sealed against her. It took great effort.

Daniel, she read in tearful fury, jealousy: *Daniel, Daniel,
his thoughts, he—*

Human beings: human ethics, human foulness—the experience of an alien being who had known the worst of his own
species and of the amaut, things she had known of, but that
only he had owned: the attitudes, the habits, the *feeling* of
being human. *Asuthithekkhe* with Daniel had been too long,
too deep; with all the darknesses left, the secrets—to a devastating degree he *was* human.

"Aiela," she pleaded, put her arms about his neck and
touched face to face, one side and the other. Humans showed
tenderness for each other differently. Even at such a moment
he had to be aware of it, and took her hands from him—too
forcefully: he touched his fingers to her cheek, trembling.

A human might have cursed, or struck at something, even
at her. Aiela removed himself to the foot of the bed and sat
there with his back to her, his hands laced until his azure
knuckles paled; and for several moments he strove to gather
up the fragments of his *kastien*. To strike was unproductive.
To hate was unproductive. To resent Daniel, perfect in his
humanity, was disorderly; for Order had drawn firm lines between their species: it was the iduve that had muddled the
two of them into one, and the iduve, following their own
ethic, were highly orderly.

He felt Isande stir, and foreknew that her slim hand would
reach for him; and she, that he would refuse it. *It is not
elethia to shut me out,* she sent at him. *No. You think you
are going to leave me and do things your own way, but I will
follow you, even if my mind is all I can send.*

Stop it. He arose, shut out her thoughts, and went out to
the balcony.

Ashanome burned aloft like the earliest star of evening, a star of ill omen for Priamos, ineluctable destruction. A time ago he had been a ship's captain in what now seemed the safety of the Esliph, a *giyre* hardly complicated. Now he was the emissary of the Orithain, holding things the amaut could in no wise know: a day lost, the night advancing, his asuthe crippled, a mission that he could not possibly fulfill. The next noon would see the deadline expire.

Suddenly he doubted Chimele had meant for him to succeed. He was no longer even sure her *arastiethe* would permit her to rescue a pair of lost kamethi before the world turned to cinders. If he defied her and ran through the streets crying the doom to come, it would save no one: the amaut could not evacuate in time. He must witness all of it. Bitterly he lamented that the *idoikkhei* could not send. He would beg, he would implore Chimele to take Isande home at least.

She will not desert us, Isande sent him. But doubt was in it. Chimele did not do things carelessly: it was not negligence that had set them, unconscious and helpless, among amaut. Motives with iduve were always difficult to reckon.

Aiela's pulse quickened with anger that Isande tried to damp, frightened as she always was at defiance of the iduve. But there was one iduve ship at hand, one that would have to leave before the attack. At that remembrance, purpose crystallized in his mind; and Isande clung to the bedpost and radiated terror.

Send me to him? Blast you, no, Aiela! No!

Aiela shut out her objections, returned to the bedside and opened his case, donned a jacket against the cool of evening, and strapped on his service pistol. Isande's rage washed at him, frustrated by his relief at having found help for her.

She sent memories: a younger Khasif seen through the eyes of a frightened kalliran girl, attentions that had gone far beyond what she had ever admitted to anyone—being touched, trapped in a small space with an iduve whose intentions were far more dangerous than *katasukke*. She made him feel these things: it embarrassed them both.

"Chimele forbade us to go to Khasif," she said, foreknowing failure. He would have a *vaikka* to suffer for that: he reckoned that and hoped that he would even have the chance. His mind already drifted away from her, toward the dark of Daniel's consciousness, toward the thing he had come to do.

He is HUMAN! The word shrieked through her thoughts with a naked ugliness from which even Isande recoiled in shame.

You see why I cannot touch you, Aiela said, and hated himself for that unnecessary honesty. She could not help it: something there was that set her inner defenses working when she found Daniel coming close to her, though she strove on the surface to be amiable with him. *Male and alien,* her reactions screamed, and in that order.

Did Khasif do that to you? Aiela wondered, not meaning her to catch it; perhaps it was too accurate—she threw up screens and would not yield them down. Her hands sought his, her mind inaccessible.

"How do you think you can help him?" she asked aloud.

"There are all the resources of Weissmouth. Out of the amaut and the human mercenary forces, there has to be some reasonable chance of finding a way to him."

What she thought of those chances leaked through, dismal and doomsaying. Dutifully she tried to suppress it.

"Khasif favors me," she said. "Greatly. He will listen to me. And I am going to seal myself somewhere I won't compromise his security or Chimele's, so that you can communicate with *Ashanome* through me—instantly, if you need to. Maybe Chimele will tolerate it—and maybe we're lucky it's Khasif: outside the *harachia* of Chimele he can be a very stubborn and independent man; he may decide to help us."

He might be stubborn about other matters: she feared that too, but she would risk that to influence him to Aiela's help. Aiela caught that thought in dismay, almost dissuaded from his plans. But there was no other way for Isande, no other hope at all. He took her small valise from the bureau and helped her, arm about her waist, toward the door. Her faint hope that mobility would overcome the sensation of falling vanished at once: it was no better at all, and she dreaded above all to be in open spaces, with the sky yawning bottomless overhead.

Aiela expected Kleph outside. To his dismay there were three amaut, bowing and bobbing in courtesy: Kleph had acquired companions. He was surprised to see the gold disc of command on the collar of one, a tall amaut of middling years and considerable girth. That one bowed very deeply indeed.

"Lord and lady," the amaut exclaimed. *"Sushai."*

"*Sushai-khruuss,*" Aiela responded to the courtesy. "*Bnesych* Gerlach?"

Again the bow, three-leveled. "Most honored, most honored am I indeed by your recognition, lord nas kame. I am Gerlach son of Kor son of Thagrish son of Tophash son of Kor son of Merkush fourteenth generation son of Gomek of *karsh* Gomek." The *bnesych*, governor of the colony, was being brief. In due formality he might have named his ancestors in full. This was the confidence of an immensely important man, for anyone who had been in trade in the *metrosi* knew *karsh* Gomek of Shaphar in the Esliph. They were the largest and wealthiest of the *karshatu* of the colonial worlds. Gomek already controlled the economy of the Esliph, and their intrusion into human space had been no haphazard effort of a few starveling colonials. *Karsh* Gomek had the machinery and the support to make the venture pay, transporting indentured amaut vast distances at small cost to the company, great peril to the desperate travelers, and everlasting misery for the humans docile enough and tough enough to survive the life of laborers for the amaut. This place could be made a viable base of further explorations in search of richer prizes. Daniel's kind were indeed in danger, if struggle with the iduve had weakened them or thrown them into disorder. As long as the human culture had within it the potential for another and another Priamos, with humans selling each other out, the amaut, who did not fight, could keep spreading.

"And this," added the *bnesych*, bending a long-fingered hand at the young amaut female that stood at his elbow, "this is my aide Toshi."

"Toshi daughter of Igrush son of Toshiph son of Shuuk of *karsh* Shuuk." A person of middling stature, Toshi was as fair as Kleph was ugly—not by kalliran standards, surely, but palest gray. Her flat-chested figure was also flat-bellied and her carriage was graceful, but her pedigree was modest indeed, and Aiela surmised uncharitably what had recommended the young lady to the great *bnesych*.

Are you satisfied with your allies? Isande's xenophobia pricked at him, she restless within the circle of his arm. In her vision they were pathetic little creatures, ineffectual little waifs of dubious morality.

Mind your manners, Aiela fired back. *I need the* bnesych's *good will.*

Don't trouble yourself. Kick an amaut *and he will bow and thank you for the honor of your attention. You are* nas kame. *You do not ask in the outside world: you order.*

"You may serve us," said Aiela, ignoring her, "by providing us transportation to the port."

"Ai, my lord," murmured *bnesych* Gerlach, "but the noi kame said you were to remain here. Are the accommodations perhaps not to your liking? They are humanish foul, yes, for which we must humbly beg your pardon, but you have been among us so short a time—we have gathered workmen who will repair and suit quarters to your most exacting order. Anything we may do for you, we should be most honored."

"Your courtesy does you credit." The kalliran phrase fell quite naturally from Aiela's lips, irritating Isande. The *arastiethe* of *Ashanome* had been damaged; Chimele would have bristled had she heard it. "But you see," Aiela continued over her objections, "I shall be staying. My companion will not. And I still require a means to go to the port, and I am in a hurry."

Bnesych Gerlach opened and shut his mouth unhappily, rolled his lips in, and bowed. Then he began to give orders, hustled Toshi and Kleph off, while he clung close to Aiela and Isande, managing amazingly enough to scurry along with them and bow and talk at the same time, assuring them effusively of his cooperation, his wish to be properly remembered to the great lords, his delight at the honor of their presence under his roof, which he would memorialize with a stone of memory in his *karsh* nest on Shaphar.

Isande, ill and dizzied, fretted miserably at his attendance, but bowing to Aiela's wishes she did not bid the creature begone. When they descended in the antiquated cable lift, she lost all her combative urges and simply leaned against Aiela, cursing the nine thousand years of noi kame which had produced a being such as herself.

On ground level they found themselves in an immense foyer with glass doors opening onto a street busy with amaut pedestrians. A hovercraft obscured the view, dusting all and sundry, and settled to an awkward halt outside their building.

"Your car," said the *bnesych* as Toshi and Kleph rejoined them. "Is it not, Toshi?"

"Indeed so," said Toshi, bowing.

"Please escort our honorable visitors, Kleph."

Now Kleph began the series of bows, curtailed as Aiela impatiently paid a nod of courtesy to the *bnesych*, to Toshi, and helped his ailing asuthe toward the door. Kleph hurried ahead to open the door for them, pried the valise from Aiela's fingers, rushed ahead to the door of the hovercraft, and had the steps down for them in short order, scrambling in after they settled in the tight passenger space.

"To which ship?"

Aiela stared at him. "Which?"

"A second landed at noon today," Kleph explained, moistening his lips. "I had thought perhaps it—in my presumption—forgive me, most honorable lord nas kame. To the original ship, then? Of course I did not mean to meddle, oh, most assuredly not, most honorable noi kame. I am not in the habit of prying."

Ashakh must have returned, Isande sent, which worried her, for Ashakh was an unknown quantity in their plans.

"The original ship," said Aiela, and Kleph extracted his handkerchief and mopped at his face. Occupying the cab of the hovercraft with two nervous amaut at close quarters, one could notice a slight petroleum scent. The cleanliness of *Ashanome* and its filtered air rendered them unaccustomed to such things. The scents of amaut and wet earth, decaying matter, wet masonry, and the river—even Aiela noticed these things more than casually, and for Isande they were loathsome.

The little hovercraft proceeded on its way, a humming thunder kicking up sand in a cloud that often obscured their vision. It was getting on toward dark, that hour the amaut most loved for social occasions. Sun-hating, they stayed indoors and underground during the brightest hour and sought the pleasant coolness of the evening to stroll above-ground. *Habishu* were opening, and from them would be coming the merry notes of *geshe* and *rekeb*; their tables were set out of doors, disturbed by the passage of the hovercraft. Irritated *habishaapu* would be forced to wipe the tables again, and amaut on the streets turned their backs on the dust-raising hovercraft and shielded their faces. Such things were not designed for the streets, but then, streets and cities were a novelty to the amaut. It went against their ethic to spoil land surface with structures.

The hovercraft crossed the river in a cloud of spray and came up dripping on an earthen ramp, a bridge accessible but with some of its supports in doubtful condition. The fighting had badly damaged this sector. Hollow, jagged-rimmed shells reared ugliness against a heaven that had now gone dull. They followed a street marked with ropes and flags, at times riding one edge up and over rubble that spilled from shattered buildings.

The port was ahead, the base ship brightly lighted, rising huge and silver and beautiful among the amaut craft, a second ship, a sleek probe-transport, its smaller double. One thought of some monstrous nest, amaut vessels like gray, dry chrysalides, with the bright iduve craft shining among them like something new-hatched.

The hovercraft veered toward the larger, the original ship, but the amaut driver halted the vehicle well away from it. Human attendants came running to lower the hovercraft's ramp, crowding about.

Isande misliked being set down among such creatures. She had accustomed herself to Daniel's face; indeed there were times when she could forget how different it was. These were ugly, and they had an unwashed human stench. Even Aiela disliked the look of them, and helped Isande down himself, protecting her from their hands. He stepped to the concrete and looked at the two ships that shone before them under the floodlights, still a goodly walk distant. But Isande felt steadier: the dimming of the sun had brought out the first stars, and those familiar, friendly lights brought sanity to the horror of color that was the day sky.

I think I can walk, she said, and wistfully: *if it were only a question of moving at night, I could probably——*

No. No. You're safer with him. Come, we'll never get these amaut closer to those ships. Besides, arastiethe *won't permit Khasif to argue with us with them to witness it. If we want that ship to open to us, we had better be alone.*

You are learning the iduve, Isande agreed. *But he will take us inside before he asks why. Then——*

The *idoikkhei* burned, jolted, whited out their minds. When Aiela knew that he was still alive and that Isande was, he found himself fallen partially on her, his head aching from an impact with the pavement, his right arm completely paralyzed to the shoulder. He touched Isande's face with his left hand, cold and sick as he saw a line of blood between her lips; and this was the iduve's doing, a punishment for their presumption. He hated. *Ikas* as it was to hate, he did so with a strength that made Isande cringe in terror.

"They will kill you," she cried. And then the *idoikkhei* began to pulse again.

It was different, not pain, but an irregular surge of energy that made one anticipate pain, and it had its own variety of torment.

Two minds, Aiela realized suddenly, remembering the sensation: *two opposing minds,* and his anger became bewilderment. Isande tried to rise with his help, found she could not, and then through her vision came a view of the other ship, hatch opening, a tall slim figure in black descending.

An iduve, onworld, among outsiders.

Even Tejef had maintained his privacy; that a *nasul* so exposed itself was unthinkable. Even in the midst of their private terror it occurred to the asuthi simultaneously that Priamos might die for seeing what it was seeing, an iduve among them. Had it happened on Kartos there would have been panic and mass suicides.

Mejakh! Isande recognized the person, and her thoughts became a babble of terror. The iduve was coming toward them. The *idoikkhei* were beginning to cause pain as Mejakh's nearness overcame Khasif's interference.

Aiela hauled Isande to her feet and tried to run with her. The pain became too much. They stumbled again, trying to rise.

The hatch of the base ship opened and another iduve descended, careless of witnesses. Aiela forgot to struggle, transfixed by the sight. It was incredible how fast the iduve could move when they chose to run. Khasif crossed the intervening space and came to an abrupt halt still yards distant from Mejakh.

Sound exploded about them all, light: the ground heaved and a wall of air flung Aiela down, dust and cement chips showering about him as he tried to shield Isande. Choking black smoke confounded itself with the darkness: lights on the field had gone out. Amaut poured this way and that, gabbling alarm, human shapes among them. Powerful lights from off the field were sweeping the clouds of smoke, more obscuring than aiding.

Isande! he cried; but his effort to reach her mind plunged him into darkness and pitched him off balance: he felt her body loose, slack-limbed. His hand came away wet from hers, and he wiped the moisture on his jacket, sick with panic.

Hands seized him, hauled him up, attempted to restrain him: humans. He fired and dropped at least one, blind in the dark and smoke.

But when he was free again and sought Isande, he could not find her. Where she should have been there was no one, the pavement littered with stone and powder.

And close at hand an airship thundered upward, its twin lights glaring barefully through the roiling smoke.

Don't let it go, Aiela implored the silent form of the base ship; but both his asuthi were dark and helpless, and the base ship made no effort to intervene. Weaponsfire laced the dark. More shadows, human-tall, raced toward him. Of the hovercraft there was no sign at all. It had deserted them.

A projectile kicked up the pavement near him. The chips stung his leg.

He ran, falling often, until the pounding in his skull and the pain in his side made him seek the shelter of the ruins and wait the strength to run again.

10

TEJEF CAME INFREQUENTLY to the outside of his ship. Considering the proximity of *Ashanome* he did not think it wise to put too great a distance between himself and controls at any moment. But the burden this aircraft brought was a special one. First off the ramp was Gordon, a thin, wiry human with part of two fingers missing. He was not a handsome being, but he had been even less so when he arrived. He was senior among the kamethi, and of authority second only to Margaret.

"Toshi has a report to give," Gordon said, gesturing toward the little amaut who was supervising the unloading of three stretchers. "She can tell it better than I can. We took casualties: Brown, Ling, Stavros, all unrecovered."

"Dead, you say. Dead."

"Yes."

"A sadness," Tejef said. The three had been devoted and earnest in their service. But his attention was for the three being unloaded.

"A male and female of your kind," said Gordon. "And another—something different. Toshi says she's kallia."

The litters neared them, and Khasif was the first: Tejef looked into the face that was so nearly the mirror image of his own, felt the impact of *takkhenes* as Khasif's eyes partially opened. They must have poured considerable amounts of drug into his veins. It would have been the only way to transport him, else he would seize control of the aircraft and wreck them all. Even now the force of him was very tangible.

"Mainlevel compartment twelve is proof against him," Tejef told the bearers. "Put a reliable guard there to warn the humans clear of that area. I think you understand the danger of confronting him once the drug has worn off."

"Yes, sir. We will be careful."

And there was Isande. The kallia and he were of old acquaintance. He was glad to see that she was breathing, for she was of great *chanokhia*.

"She must go to the lab," he told the amaut. "Dlechish will see to her."

And the third one was shrouded in a blanket, darkish blood seeping through it. So the humans treated the dead, concealing them.

This would be the female of his kind. He reached for the blanket, unknowing and uneasy. Chimele it would not be: the Orithain of *Ashanome* would not die by such a sorry mischance, or so shamefully. But for others, for gentle Chaikhe, for fierce old Nophres or Tahjekh, he would feel a certain regret.

The ruined face that stared back at him struck him with a *harachia* that drained the blood from his face and wrung from him a hiss of dismay. Mejakh. Quickly he let fall the blanket.

"Are there rites you do, sir?" asked Gordon.

"How you say?" Tejef asked, not knowing the word.

"Ceremonies. Burial. What do you do with the dead?"

She was *sra* of his. It was not *chanokhia* to let her be bundled into the disintegration chamber by the hands of *m'metanei*. He must dispose of her, he. He conceded Mejakh that final *vaikka* upon him, to force him to do her that honor. There was no other iduve able to do so.

"I see to her. Put her down. Put down!"

He had raised his voice, *e-chanokhia*, disgracing himself before the shocked faces of the *m'metanei*. He walked away from the litter to take himself from the *harachia* of the situation, to compose himself.

"Sir." Toshi came up at his elbow and bowed many times, so that he was forewarned he might not have reason to be pleased with her. "Have I done wrong or right?"

"How was this done?"

"I urged the authorities in Weissmouth to remember their loyalty to you, my lord, and they heard me, although it needed utmost persuasion. There were delays and delays: transportation must be arranged; human mercenaries must be engaged; it must not be done in the headquarters itself. All was prepared. We aimed only for the kamethi, who were accessible; but when the great ships opened and presented us such a chance—my lord, your orders did direct us to seize any opportunity against such personnel—"

"It was most properly done," said Tejef, and Toshi gave a sigh of utmost relief and bowed almost double, long hands folded on her breast.

"But sir—the other *nas kame*—I confess fault: we lost him in the dark. Our agents are scouring Weissmouth for him at this moment. We felt pressed to lift off before the great lords your enemies could resolve to stop us. I think it was our good fortune we escaped even so."

"Few things are random where Chimele is concerned. This *kallia* that escaped: his name?"

"Aiela."

"Aiela." Tejef searched his memory and found no such name. "Go back to Weissmouth and make good your omission, Toshi. You acted wisely. If you had waited, you would surely have been taken. Now see if you can manage this thing more discreetly."

"Yes, sir." Toshi gave a deep breath of relief and bowed, then backed a pace and turned, hurried off shouting orders at the crew of her aircraft. Tejef dismissed the matter into her capable hands.

There was still the unpleasant necessity of Mejakh. Harshly he ordered the *kamethi* to stand aside, and he knelt and gathered the shattered body into his arms.

Tejef washed meticulously and changed his clothes before he entered the *paredre* again. The remembrance of Mejakh's face, the knowledge of Khasif a prisoner in the room down the corridor, worked at his nerves and his temper with the corrosive effect of *takkhenes* out of agreement. It grew stronger. Khasif must be coming out from under the effect of the drug.

Tejef mind-touched the projection apparatus where he stood and connected it to the unit in Khasif's cell.

The *nasith* was a sorry sight. He had gained his feet, and he was dusty and bruised and bleeding, but he attempted a show of hostility.

Tejef was amazed to find that he did have the advantage of his proud *iq-sra*. Perhaps it was the drug still dulling Khasif's mind, or perhaps it was the knowledge that Mejakh was dead and that he had fallen to *m'metanei* and amaut. Undoubtedly

Khasif had already attempted the door with his mind, and found its mechanism proof against an iduve's peculiar kind of tampering—the lock primitive and manual. Now Khasif simply withdrew to the farthest corner, stumbled awkwardly into the wall he could not see in his vision of the *paredre*. He leaned there as if it were difficult to hold his feet.

"I have sent Mejakh hence," Tejef said softly, "but she had nothing for *serach* but what she wore and the blanket they wrapped her in, and I vented the residue world-bound. Hail Mejakh, who was *sra* to us both."

Khasif ought to have reacted to that pretty *vaikka*. He did not move. Tejef felt his own strength coursing along his nerves, felt Khasif's weakness and his fear.

"You could be free," Tejef assured him, "if you declared yourself *arrhei-nasul* and made submission to me. I would take it."

Khasif made a small sound of anger. That was all. It was a beaten sound.

"Sir." Gordon's voice sounded beyond the walls of Khasif's room, and Tejef ceased the projection and stood in the *paredre* once more, facing Gordon and the man Daniel.

"Let him go," said Tejef. "The restraint is not necessary."

Gordon released his prisoner, who showed a disheveled appearance that had no reasonable connection with his having been aroused from sleep. There was blood on his mouth. The human wiped at it at his first opportunity, but he seemed indisposed to quarrel with an iduve. Tejef dismissed Gordon with a nod.

"I assume you are in contact with your asuthe," said Tejef.

"Is Isande on this ship?" the human demanded, and Tejef would have corrected his belligerence instantly had the man worn the *idoikkhe*. He did not, and risked a chastisement of more damaging nature if his insolence persisted.

"Isande is here; but I would surmise that the man who asked that question is named Aiela."

"I thought *arastiethe* forbade guesswork."

"Hardly an unreasonable assumption. And I am not wrong, am I? It was Aiela who asked."

"Yes," Daniel admitted.

"Tell this Aiela that should he wish to surrender himself, I will appoint him the place and the person."

"Arle—the little girl." Daniel ignored the barb to make that broken-voiced plea. "Where is she? Is she alive?"

Vaikka was practically meaningless against such a vulnerable creature as this, one so lacking in pride. Tejef had allowed himself to be vexed; now he dismissed his anger in disgust, made a gesture of inconsequence. He dealt with humans—it was all that could be expected.

"Chimele sent you to Priamos with asuthi to guide you, but without the *idoikkhe*—without its danger and its protection. Was it in order to kill me—to draw near to me, and to seem only human?"

"Yes," said Daniel, so plainly that Tejef laughed in surprise and pleasure. And at once the human's face changed, anger flaring; unprepared for the creature's maniacal lunge, Tejef slapped the human in startled reaction—open-handed, not to kill. The blow was still hard enough to put the fragile being to the floor, and Tejef waited patiently until the human began to stir, and bent and seized his arm, dragging him to his feet.

"Probably you are recently kameth, for I cannot believe that Chimele would have chosen a stupid being to serve her. I could have broken your neck, *m'metane*. I simple did not choose to."

And he let the human go, steadying him a moment until he had his balance; the *m'metane* seemed more defensive now than hostile; he stumbled backward and nearly tripped over a chair.

"I should prefer to reason with you," said Tejef.

"If *that's* your aim, try reasoning with Chimele. Haven't you sense enough to know you're going to get yourself killed?"

"Then it is important," said Tejef, "to do so properly, is it not? What does your asuthe say to that?"

Daniel told him, plainly; and Tejef laughed.

"Please," Daniel pleaded. "Where is Arle? Is she all right?"

"Yes. Quite safe."

"Please let me see her."

"No," said Tejef; but he knew his anger on the subject was, in human terms, irrational. The child herself incessantly begged for this meeting, and, child of the *dhis* as she was, she was human, only human, and knew Daniel for *nas*—a friend, as she put it. It was not the same as if she had been iduve young, and it was well for him to remember it.

Then it occurred to him that a human according to hi peculiar ethic would feel a certain obligation for the favor: *niseth-kame*, paradoxical as the term was.

"Arle is not from *Ashanome*," Daniel persisted. "She is n possible harm to you."

Tejef reasoned away his disgust, reminding himself that sometimes it was necessary to deal with *m'metanei* a *m'metanei*, expecting no *arastiethe* in them.

"I shall take you where she is," said Tejef.

Margaret answered the call to the door of the *dhis*, bu Arle was not far behind her, and Tejef was quite unprepared for the child's wild shout and her plunge out the door int Daniel's arms. The man embraced her tightly, asking ove and over again was she well, until she had lost her breath an he set her back. But then the child turned to Tejef an wanted to embrace him too. He stiffened at the thought, bu as he recoiled she remembered her manners and refrained hands still open as if she did not know what else to do wit them.

"You see," Tejef told her. "Daniel walks; he is well. Be no so uncontrolled, Arle."

She dried her face dutifully and crept back to the shelte of Daniel's arm: the touch between them frayed at Tejef sensibilities.

"He hasn't hurt you—he hasn't touched you?" Daniel in sisted to know, and when Arle protested that she had beer treated very well indeed, Daniel seemed both confused an relieved. He caressed the side of her face with the edge of hi hand and gave a slight nod of courtesy to Margaret and t Tejef. "Thank you," he said in the kalliran tongue. "Bu when your time is up and Chimele attacks—what is you kindness to her worth?"

"For my own kamethi," Tejef admitted, "I have great re gret. But I shall not regret having a few of Chimele's fo *serach*."

"There's no sense in all these people dying. Where is th *arastiethe* in that? Give up."

"Hopelessly irrational, *m'metane*. *Arastiethe* is to posses and not to yield, I am iduve. Express me that thought of yours in my own language, if you can."

That set the human back, for of course it was a contradiction and could not be translated to mean the same thing. "But," Daniel persisted, "you iduve claim to be the most intelligent of species—and can't you and Chimele resolve a quarrel short of this?"

"Yet your species fights wars," said Tejef, "and mine does not. I have a great *m'melakhia* for your kind, human, I truly do. I do not willingly harm you, and if I were able, I would spend time among your worlds learning what you are. But you know my people, however lately you are kameth and asuthe. I think you know enough to understand. There is *vaikka* involved; and to yield is to die; morally and physically, it is to die. One cannot survive without *arastiethe*."

"And what *arastiethe* have you," Daniel cried, "if you are unable to save even your own kamethi, that trust you?"

"They are *mine*," Tejef answered, lost in Daniel's tangled logic.

"Because you have taken advantage of them, because you hold the truth from them—because they trust you're going to protect them."

"Daniel!" Arle cried, alarmed by the shouting if not the knowledge of what he had said. That was what saved him, for she thrust herself between, and her high, thin voice chilled the air.

Tejef turned away abruptly, painfully aware of the illogicalities at war in him. His pulse raced, the skin at the base of his scalp tightened, his respiration quickened. He knew that he must remove himself from the *harachia* of these beings before he lost his dignity entirely. Khasif's *takkhenois* and the *harachia* of Mejakh's corpse had upset him: the nearness of other iduve reminded him of reality, of forgotten *chanokhia*. He had set humans in the *dhis;* and now he had lost control of them. The child should not have come out. He himself had brought a strange male to them, reckoning human *chanokhia* different: but he had erred. He had been disadvantaged, had affronted the honor of Margaret, who was almost *nas*, and this child he had given to her he had allowed to be seen—to be touched—by this *m'metane-toj*. All his careful manipulation of humans lost its important in the face of simple decency. *Harachia* tore at his senses, almost as if they three, human: male, female, and child, possessed a *takkhenes* united against him—when *m'metanei* could possess no such thing. *He* was the one who had given them power against him. Perverted, the kalliran language expressed it: his own had not even the concept to lend shape to his fears about himself.

"Tejef." Margaret's light steps came up behind him; her hand caught his arm. "Tejef? What's wrong? What did he say?"

"Go back!" he cried at her, realizing with a tightening of his stomach she had abandoned Arle and the open *dhis* to Daniel. "Go!"

"What's wrong?" she asked insistently. "Tejef—"

He had wanted this female, still wanted her; and her contaminating touch brought a swell of rage into his throat. What else she said he did not hear, and only half realized the reflexive sweep of his arm, her shriek of terror abruptly silenced. It shocked the anger out of him, that cry: he was already turning, saw her hit the wall and the wall bow before she slid down, and the child screamed like an echo of Margaret. He fell to his knees beside her, touched her face and tried to ease the limbs that were twisted and broken, strained by the way she was lying.

Daniel grasped his shoulder to jerk him back, and Tejef hit him with a violence that meant to kill: but the human was quick and only the side of his arm connected, casting him sprawling across the polished floor. He rolled and scrambled up to the attack.

"No!" Arle wailed, stopping him, wisely stopping him; and Tejef turned his attention back to Margaret.

She was conscious, and sobbed in pain as he tried to ease her legs straight; and Tejef jerked back his hands, wiping them on his thighs, desiring to turn and kill the human for witnessing this, for causing it. But Arle was between them, and when Margaret began to cry Daniel moved the child aside and knelt down disregarding Tejef, comforting Margaret in her own language with far more fluency than Tejef could use.

Tejef seized Daniel's wrist when he ventured to touch her, but the human only stared at him as if he realized the aberrance of an iduve who could not rule his own temper.

The amaut must be called. Tejef arose and did so, and in a mercifully little time they had Margaret bundled neatly onto a stretcher and on her way to Dlechish and the surgery. Tejef watched, wanting to accompany them, ill content to wait and not to know; but he would not be further shamed before the amaut, and he would not go.

He felt Arle's light fingers on his hand and looked down into her earnest face.

"Can I please go with her, sir?"

"No," said Tejef; and her small features contracted into tears. He cast a look over her head, appealing to Daniel. "What is your custom?" he asked in desperation. "What is right?"

Daniel came then, hugged Arle to him and quieted her sobs, saying all the proper and fluent human things that comforted her. "Perhaps," he said to her insistence, "perhaps they'll let you come up and sit with her later, when she's able to know you're there. But she'll be asleep in a moment. Now go on, go on back into your apartments and wash your face. Come on, come on now, stop the tears."

She hugged him tightly a moment, and then ran away inside, into the echoing hall of the *dhis* where neither of them could follow.

"I will honor your promises to her," Tejef told Daniel with great restraint. "Now go up to surgery. I want someone with her who can translate for the amaut. Dlechish does not have great fluency in human speech."

"And what happens," Daniel asked, "when you lose your temper with Arle the way you just did with her?"

Tejef drew a quick breath, choking down his anger. "I had no wish to harm my kamethi."

Daniel only stared at him, thinking, or perhaps receiving something from his asuthe. Then he nodded slowly. "You care for them," he observed, as if this were a highly significant thing.

"*M'melakhia* does not apply. They *are* mine already." He did not know why he felt compelled to argue with a *m'metane*, except that the human had puzzled him with that word. He felt suddenly the gulf of language, and wished anew that he understood *metane* behavior. *Arastiethe* would not let him ask.

"Call *Ashanome*," Daniel said softly. "Surrender. The kamethi do not have to die."

Tejef felt a chill, for the human's persistent suggestion

quite lost its humor; he meant it seriously. It was human to do such a thing, to give up one's own *arastiethe* and become nothing. The inverted logic that permitted such thinking seemed for the moment frighteningly real.

"Did I ask your advice?" Tejef replied. "Go up to surgery."

"She might take it kindly if you came. That is our *arastiethe*, knowing someone cares. We also tend to die when we are denied it."

Tejef pondered that, for it explained much, and posed more questions. Was that *caring*, he wondered; and did it always demand that one yield *arastiethe* by demonstrating concern? But if human honor were measured by gathering concern to one's self, then it was by seeking and accepting favors: the perversity of the idea turned reason itself inside out. In that realization the cleanliness of death at the hands of *Ashanome* seemed almost an attractive prospect. His own honor was not safe in the hands of humans; and perhaps he wounded his own kamethi—and Margaret—in the same way.

"Will you come up?" Daniel asked.

"Go," Tejef ordered. "Put yourself in the hands of one of the kamethi and he will escort you there at your asking."

"Yes, sir." Daniel bowed with quiet courtesy and walked away to the lift. It was kalliran, Tejef realized belatedly, and was warmed by the fact that Daniel had chosen to pay him that respect, for humans did not generally use that custom. It filled him with regret for the clean spaciousness of *Ashanome*, for familiar folk of honorable habits and predictable nature.

The lift ascended, and Tejef turned away toward the door of the *dhis*, troubled by the *harachia* of the place where Margaret had lain, a dent in the metal paneling where her fragile body had hit. She had often disadvantaged him, held him from *vaikka* against humans and amaut, shamed him by her attentions. It was not the deference of a kameth but the tenacious *m'melakhia* of a *nasith-tak*—but of course there was no *takkhenes*, no oneness in it; and it depended not at all on him. She simply chose to belong to him and him to belong to her, and the solitary determination of her had an *arastiethe* about it which made him suspect that he was the recipient of a *vaikka* he could only dimly comprehend.

He was bitterly ashamed of the grief his perverted emotion had brought her in all things, for in one private part of his thoughts he knew absolutely what he had done, saw through his own pretenses, and began now to suspect that he had hurt her in ways no iduve could comprehend. For the first time he felt the full helplessness of himself among a people who could not pay him the *arastiethe* his heart needed, and he felt fouled and grieved at the offering they did give him. The contradictions were madness; they gathered about him like a great darkness, in which nothing was understandable.

"Sir?" Arle was in the doorway again, looking up at him with great concern (*arastiethe? Vaikka?*) in her kallia-like eyes. "Sir, where's Daniel?"

"Gone. Up. With Margaret. With Dlechish. He can talk for her. She has great avoidance for amaut: I think all humans have this. But Dlechish—he cares for her; and Daniel will stay with her." It was one of the longest explanations in the human language he had attempted with anyone but Margaret or Gordon. He saw the anger in the child's eyes soften and yield to tears, and he did not know whether that was a good sign or ill. Humans wept for so many causes.

"Is she going to die?"

"Maybe."

The honest answer seemed to startle the child; yet he did not know why. Plainly the injuries were serious. Perhaps it was his tone. The tears broke.

"Why did you have to hit her?" she cried.

He frowned helplessly. He could not have spoken that aloud had he been fluent. And out of the plenitude of contradictions that made up humans, the child reached for him.

He recoiled, and she laced her fingers together as if the compulsion to touch were overwhelming. She gulped down the tears. "She loves you," she said. "She said you would never want to hurt anybody."

"I don't understand," he protested; but he thought that some gesture of courtesy was appropriate to her distress. Because it was what Margaret would have done, he reached out to her and touched her gently. "Go back to the *dhis*."

"I'm afraid in there," she said. The tears began again, and stopped abruptly as Tejef seized her by the arms and made her straighten. He cuffed her ever so lightly, as a *dhisais* would a favored but misbehaving child.

"This is not proper—being afraid. Stand straight. You are *nas.*" And he let her go very suddenly when he realized the phrase he had thoughtlessly echoed. He was ashamed. But the child did as he told her, and composed herself as he had done for old Nophres.

"May I please go up and stay with Margaret too, sir?"

"Later. I promise this." The prospect did not please him, having her outside the *dhis,* but the illusions must cease, for both their sakes: the child was human, and there was no one left in the *dhis* to care for her. The time was fast running out, and it was not right that the child should be alone in this great place to die. She should be near adults, who would show her *chanokhia* in their own example.

"Are you going there now?" Arle asked.

"Yes," he conceded. He looked back at her standing there, fingers still clenched together. "Come," he said then, holding out his hand. "Come, now. With me."

Most of the lights in the *paredre* of *Ashanome* were out save the ones above the desk, but Chimele knew well the shadowy figure that opened the hall door, a smallish and somewhat heavy iduve who crossed the carpets on silent feet. She straightened and lifted her chin from her hand to gaze on Rakhi's plump, earnest face.

"You were to sleep," he chided. "Chimele, you must sleep."

"I shall. I wanted to know how you fared. Sit, Rakhi. How is Chaikhe?"

"Well enough, and bound for Weissmouth. We considered, and decided it would be best to pursue this adjustment long-distance."

"But is the *asuthithekkhe* bearable, Rakhi?"

The *nasith* gave a weak grin and massaged his freshly scarred temple. "Chaikhe bids your affairs prosper, Chimele-Orithain. She is very much with me at this moment."

"I bid hers prosper, most earnestly. But now you must close down that contact. We two must talk a moment. Can you do so?"

"I am learning," he replied, and leaned back with a sigh. "Done. Done. *Au,* Chimele, this is a fearsome closeness. It is embarrassing."

"O my Rakhi," said Chimele in distress, "Khasif is gone.

Now I have sent Ashakh in his place, and to risk you and Chaikhe at once—"

"Why, it is a light thing," he said. "Do not mere *m'metanei* adjust to this? Is our intelligence not equal to it? Is our self-control not more than theirs?"

She smiled dutifully at his spirit. It was not as easy as Rakhi said, and she did not miss the trembling of his hands, the pain in his eyes; and for Chaikhe, *katasathe*, such proximity to a half-*sra* male must be torment indeed. But of the three remaining *nasithi-katasakke* this pairing had seemed best, for Ashakh's essentially solitary nature would have made *asuthithekkhe* more painful still.

"Chaikhe is really bearing up rather well," said Rakhi, "but I fear I shall have Ashakh to deal with when he sees her on Priamos and knows that I have—in a manner—touched her. I really do not see how we will keep this from him if he is still to direct Weissmouth operations. He will sense something amiss a decad of *lioi* distant."

"Well, you must advise Chaikhe to avoid *harachia*. Ashakh must remain ignorant of this arrangement, for I fear he could complicate matters beyond redemption. And do not you fail me, Rakhi. I have been confounded by one *dhisais* male human, and if you develop any symptoms I insist you warn me immediately."

Rakhi laughed outright, although he flushed dark with embarrassment. "Truly, Chimele, *asuthithekkhe* is not so impossible for iduve as it was always supposed to be. Chaikhe and I—we maintain a discreet distance in our minds. We leave one another's emotions alone, and I suppose it has helped that I am a very lazy fellow and that Chaikhe's *m'melakhia* is directed toward her songs and the child she carries."

"Rakhi, Rakhi, you are always deprecating yourself, and that is a *metane* trait."

"But it is true," Rakhi exclaimed. "Quite true. I have a very profound theory about it. Chaikhe and I would be at each other's throats otherwise. Could you imagine the result of an *asuthithekkhe* between Ashakh and myself? I shudder at the thought. His *arastiethe* would devour me. But the direction of *m'melakhia* is the essential thing. Chaikhe and I have no *m'melakhia* toward each other. In truth," he added upon a thought, "the *m'metanei* misinformed us, for they said strong *m'melakhia* one for the other is essential. I shall make a detailed record of this experience. I think it is is unique."

"I shall find it of great interest," Chimele assured him. "But it would be a great bitterness to me if harm comes to you or to her."

"The novelty of the experience is exhilarating, but it is a great strain. I wonder if the *m'metanei* predict correctly when they say that the strain grows less in time. Perhaps the converse will occur for iduve there too. I surely hope not."

"As do I, *nasith*. Will you go rest now?"

"I will, yes."

"Only do this: advise Chaikhe that Ashakh will be within Weissmouth itself, and she must remain in isolation and wait for my orders. I am summoning up all ships save the two that will remain in port. Mejakh has cost us. I fear the cost may run higher still."

"Ashakh?"

She ignored the question. "May your sleep be secure, o' *nas.*"

"Honor be yours, Chimele."

She watched him go, heard the door close, and rested her forehead once more on her hands, restoring her composure. Rakhi was the last, the last of all her brave *nasithi*, and it was lonely knowing that others had the direction of *Ashanome*, that for the first time in nine thousand years the controls were not even under the nominal management of one of her *sra*. She bore the guilt for that. Of the fierceness of her own *arastiethe*, she had postponed bearing the necessary heir until it was too late for the long ceremonies of *kataberihe*, and *vaikka* had taken heavy toll of those about her. Mejakh was gone, her *sra* on the point of extinction: Khasif and Tejef together. Tamnakh's *sra* was in imminent danger: Ashakh and Chaikhe and the unborn child in her; and if Rakhi *sra*-Khuretekh suffered madness and died, then the *orith-sra* of *Ashanome* came down to her alone.

She felt a keen sense of *m'melakhia* for Tejef, for the adversary he had been, a deep and fierce appreciation. He had run them a fine chase indeed, off the edge of the charts and into *likatis* and *tomes* unknown to iduve. And *Ashanome's* victory would be bitter indeed to *Tashavodh*, dangerously bitter.

Perhaps to ease the sting of it a *nas-katasakke* of

Kharxanen could be requested for *kataberihe*, for *Tashavodh's m'melakhia* to gain *sra* within the *orith-sra* of *Ashanome* was of long standing. Chaxal her predecessor had refused it, and Chimele bristled at the thought: she would bear the heir *Ashanome* needed, perhaps two for safety's sake, as rapidly as her health could bear. Then she could declare dissatisfaction with her mate and send him packing to his own *nasul* in dishonor; that would not be a proper *vaikka*—the Orithanhe forbade—but it would be pleasant.

But defeat—at the hands of Tejef and *Tashavodh*—to see him welcomed in triumph—was unthinkable. She would not bear it.

And there was that growing fear. *Ashanome* had been set back, and this was not an accustomed thing. It had been a hard decision, to sacrifice Khasif. In accepting risk, iduve disliked the irrational, a situation with too many variables. Were there any choice, common sense would dictate withdrawal; but there was no choice, and Tejef would surely seize upon the smallest weakness, the least hesitation: he was unorthodox and rash himself, *e-chanokhia*—but such qualities sometimes made for unpleasant surprises for his adversaries. Occasionally Isande could win at games of reason; the human Daniel had confounded skillfully laid plans by doing what no iduve would have done; and Qao-born Aiela managed to have his own way of an Orithain much more often than was proper. The fact was that *m'metanei* often bypassed the safe course. At times they did bluff, opposing themselves empty-handed to forces they ill understood, everything in the balance. This was not courage in the iduve sense, to whom acting as if one had what one did not smacked of falsity and unreason, which indicated a certain bent toward insanity. For the Orithain of *Ashanome* to bluff was indeed impossible: *arastiethe* and *sorithias* forbade.

But reversing the proposition, to allow another to assume he had what he did not, that was *chanokhia*, a *vaikka* with humor indeed, if it worked. It it did not—the loss must be reckoned proportional to the failure of gain.

Her eyes strayed to the clock. As another figure turned over, the last hour of the night had begun. Soon the morning hour would begin the last day of Tejef's life, or of her own.

"Chimele," said the voice from control: Raxomeqh, fourth of the Navigators. "Projection from *Mijanothe*."

Predictable, if not predicted, Chimele sighed wearily and rose. "Accepted," she said, and saw herself and her desk suddenly surrounded by the *paredre* of *Mijanothe*. She bowed respectfully before aged Thiane.

"Hail Thiane, venerable and honored among us."

"Hail *Ashanome*," said Thiane, leaning upon her staff, her eyes full of fire. "But do I hail you reckless or simply forgetful?"

"I am aware of the time, eldest of us all."

"And I trust memory also has not failed you."

"I am aware of your displeasure, reverend Thiane. So am I aware that the Orithanhe has given me this one more day, so despite your expressed wish, you have no power to order me otherwise."

Thiane's staff thudded against the carpeting. "You are risking somewhat more than my displeasure, Chimele. Destroy Priamos!"

"I have kamethi and *nasithi* who must be evacuated. I estimate that as possible within the limit prescribed by the Orithanhe. I will comply with the terms of the original and proper decree at all deliberate speed."

"There is no time for equivocation. Standing off to moonward is *Tashavodh,* if you have forgotten. I have restrained Kharxanen with difficulty from seeking a meeting with you at this moment."

"I honor you for your wisdom, Thiane."

"Destroy Priamos."

"I will pursue my own course to the limit of the allotted time. Priamos will be destroyed or Tejef will be in our hands."

"If," said Thiane, "if you do this so that it seems *vaikka* upon *Tashavodh*, then, *Ashanome,* run far, for I will either outlaw you, Chimele, and see you hunted to Tejef's fate, or I will see the *nasul Ashanome* itself hunted from star to star to all time. This I will do."

"Neither will you do, Thiane, for if I am declared exile, I will seek out *Tashavodh* and kill Kharxanen and as many of his *sra* as I can reach when they take me aboard. I am sure he will oblige me."

"Simplest of all to hear me and destroy Priamos. I am of many years and much travel, Chimele. I have seen the treasures of many worlds, and I know the value of life. But

Priamos itself is not unique, not the sole repository of this species nor essential to the continuance of human culture. Our reports indicate even the human authorities abandoned it as unworthy of great risk in its defense. Need I remind you how far a conflict between *Tashavodh* and *Ashanome* could spread, through how many star systems and at what hazard to our own species and life in general?"

"It is not solely in consideration of life on Priamos that I delay. It is my *arastiethe* at stake. I have begun a *vaikka* and I will finish it on my own terms."

"Your *m'melakhia* is beyond limit. If your *arastiethe* can support such ambition, well; and if not, you will perish miserably, and your dynasty will perish with you. *Ashanome* will become a whisper among the *nasuli*, a breath, a nothing."

"I have told you my choice."

"And I have told you mine. Hail *Ashanome*. I give you honor now. When next we meet, it may well be otherwise."

"Hail *Mijanothe*," said Chimele, and sank into her chair as the projection flicked out.

For a moment she remained so. Then with a steady voice she contacted Raxomeqh.

"Transmission to Weissmouth base two," she directed, and the *paredre* of the lesser ship in Weissmouth came into being about her. Ashakh greeted her with a polite nod.

"Chaikhe is landing," said Chimele, "but I forbid you to wait to meet her or to seek any contact with her."

"Am I to know the reason?"

"In this matter, no. What is Aiela's status?"

"Indeterminate. The amaut are searching street by street with considerable commotion. I have awaited your orders in this matter."

"Arm yourself, locate Aiela, and go to him. Follow his advice."

"Indeed," Ashakh looked offended, as well he might. His *arastiethe* had grown troublesome in its intensity in the *nasul*: it had suffered considerably in her service already. She chose not to react to his recalcitrance now and his expression became instead bewildered.

"For this there is clear reason," she told him. "Aiela's thinking will not be predictable to an iduve, and yet there is *chanokhia* in that person. In what things honor permits, seek and follow this kameth's advice."

"I have never failed you in an order, Chimele-Orithain, even at disadvantage. But I protest Chaikhe's being—"

She ignored him. "Can you sense whether Khasif or Mejakh is alive?"

"Regarding Mejakh, I—feel otherwise. Regarding Khasif, I think so; but I sense also a great wrongness. I am annoyed that I cannot be more specific. Something is amiss, either with Tejef or with Khasif. I cannot be sure with them."

"They are both violent men. Their *takkhenes* is always perturbing. It will be strange to think of Mejakh as dead. She was always a great force in the *nasul*."

"Have you regret?"

"No," said Chimele. "But for Khasif, great regret. Hail Ashakh. May your eye be keen and your mind ours."

"Hail Chimele. May the *nasul* live."

He had given her, she knew as the projection went out, the salutation of one who might not return. A kameth would think it ill-omened. The iduve were not fatalists.

11

ISANDE CAME AWAKE slowly, aware of aching limbs and the general disorientation caused by drugs in her system. Upon reflex she felt for Aiela, and knew at once that she did not lie upon the concrete at the port. She was concerned to know if she had all her limbs, for it had been a terrible explosion.

Isande. Aiela's thoughts burst into hers with an outpouring of joy. Pain came, cold, darkness, and the chill of earth, but above all relief. He read her confusion and fired multilevel into her mind that she must be aboard Tejef's ship, and that amaut treachery and human help had put her there. A shell had exploded near them. He was whole. Was she? And the others?

Under Aiela's barrage of questions and information she brought her blurred vision to focus and acknowledged that indeed she did seem to be aboard a ship. Khasif and Mejakh—she did not know. *No. Mejakh—dead, dead*—a nightmare memory of the inside of an aircraft, Mejakh's corpse a torn and bloody thing, the explosion nearest her.

Are you all right? Aiela persisted, trying to feel what she felt.

I believe so. She was numb. There was plasmic restruct on her right hand. The flesh was dark there. And hard upon that assessment came the realization that she, like Daniel, like Tejef, was trapped on the surface of Priamos. Aiela could be lifted offworld. She could not. Aiela would live. At least she had that to comfort her.

No! and with Aiela's furious denial came a vision of sky with a horizon of jagged masonry, the cold cloudy light of stars overhead. He hurt, pain from cracking his head on the pavement, bruises and cuts beyond counting from clambering through the ruins to escape—*Escape what? The ship inaccessible?* Isande began to panic indeed; and he pleaded with her to stop, for her fear came to him, and he was so overwhelmingly tired.

Another presence filtered through his mind—Daniel. Although his thoughts reached to Weissmouth and back, he stood in a room not far away. A pale child—Arle, her image never before so clear—slept under sedation: he worried for her. And in that room was a woman whose name was Margaret, a poor, broken thing kept alive with tubings and life support. A dark man sat beside the woman, talking to her softly, and this was Tejef.

Rage burned through Isande, rejected instantly by Daniel: *Murderer!* she thought; but Daniel returned: *At least this one cares for his people, and that is more than Chimele can do.*

Blind! Isande cried at him, but Daniel would not believe it. *Chimele would be a target I would regret less.*

And that disloyalty so upset Isande that she threw herself off the bed and staggered across the little room to try the door, cursing at the human the while in such thoughts as she did not use when her mind was whole.

I cannot reason with Daniel, said Aiela; *but he knows the choice this world has and he will remember it when he must. Humans are like that.*

Kill him, Isande raged at Daniel. *You have the chance now: kill him, kill him, kill him!*

Daniel foreknew defeat, weaponless as he was; and Isande grew more reasoning then and was sorry, for Daniel was as frightened as she and nearly as helpless. Yet Aiela was right: when the time came he would make one well-calculated effort. It was the reasonable thing to do, and that, he had learned of the iduve—to weigh things. But he resented it: Chimele had more power to choose alternatives than Tejef, and stubbornly refused to negotiate anything.

Iduve do not negotiate when they are winning or when they are losing. Isande flared back, hating that selective human blindness of his, that persistence in reckoning everyone as human; *and that Tejef you honor so has already killed millions by his actions; by iduve reckoning, his was the action that began this. He knew what would happen when he sheltered here among humans.*

Tejef has given us our lives, Daniel returned, with that reverence upon the word *life* that a kallia would spend upon *giyre.* Tejef was fighting for his own life, and that struck a response from the human at a primal level. Still Daniel would kill him. The contradictions so shocked Isande that she withdrew from that tangle of human logic and fiercely agreed that it would certainly be his proper *giyre* to his asuthi and *Ashanome* to do so.

The thought that echoed back almost wept. *For Arle's life, for this woman Margaret's, for yours, for Aiela's, I will try to kill him. I am afraid that I will kill him for my own—I am ashamed of that. And it is futile anyway.*

You are not going to die, Aiela cast at them both, and the stars lurched in his vision and loose brick rattled underfoot as he hurled himself to his feet. *I am going to do something. I don't know what, but I'm going to try, if I can only get back to the civilized part of town.*

Through his memory she read that he had been trying to do that for most of the night, and that he had been driven to earth by human searchers armed with lights, hovercraft thundering about the ruined streets, occasional shots streaking the dark. He was exhausted. His knees were torn from falling and felt unsure of his own weight. If called upon to run again he simply could not do it.

Try the ship, she pleaded with him. *Chimele will want you back. Aiela, please—as long as you can hold open any communication between Daniel and myself*—the revulsion crept through even at such a moment—*we are a threat to Tejef.*

Forget it. I can't reach the port. They're between me and there right now. But even if I do get help, all I want is an airship and a few of the okkitani-as. I'm going to come after you.

Simplest of all for me to tell Tejef where you are, she sent indignantly, *and I'm sure he'd send a ship especially to transport you here. Oh, you are mad, Aiela!*

One of Tejef's ships is an option I'm prepared to take if all else fails. That was the cold stubbornness that was always his, world-born kallia, ignorant and smugly self-righteous; but she recognized a touch of humanity in it too, and blamed Daniel.

Aiela did not cut off that thought in time: it flowed to his asuthe. *No,* said Daniel, *I'm afraid that trait must be kalliran, because I've already told him he's insane. I can't really blame him. He loves you. But I suppose you know that.*

Daniel was not welcome in their privacy. She said so and then was sorry, for the human simply withdrew in sadness. In his way he loved her too, he sent, retreating, probably because he saw her with Aiela's eyes, and Aiela's was not capable of real malice, only of blindness.

Oh, blast you, she cried at the human, and hated herself.

Stop it, Aiela sent them both. *You're hurting me and you know it. Behave yourselves or I'll shut you both out. And it's lonely without you.*

"Your asuthi," asked Tejef, coming through Daniel's contact. He had risen from Margaret's side, for she slept again, and now the iduve looked on Daniel with a calculating frown. "Does that look of concentration mean you are receiving?"

"Aiela comes and goes in my mind," said Daniel. *Idiot,* Aiela sent him: *Don't be clever with him.*

"And I think that if Isande were conscious, you might know that too. Is she conscious, Daniel? She ought to be."

"Yes, sir," Daniel replied, feeling like a traitor. But Isande controlled the panic she felt and urged him to yield any truth he must: Daniel's freedom and Tejef's confidence that he would raise no hand to resist him were important. Iduve were unaccustomed to regard *m'metanei* as a threat: they were simply appropriated where found, and used.

Through Daniel's eyes she saw Tejef leave the infirmary, his back receding down the corridor; she felt Daniel's alarm, wishing the amaut were not watching him. Potential weapons surrounded him in the infirmary, but a human against an amaut's strength was helpless. He dared go as far as the hall, closed the infirmary door behind him, watching Tejef.

Then came the audible give of the door lock and seal. Isande backed dizzily from the door, knocking into a table as she did so. Tejef was with her: his *harachia* filled the little room, an indigo shadow over all her hazed vision. The force of him impressed a sense of helplessness she felt even more than Aiela's frantic pleading in her mind.

"Isande," said Tejef, and touched her. She cringed from his hand. His tone was friendly, as when last they had spoken, before Reha's death. Tejef had always been the most unassuming of iduve, a gentle one, who had never harmed any kameth—save only Reha. Perhaps it did not even occur to him that a kameth could carry an anger so long. She hated him, not least of all for his not realizing he was hated.

"Are you in contact with your *asuthi?*" he asked her. "Which is yours? Daniel? Aiela?"

Admit the truth, Aiela sent. *Admit to anything he asks.* And when she still resisted: *I'm staying with you, and if you make him resort to the* idoikkhe, *I'll feel it too.*

"Only to Aiela," she replied.

"This *kameth* is not familiar to me."

"I will not help you find him."

A slight smile jerked at his mouth. "Your attitude is under-standable. Probably I shall not have to ask you."

"Where is Khasif?" Aiela prompted that question. She asked it.

The room winked out, and they were projected into the room that held Khasif. The iduve was abed, half-clothed. A distraught look touched his face; he sprang from his bed and retreated. It frightened Isande, that this man she had feared so many years looked so vulnerable. She shuddered as Tejef took her hand in his, grinning at his half-brother the while.

"*Au, nasith sra-Mejakh,*" said Tejef, "the *m'metane-tak* did inquire after you. I remember your feeling for her: Chimele forbade you, but any other *nas* has come near her at his peril, so she has been left quite alone in the matter of *katasukke.* I commend your taste, *nasith.* She is of great *chanokhia.*"

Knowing Khasif's temper, Isande trembled; but the tall iduve simply bowed his head and turned away, sinking down on the edge of his cot. Pity touched her for Khasif: she would never have expected it in herself—but this man was hurt for her sake.

The room shrank again to the dimensions of Isande's own quarters, and she wrenched herself from Tejef's loose grip with a cry of rage. Aiela fought to tell her something: she would not hear. She only saw Tejef laughing at her, and in that moment she was willing to kill or to die. She seized the metal table by its legs and swung at him, spilling its contents.

The metal numbed her hands with the force of the blow she had struck, and Tejef staggered back in surprise and flung up an arm to shield his face. She swung it again with a force reckless of strained arms and metal-scored hands, but this time he ripped the wreckage aside and sprang at her.

The impact literally jolted her senseless, and when she could see and breathe again she was on the floor under

Tejef's crushing weight. He gathered himself back, jerked her up with him. She screamed, and he bent both her arms behind her and drew her against him with such force that she felt her spine would be crushed. Her feet were almost off the floor and she dared not struggle. His heart pounded, the hard muscles of his belly jerked in his breathing, his lips snarled to show his teeth, a weapon the iduve did not scorn to use in quarrels among themselves. His eyes dilated all the way to black, and they had a dangerous madness in them now. She cried out, recognizing it.

The rubble gave, repaying recklessness, and Aiela went down the full length of the slide, stripping skin from his hands as he tried to stop himself, going down in a clatter of brick that could have roused the whole street had it been occupied. He hit bottom in choking dust, coughed and stumbled to his feet again, able to take himself only as far as the shattered steps before his knees gave under him. In his other consciousness he lurched along a hallway—Isande's contact so heavily screened by shame he could not read it: guards at the door—Daniel crashed into them with a savagery unsuspected in the human, battered them left and right and hit the door switch, unlocking it, struggling to guard it for that vital insant as the recovering guards sought to tear him away.

"Khasif!" Daniel pleaded.

One of the guards tore his hand down and hit the close-switch, and Daniel interposed his own body in the doorway. Aiela flinched and screamed, anticipating the crushing of bones and the severing of flesh—but the door jammed, reversed under Khasif's mind-touch. The big iduve exploded through the door and the human guards scrambled up to stop him—madness. One of them hit the wall, the echo booming up and down the corridor; the other went down under a single blow, bones broken; and Daniel flung himself out of Khasif's way, shouting at him Isande's danger, the third door down.

Khasif reached it, Daniel running after, Aiela urging him to get Isande out of the way—clenching his sweating hands, trying to penetrate Isande's screening to warn her.

She gave way: Tejef's face blurred in double vision over Daniel's sight of the door. Khasif's ominous tall form outlined in insane face and back overlay, receding and advanc-

ing at once. Isande cried out in pain as Khasif tore her from
Tejef and hurled her out the door into Daniel's arms: Daniel's face superimposed over Khasif's back, and then nothing,
for Isande buried her face against the being that had lately
been so loathsome to her, and clung to him; and Daniel,
shaken, held to her with the same drowning desperation.

Metal crashed, and little by little Khasif was giving ground,
until he was battling only to hold Tejef within the room.

Ship's controls! Aiela screamed at his asuthi.

They tried. Section doors prevented them, and amaut
guards and humans converged from all sides, forcing them
into retreat. Khasif stood as helpless as they under the threat
of a dozen weapons.

Tejef occupied the hallway, a dark smear of blood on his
temple. He gave curt orders to the armed humans to hold the
nasith for him at the end of the hall. Aiela shuddered as he
found that look resting next on Isande and on Daniel.

"Go to your quarters," Tejef said very quietly. But when
Daniel started to obey, too, Tejef tilted his head back and
looked at him from eyes that had gone to mere slits. "No,"
he said, "not you."

Aiela, Isande appealed, *Aiela, help him, oh help him!* For
she knew what Daniel had done for her.

Do as Tejef tells you, said Aiela. *Daniel—give in, whatever
happens: no temper. No resistance. They react to resistance.
They lose interest otherwise.*

"Sir," said Daniel in a voice that needed no dissembling to
carry a tremor, "sir—I acted not against you. For Isande, for
her. Please."

The íduve stared at him for a long cold moment. Then he
let go a hissing breath. "Get out of my sight. Go to your
quarters, and stay there or I will kill you."

Go! Aiela hurled at Daniel: *Bow your head and don't look
him in the eyes! Go!* And blessedly the human ignored his
own instincts, took the advice, and edged away carefully.
He's all right, he's all right, Aiela said then to Isande, who
collapsed in the wreckage of her quarters, crying. He probed
gently to know if she were much hurt.

No, she flung back. *No.* Fear leaked through, shame, the
ultimate certainty of defeat. *Go away, go away,* she kept
thinking, *o go away, reach the ship and leave. I learned to
survive after losing Reha. It's your turn. We've lost whatever*

chance we had because of me, because I started it, I did, I did, nothing gained.

It's all right, came Daniel's unbidden intervention. He shook all over, he was so afraid, alone in his quarters. It was a terrible thing for a man of his kind to yield down screens at such a moment: but along with the fear another process was taking place: he was gathering his mental forces to replot another attack. Of a sudden this humanish stubbornness, so different from kalliran methodical process, came to Isande as a thing of *elethia*. She wept, knowing his blind determination; and she appealed to Aiela to reason with him.

Luck, said Aiela, *is what humans wish each other when they are in that frame of mind. I do not believe in luck:* kastien *forbids. But trust him, Isande. You're going to be all right.*

And that was a hope as irrational as Daniel's, and as little honest. He did not want to tear his mind away, but the triple flood of thoughts distorted his perceptions and tore at his emotions. At last he had to let them both go, for he, like Daniel, was determined to try; and he knew what they would both say to that.

He had come at last near the streets of the occupied quarter. The sounds and smells of a *habish* told him so, and guided him down the alley. It lacked some few hours until daylight, but by now even most of the night-loving amaut had given up and gone home. The place was quiet.

This, at the most one other street lay between him and the safety of headquarters, but far more effort would be needed to thread the maze of Weissmouth's alleys, with their turnings often running into the impassable rubble of a ruined building. Aiela had no stomach for recklessness at this stage; but neither had he much more strength to spend on needless effort. He tried the handle of the *habish's* alley door, jerked it open, and walked through, to the startled outcries of the few drunken patrons remaining.

He closed the front door after him and found to his dismay that it was not the headquarters street after all: but at least it was clear and in the right section of town. He knew his way from here. The headquarters lay uphill and set out in that direction, walking rapidly, hating the spots of light thrown by the occasional streetlamps.

A dark cross-street presented itself. He took it, hurrying yet faster. Footsteps sounded behind him, silent men, running. He gasped for air and gathered himself to run too, racing for what he hoped was the security of the main thoroughfare.

He rounded the corner and had sight of the bulk of the headquarters building to his left, but those behind him were closing. He jerked out his gun as he ran, almost dropping it, whirled to fire.

A hurtling body threw him skidding to the pavement. Human bodies wrestled with him, beat the gun from his hand and pounded his head against the pavement until he was half-conscious. Then the several of them hauled him up and forced him to the side of the street where the shadows were thick.

He went where they made him go, not attempting further resistance until his head should clear. They held him by both arms and for half a block he walked unsteadily, loose-jointed. They were going toward the headquarters.

Then they headed him for a dark stairs into the basement door of some shop.

He had hoped in spite of everything that they were mercenaries in the employ of the amaut authorities that had muddled their instructions or simply seized the opportunity to vent their hate on an alien of any species at all. He could not blame them for that. But this put a grimmer face on matters.

He lunged forward, spilling them all, fought his way out of the tangle at the bottom of the steps, kneed in the belly the man quickest to try to hold him. Other hands caught at him: he hit another man in the throat and scrambled up the stairs running for his life, expecting a shot between the shoulders at any moment.

The headquarters steps were ahead. For that awful moment he was under the floodlights that illumined the front of the building, and rattling and pounding at the glass doors.

An amaut sentry waddled into the foyer and blinked at him, then hastened to open. Aiela pushed his way past, cleared the exposed position of the doors, leaned against the wall to catch his breath, staggered left again toward *bnésych* Gerlach's darkened office door, blazoned with the symbols of *karsh* Gomek authority.

"Most honorable sir," the sentry protested, scurrying along
at his side, "the *bnesych* will be called." He searched among
his keys for that of the office and opened it. "Please sit down,
sir. I will make the call myself."

Aiela sank down gratefully upon the soft-cushioned low
bench in the outer office while the sentry used the secretary's
phone to call the *bnesych*. He shook in reaction, and shivered
in the lack of heating.

"Sir," said the sentry, "the *bnesych* has expressed his profound joy at your safe return. He is on his way. He begs your
patience."

Aiela thrust himself to his feet and leaned upon the desk,
took the receiver and pushed the call button. The operator's
amaut-language response rasped in his ear.

"Get me contact with the iduve ship in the port," he ordered in that language, and when the operator protested in
alarm: "I am nas kame and I am asking you to contact my
ship or answer to them."

Again the operator protested a lack of clearance, and Aiela
swore in frustration, paused open-mouthed as an amaut appeared in the doorway and bowed three times in respect. It
was Toshi.

"Lord Aiela," said the young woman, bowing again.
"Thank you, Aphash. Resume your post. May I offer you
help, most honorable lord nas kame?"

"Put me in contact with my ship. The operator refuses to
recognize me."

Toshi bowed, her long hands folded at her breast. "Our
profound apologies. But this is not a secure contact. Please
come with me to my own duty station next door and I will be
honored to authorize the port operator to make that contact
for you with no delay. Also I will provide you an excellent
flask of *marithe*. You seem in need of it."

Her procedures seemed improbable and he stood still, not
liking any of it; but Toshi kept her hands placidly folded and
her gray-green eyes utterly innocent. Of a sudden he welcomed the excuse to get past her and into the lighted lobby;
but if he should move violently she would likely prove only a
very startled young woman. He took a firmer grip on his
nerves.

"I should be honored," he said, and she bowed herself
aside to let him precede her. She indicated the left-hand cor-

ridor as he paused in the lobby, and he could see that the second office was open with the light on. It seemed then credible, and he yielded to the offering motion of her hand and walked on with her, she waddling half a pace behind.

It was a communications station. He breathed a sigh of relief and returned the bow of the technician who arose from his post to greet them.

And a hard object in Toshi's hand bore into his side. He did not need her whispered threat to stand still. The technician unhurriedly produced a length of wire from his coveralls and waddled around behind him, drawing his wrists back.

Aiela made no resistance, enduring in bitter silence, for if Toshi were willing to use that gun, he would be forever useless to his asuthi. He was surely going to join Isande and Daniel, and all that he could do now was take care that he arrived in condition to be of use to them. It was by no means necessary to Tejef that he survive.

They faced him about and took him out the door, down a stairs and to a side exit. Toshi produced a key and unlocked it, locked it again behind them when they stood on the steps of some dark side of the building.

Fire erupted out of the dark. The technician fell, bubbling in agony. Toshi crumpled with a whimper and scuttled off the steps against the building, while Aiela flung himself off, fell, struggled to his feet and sprinted in blind desperation for the lights of the main street.

Faster steps sounded behind him and a blow in the back threw him down, helpless to save himself. His shoulder hit the pavement as he twisted to shield his head, and humans surrounded him, hauled him up, and dragged him away with them. Aiela knew one of them by his cropped hair: they were the same men.

They took him far down the side street away from the lights and pulled him into an alley. Here Aiela balked, but a knee doubled him over, repaying a debt, and they forced him down into the basement of a darkened building. When they came to the bottom of the steps, he began to struggle, using knee and shoulders where he could; and all it won him was to be beaten down and kicked.

A dim light swung in the damp-breathing dark, a globe-lamp at the wrist of an amaut, casting hideous leaping shadows about them. Aiela heaved to gain his feet and scrambled for the stairs, but they kicked him down again. He saw the amaut thrust papers into the hands of one of the humans, snatching the stolen kalliran pistol from the man's belt before he expected it and putting it into his own capacious pocket.

"Ffife ppasss," the amaut said in human speech. "All ffree, all run country, go goodpye."

"How do we know what they say what you promised?" one made bold to ask.

"Go goodbpye," the amaut repeated. "Go upplandss, ffree, no more amautss, goodbpye."

The humans debated no longer, but fled, and the amaut went up and closed the street door after them, waddling down the steps holding up his wrist to cast a light that included Aiela upon the floor.

It was Kleph, his ugly face more than usually sinister in the dim lighting. Cold air and damp breathed out from some dark hole beyond the light, an amaut burrow, tunnels of earth that would twist and meet many times beneath the surface of Weissmouth. Aiela had not been aware that this maze yet existed, but it was expected. He knew too that one hapless kallia could be slain and buried in this earthen maze, forever lost from sight and knowledge save for the *idoikkhe* on his wrist, and amaut ingenuity could solve that as well.

"What are you after?" Aiela asked him. "Are you here to cover your high command's mistakes?"

"Most honorable sir, I am devastated. You were given into my hands to protect."

Aiela let go a small breath of relief, for the fellow did not reasonably need to deceive him; but it was still in his mind that Kleph had access to humans such as had attacked them at the port, and had just evidenced it. The little fellow waddled over and freed him, put his arm about him, helping him and compelling him at once as they sought the depths of the tunnel. Shadows rippled insanely over the rudimentary plaster of the interior, the beginnings of masonry.

"Kleph," Aiela protested, "Kleph, I have to find a way to contact my ship."

"Impossible, sir, altogether impossible."

The squat little amaut forced him around a corner despite his resistance; and there Aiela wrenched free and sought to run, striking the plaster wall in the dark, turning and running again, following the rough wall with his hands.

He did not come to the entrance when he expected it, and after a moment he knew that he was utterly, hopelessly lost. He sank down on the earthen floor gasping for breath, and leaned his shoulders against the chill wall, perceiving the bobbing glow of Kleph's lamp coming nearer. In a moment more Kleph's ugly face materialized at close quarters around the corner, and he made a bubbling sound of irritation as he squatted down opposite.

"Most honorable sir," said Kleph, rocking back on his heels and clasping his arms about his knees in a position the amaut found quite comfortable. "There is a word in our language: *shakhshoph.* It means the hiding-face. And, my poor lord, you have gotten quite a lot of *shakhshoph* since you arrived in our settlement. One is always that way with outsiders: it is only decency. Sometimes too it hides a lie. Pay no attention to words with my people. Watch carefully a man who will not face you squarely and beware most of all a man who is too polite."

"Like yourself."

Kleph managed a bow, a rocking forward and back. "Indeed, most honorable sir, but I am fortunately your most humble servant. Anyone in the colony will tell you of Kleph. I am a man of most insignificant birth; I am backworld and my manners want polish. I have come from the misfortune of my origin to an apprentice clerkship with the great *karsh* Gomek, to ship's accountant, to my present most honored position. My lord must understand then that I am very reluctant to defy the orders of *bnesych* Gerlach. But we observe a simple rule, to choose a loyalty and stay by it. It is the single wisdom of our law. *Bnesych* Gerlach gave my service to the ship in the port, and as you serve the lord of that ship, I am interested in saving your life."

"You—chose a remarkable way of demonstrating it."

"They have injured you." Kleph's odd-feeling hand most unwelcomely patted Aiela's neck and shoulder. "Ai, most honorable sir, had I the opportunity I would have shot the lot of them—but they will take the passes and disappear far into the uplands. If one wishes to corrupt, one simply must pay his debts like a gentleman. They are filthy animals, these humans, but they are not stupid: a few corpses discovered could make them all flee my employ in the future. But for the passes to get them clear of our lines, they will gladly do anything and suffer anything and seek my service gladly."

"Like those that fired a shell among us at the port?"

Kleph lifted a hand in protest. "My lord, surely you have realized that was not my doing. But I am Master of Accounts, and so I know when men are moved and ships fly; and I have human servants, so I know when these things happen and do not get entered properly in the records. Therefore I am in danger. There are only two men on this world besides myself who can bypass the records: one is under-*bnesych* Yasht, and the other is *bnesych* Gerlach."

"Who hired it done?"

"One or the other of them. No *shakhshoph*. It is what I told you: one chooses a loyalty and remains constant; it is the only way we know to survive—as for instance my own lords know where my loyalty in this matter must logically lie, and so I shall need to stay out of sight until the crisis is resolved: a cup of poisoned wine, some such thing—it is only reasonable to eliminate those men known to serve the opposition. I am highly expendable; I am not of this *karsh*, and therefore I was given to the lord in the port. I also was meant to be eliminated at the port; and now it is essential that we both be silenced."

"Why?" Aiela had lost his power to be shocked. His mind simply could not grasp the turns of amaut logic.

"Why, my lord nas kame, if the population of this colony realizes the *bnesych* serves the other lord, it would split the colony into two factions, with most bloody result. We are not a fighting people, no, but one protects his own nest, after all—and the *bnesych* has many folk in this venture who are not of *karsh* Gomek: out-*karsh* folk, exiles, such as myself. Such loyalties can be lost quickly. There is always natural resentment toward a large *karsh* when it mismanages. And if it no longer appears the action at the port was on human initiative, it would be most, most distressing in some quarters." He pressed his broad-tipped fingers to Aiela's brow, where there was a swelling raised. "Ai, sir, I am sorry for your unhappy state, and I did try to find you before you wandered into a trap, but you were most elusive. When I knew you had entered the headquarters and when I saw the northside lights

out, I acted and disposed my human agents at once, or you
would be in the other lord's hands before dawn."

"Get me to the ship at the port," Aiela said, "or get me a
means to contact them, or there are going to be people hurt."

"Sir?" asked Kleph, his squat face much distressed. He
gulped several times in amaut sorrow. "O sir, and must the
great lords blame those who are guiltless? See, here am I,
out-*karsh*, helping you. Surely then your masters will understand that not all of us in this colony are to blame. Surely
they will realize how faithfully we serve them."

It was impossible to tell Kleph that the iduve did not understand the custom of service and reward, or that harm and
help were one and the same to them. Aiela made up his mind
to a half-truth. "I will speak for you," he said, "maybe—if
you help me."

"Sir, what you ask is impossible just now, if you only under—"

"It had better not be impossible," Aiela said.

Kleph rocked back and forth uncomfortably. "The port—
these tunnels are not complete, nor shored properly all the
way, and your—*hhhunh*—size will not make the passage
easy. But at this hour, honest folk will be abed, and no human mercenary would be down here; they fear such places."

"Then take me to the port." Aiela gathered his stiffening
legs under him, straightening as much as he could in this
low-ceilinged chamber. Kleph scrambled up with much more
agility and Aiela snatched at his collar, for it occurred to him
Kleph could run away and leave him to die in these tunnels,
lost in a dark maze of windings and pitfalls. He knew of a
certainty that he could not best the creature in a fight or hold
him if he were determined, but he intended to make it clear
Kleph would have to harm him to avoid obeying him.

"You recovered my gun," Aiela said. "Give it back."

Kleph did not like it. He bubbled and boomed in his
throat and twisted about unhappily, but he extracted the
weapon from his belly-pocket and surrendered it. Aiela hol-
stered it without letting go Kleph's collar, and then pushed at
the little fellow to start him moving. They came to tunnel
after tunnel and Kleph chose his way without hesitation.

Light burst suddenly like a sun exploding, heat hit their
faces, and the stench of ozone mingled with the flood of outside air. A shadow of manlike shape dropped from above

into their red-hazed vision, and Aiela hauled back on Kleph to flee. But the pain of the *idoikkhe* paralyzed his arm and he collapsed to his knees, while beside him on his face Kleph groveled and gibbered in terror, his saucer eyes surely agony, for the amaut could scarcely bear noon daylight, let alone this.

"Aiela," said a chill, familiar voice, and the *idoikkhe's* touch was gentle now, a mere signature: *Ashakh.*

Aiela expelled his breath in one quick sob of relief and picked himself up to face the iduve, who stood amid the rubble of the tunnel and in the beam of light from the street above.

What of the amaut? asked the pulses of the *idoikkhe. Will you be rid of him?*

"No," Aiela said quickly.

A response in which I find no wisdom, Ashakh replied. But he put the small hand weapon back in his belt and looked down on the amaut, coming closer. "Get up."

Kleph obeyed, crouching low and bowing and bobbing in extreme agitation. The light at his wrist swung wildly, throwing hideous shadows, leaping up and down the rough walls. Ashakh was a darkness, dusky of complexion and clad in black, but his eyes cast an uncanny mirror-light of dim rose hue, damped when he moved his head.

This person was aiding you? Ashakh asked.

"If Kleph is right, *bnesych* Gerlach was behind what happened at the port, and Kleph risked a great deal helping me."

"Indeed," mused Ashakh aloud. "Do you believe this?"

"I have reason to."

As you have reason for letting this amaut live? I fail to understand the purpose of it.

"Kleph knows Weissmouth," said Aiela, "and he will be willing to help us. Please," he added, sweating, for the look on Ashakh's grim face betokened a man in a hurry, and the iduve understood nothing of gratitude. He misliked being advocate for Kleph, but it was better than allowing the little fellow to be killed.

Chimele values your judgment; I do not agree with it.

But Ashakh said no more of killing Kleph, and Aiela understood the implication: it was on his shoulders, and *vaikka* was his to pay if his judgment proved wrong.

"Yes, sir," said Aiela. "What shall we do?"

"Have you a suggestion?"

"Get a ship and get the others out of Tejef's hands."

Ashakh frowned. "And have you a means to accomplish this?"

"No, sir."

"Well, we shall go to the port, and this person will guide us." Ashakh fixed the trembling amaut with a direct stare and Kleph scurried to get past him and take the lead. The tall iduve must bend to follow as they pursued their way through the winding passages.

"Do they know—does the Orithain know," Aiela asked, "what happened?"

We had a full account from Tesyel, who commands the base ship. And then in un-Ashakh fashion, the iduve volunteered further conversation. *Chimele sent me to find you. I was puzzled at first by the direction of the signal, but remembering the amaut's subterranean habits I resolved the matter—not without giving any persons trying to track us a sure indication of the direction of our flight. We had best make all possible haste. And I still mislike this small furtive person, Aiela-kameth.*

"I can only decide as a kallia, sir."

Honor to your self-perception. What are your reasons for mistrusting Gerlach?

12

━━━━◆━◆━◆━━━━

THE TOUCH OF Rakhi's mind came softly, most softly. It had hurt before, and Chaikhe accepted it cautiously, her nape hairs bristling at the male presence. She fought to subdue the rage that beat along her veins, and she felt Rakhi himself struggling against a very natural revulsion, for *chanokhia* forbade intimacy with a *katasathe*. She was for gift-giving and for honor, not for touching.

And there was his own distinctive *harachia*, a humorous, subdued presence. His *arastiethe* suffered terribly at close range, much more than hers did, for although folk judged Rakhi scandalously careless of his reputation, he was not really a person of *kutikkase* and his sense of *chanokhia* was keen in some regards. He cared most intensely what others thought of him, and found even the disapproval of a nas kame painful; but where others bristled and had recourse to the *idoikkhei* or engaged in petty *vaikka*, Rakhi laughed and turned inward. It was the shield of a nature as solitary in its own way as Ashakh's, and of a man of surprising intelligence. Even Chimele scarcely understood how much Rakhi dreaded to be known, how much he loathed to be touched and to touch; but Chaikhe felt these things, and kept her distance.

"*Nasith*," Rakhi voiced. He used this means, although other communication was swifter and carried sensory images as well; but this let him keep the essence of himself in reserve. "*Nasith*, Chimele is with me. She asks your state of health."

"I am quite well, *nasith-toj*."

"She advises you that Ashakh is presently attempting to recover the kameth Aiela. He has not communicated with you?"

"*Nasith*, I certainly would not have thought of violating

192

Chimele's direct order in this regard. No, nor would I accept it if he contacted me."

But you are iq-sra through both lines, he thought, *and Ashakh does as Ashakh pleases when he likes his orders as little as he likes the one that separated you. We shall have him to deal with sooner or later.* "Contact *bnesych* Gerlach and re-establish communications with the amaut authorities. Under no circumstance admit humans within your security. They do not know us, and they have a great *m'melakhia,* tempered with very little judgment of reality, as witness their actions against Khasif and Mejakh. They also have a certain tendency toward *arrhei-akita,* which makes *vaikka* upon the few no guarantee that the example will deter others. Many of their actions arise from logical processes based on biological facts we do not yet understand, or else from their ignorance of us. Remember Khasif and use appropriate discretion.'

"I will bear this in mind."

"*Ashanome* has suffered *vaikka* at the hands of someone in Weissmouth in the matter of Khasif. Chimele puts the entire business into your capable hands, *nasith-tak.* Whatever the fate of Priamos as a whole, this *vaikka* must be paid. Look to it, for we have been disadvantaged under the witness of both *Mijanothe* and *Tashavodh.*"

"Does Chimele not suggest a means?" inquired Chaikhe, proud and anxious at once, for the *arastiethe* of *Ashanome* was a great burden to bear alone.

Chimele's *harachia* came over Rakhi's senses, a rather uncertain contact at the distance he preserved: her *takkhenois* was full of disturbance, so that Chaikhe shivered. " 'Tell Chaikhe that Weissmouth is hers, and what she does with those beings is hers to determine, but I forbid her to risk her loss to us without consulting me.' "

"Tell Chimele I will handle the matter on those terms," she said, uncomforted. Chimele's disturbance lingered, upsetting her composure and making her stomach tight.

Chaikhe. Rakhi let Chimele's image fade. "Dawn is beginning in Weissmouth. I urge you make all possible haste."

"I shall. Leave me now. I shall begin at once."

He broke contact, but he was back before she had crossed the deck to the command console. *Chaikhe, understand: I must—*

His trouble set her teeth on edge and backlashed to such an extent that he hastily withdrew the feeler. She took firm grip on her rational faculty and invited his return.

Chaikhe, I—must stay. I do not lack chanokhia, I protest I am not sensitive to your distress. I dislike this proximity. It grates, it hurts—"I must remain in contact. Chimele's order, *nasith*. She judges it necessary." *But Chimele does not suffer, she does not feel this.*

Chaikhe shuddered as he did. The consciousness of the child within her sent a quick pulse of fury over her, an impulse to kill: and that impulse directed at Rakhi distressed her greatly. Something powerful stirred in her blood. Chemistry beyond her control was already beginning subtle changes in her; her temper almost ruled her. Her *takkhenois* was devastating. Her own power frightened her. *Is it this, to be* katasathe?

"Chaikhe," Rakhi's thought reached her, faint and timid, "Chaikhe, honor to you, *nasith-tak*, but I must do as I am told. Chimele—"

"I perceive, I perceive, I perceive." For a moment the faculty of reasonable response left her, and she was a prey to the anger; but then there was the cold clarity of Rakhi's thought in her mind. *Au, Chaikhe, Chaikhe, what is happening?*

And Chaikhe looked down at the green robes that were the honor of a *katasathe* and felt a moment of panic, a wish to shed these and the child at once and to be Chaikhe again. The violence growing in her mind went against everything she had always honored; and it was the child's doing.

Yet the thought of yielding up the child before the time shocked her. She could not. The process would complete itself inexorably and the madness, the honorable madness, would fasten itself upon her, a possession over which logic had no power.

Dhisais!

Long moments later Rakhi felt again toward her mind, fear at first, and then that characteristic humor that was Rakhi. "O *nasith-tak*, being *katasathe* is a situation of ultimate frustration to a male. If I should also become *dhisais*, I know not what I shall do with myself. Will they let me in the *dhis*, do you think?" *Or shall I die*, nasith-tak? *I should rather that, than to lose my mind.*

In another male his language would have been unbearably

offensive to her condition—for to be *katasathe* was to hold a *m'melakhia* so private and so possessive that proximity to others as equals was unbearable. Had she been aboard *Ashanome*, she would have resigned her other activities and settled into a period of waiting, accepting gifts of the *nasul*, protection of Ashakh, increasingly occupied with her own thoughts. But in a strange way Rakhi did share with her, and could not really share or threaten; and she felt his disadvantage as her own. Their *arastiethe* had become almost one, and Rakhi had a right to such frankness.

We have begun to merge, he thought suddenly. *Au, Chaikhe, Chaikhe-nasith, what will become of me?*

Go away. Chimele's orders notwithstanding, go, now! Give me my privacy for a moment. Something is happening to me. I fear—I fear—

She is ill, she perceived Rakhi telling Chimele in great alarm, sweating, for he felt it too.

" 'No,' " came Chimele's answer, and in her mind she could see Chimele's brooding face sketched by the tone of the answer. "No, no illness. What was put into Chaikhe's veins while she slept was no more than nature would have sent soon enough. My profound regret, Chaikhe.' "

You are driving me to this state! she realized suddenly, with a flood of anger that hurt Rakhi no less; she felt the tremor that ran through him and his shame at having unwittingly participated. Then bitter laughter rose in her. *Honor to Chimele sra-Chaxal. Vaikka, vaikka, o Chimele, shadowworker. From all others I knew how to defend myself; but those that come between Chimele and necessity must suffer for it. Honor to you indeed,* nasith.

"I knew nothing of it," Rakhi protested. "I did not, Chaikhe."

We are both disadvantaged, nasith-toj. *But when did one ever deal with Chimele and profit from it? Go. Go away.*

He fled in great discomfort, and Chaikhe sank down at the control console, her indigo fingers clenched together until the knuckles turned pale. Then with an abrupt act of will she forced her mind to business and fired an impulse to Tesyel, nas kame in charge of the base ship. *Tesyel,* she sent him, *have Neya escort the* bnesych *Gerlach to me immediately, giving him no opportunity for delay. If he be sleeping or naked as the day he was born, still give him no time to turn*

aside. If there are others with him, bring them. If they resist,
destroy them. Use whatever of the okkitani-as *you need in*
this.

A light flashed on the board, Tesyel's signaled acknowledgment. Chaikhe noted it as a matter expected and
put the wide scan from the base ship on her own screens.

Something flashed there, coming hard, at the far limit of
the screen. She exerted herself to fire, almost a negligent gesture, for she meant to seal Weissmouth against all aircraft
until Ashakh was heard from, and had it been Ashakh, she
was sure she would have been advised.

The incoming ship brushed off the fire and varied nothing
from its course, far outstripping amaut capabilities in its
speed and defenses. It was huge, just inside the limits for in-
tra-atmosphere operation.

The recognition occupied less than a second in Chaikhe's
mind, as long as it took to flash a warning to Tesyel aboard
the base command ship.

Tejef! her mind cried at Rakhi, shamefully hysterical, and
rage and the wish to kill washed over her to the depths of her
belly. Her ship blasted out a futile barrage at the incoming
vessel, which showed every evidence of intending a landing:
stalemate. Greater expense of energy could wipe out Weissmouth and the surrounding valley and still not penetrate the
other's defenses.

Calm! Rakhi insisted. *Calm! Think as Chaikhe, not as a*
dhisais. *O nasith-tak, if ever you needed your wits it is now.*
Conserve power, conserve, waste nothing and do not let him
harm our people in the city. You are the citadel of our power
on Priamos. If you fall, it is over. Do not add yourself to
Tejef *for search.*

Power fluctuated wildly. In mental symbiosis with the ship's
mechanisms, Chaikhe felt it like a wound and shuddered.
We are attacked. And Tesyel cannot control the base ship
like an iduve. But while the attack continued, her mind cen-
tered on one delicate task, an electronic surgery that altered
contacts and began to unite her little ship with Tesyel's larger
one, putting systems into communication so that she could
draw upon the greater weapons of the base ship and command the computer that regulated its defensive systems. This
would hold as long as her ship retained power to send command impulses. When that faded, she would lose command

of the base ship. When that happened, Tejef would hold Priamos alone.

A half-day remained. When the sun stood at zenith over Weissmouth, the deadline would have expired; and Tejef's ship could force her to exhaust her power reserves well before that time, pounding at her defenses, forcing her to extend the power of her ship simply to survive.

13

"THEY ARE DOWN," said Aiela. His mind wrenched from his asuthi and became again aware of Ashakh's face looking into his in the dim light of Kleph's wrist-glove, a witchfire flicker of color in the eyes of the iduve. Insanely he thought of being pent in a close space with a great carnivore, felt his heart laboring at the mere touch of the iduve's sinewy hand on his shoulder. Iduve weighed more than they looked. They were hard muscle, explosive power with little long-distance endurance. Even the touch of them felt different. Aiela tried not to flinch and concentrated anew on what his asuthi were sending now—awareness of engine shutdown, their own frustration and helplessness, locked as they were within their own quarters.

I was not secured until we lifted, Daniel sent him, bitter with self-accusation. *I waited, I waited, hoped for a better chance. But now that door is sealed and locked.*

And that communication flowed to the tunnels of Weissmouth through Aiela's lips, a hoarse whisper.

"Is Khasif possibly conscious?" Ashakh asked.

" 'No,' " Daniel responded. " 'At least I doubt it.' "

"It agrees with my own perception. But free him, if you should find the chance. Bend all your efforts to free him."

" 'I understand,' " sent Isande. " 'Where are you?' "

"Do not ask," Ashakh sent sharply and used Aiela's *idoikkhe* enough to sting. Aiela pulled back from the contact, for he was weary enough to betray things he would not have sent knowingly. His asuthi sent him a final appeal, private: *Get off this world; if you have the option, take it to get out of here.* And Isande sent him something very warm and very sad at once, which he treasured.

"What are they saying?" Ashakh asked, pressing his shoulder again; but the iduve might have broken the arm at that

198

moment and Aiela would still have returned the same blank
refusal to say. His mind was filled with two others and his
eyes were blinded with diffused light.

Get out, Daniel sent him, pushing through his faltering
screens, and Isande did the same, willing him to go, warning
him of Ashakh and of trusting the amaut. They left a great
emptiness behind them.

"*M'metane.*" Ashakh's grip hurt, but he did not use the
idoikkhe this time. "What is wrong?"

"They—cannot help. They don't know what to do."

The iduve's brows were drawn into a frown, his thin face
set in an anger foreign to his harsh but disciplined person. "I
sense his presence, whether he senses mine or not—and
Chaikhe—Chaikhe—"

Something troubled Ashakh. His eyes were almost wild, so
that Kleph shrank from him and Aiela stayed very still, fearing the iduve might strike at any sudden move. But the iduve
rested kneeling, as if he were listening for a voice that no
other could hear, like a man hearing the inner voice of an
asuthe. His eyes stared into space, his lips parted as if he
would cry out, but with an apparent effort he shook off the
thing that touched him.

"There is a wrongness," he exclaimed, "a fear—one of my
nasithi is afraid, and I do not know which. Perhaps it is
Tejef. We were once of the same *nasul* and we were *takkhe*.
Perhaps it is his dying I feel."

And it was indicative of his confusion that he spoke such
things aloud, within the hearing of a *m'metane* and an outsider. In another moment he looked aware, and his face took
on its accustomed hardness.

"You are empaths," Aiela realized, and said it without
thinking.

"No—not—quite that, *m'metane*. But I feel the *takkhenes*
of two minds from the port—Chaikhe—Tejef—I cannot sort
them out. If she and he are diverting a great portion of their
attention to managing ships' systems, it could account for the
oddness—but it is wrong, *m'metane*, it is wrong. And from
Khasif, I receive nothing—at least I surmise that his mind is
the silent one." He had spoken in his native tongue, conced-
ing this to Aiela, but not to Kleph, who huddled in terror
against the wall, and now he turned a burning look on the
amaut.

"We are still going to the port," he said to Kleph, "and you are involved in our affairs to an extent no outsider may be. From now on you are *okkitan-as* to *Ashanome*, the *nasul* of which we two are part."

"Ai, sir, great lord," wailed Kleph, making that gulping deep in his throat which was amautish weeping. "I am nothing, I am no one, I am utterly insignificant. Please let this poor person go. I will show you the port, oh, most gladly, sir, most gladly, serving you. But I am a clerk, no fighter, and I am not accustomed to weapons and I do not wish to be *okkitan-as* and travel forever."

Ashakh said nothing, nor glowered nor threatened; there was only a quiet thoughtfulness in his eyes, a wondering doubtless when would be the most rationally proper time to dispose of Kleph. Aiela moved quickly to interpose his calming *harachia* and to warn Kleph with a painful grip of his fingers that he was going too far.

"Kleph is indeed a clerk," Aiela confirmed, "and wished to become a farmer, quite likely; his mind is unprepared for the idea of service to a *nasul*. But he is also sensible and resourceful, and he would be an asset."

"He has a choice. I have a homing sense adequate to return us to the port even in these tunnels, but it would be a convenience if this person showed us the quickest way."

"Yes, sir." Kleph seemed to catch the implication of the alternative, for his pale saucer eyes grew very wide. "I shall do that."

And the little fellow turned upon hands and feet and scrambled up to go, they following; and ever and again Aiela could detect small thudding sounds which were sobs from the amaut's resonant throat. It was well for Kleph that the iduve allowed his species liberties in accordance with their (from the kalliran view) amoral nature. But quite probably Ashakh no more understood the workings of Kleph's mind than he did that of a serpent. The drives and needs that animated this little fellow could scarcely be translated into iduve language, and it would probably be Ashakh's choice to destroy him if the perplexity grew great enough to overpower advantage. The iduve were essentially a cautious people.

As for Kleph, Aiela thought, Ashakh might have bought him body and soul if he had offered him ten *lioi* of land; but it was too late for that now.

Suddenly Kleph thrust his light within the belly-pocket of his coveralls and Ashakh made a move for him that threw Aiela against the earthen wall, bruised; the little fellow hissed like a steam leak in the grip of the iduve, the wrong sound to make with an angry starlord; but he tried to gabble out words amid his hissing sounds of pain, and Aiela groped in the dark to try to stop the iduve from killing the creature.

"Stop, ai, stop," wailed Kleph, when Ashakh let up enough that he could speak. He restored a bit of light from his pocket: his face was contorted with anguish. "No trick, sir, no trick—please, we are coming to an inhabited section. O be still, sirs, please."

"Are there no other paths?" asked Ashakh.

"No, lord, not if my lord wishes to go to the port. Only a short distance through. All are sleeping. We post no guards. No humans dare come down. They hate the deeps."

Ashakh looked at Aiela for an answer, putting the burden of judging Kleph on his shoulders, treating him as *nas*; and he would be treated as *nas* if he erred, Aiela realized with a sinking feeling; but refusing would lower him forever in this iduve's sight. Suddenly he comprehended *arastiethe*, the compulsion to take, and not to yield: *giyre* in truth did not apply with Ashakh: one did not abdicate responsibility to the next highest—one assumed, and assumed to the limit of one's ability, and paid for errors dearly. *Arastiethe* was in one's self, and had great cost.

"I'll deal with Kleph, sir," said Aiela, "either for good or for ill, I'll deal with him, and he had better know it."

"I do not mean to lead you astray," Kleph protested again in a whisper, and he pointed and doused the wan light. There appeared in the distance a faint, almost illusory glow.

Aiela kept a firm hold on Kleph's arm while they went, and now they trod on stone, and a masonry ceiling arched overhead high enough that Ashakh might straighten without fear for his head. They came to a place where light came from dim globes mounted along the ceiling—a path that broadened into a hall, and rimmed a descending trail that wound down and down past amaut residences, side-by-side dwellings cut into the stone of the city's foundations. A chill damp breathed out from that pit, a musty scent of water. Aiela imagined that did he find a pebble to dislodge on the rim of that place, it would fall a great way and then—as it reached the level of the river and the water table—it would splash. They were still on the heights of Weissmouth, where the tunnels could reach to great depth. In amaut reckoning, it was a fine residential area, a pleasant place of cool dark and damp. And a sound from Kleph now would bring thousands of startled sleepers awake. It occurred to Aiela that Kleph's strength would easily suffice to hurl him to his death in the pit, were it not fear of an armed starlord behind him.

They passed on to a closer tunnel, still one where they had headroom, and where lights glowed at the intersection of all the lesser tunnels, so that they had no need of Kleph's little globe.

And around a corner came a startled party of amaut, who carried picks upon their shoulders and light-globes on their wrists, and who scattered shrieking and hissing in terror when they saw what was among them. In a moment all the tunnels were resounding with alarm, mad echoes pealing up and down the depths, and Aiela looked back at Ashakh, who was grimly returning his weapon to his belt.

"They would not understand nor would it stop the alarm," said Ashakh. He turned on Kleph a look that withered. "Redeem your error. Get us to safety."

Kleph was willing. He seized Aiela's arm to make him hurry, but shrank from contact with Ashakh, whom he urged with gestures, and took them off into one of the side corridors. The light-globe glowed into new life, their only source of illumination now, Kleph leading them where they knew not, further and further, until Aiela refused to follow more and backed the little fellow into a wall. Kleph gave a shrieking hiss and tried to vanish into another passage, but Ashakh brought his struggling to an end by his fingers laid on Kleph's broad chest and a look that would freeze water.

"Where do you intend to take us?" Aiela demanded, seeing that Ashakh waited his intent with the creature. "I feel us going down and down."

"Necessary, necessary, o lord nas kame. We are near the river, descending—listen! Hear the pumps working?"

It was true. In an interval of deep silence there was a faint pulsing, like a giant's heartbeat within the maze. When they did not move, nowhere was there another sound but that. The alarm and the shouting had long since died away. Wherever they were, it seemed unlikely that this was a main corridor.

"Is there no quicker way?" Aiela asked.

"But the great lord said to take you to safety, and I have been doing that. See, there is no alarm."

"Be silent," said Aiela, "and stop pretending you have forgotten what we want. Whatever your personal preference, we had better come out near the port, and quickly."

Kleph's ugly face contorted in the swaying light, making his grimace worse than usual. He bubbled in his throat and edged past them without looking either of them in the eyes, retracing his steps to a tunnel they had bypassed. It angled faintly upward.

"O great lords," Kleph mourned in audible undertone, "your enemies are so great and so many, and I am not a fighter, my lords, I could not hurt anyone. Please remember that."

Ashakh hit him—no cuff, but a blow that hurled the little fellow stunned into the turning wall of the corridor; and Kleph cowered there on his knees and covered his head, shrilling a warble of alarm, a thin, sickly note. Aiela seized the amaut's shoulder, frightened by the violence, no less frightening when he looked back at Ashakh. The iduve leaned against the stone wall, clinging by his fingers to the surface. His rose-reflecting eyes were half-lidded and pale, showing no pupil at all.

A scramble of gravel beside him warned Aiela. He spun about and whipped out his gun. Kleph froze in the act of rising.

"If you douse that light," Aiela warned him, "I can still stop you before you get to the exit. I've stood between you and Ashakh until now. Don't press my generosity any further."

"Keep him away," Kleph bubbled in his own language. "Keep him away."

Aiela glanced at Ashakh, feeling his own skin crawl as he looked on that cold, mindless face: Ashakh, most brilliant of the *nasithi*, cerebral master of *Ashanome's* computers and director of her course—bereft of reason. Kallia though he was, he felt *takkhenes*, the awareness of the internal force of that man, a life-force let loose with them into that narrow darkness, at enmity with all that was not *nas*.

A slow pulse began from the *idoikkhe*, panic multiplying in Aiela's brain as the pulse matched the pounding of his own

heart; his asuthi knew, tried to hold to him. He thrust them
away, his knees in contact with the ground, the gravel burning his hands, his paralyzed right hand losing its grip on the
gun. Kleph was beside him, gray-green eyes wide, his hand
reaching for the abandoned gun.

The pain ceased. Aiela struck left-handed at the amaut and
Kleph cowered back against the wall, protesting he had only
meant to help.

Aiela, Aiela, his asuthi sent, wondering whether he was all
right. But he ignored them and lurched to his feet, for
Ashakh still hung against the wall, his face stricken; and
Aiela sensed somehow that he was not the origin of the pain,
rather that Ashakh had saved him from it. He seized the
iduve, felt that lean, heavy body shudder and almost collapse.
Ashakh gripped his arms in return, holding until it shut the
blood from his hands, and all the while the whiteless eyes
were inward and blank.

"Chaikhe," he murmured, "Chaikhe, *nasith-tak, prha-
Ashanome-ta-e-takkhe, au,* Chaikhe—Aiela, Aiela-*kameth*—"

"Here. I am here."

"A being—whose feel is *Ashanome,* but a stranger, a stranger to me—*he,* he, reaching—hypothesis: Tejef, Tejef one-
and-not-one, Khasif—Chaikhe—Chaikhe, operating machinery, extended, mindless life-force—*e-takkhe, e-takkhe, e-takkhe!*"

Stop him! Isande cried in agony. *Stop him! He is deranged,
he can die*—

He—needing something? Daniel wondered. He hated
Ashakh to the depth of all that was human. Tejef had a little
compassion. Ashakh was as remorseless as *Ashanome's*
machines. In a perverse way it pleased Daniel to see him suffer something.

Daniel, what is the matter with you? Isande exclaimed in
horror.

Aiela broke them asunder, for their quarreling was like to
drive him mad. Isande's presence remained on the one side,
stunned, fearing Daniel; and Daniel's on the other, hating the
iduve of *Ashanome,* hating dying. That was at the center of
it—hating dying, hating being sent to it by beings like
Ashakh and Chimele, who loved nothing and feared nothing
and needed no one.

"Ashakh." Aiela thrust that yielding body hard against the

wall and the impact seemed to reach the iduve; but moments
passed before the gazed look left his eyes and he seemed to
know himself again. Then he looked embarrassed and
brushed off Aiela's hands and straightened his clothing.

"*Niseth*," he said, avoiding Aiela's eyes. "I am disadvantaged before you."

"No, sir," said Aiela. "You saved my life, I think."

Ashakh inclined his head in appreciation of that courtesy
and felt of the weapon at his belt, looking thoughtfully at the
amaut. It could not comfort Ashakh in the least that an outsider had witnessed his collapse, and if Kleph could have
known it, he was very close to dying in that moment. But
Kleph instinctively did the right thing in crouching down very
small and appearing not at all to joy in the situation.

"You are correct," said Ashakh to Aiela. "You were in
danger, but it was side effect, a scattering of impulses. I
feel—even yet—a disconnection, a disharmony without resolution. Tejef turned his mind to us and he is stronger than
ever I felt him. He is—almost an outsider, not—outsider in
the sense of *e-nasuli* but *e-iduve*. I cannot sort the minds out;
they—he—Chaikhe—are involved with the machines—their
impulses—hard to untangle. The strangeness burns—it con-
fuses—"

"Perhaps," said Aiela, ignoring Daniel's silent indignation,
"perhaps he has been too long among humans."

Ashakh frowned. "You are *m'metane*, and you are not expected to go further in this. Tejef is a formidable man, and
whatever Chimele's orders, you are free of bond to me. It is
not reasonable to waste you where there is no cause, and I
doubt I shall have to face Chimele's anger for disobeying her.
Could you really aid me in some way, it would be different,
but Tejef's arrival in the city has altered the situation. She
did not anticipate this when she instructed you."

"My asuthi are aboard that ship."

"*Au*, kameth, what do you expect to do? I shall be hard
put to defend myself, and I can hardly hold him from you
forever. Should I fall in the attempt, as I doubtless will, there
you will stand with *that* upon your wrist and that ridiculous
weapon of yours, quite helpless. In the first place you will
hinder me, and in the second event, you will die for nothing."

Aiela rested his hand on the offending pistol and looked up
at the iduve with a hard set to his jaw. "My people are not

killers," he said, "but it doesn't mean we can't fend for ou[r] selves."

Ashakh hissed in contempt. "*Au.* Kallia have had th[e] luxury to be so sparing of life ever since we came an[d] brought order to your worlds. But Tejef will bend every effo[rt] to destroy me. If he succeeds, you are disarmed. I woul[d] cheerfully give you this weapon of mine instead, but se[e] there is no external control, and you can neither calibrate no[r] fire it. No, Chimele gave her orders, and I assume she is cas[t]ing me away as she did Khasif. She forbade me to seek ou[t] Chaikhe, but you are under no such bond. I do not requi[re] you for *serach*, though it would do me honor; and I shoul[d] prefer to have you providing Chaikhe contact with you[r] asuthi aboard Tejef's ship."

Listen to him, Isande urged, joy and relief flooding ove[r] her. But her happiness died when she met his determine[d] resistance.

"No, sir," said Aiela. "I'm going with you."

He half expected a touch of the *idoikkhe* for his im[]pudence, but Ashakh merely frowned.

"*Tekasuphre*," the iduve judged. "Chimele said you wer[e] prone to unpredictable action."

"But I am going," Aiela said, "unless you stop me."

Ashakh broke into a sudden grin, a thing more terrib[le] than his frown. "A *vaikka-dhis*, then, kameth. We will d[o] what we can do, and he will notice us before Chimele burr[s] this wretched world to cinders."

"Ai, sir!" wailed Kleph, and applied his hands to his mout[h] in dismay at his own outburst.

In the next moment he had doused the light and attempte[d] flight. Aiela snatched at him and seized only cloth, b[ut] Ashakh's arm stopped the amaut short, restoring light th[at] flashed wildly about the tunnel with the flailing of Kleph[']s arms, and he had the being by the throat, close to crushing i[t] had Aiela not intervened. Ashakh simply dropped the littl[e] wretch, and Kleph tucked himself up in a ball and moane[d] and rocked in misery.

"Up," Aiela ordered him, hauling on his collar, and th[e] amaut obediently rose, but would not look him in the fac[e,] making little hisses and thuds in his throat.

"This person is untouchable," said Ashakh; and in his la[n]guage the word was *e-takkhe*, out of *takkhenes*. No close[r] word to enemy existed in the iduve vocabulary, and the killing impulse burned in Ashakh's normally placid eyes.

"I have a bond on him," Aiela said.

"Be sure," Ashakh replied, no more than that: iduve manners frowned on idle dispute as well as on interference with another's considered decisions.

What do you think you are? Isande cried, slipping through his screening. *Aiela, what do you think you're doing?*

He shut her out with a mental wince. *Not fair, not fair,* her retreating consciousness insisted. *Aiela, listen!*

He seized poor Kleph by the arm and shook at the heavy little fellow. "Kleph: now do you believe I meant what I said? Does it offend your precious sensibilities, all this fine world gone to cinders? If you have any other plans for it, then get us to the port. Maybe we can stop it. Do you understand me this time?"

"Yes," said Kleph, and for the first time since Ashakh's arrival the saucer eyes met his squarely. "Yes, sir."

Kleph edged past him to take the lead. His low brow furrowed into a multiplication of wrinkles so that his eyes were fringed by his colorless hair. His thin lips rolled in and out rapidly. How much he honestly could understand, Aiela was not sure. Almost he wished the little amaut would contrive to escape as soon as they made the port.

Aiela, Isande sent, *what are you doing? Why are you screening?*

Aiela shut her out entirely. Pity was dangerous. Let it begin and screens tumbled one after the other. He had to become for a little time as cold as the iduve, able to kill.

His mind fled back to the safe and orderly civilization of Aus Qao, where crime was usually a matter of personal disorder, where theft was a thing done by offworlders and the clever rich, and where murder was an act of aberration that destined one for restructuring. No kalliran officer had fired a lethal weapon on Aus Qao in five thousand years.

He was not sure that he could. Ashakh could do so without even perceiving the problem: he only reacted to the urgings of *takkhenes,* of the two of them the more innocent. A kallia must somehow, Aiela thought, summon up the violence of hate before he could act.

He could not kill. The growing realization panicked him. Conscience insisted that he tell his iduve companion of this

weakness in himself before it cost Ashakh his life. Something—*arastiethe* or fear, he knew not which—kept him
silent. *Giyre* was impossible with this being: did he try to explain, Ashakh would send him away. All that he could do
was to expend everything, conscience and *kastien* as well, and
stay beside the iduve as far as his efforts could carry him.

14

RAKHI SWEATED. Great beads of perspiration rolled down the sides of his face, and the serenity of the *paredre* of *Ashanome* flashed in and out with the nervous flicker of a half-hearted mind-touch at the projection apparatus. But it was not projection. Between pulses the air was close and stank of burning; he occupied a woman's body, felt the urge to *takkenes* with the life within it, a strangeness of yearning where there was yet neither movement nor fully mind—only the most primitive sort of life, but selfed, and precious. Rage surged coldly over his nerves: lights dimmed, lights flashed, screens flared and went dark. He dared do nothing but ride it out, joined, aware, occasionally guiding Chaikhe's tired mind when she faltered in reaction. His body had limbs of vast size, his mind extended into a hundred circuits; he felt with her as her mind touched and manipulated contacts, shunted power from one system to another with a coordination as smooth as that of a living body.

And he perceived the hammering of Tejef's weapons against the ship/body, the flow of energies on the shields, a debilitating drainage of power that required a great effort to balance defense between weakness and waste and destruction to the city. It began to be evident: Tejef's ship, a small *akites*, had Chaikhe's power supply from two lesser ships at a disadvantage. Chaikhe could, by skill and efficient management, prolong the struggle, but she was incapable of offensive action. Tejef could not down her shields, for probe and transfer ships such as Chaikhe commanded were heavily shielded, but their combined weaponry, while adequate to level a city, had no effect against an *akites*. The chronometer continued its relentless progress, ticking off the moments as *Ashanome*-time proceeded toward main-dark, and Kej, light-years away, had fled the ambered sea of Thiphrel: shadow flooded the coastal

209

plain to the east of Mount Im, advancing toward ancient
Cheltaris. Priamos-time, on the inner track, went more
slowly, but had less time to run. Nine hours had passed since
midnight. When three more had gone, Priamos would blaze
like a novaed star and die.

Life-support/cooling had shut down entirely save for the
control room. Lights were out everywhere but the panel even
there. In the base ship Tesyel and the remaining crew huddled on the bridge, five degrees cooler than Chaikhe's command center. The amaut with Tesyel suffered cruelly in the
heat, mopping dry skin with moistened cloths, lying still,
listless. Communications were almost out. Only the sensors
that maintained the field and the shields were still fully
operative.

The attack slacked off. It did so at irregular intervals, and
Chaikhe allowed the automatic cutback to the secondary
shields. But groundscan was picking up movement in what
had been a dead zone; Chaikhe mentally reached for the
image and the dark silhouette of an iduve appeared on the
screen—no human, that lean quick shadow. *Takkhenes*
reached and confirmed it: she saw the image hesitate at the
touch, felt the ferocity that was Ashakh.

Chimele's orders! Rakhi sent. *Break, break contact, now!*
And Chimele in the *paredre* was on her feet, her face dark
with anger. Chaikhe flinched from the wrath Rakhi transmit-
ted; but her attack reflexes had reacted before Rakhi's cooler
counsel prevailed, shunted power to the attack and expended
heavily against Tejef's shields.

Think! Rakhi sent. *Nothing can live amid those energies.
Hold back before you kill Ashakh.*

She cut back suddenly—return fire damaged systems. She
began to replot. But in another part of her mind she knew
Ashakh still alive, about to die if she kept her shields extended as she must. *Warn him, warn him,* she thought. *Does
he expect me to lower defenses for him and die? What is he
doing?*

Calm! Rakhi insisted, and winced from the fury of her
mind, *m'melakhia* for Ashakh in deadly conflict with that
for the child in her, fury washing out reason. *Kill!* The impulse surged through her being, but Rakhi's singleminded
negative imposed control and she extended her mind to watch
Ashakh's progress.

More of the witless humans were creeping out from cover, as if the lesson of scores of human and amaut dead were not enough to teach them the peril of the field about the embattled ships; and like the stubborn creatures they were they moved out, stalking Ashakh and his two companions.

Aiela, Chaikhe recognized the azure-skinned being that moved beside Ashakh, but the small person with them, an amaut—

Tesyel, she sent by the *idoikkhe: Have you dispatched any* okkitan-as *to Weissmouth?*

"Negative," came the nas kame's voice. "We had no time. I scan that one, but I do not know him."

A Priamid amaut. Ashakh's witlessness appalled her, his lack of *m'melakhia* for *Ashanome* in taking on such a servant sent waves of heat to her face. *Ashakh!* she hurled an impact of mind at him that he had no means to receive, but perhaps *takkhenes* itself carried her anger. Ashakh hesitated, looked full toward the ship.

—And arched his back and fell, trying even in the motion to bring his weapon to bear. Chaikhe gave a shrill hiss of rage, seeing the humans that had done it, a shot from beyond him. Ashakh fired: a hundred *ehsim* of port landscape became a hemisphere of light and a handful of humans and an amaut aircraft were not there when it imploded into darkness, nor again when normal light returned, Tejef's shields tightened and flared at the rippling of that energy, sucked outward toward Ashakh. Chaikhe reacted instantly, aware of the distant figures of the nas kame and the amaut trying to drag Ashakh back out of the exposed area. She hit at Tejef's shields, and as her searching mind found no consciousness in Ashakh a rage grew in her, a determination to destroy everything, to force *Ashanome* to wipe out *akites* and port and population entire. If her *sra* was to die, it deserved that for *serach*, she and Ashakh and her child.

"No!" Rakhi shouted into her mind. "Chimele forbids! Chimele forbids, Chaikhe!"

She gave a moan, a keening of rage, and desisted. But another impulse seized her, a fierceness to *vaikka* upon the power against whom she and Ashakh struggled, be it Chimele, be it Tejef.

Chaikhe! Rakhi cried. Through his mind Chimele radiated terrible anger. But Chaikhe wrapped herself in the chill of

her own *arastiethe*, suddenly diverted power from the shields
to communications, playing mental havoc with the circuitry
of the ship until she patched into amaut communications
citywide. The whole process took a few blinks of an eye. The
frightened chatter of amaut voices came back to her.

Be sure what you do, Rakhi advised her, Chimele's order;
but Chimele's *takkhenois* lost some of its fierceness and
flowed into alignment, feeding her will, supporting her now
that her mind was clear.

"Open citywide address channels," Chaikhe ordered, and
received the acknowledgment of the terrified amaut in command of their communications.

"I am the emissary of the Orithain," Chaikhe began softly,
the phrase that had heralded the terror of iduve decrees since
the dawn of civilization in the *metrosi.* "Hail Priamos. We
pose you now alternatives. If this rebel iduve is not ours before midday, we shall destroy as much of Weissmouth and of
Priamos as is necessary to take or destroy him; if this colony
seems to side with him, we shall eliminate it. Evacuation is
logistically impossible and the use of this field is extremely
hazardous. I counsel you against it. I have said."

She ceased, and listened in satisfaction as amaut communications went chaotic with incoming and outgoing calls, amaut
asking orders, officers reacting in harried outbursts of emotion, sometimes a human's different voice calling in, incom-
prehensible and distraught.

The panic had begun. It would run through the city, into
the tunnels, and into every command station in the amaut
colony. *Vaikka,* Chaikhe told herself with satisfaction. *They
are sure we are among them now.* And the knowledge that
these pathetic beings scattered before her attack filled her
with a shuddering desire to pursue the *vaikka* further; but
other duties called. Tejef. Tejef was the objective.

Attack resumed, ineffectual *vaikka* from Tejef for the damage done him among the amaut who trusted him for protection. Aiela had taken Ashakh beyond the range of weapons
fire, and there was the grateful feel of returning consciousness
from Ashakh. Her heart swelled with gladness.

No! cried Rakhi. "Chimele will not permit contact,
Chaikhe."

The attack increased. Systems faltered. There was no time
to dispute.

The spate of fire was a brief one; the glow about the iduve ships dimmed and the humans dared come from cover again. Aiela saw them moving far across the field and fired his own pistol to put a temporary stop to it. The humans were not yet aware that the weapon could not kill. He feared they would not be long in learning, about as long as it took for the first that he had fired on to recover; and as for the iduve weapon, that black thing like an elongate egg, there was indeed no way to operate it save by mind-touch.

"Let us go back, please, let us go back," Kleph pleaded. "Let us get off this awful field, into the safe dark, o please, sir."

A small projectile exploded not far away, and Kleph winced into a tighter crouch, almost a single ball of knees and arms, moaning.

It was indeed too close. Aiela seized Ashakh's limp arm and snapped at Kleph in order to take the other. It was the first order Kleph had obeyed with any enthusiasm, and they hurried, pulling the iduve back into the cover of the basement from which they had emerged onto the field. There they had only the light of Kleph's lamp and what came from the open door; and the very foundations shook with the pounding of fire out on the field. The wailing of sirens went on and on.

Ashakh stirred at last. He had been conscious from time to time, but only barely so. The shot that had struck him in the back would have likely been a mortal wound had he been kallia; but Ashakh's heart, which beat to right center of his chest, had kept a strong rhythm. This time when he opened his eyes they were clear and aware.

"A human weapon?" Ashakh asked.

"Yes, sir."

"*Niseth,*" murmured the proud iduve for the second time. "*Au, kameth, Tejefu-prha-idoikkhe—*"

"He has not used it."

That much puzzled Ashakh. Aiela could see the perplexity go through his eyes. Then he struggled to get his hands under him, Aiela's protests notwithstanding. "Either Tejef is too busy to divert his attention to you or Chaikhe has been taking care of you, kameth. I think the latter. This would be a serious error on his part."

"Chaikhe gave him something to worry about," said Aiela. "It was over the loudspeakers all over the field. She advised

Priamos what it could expect—I don't doubt it went to the
city too. The field emptied quickly after that announcement,
except for a determined few. We saw one aircraft try to take
off."

"It hit the shields," burst out Kleph, his saucer eyes wide.
"O great lord, it went in a puff of fire."

"Tekasuphre," judged Ashakh. He struggled to sit upright,
and it was probable that he was in great pain, although he
gave no demonstration of it. He suffered in silence while
Aiela made a bandage of Kleph's folded handkerchief and attempted to wedge it into position within Ashakh's belt. There
was surprisingly little bleeding, but the iduve's normally hot
skin was cold to the touch, and the iduve seemed distracted,
mentally elsewhere. So much of the iduve's life was mind:
Aiela wondered now if mind were not being diverted toward
other purposes, sustaining body.

"Sir," he said, "Ashakh—you have to have help, and we
don't know what to do. How bad is it?"

It was badly asked: Aiela realized it at once, for Ashakh's
face clouded and the *idoikkhe* tingled, the barest prickling.
Arastiethe forbade—and yet Ashakh forebore temper.

"I meant," Aiela amended gently, "that I can't tell what it
hit, or how to deal with it. In a kallia, it would be serious. I
have no knowledge of iduve anatomy."

"It is painful," Ashakh conceded, "and my concentration is
necessarily impaired. I regret, kameth, but I advise you to
seek Chaikhe at your earliest opportunity. I remind you I
predicted this."

"I have long since found it is futile to expect explanations
between iduve and kallia to make sense," said Aiela, all the
while his asuthi heard and pleaded·with him to take Ashakh's
offer. "My interests lie with my asuthi and with you, and
once with Chaikhe I can't do much for either."

Ashakh frowned. "You are kameth, not *nas.*"

Aiela shrugged. It was not productive to become involved
in an argument with an iduve. Silence was the one thing they
could not fight. He simply did not go, and looked up toward
Kleph, who, ignored, had begun to creep toward the dark of
the tunnel opening.

"Stay where you are," Aiela warned him.

"Ai, sir," said Kleph, "I did not—" And suddenly the
amaut's mouth made one quick open and shut and he

scrambled backward, while Ashakh reached wildly for the weapon that was no longer in his belt but in Aiela's, rescued from the outside pavement.

Toshi and Gerlach and two humans were in the tunnel opening, weapons leveled.

Fire! Daniel screamed at Aiela; and Isande sent a negative.

Aiela, cursing his own lack of foresight, simply gathered himself up in leisurely dignity, dropped Ashakh's weapon and his own from his belt, and bent again to assist Ashakh, who was determined to get to his feet. Kleph shrugged and dusted himself off busily as if his presence there were the most natural thing in the world.

"Sir," exclaimed Kleph to Gerlach, "I am relieved. May I assist you with these persons?"

Never had Aiela seen an amaut truly overcome with anger, but Gerlach fairly snarled at Kleph, a spitting sound; and Kleph scampered back out of his reach, forgetting to bow on the retreat, his face twisted in a grimace of fright and rage.

"Kleph double-heart, Kleph glib of speech," exclaimed Gerlach, "you are to blame for this disaster." He seemed likely to rush at Kleph in his fury; but then he fell silent and seemed for the first time to realize the enormity of his situation, for Ashakh drew himself up to his slim towering height, folded his arms placidly, and looked down at their diminutive captor.

"*Prha*, kameth?" Ashakh asked of Aiela. *Arastiethe* forbade he should take direct account of the likes of Gerlach and Toshi.

"Gerlach knows well enough," said Aiela, "that *karsh* Gomek would pay dearly should he kill you, sir; they would pay with every Gomek ship in the Esliph and the *metrosi*. If he were wise at all, he would leave iduve business to the iduve."

"We want Priamos," Gerlach protested, "Priamos with its fields undamaged."

"That will not be," said Aiela, "unless you stand aside."

"If my lords will yield gracefully, I shall see that this matter is indeed settled by iduve, by the lord-on-Priamos."

"You have chosen the wrong loyalty," said Aiela.

"We had only one knowable choice," said Gerlach. "We know that the lord-on-Priamos wants this world intact and the lord-above-Priamos wants to destroy us. Perhaps our choice was wrong; but it is made. We know what the lord-above-Priamos will do to us if we lose the lord-on-Priamos to protect us. We are little people. We shelter in what shade is offered us, and only the lord-on-Priamos casts a shadow on this world."

Aiela thought that was for Ashakh to answer; but the iduve simply stared at the little fellow, and of course it was unproductive to argue. *Elethia* insisted upon silence where no proof would convince; and Gerlach was left to sweat in the interval, faced with the necessity of moving a starlord who was not in a mood to reason.

"Guard them," he said suddenly to Toshi. "I have other matters to attend." And he scurried up the steps to daylight, not without a snarl at Kleph. "Shoot this one on the least excuse," he told Toshi, looking back. Then he was gone.

"What good do you get from this?" Aiela asked then in human speech, addressing himself to the mercenaries with Toshi. "What's your gain, except a burned world?"

"We know you," said the dark-faced one. "You and your companions cost us three good friends the last trip into this city."

"But what," asked Aiela, "do you have to gain from Tejef?"

The man shrugged, a lift of one shoulder, as humans did. "We aren't going to listen to you."

How do I reason with that? Aiela asked of Daniel.

Forget it, Daniel sent. *Tejef's kamethi chose to be with him.*

They have giyre.

Believe this, sent Daniel. *They'll kill you where you stand. If Ashakh drops, that little devil of an amaut will send them for your throat, and you'll have no more mercy out of them than from her.*

Aiela looked uneasily at Ashakh, who with great dignity had withdrawn to the brick wall and leaned there in the corner, arms folded, one foot resting on a bit of pipe. The iduve merely stared at the humans and at Toshi, looking capable of going for their throats, but a moment ago he had been in a state of complete collapse, and Aiela had the uncomfortable feeling that *arastiethe* alone was keeping the man on his feet, pure iduve arrogance. It would not hold him there forever.

Something was mightily amiss in the ship. Amaut bustled up and down the corridor, and the lights had been dimming periodically. Arle watched from the security of the glass-fronted infirmary and saw the hurrying outside become frantic. The lights dimmed again. She scurried back to the banks of instruments at Margaret's bedside and wondered anxiously whether they varied because the power was going out or because there was something wrong with Margaret.

She slept so long.

("You stay, watch," Tejef had told her personally, setting her at this post and making her secure before the sickening lunge the ship had made aloft and down again; and Dlechish, the awful little amaut surgeon, had been there through that, making sure all went well with Margaret.)

Dlechish was gone now, Arle had had the infirmary to herself ever since this insanity with the lights had begun, and she was glad at least not to have to share the room with amaut.

But Margaret was so pale, and breathed with such difficulty. When the instruments faltered, Arle would clench her hands on the edge of her hard seat and hold her own breath until the lines resumed their regular pattern. Of the machines themselves she understood nothing but that these lines were Margaret's life, and when they ceased, Margaret's existence would have ceased also.

The lights dimmed again and flickered lower. Margaret stirred in her sleep, tossing, struggling to move against the restraints and the frames and the tubing. When Arle attempted to hold her still, Margaret tried the harder to rid herself of the encumbrances, and began to work her hand free. Arle pleaded. Margaret's movements were out of delirium and nightmare. She began to cry out in her pain.

"Tejef!" Arle cried at the intercom. And when no answer came she went out and tried to find someone, one of the guards, anyone at all. She began to run, hard-breathing, to one and another of the compartments off the infirmary, trying to find at least one of the amaut attendants.

The fourth door yielded an amaut who gibbered at her and thrust an ugly black gun at her. She screamed in fright, and her eyes widened as she saw the dark man who lay inside the room, unconscious or dead, in the embrace of restraints and strange instruments.

She tried to dart under the amaut's reach. He seized her

arm in one strong amautish hand and twisted it cruelly. Of a
sudden he let her go.

She kicked him and fled, and met a black-clad man chest-
on. She looked up and was only realizing it was Tejef when
his hand cracked across her face.

It threw her down, hurt her jaw, and made her deaf for a
moment; but dazed and hurt as she was she knew that he had
slapped, not hit, and that the tempers which gripped him
would pass. She gave a desperate sob of effort, scrambled to
her feet, and raced for the infirmary, for Margaret, and
safety.

He had followed her, coming around the corner not long
after she had shut and locked the door; and to her horror she
saw the door open despite the lock, without his touching it.
She fled back to Margaret's bedside and sank down there
hard-breathing. She sought to ignore him by way of defense,
and did not look at him.

"You're not hurt?" Tejef demanded of her. Arle shook her
head. One did not talk to Tejef when he was angry. Margaret
had advised her so. She was sick with fear.

"I say stay with Margaret, *m'metane-tak*. Am I mistaking
meaning—*stay?*"

"Margaret got worse. And I thought it was you in there.
I'm sorry, sir."

"I?" Tejef seemed greatly surprised, even upset, and fingered gently the hot place his blow had left on her cheek.
"You are a child, Arle. A child must obey."

"Yes, sir."

"*Niseth.* I regret the blow."

She looked up at him, perceiving that he was indeed sorry.
And she knew that it embarrassed him terribly to admit that
he was wrong. That was to be a man—not being wrong. Her
father had been like that.

"Tejef," said Margaret. Her eyes had opened. "Tejef,
where are we?"

"Still on Priamos." As if it were a very difficult thing he
offered his hand to her reaching fingers.

"I thought I felt us move."

"Yes."

The confusion seemed to overwhelm her. She moaned a
tiny sound and clenched her fingers the more tightly upon
his; but he disengaged himself gently and quietly went about

preparing Margaret's medicines himself. The lights dimmed. Things shook in his hands.

"Sir?" Arle exclaimed, half-rising.

The lights came on again and he continued his work. He returned to Margaret's side, ignoring Arle's questions of lights and machines, administered another injection and waited for it to take effect.

"Tejef," Margaret pleaded sleepily.

His lips tightened and he kept his eyes fixed upon the machines for a moment; but then he bent down and let her lips brush his cheek. Gently he returned the gesture, straightened, hissed very softly, and walked out, his long strides echoing down the hall.

When Arle looked at Margaret again, she was quiet, and slept.

"Priamos-time," said Rakhi, "one hour remains."

Then let me use it unhindered, Chaikhe retorted, not caring to voice or to screen. Rakhi's periodic reminders of the time disrupted her concentration and lessened her efficiency. She had her own internal clock; cross-checking with Rakhi's was a nuisance.

Exhaustion is lowering your efficiency, dimming your perceptions, and rendering you most difficult, Chaikhe. His mind seemed a little strained also. Chimele hovered near him like a foreboding of ruin to come. *I know you are tired and short of temper. So am I. It is senseless to work against me.*

Go away. Chaikhe flung herself back from the console, abandoning manual and mental controls. It was rashness. Tejef's attacks were fewer during the last half-hour, but no less fierce. Tejef also knew the time. He was surely saving what he could for some last-moment effort.

"Do you think this man who has run us so long a chase will be predictable at the last?" Rakhi restrained his impatience; he fought against the vagaries of her hormone-heightened temper with a precise, orderly process quite foreign to his own tastes, but he could use it when he chose.

Rakhi, thought Chaikhe distractedly, *there is a bit of Chaxal in your blood after all. You sound like Ashakh, or Chimele.*

Sit down, he ordered rudely, *and remember that Tejef has arastiethe enough to choose his own moment. What chance *has he of outlasting us, with* Ashanome *overhead? He knows that he must die, but he will try to make the terms not to our liking. This is not the moment for tempers,* nasith-tak.

She flared for a moment, but acknowledged reason when she heard it, and scanned the instruments for him, feeding him knowledge of fading power levels, blown systems. *I have done as much for this little ship as reasonably possible,* she told him, *and being of the order of Artists, I consider I have exceeded expectations.*

"Quite true, *nasith-tak.*"

And at this point even Ashakh could not keep this ship functioning, she continued bitterly. *Chimele knew my power on this world and she knew Tejef's, and she drew back one ship that we might have had down here. She might have made me capable of attack, not only of defense. Am I only bait, nasith? Was I only a lure, and did she deceive me with half-truths as she did Khasif and Ashakh?*

" 'Impertinence!' " Chimele judged, when Rakhi conveyed that to her; and the impact of her anger was unsettling.

Did you deceive me?

" 'Your question was not heard and your attitude was not perceived, *nasith*. However I use you, I will not be challenged. Follow my orders.' "

Tell her my shields are failing.

" 'Continue in my orders.' "

Hail Chimele, she said bitterly, but Rakhi did not translate the bitterness. *Tell me I am honored by her difficulty with me. But of course I am going to comply. Honor to* Ashanome, *and to the last of us. Walk warily, Rakhi. May the* nasul *live.*

Rakhi stopped translating. *A* katasthe *ought to show more respect for one who can destroy her or exile her forever. Be sensible. The Orithain's honor is* Ashanome's. *Are you* takkhe? *Au, Chaikhe, are you?*

I am dhisais! she raged at him. *I am* akita! *Not even Chimele has power over me.* And Rakhi fled for a moment, struggling with the impulses of his own body. His blood raced faster, his borrowed fierceness tore at his nerves, tormented by Chimele's *harachia*.

"We shall both be fit for the red robes," came Rakhi's slight mindtouch, his wonted humor a timorous thing now, and soft. "Chaikhe, do not press me further, do not."

About the ship the shields flared once more under attack,

shimmering in and out of the visible spectrum as they died, an eerie aurora effect in the late morning sun. Chaikhe shuddered, feeling the dying of the ship, wild impulses in *serach* and to death at war with the life in her.

Think! Rakhi's male sanity urged.

Tesyel: her mind reached for the *idoikkhe* of the kameth of the base ship, a last message. *I shall leave you power enough to safeguard yourself and get offworld. I do not require you for* serach. *A world will be quite enough. See to your own survival.*

"Are you hurt?" His kalliran voice came through with anxious stress. Tesyel was a good man, but he had his people's tendency to become personally involved in others' crises. Perhaps in the labyrinthine kalliran ethic he conceived that he had suffered some sort of *niseth* in being shown inadequate to ward off the misfortune of *Ashanome*, *m'metane* though he was. In some situations a kallia had a fierce *m'melakhia* of responsibility.

I am not injured, said Chaikhe, *and you are without further responsibility,* kameth. *You have shown great* elethia *in my service. Now I return you to the* nasul. *Do nothing without directly consulting* Ashanome.

"I am honored to have served you," murmured the kameth sadly. His voice was almost lost in static. "But if I—"

The static drowned him out. In the next moment the shields collapsed. The control room went black for a few seconds. Chaikhe sought desperately to restructure the failed mechanisms, bypassing safety devices.

The attack resumed. Overheated metal stank. Light went out and dimly returned. A whining of almost harmonic sound pulsed through the ship's structure. Power was dying altogether.

Chaikhe mind-touched the doors through to the airlock, desperately seeking air. Reserve batteries were fading too, and she fought to reach the door in the dark and the roiling smoke, choking. She fell.

Long before she knew anything else she was aware of Rakhi's frantic pleading, trying with his own will to animate her exhausted body.

And then she knew another thing, that someone trod the inner corridor of the ship, and *m'melakhia* drove her to her feet, graceless and stumbling as she sought a weapon in the dark.

"Chimele forbids," Rakhi told her, and that stunned her into angry indecision.

Forbids? What is she about to do?

Her senses reeled. Her eyes poured water, stung by the smoke, and she hurled herself blindly down the corridor.

A squat amaut shadow stood outlined against the smoke-filled light from the airlock. Chaikhe had never felt real menace in a non-iduve before: this being radiated it, a cold sickly *m'melakhia* that came over her crisis-heightened sensitivity. It was repugnant. She had received from kalliran minds before, particularly in *katasukke;* it was a talent suspect and embarrassedly hidden, *e-chanokhia.* Kallia held a cleanly muddle of stresses and inhibitions, cramped but intensely orderly. This creature was venomous.

"My lady," it said with a bow, "*Bnesych* Gerlach at your service, my lady."

Chaikhe felt the almost-*takkenes* of the child in her. Her lips quivered. Her vision blurred at the edges and became preternaturally clear upon Gerlach's vulnerable self. She could crack his brute neck so easily, so satisfyingly. He would know it was coming; his terror would be delightful.

No! Rakhi cried. *Chaikhe, rule yourself. Control. Calm.*

M'melakhia focused briefly upon her asuthe, sweet and satisfying, full of the scent of blood.

I am you, he protested, horrified. *It is not reasonable.*

He suffered; their *arastiethe* was one, and to live they each must yield. The situation defied reason.

Leave me, she pleaded, aware of Gerlach's eyes on her, a shame that Chimele's orders left her powerless to remedy.

He lacked the control to break away. Their joined *arastiethe* made him fear her fear, suffer shame with her, dread injury to the child, feel its *takkhenois* within his own body—things rationally impossible.

Is this what m'metanei *mean by* m'melakhia *one for the other?* Rakhi wondered out of the chaos of his own thoughts. *Au, I am drowning, I am suffocating, Chaikhe, and I am too weary to let go. If he touches you, I think I shall be ill.*

Gerlach was beside her. Fire had leapt up in the corridor, control room systems too damaged to prevent it, smoke choking them as the ship deteriorated further. Gerlach seized her

arm and drew her on. The collapse of systems with which her
mind was in contact dazed and confused her.

Let go, Rakhi urged her, *let go, let go.*

Her mind went inward, self-seeking, dead to the outside.
She saw the *paredre* of *Ashanome* briefly; and then Rakhi
performed the same inwardness and that vision went. She
knew her limbs had lost their strength. She knew Gerlach's
coarse broad hands taking her, a loss of breath as she was
slung across his shoulder. For a moment she was in complete
withdrawal; then the pain of his jolting last step to the pavement jarred her free again.

Kill him! Rakhi's voice in her mind was a shuddering echo
and reecho, down vast corridors of distance. Chimele's strong
nails bit into his/her shoulder, reminding them of calm.
Other minds began to gather: Raxomeqh's cold brilliance,
Achiqh, Najadh, Tahjekh, like tiny points of light in a vast
darkness. But Chaikhe concentrated deliberately on the horror of Gerlach, his oiliness, the grotesqueries of his waddling
gait and panting wheezes for breath, learning what *m'metanei*
called hate, a disunity beyond *e-takkhe*, a desire beyond
vaikka-nasul, a lust beyond reason.

Dhisais, dhisais, Rakhi reminded her, Chimele's incompre-
hensible orders twisted through his hearing and his mind. *Be
Chaikhe yet for a little time more. Restraint!*

She had never been so treated in her life. Not even in the
fierceness of *katasakke* had she been compelled to be touched
against her will. Did *m'metanei* suffer such self-lessening in
being kameth, in taking part in *katasukke*? The thought ap-
palled her.

Stop it, Rakhi shuddered. *Au, Chaikhe, this is obscene.*

Male, he, it, this—dhisais, dhisais, akita, *I—kill him. My
honor, mine, male, male, male, e-takkhe, I—*

Rakhi's fists slammed into the desk top, pain, pain, shattered plastics, bleeding, his wrists lacerated. The physical
shock shuddered through Chaikhe's body. She felt the wounds
on her own wrists, the flow of the warm blood over her
hands, tension ebbing.

We, he kept repeating into her mind, *we, together, we.*

For the last few moments, Ashakh had not moved. Aiela
stared at him tensely, wondering how much longer the iduve
could manage to stand. He rested still with his back against

the corner, his arms folded tightly across his chest, eyes closed; and whether the bleeding had started again the cellar was too dark to show. From time to time his eyes would still open and glimmer roseate fire in the light of Toshi's wrist-globe. The little amaut never varied the angle of the gun she trained upon the both of them. Aiela began to fear that it would come soon, that Ashakh's growing weakness would end the stalemate and render them both helpless.

Dive for an exit, Daniel advised him. *The second Ashakh falls, they'll see only him. Dive for any way out you can take. Isande, Isande, you reason with him.*

Peace, Aiela pleaded. He had another thing in mind, an attack before necessity came upon them. Toshi had one hand bandaged, thanks, no doubt, to Kleph's hirelings outside the headquarters; and if Kleph, who huddled near Ashakh, had the will to fight, Kleph could handle Toshi—the only one of them now who had the strength for that. Aiela began instead to size up the two humans, wondering what chance he would have against the two of them.

Precious little, Daniel estimated. *You've no instinct for it. Get yourself out of there. Get to Chaikhe. If you can't send any more, Isande and I are cut apart, as good as dead too. We have nothing left without you.*

Isande had no words: what she sent was yet more unfairly effective, and it took the heart from him. He hesitated.

Ashakh's eyes opened slightly. "You still have the option," he told Toshi, "to cast down your weapons and rescue yourselves."

Toshi gave a nervous bubbling of laughter, to which the humans did not respond, not understanding.

"He said get out of here," said Aiela, and the men looked at Ashakh as if they thought of laughing and then changed their minds. Iduve humor was something outsiders would not recognize, nor appreciate when they saw it in action. Ashakh was indulging in a bit of *vaikka,* he realized in chill fear, absolutely straight-faced and far from bluffing; likely as his own death was at the moment, *arastiethe* forbade any unseemly behavior.

One human fled. Toshi did not let herself be distracted.

The cellar went to eye-wrenching light and dark and rumbled in collapse. Aiela and Kleph clenched themselves into a unified ball, seeking protection from the cascading ce-

ment and brick, and for a moment Aiela gave himself up to
die, uncertain how much weight of concrete there was above.
A large piece of it crashed into his head, bruising his protecting fingers, and at that he thought of Ashakh and scrambled
the few feet to try to protect him.

In the next breath it was over, and Aiela found daylight
flooding in through a gap where the door had been, and the
side of the room where Toshi and the human had been was a
solid mound of rubble.

A dusty and bloodied Ashakh dragged himself to his feet
and leaned unsteadily on the edge of the basement steps.
"Niseth," he proclaimed. "The effect considerably exceeded
calculations."

And upon that he nearly fainted, and would have fallen,
but Kleph and Aiela held him on his feet and helped him up
to daylight, where the air was free of dust.

"What was it, great lord?" Kleph bubbled nervously.
"What happened?"

"Aiela," said Ashakh, catching his breath, "Aiela, go down,
see if you can locate our weapons."

Aiela hurried, searching amid the grisly rubble, pulling
brick aside and fearing further collapse. He knew by now
what Ashakh had done, delicately mind-touching the weapon
he had so casually dropped, and negating a considerable portion of the cellar.

His own gun lay accessible. When he found Ashakh's, it
looked unscathed too, and he brought it up into the daylight
and put it into the iduve's hand.

"Damaged," Ashakh judged regretfully. His indigo face
had acquired a certain grayish cast, and his hand seemed to
have difficulty returning the weapon to his belt.

"Chaikhe," he said, and could tell them little more than
that. He shook off Kleph's hand with a violence that left the
little amaut nursing a sore wrist, and stumbled forward, un-
reasoning, heedless of their protests. There was nothing before
them but open ground, the wide expanse of the port,
Chaikhe's ship with its ramp down and the base ship beyond:
closest was Tejef's ship, hatch opened, and a smallish figure
toiling toward its ramp.

"Come back," Kleph cried after Ashakh. "O great lord,
come back, come back, let this small person help you."

But Aiela hesitated only a moment: mad as the iduve was,

that ramp was indeed down and access was possible. There would not be another chance, not with the sun inching its way toward zenith. He ran to catch up, and Kleph, with a squeal of dismay, suddenly began to run too, seizing the iduve's other arm as Aiela sought to keep him from wasting his strength in haste.

Ashakh struck at Aiela, half-hearted, his violet eyes dilated and wild; but when he realized that Aiela meant only to keep him on his feet, he cooperated and leaned on him.

And after a few *meis* more, it was clear that Ashakh could summon no more strength: *arastiethe* insisted, but the iduve's slender body was failing him. His knees buckled, and only Kleph's strength saved him from a headlong collapse.

"We must get off this field," cried Kleph in panic. "O lord nas kame, let us take him to the other ship and beg them to let us in."

Ashakh pushed away from the amaut. His effort carried him a few steps to a fall from which he could not rise.

"Let us go," cried Kleph.

Self-preservation insisted go. The base ship would lift off before *Ashanome* struck. Daniel and Isande insisted so; but before them was Ashakh's objective, and an open hatch that was the best chance and the last one.

"Get him to the greater ship," Aiela shouted at Kleph, and began to run. "He can mind-touch the lock for you, get you in—move!"

He thought then that he had saved Ashakh's life at least, for Kleph would not abandon him, thinking Ashakh his key to safety; and the bandy-legged fellow had the strength to manage that muscle-heavy body across the wide field.

Aiela, Aiela, mourned Isande, *oh, no, Aiela.*

He ran, ignoring her, mentally calculating a triangle of distance to that open hatch for himself and for the amaut that struggled along with his burden. He might make it. His side was splitting and his brain was pounding from the effort, but he might possibly make it before one instant's notice from the iduve master of that ship could kill him.

Distract Tejef, he ordered his asuthi. *Do anything you can to get free. I'm going to need all the help possible. Keep his mind from me.*

Daniel cast about for a weapon, seized up a chair from its transit braces, and slammed it into monitor panel, door, walls, shouting like a madman and trying to do the maximum damage possible.

Only let one of the human staff respond to it, Daniel kept hoping. He meant to kill. The ease with which he slipped into that frame of mind affected Aiela and Isande with a certain queasiness, and stirred something primitive and shameful.

Isande began to pry at the switchplate, seeking some weakness that could trigger even the most minor alarm, but Aiela could not advise her. He could no longer think of anything but the amaut that was now striving to run under his burden.

Then his vision resolved what Ashakh's *takkhenois* had told him from a much greater distance.

That bundle of green was a woman, indigo-skinned and robed as a *katasathe*.

Aiela had his gun in hand: though it was not designed to kill, firing on a pregnant woman gave him pause—the shock and the fall together might kill her.

And the amaut whirled suddenly in midstep, and his hand that was under Chaikhe's body held a weapon that was indeed lethal.

Aiela fired, reflexes quicker than choice, tumbling both amaut and iduve woman into a heap, unconscious.

There was no stopping to aid Chaikhe. He ran, holding his side, stumbled onto the glidewalk of the extended ramp, daring not activate it for fear of advising Tejef of his presence. He raced up it, the hatchway looming above. It came to him that if it started to close, it could well cut him in half.

It stayed open. He almost fell onto the level surface of the airlock, ran into the corridor, his boots echoing down the emptiness.

Then the *idoikkhe's* pain began, slowly pulsing, unnerving in its gradual increase. Coordination failed him and he fell, reaching for his gun, trying to brace his fingers to hold that essential weapon, expecting, hoping for Tejef's appearance, if only, if only the iduve would once make the mistake of overconfidence.

Leave me, go! he cried at his asuthi, who tried to interfere between him and the pain.

Something was breaking. The light-dimming had ceased for a time, but now a steady crashing had begun down the hall,

a thunderous booming that penetrated even Margaret's
drugged sleep. She grew more and more restless, and Arle's
soothing hand could not quiet her.

Someone cried out, thin and distant, and when Arle
opened the infirmary door she could hear it more plainly.

It was Daniel's voice, Daniel as she had heard him cry out
once before in the hands of the amaut, and such crashing as
Margaret's body had made when Tejef struck her. That
flashed into her mind, Margaret broken by a single unintended blow.

She cried out and began to run, hurrying down the hall to
that corner room, the source of the blows and the shouting.
Her knees felt undone as she reached it; almost she had not
the courage to touch that switch and free it, but she did, and
sprawled back with a shriek as a chair hurtled down on her.

The wreckage crashed down beside her on the floor; and
then Daniel was kneeling, gathering her up and caressing her
bruised head with anxious fingers, stilling her sobs by crushing her against him. He pulled her up with him in the next
breath and ran, hitting another door-switch to open it.

A woman met them, of a kind that Arle had never seen, a
woman whose skin was like a summer sky and whose hair
was light through thistledown; and no less startling was the
possessive caress she gave, assuming Arle into her affections
like some unsuspected kin, taking her by the arm and compelling her attention.

"Khasif," she said, "Arle—a man like Tejef, an iduve—
have you seen him? Do you know where he is?"

Her command of human language was flawless. That alone
startled Arle, who had found few of the strangers capable of
any human words at all; and her assumption of acquaintance
utterly robbed her of her power of thought.

"Arle," Daniel pleaded with her.

Arle pointed. "There," she said. "The middle door in the
lab. Daniel!" she cried, for they left her at a run. She went a
few paces to follow them, and then did not know what to do.

The kameth no longer resisted. Tejef saw the fingers of his
left hand jerk spasmodically at the pistol, but the kallia no
longer had the strength to complete the action. Tejef kicked
the weapon spinning down the corridor, applied his foot to
the kameth's shoulder, and heaved him over onto his back.

Life still remained in him and the *harachia* of that force worked at his nerves; but there was little enough point in killing one who could not feel, nor in committing the *e-chanokhia* of destroying a kameth. The eyelids jerked a little but Tejef much doubted there was consciousness. He abandoned him there and went down the corridor to the air-lock. It lacked a little of noon. Chimele had cast her final throw. He felt greatly satisfied by the realization that she had failed any personal *vaikka* upon him, even though she would not fail to destroy him; and then he felt empty, for a moment only empty, the minds about him suddenly stilled, *takkhenes* almost gone, the air full of a hush that settled about his heart.

Then came a touch, faint and bewildered, a thing waking, female and sensitive.

Chaikhe.

He willed the monitor into life and saw the field, four forms, three of which moved—a squat amaut dragging Ashakh's limp body in undignified fashion. Ashakh too tall a man for such a small amaut to handle; and Gerlach lying very still by the ramp, and a mound of green stirring toward consciousness, feebly trying to rise.

Katasathe. The *harachia* of the green robes and the realization that he had fired on her, once *nas*, hit his stomach like a blow. The sight of her tangled with Gerlach's squat body— beautiful Chaikhe tumbled in the dust of the pavement—was a painful one. Such a prisoner as she was a great honor to a *nasul*, a prize for *katasakke* or *kataberihe* to an Orithain, the life within her for the *dhis* of her captors, great *vaikka* could that *nasul* bend her to its will.

So long alone, always mateless; the illusions of kamethi melted into what they were—*e-chanokhia*, emptiness.

She arose, lifted her face: *takkhenes* reached and touched, an impact that slammed unease into his belly. She seemed to know he watched. Anger grew in her, a fierceness that overwhelmed.

He must kill her. Obscene as the idea was, he must kill her. He faltered, hesitated between the hatch control and the weaponry, and knew that the indecision itself was a sickness.

Her mind-touch seized the lock control, held it, felt toward other mechanisms. Uncertain then, he gave backward, realizing she would board the ship—*dhisais, e-takkhe* with him. He could not let it happen. In cold sanity he knew it was a risk to face her, but he could not reach her with the weapons now. She was ascending the ramp in firm control of the mechanisms. He gathered himself to wrest that control from her.

Takkhenes reached out for him, a fierceness of *we* incredibly strong, as if a multiplicity of minds turned on him—not Chaikhe's alone, not Ashakh's, whose mind was silent. It was as if thousands of minds bore upon him at once, focused through the lens of Chaikhe's, like the *takkhenes-nasul* of all *Ashanome*, willing his death, declaring him *e-takkhe*, anomaly, ugliness, and alone, cosmically alone.

It acquired a new source, a muddled echo that had the essence of Khasif about it, leftward, same-level. Tejef realized that presence, felt it grow, and desperately reached his mind toward intervening door locks, knowing he must hold them.

They activated, opening, one after the other. Khasif was nearer, fully alert now, a fierceness and anger that yet lacked the force that Chaikhe sent.

Death took root in him, cold and certain, and the rage that he felt at Chimele was all that held it from him. He could not decide—Khasif or Chaikhe—he could not find strength to face either, caught between.

And Chimele, knowing: he felt it.

He turned, flight in his mind, to seize manual control of the ship and tear her aloft, self-destroying, taking the *e-takkhei* with him to oblivion.

"*Nasith.*"

Chaikhe's image occupied the screens now at her own will. Her dark and lovely face stared down at him. Doors refused to open to his mind: he operated them manually and ran.

A last sprang open before he touched it. Khasif was there, the kamethi Isande and Daniel with him—and with a reaction quicker than reason Tejef went for Khasif, Khasif yet weak from his long inactivity and his wounds—Tejef's *takkhenois* gathered strength from that realization. The kamethi themselves attempted interference, dragging at them from behind.

He spun, swung wildly to clear them from him, and saw Isande's face, in his mind Margaret, her look; that it was which kept the strength from his blow.

And a shout of anger beyond, from her asuthe the kallia,

who had stumbled after, gun in hand. Tejef's eyes widened, foreknowing.

Aiela fired, left-handed, saw Isande and the iduve hit the floor at once. He tried to reach her, but it was all he could do to lean against the wall and hold himself on his feet. Daniel was first to her side, gathered her up and held her, assuring him over and over again that she was alive. Above them both stood Khasif, whose sharp glance away from Isande warned Aiela even as a soft step sounded behind him.

Chaikhe.

The very act of breathing grew difficult, concentration impossible. The gun tumbled from Aiela's fingers and crashed against the flooring, sounding distant.

"She is *dhisais*," said Khasif. "And it was not wise for you to have interfered among iduve, kamethi. You have interfered in *vaikka*."

Run, Daniel thought desperately; burdened with Isande's weight, he tensed his muscles to try.

No! Aiela protested. He leaned against the wall, shut his eyes to remove the contact of Chaikhe's; and hearing her move, he dared to look again.

She had turned, and walked back in the direction of controls.

Doors closed between them, and Khasif at last stirred from where he stood, looking down at Tejef with a long soft hiss.

The ship's engines stirred to life.

"We are about to lift," said Khasif softly, "and Tejef will give account of himself before Chimele; perhaps that is the greater *vaikka*. But it was not wise, kameth."

"Ashakh," Aiela exclaimed, remembering, hardly recognizing his own voice. "Ashakh—is still out there."

"I am instructing Teysel on the base ship to take him up to *Ashanome*. For Priamos there is no longer need of haste. For us, there is. See to yourselves, kamethi."

15

THE MELAKHIS WAS in session, and the entire body of the *nasul* with them, in the great hall beyond the *paredre*. The *paredre* projected itself and a hundred Chimeles, reflection into reflection, down the long central aisle of the hall, and thousands of iduve gathered, a sea of indigo faces, some projections, some not. There were no whisperings, for the synpathic iduve when assembled used other than words. *Takkhenes* gathered thick in the room, a heaviness of the air, a possession, a power that made it difficult even to draw breath, let alone to speak. Words seemed out of place; hearing came as through some vast gulf of distance.

And for a handful of *m'metanei* summoned into the heart of the *nasul*, the silence was overwhelming. Hundreds, thousands of iduve faces were the walls of the *paredre*; and Chimele and Khasif were in the center of it. Another pair of figures materialized among those that lined the hall, Ashakh's slim dark form and the shorter, stouter one of Rakhi—solid, both of them, who silently joined the company in the center. Ashakh's presence surprised Aiela. The base ship had hardly more than made itself secure in the hangar deck, and here was the *nasith*, stiff with his injuries, but immaculately clean, bearing little resemblance to the dusty, bloody being that had exited the collapse of the basement. He joined Chimele, and received a nod of great respect from her, as did Rakhi.

Then Chimele looked toward the kamethi and beckoned. They moved carefully in that closeness of iduve, and Daniel kept a tight grip on Arle's shoulder. Chimele greeted them courteously, but only Aiela and Isande responded to it: Daniel kept staring at her with ill-concealed anger. It rose in a surge of panic when he saw her take a black case and open it. The platinum band of an *idoikkhe* gleamed within.

No! was in Daniel's mind, frightening his asuthi. But they

232

were by him, and Arle was there; and Daniel was prisoner of more than the iduve. He took it upon his wrist with that same helpless panic that Aiela had once felt, and was bitterly ashamed.

Is this what takkhenes *does to* m'metanei? Aiela wondered to himself. Daniel hated *Ashanome;* indeed, he had not feared Tejef half so much as he feared Chimele. But he yielded, and Aiela himself could not imagine the degree of courage it would take for one *m'metane* to have defied the *nasul.*

Outsiders both of you, Isande judged sadly. *Oh, I am glad I never had to wrestle with your doubts. You are simply afraid of the iduve. Can't you accept that? We are weaker than they. What does it take to make you content?*

Chimele had grown interested in Arle now, and gazed upon the child's face with that look Aiela knew and Daniel most hated, that bird-of-prey concentration that cast a spell over the recipient. Arle was drawn into that stillness and seemed more hypnotized than afraid.

"This is the child that was so important to you, Daniel-kameth, so important that your asuthi could not restrain you?"

Daniel's heart thudded and seemed to stop as he realized that *vaikka* need not involve the real offender, that reward and punishment had no human virtue with the starlords. He would have said something if he could have gathered the words; as it was, he met Chimele's eyes and fell into that amethyst gaze, that chill calm without pity as *m'metanei* knew it. Perhaps Chimele was laughing. None of the kamethi could detect it in her. Perhaps it was a *vaikka* in itself, a demonstration of power.

"She has a certain *chanokhia*," said Chimele. "Arrangements will be made for her proper care."

"I can manage that," said Daniel. It was the most restrained thing he could manage to say.

And suddenly the center of the *paredre* itself gave way to a projection, red and violet, *Tashavodh* and *Mijanothe,* Kharxanen and Thiane.

"Hail *Ashanome*," said Thiane. "Are you satisfied?"

Chimele arose and inclined her head in reverence to the eldest of all iduve. "You are punctual, o Thiane, long-living."

"It is the hour, o *Ashanome*, hunter of worlds, and

Priamos still exists. We have seen ships rejoining you. I ask again: are you satisfied?"

"You have then noted, o Thiane, that all of our interference on the world of Priamos has ceased ahead of the time, and that all equipment and personnel have been evacuated."

Thiane frowned, nettled by this mild *vaikka*. "There is only one being whose whereabouts matters, o *Ashanome*."

"Then see." Chimele looked to her left and extended her hand. Another projection took shape, a man in dark clothing, seated. His eyes widened as he realized where he was: he arose and Arle began an outcry, stopped by Isande's fierce grip on her arm.

"This person," said Chimele softly, "was once of *Ashanome*. We have him among us again, and we are capable of settling our own internal matters. We give you honor, *Mijanothe*, for the propriety you constantly observed in *harathos*. And, o Kharxanen of *Tashavodh*, be advised that *Ashanome* will be ranging these zones for some time. In the interests of the ban on *vaikka* which the Orithanhe set upon us both, it seems to us that it would be proper for the *nasul Tashavodh* to seek some other field. We are in prior occupation of this space, and it is not proper for two *orith-nasuli* to share so close quarters without the decency of *akkhres-nasuli* and its binding oaths."

There was a silence. Kharxanen's heavy face settled into yet a deeper frown; but he inclined himself in a stiff bow. "Hail *Ashanome*. We part without *vaikka*. These zones are without interest to us; we delight that *Ashanome* is pleased to possess them. It seems to us an excellent means of disentangling our affairs. I give you farewell, Chimele."

And without further courtesy, his image winked out.

It seemed, though one could not be certain, that a smile touched the face of Thiane, a smile which was no longer present as she turned to stare at the being who stood in the shaft of pale light. Then she inclined her head in respect to Chimele.

"Honor is yours, *Ashanome*," declared Thiane. She set both hands on her staff and looked about her at all the assembly, the confident attitude of a great power among the iduve. Chimele resumed her chair, easy and comfortable in the gesture, undisturbed by the *harachia* of Thiane.

And Thiane turned last to the image of Tejef in its shaft of light, and he bowed his head. All threat, all strength was gone from him; he looked far less imposing than Thiane.

"He is near," said Chimele softly. "He is not held from joining us in the *paredre*: it has not been necessary to restrain him. Perhaps to honor you he would come to your summons."

"Tejef," said aged Thiane, looking full at him, and he glanced up. A low murmuring came from the *nasul*, the first sound and an ugly one. Suddenly Tejef tore himself from the area of the projection and vanished.

He was not long in coming, tangible amid the multitude of projections that lined the *paredre*. Isande's mind went cold and fearful even to look upon him, but he passed her without giving her notice, though her fair complexion made her most obvious in the gathering. He stopped before Chimele and Thiane, and gave Thiane a bow of courtesy, lifting his eyes again to Thiane, as if the action were painful.

"Tejef," said Thiane, "if you have a message for *Tashavodh*, I will bear it."

"No, eldest of us all," answered Tejef softly, and he bowed again at this exceptional courtesy from Thiane.

"Was it properly done?" asked Thiane.

Tejef's eyes went to Aiela; but perhaps to blame a *m'metane* was too great a shame. There was no anger, only recognition; he did not answer Thiane.

"You have seen," said Chimele to Thiane. "*Harathos* is satisfied. And hereafter he is *Ashanome's* and it is the business of the *nasul* what we do."

"Hail *Ashanome*, ancient and *akita*. May we always meet in such a mind as we part now."

"Hail *Mijanothe*, far-seeing. May your seekings be satisfied and your prosperity endless. And hail Thiane, whose honor and *chanokhia* will be remembered in *Ashanome*."

"As that of Chimele among us," murmured Thiane, greatly pleased, and flicked out so quickly that her echoes were still dying.

Then it broke, the anger of *Ashanome*, a murmuring against Tejef that sent him to the center of the *paredre*, looking about at them and trying to show defiance when they crowded him. Two *dhis*-guardians, Tahjekh and Nophres, drew their *ghiakai* and rested them point-down on the priceless carpets, crossed, barring his way to Chimele.

An iduve hand caught Aiela's arm and the *idoikkhei* stung the three of them simultaneously. "Out," said Ashakh. "This is no place for *m'metanei*."

Isande took a step to obey, but stopped, for Daniel was not coming, and Aiela stayed, terrified for what Daniel was likely to do.

Get the child out of here, Aiela appealed to him. But there was chaos already in the hall, iduve bodies intruding into the projection area, seeming to invade the *paredre*, real and unreal mingling in kaleidoscope combination. Tejef shrank back, less and less space for him. Someone dealt him a heavy blow; bodies were between and the kamethi could not see.

"Hold!" Khasif's voice roared, bringing order; and Chimele arose and the iduve melted back from her. An uneasy silence settled.

"Tejef," said Chimele.

He attempted to give a hiss of defiance. It was so subdued that it sounded far otherwise.

"There is a human female who claims to be your mate," said Chimele. "She will have treatment for her injuries. It was remiss of you to neglect that—but of course, your abilities were limited. The amaut who sheltered in your protection have realized their error and are leaving Priamos in all possible haste. Your *okkitan-as* Gerlach perished in the lifting of your ship: Chaikhe found no particular reason to clear him from beside the vessel. And as for *karsh* Gomek in general, I do not yet know whether we will choose to notice the inconvenience these beings have occasioned us. It is even possible the *nasul* would choose not to notice your offenses, Tejef, if you were wise, if you made submission."

The oppressive feeling in the air grew stronger. Tejef stood among them, sides heaving, sweat pouring down his indigo face. He shook his face to clear the sweat from his eyes and seemed likely to faint, a creature sadly fallen from the whole and terrible man who had faced them onworld. *To yield*, Daniel had heard from him once, *is to die; morally and physically, it is to die;* and if ever a man looked apt to die from such a cause, this one did, torn apart within.

Tejef's wild shout of anger drowned all the rising murmur of the *nasul*. Iduve scattered from his first blows, voices shrieked and hissed. Isande snatched Arle and hugged the human child's face against her breast, trying to shut out the awful sight and sound, for the *ghiakai* of the guardians faced Tejef now, points level. When he would try to break free of the circle they would crowd him; and by now he was dazed and bleeding. With a shout he flung himself for Chimele; but there were the guardians and there was Khasif, and Khasif's blow struck him to the floor.

Daniel thrust his way into the circle, jerked at the shoulder of a young iduve to push his way past before the youth realized what had happened—and cried out in pain, collapsing under the discipline of the *idoikkhe*.

Pain backwashed: Aiela forced his own way through the breach, trying to aid his stricken asuthe, cried out Chimele's name and felt the impact of all that attention suddenly upon himself.

"*M'metanei*," said Chimele, "this is not a place for you. You are not noticed." She lifted her hand and the iduve parted like grass before the wind, opening the way to the door. When Daniel opened his mouth to protect the dismissal: "Aiela," she said most quietly. It was a last warning. He knew the tone of it.

Daniel rose, turned his face to Tejef, appealing to him: he wanted to speak, wanted desperately, but Daniel's courage was the kind that could act: he had no eloquence, and words always came out badly. In pity, Aiela said it. Daniel would not yield otherwise.

"We interfered. I did. We are sorry."

And to Aiela's dismay the iduve gave back all about them, and they were alone in the center with Tejef—and Daniel moved closer to Isande, who clenched Arle's hand tightly in hers, and gazed fearfully as Tejef gained his feet.

"Kamethi," said Chimele, "I have not heard, I have not noticed this behavior. You are dismissed. Go away."

"He had honor among his kamethi," said Aiela, echoing what was in Daniel's heart. It was important Tejef know that before they left. The *idoikkhe* touched, began and ceased. Isande radiated panic, she with the child, wanting to run, foreseeing Daniel's death before their eyes—Aiela's with him. It was her unhappiness to have asuthi as stubborn as herself—her pride, too. They were both mad, her asuthi, but she had accepted that already.

And Chimele looked upon the three of them: a kallia's eyes might have varied, shown some emotion. Hers scarcely could, no more than they could shed tears. But Aiela pitied her: if he had disadvantaged her once before her *nasithi* alone and merited her anger, he could only surmise what he did to her now with the entire *Melakhis* and *nasul* to witness.

"Chimele-Orithain," he said in a tone of great respect, "we have obeyed all your orders. If a kameth can ask anything of you—"

A tall shadow joined them—Ashakh, who folded his arms and gave a nod in curt deference to Chimele.

"This kameth," said Ashakh, "is about to encounter trouble with which he cannot deal. He is a peculiar being, this *m'metane,* a little rash with us, and without any sense of *takkhenes* to feel his way over most deadly ground; but his *chanokhia* appeals to me. I oppose his disrespect, but I am not willing to see harm come to him or to his asuthi—one of whom is, after all, human as well as outsider, and even more ignorant of propriety than this one. I have borne with much, Chimele. I have suffered and my *sra* has suffered for the sake of *Ashanome.* But this kameth and his asuthi are of worth to the *nasul.* Here I say no, Chimele."

"Ashakh," said Chimele in a terrible voice, "it has not been the matter of the kamethi alone in which you have said no."

"I do not oppose you, Chimele."

"I perceive otherwise. I perceive that you are not *takkhe* with us in the matter of Tejef, that someone lends him support."

"Then you perceive amiss. My *m'melakhia* has always been for the well-being of *Ashanome.* We have been able to compose our differences before, *nasith-tak.*"

"And they have been many," said Chimele, "and too frequent. No!" she said sharply as Tejef moved: he came no closer, for there were the *dhis*-guardians between, and Khasif and Ashakh moved to shield her as reflexively as they always had. The closeness was heavy in the air again: oppressive, hostile, and then a curiously perturbing fierceness. Chimele glanced at Rakhi in alarm.

"You do not belong here," he said, but her anger seemed smothered by fright, and it was not clear to whom she spoke.

Tejef moved nearer, as near as the *ghiakai* would permit. "Chimele-Orithain. You cast me out; but Mejakh's *takkhenois* is gone and the touch of the *nasul* is easier for that, Chimele *sra*-Chaxal. I have always had *m'melakhia* for this *nasul*, and not alone for the *nasul*. I was *nas*, Chimele."

Chimele's breath was an audible hiss. "And your life in the *nasul* was always on scant tolerance and we have hunted you back again. Your *m'melakhia* is *e-takkhe—e-takkhe* and unspeakably offensive to me."

A fierce grin came to Tejef's face. He seemed to grow, and set hands on knees as he fell to kneel on the carpets. His gesture of submission was itself insolence; slowly he inclined his body toward the floor and as slowly straightened.

Arle cried out, a tiny sound, piercing the intolerable heaviness in the air. Isande hugged her tightly, silencing her, for Ashakh sent a staccato message to the three *idoikkhei* simultaneously: *Do not move!*

"Go!" Chimele exploded. "If you survive in the *nasul*, I will perhaps not seek to kill you. But there is *vaikka* you have yet to pay, o Tejef no-one's-getting."

"My *sra*," answered Tejef with cold deliberation, "will have honor." But he backed carefully from her when he had risen.

"You are dismissed," Chimele said, and her angry glance swept the hall, so that Tejef had no more than cleared the door before others began to disperse in haste, projections to wink out in great numbers, the concourse clearing backwards as the iduve departed into that part of the ship that was theirs.

"Stay," she said to the *nasithi-katasakke* when they would as gladly have withdrawn; and she ignored them when they had frozen into waiting, and bent a fierce frown on Aiela. The *idoikkhe* sent a signal that made him wince.

M'metane, it is your doing that I bear this disadvantage. It is your doing, that gave this being arastiethe *to defy me, to draw aid from others. Your ignorance has begun what you cannot begin to comprehend. You have disadvantaged me, divided the* nasul, *and some of us may die for it. What are you willing to pay for that,* m'metane *that I honored, what* vaikka *can you perceive that would be adequate?*

He stared at her, pain washing upward from the *idoikkhe*, and was stricken to realize that not only might he lose his life, he might in truth deserve it. He had Isande's misery to his account; now he had Chimele's as well.

And in the disadvantaging of an Orithain, he had threatened the existence of *Ashanome* itself.

"I did what was in me to do," he protested.

Ashakh saved him. He realized that when the pain cleared and he heard Isande and Daniel's faint, terrified presences in his mind, and felt the iduve's viselike grip holding on his feet.

"Chimele," said Ashakh, "that was not disrespect in him: it was very plain kalliran logic. And perhaps there is merit in his reasoning: after all, you found *chanokhia* in him, and chose him, so his decisions are, in a manner of speaking, yours. Perhaps when one deals with outsiders, outsider-logic prevails, and events occur which would not occur in an iduve system."

"I perceive your *m'melakhia* for these beings, Ashakh, and I am astounded. I find it altogether excessive."

The tall iduve glanced aside, embarrassed. "I comprehend the *chanokhia* that Tejef found in these beings, both human and kallia."

"You were responsible for swinging the *takkhenes* of *Ashanome* toward Tejef—your *vaikka* for Chaikhe."

Again he had looked toward her, and now bowed his head slightly. "Chaikhe is *dhisais*—as Rakhi can tell you: beyond *vaikka* and no longer appropriate for my protection. I understand what you did, since you did not spare Rakhi, for whom you have most regard, and I admire the strength and *chanokhia* of your action, o Chimele. You disadvantaged me repeatedly in your maneuvering, but it was in the interests of *Ashanome*."

"Is it in our interests—what you have done?"

"Chimele," said Rakhi softly, and such a look went between them that it seemed more than Rakhi might have spoken to her in that word, for Chimele seemed much disquieted.

"Khasif," said Chimele suddenly, "can you be *takkhe* with this matter as it is?"

Khasif bowed. "I have brought you Tejef; and that *vaikka* is enough. He is *sra* to me, Chimele, as you are. Do not ask me questions."

"Chaikhe—" Chimele said.

"Orithain," said Rakhi, "she has followed your orders amazingly well: but remember that she was scarcely out of the *dhis* when she acquired Tejef's interest."

Her lips tightened. "Indeed," she said, and after a moment: "Aiela, the *harachia* of yourself and your asuthi is a disturbance for the moment. You did serve me and I rejoice in the honor of your efforts. You are dismissed, but you still owe me a *vaikka* for your presumption today."

He owed her at least the same risk he had taken for Tejef, to restore what he had stolen from her, though every instinct screamed *run!* "Chimele," he said, "we honor you—from the heart, we honor you."

Chimele looked full into his eyes. "*M'metane*," she said, "I have a *m'melakhia* for the peculiarity that is Aiela Lyailleue. Curiosity impels me to inquire further and to refrain from dealing with you as you have so well deserved. You are the only *m'metane* I have seen who has not feared to be *m'metane* among us. You are *Ashanome's* greatest living curiosity—and so you are free with us, and you are getting into the perilous habit of taking liberties with *Ashanome*. The contagion has spread to your asuthi, I do perceive. In moderation, it has been of service to me."

"I am honored by your interest, Chimele."

Her attention turned then to Ashakh. By some impulse that passed between them, Ashakh bowed very low, hands upon his thighs, and remained in that posture until Chimele's agitation had passed. He seemed to receive that too, for he straightened without looking up before, and slowly lifted his face.

"Chimele, I protest I am *takkhe*."

"I perceive your approval of these outrageous beings."

"And I," said Ashakh, "feel your disapproval of me. I am disadvantaged, Chimele, for I do honor you. If you insist, I shall go *arrhei-nasul*, for my *m'melakhia* is not adequate to challenge you, certainly not at the peril of the dynasty itself. You are essential and I am not. Only permit me to take these kamethi with me. *Arastiethe* forbids I should abandon them."

Chimele met his eyes a moment, then turned aside and reached for Aiela's arm. Her incredibly strong fingers numbed his hand, but it was not an act of anger.

One did not often see the *nasithi-katasakke* on the kamethi level; and the presence of Rakhi caused a mild stir—only mild, for even the kamethi knew the eccentricity of this iduve. So it was not a great shock for Aiela and Isande to find the *nasith* greeting them in passing. Beside them the great viewport showed starry space, no longer the sphere of Priamos. *Ashanome* was free and running again.

"Sir," the kamethi acknowledged his courtesy, bowing at once.

"And that third person?"

"'I am here,'" said Daniel through Aiela's lips. *Trouble, Aiela? What does a* nas *want with us at this hour?*

Be calm. If Chimele meant harm, she would do that harm for herself, with no intermediary. Aiela compelled his asuthi to silence and kept his eyes on Rakhi's so the *nasith* should not know that communication flickered back and forth: this three-way communication bemused one to a point that it was hard not to appear to drift.

"Is the *asuthithekkhe* pleasant?" Rakhi wondered, with the nearest thing to wistfulness they had ever heard in an iduve.

"It has its difficulties," Aiela answered, ignoring the feedback from his asuthi. "But I would not choose otherwise."

"The silence," said Rakhi, "is awesome—without. For us the experience is not altogether pleasant. But being severed—makes a great silence."

Aiela understood then, and pitied him. It was safe to pity Rakhi, whose *m'melakhia* was not so fierce. "Is Chaikhe well, sir?"

"She is content. She is inward now—altogether. *Dhisaisei* grow more and more that way. I have felt it." Rakhi silenced himself with an embarrassed glance toward the viewport. The body of *Ashanome* passed under the holding arm. For a moment all was dark. Their reflections, pale *kallia* and dusky iduve, stared back out of the viewport. "There is a small *amaut* who mentioned you with honor. His name is Kleph. Ashakh bade me say so: *arastiethe* forbids the first of Navigators should carry messages. This person was greatly joyed by the sight of the gardens of *Ashanome*. Ashakh procured him this assignment. *Arastiethe* forbade—"

"—that Ashakh should admit to gratitude."

Rakhi frowned, even he a little nettled to be thus interrupted by a *m'metane*. "It was not *chanokhia* for this amaut to have delivered Ashakh in a helpless condition aboard the base ship. This being could not appreciate *vaikka* in any reasonable sense, save to be disadvantaged in this way. Has Ashakh erred?"

"No," said Aiela, "and Ashakh knows he has not."

The ghost of a smile touched the *nasith's* face, and Aiela frowned, suspecting he himself had just been the victim of a bit of iduve humor, straightfaced in delivery. Perhaps, he thought, the iduve had puzzled out the ways of *m'metanei* more than the iduve chose to admit. Yet not even this most gentle of iduve was to be provoked: one had to remember that they *studied* gratitude, could perhaps practice it for humor's sake. Whether anything then stirred the cold of their dark hearts was worthy of debate.

Let be with him, Isande advised. *Even Rakhi has his limits.*

"*M'metanei*," said Rakhi, "I should advise that you go soft of step and well-nigh invisible about the *paredre* for the next few days. Should Chimele summon you, as she will, be most agreeable."

"Why, sir?" asked Isande, which was evidently the desired question.

"Because Chimele has determined a *vaikka* upon *Tasha-vodh* that the Orithanhe and its ban cannot deny her." The iduve grinned despite himself. "Kharxanen's *m'melakhia* for a bond with the dynasty of *Ashanome* is of long standing—indeed, the origin of all these matters. It will go frustrated. The Orithanhe itself has compelled Kharxanen and Tejef to deny they are *sra* to each other; so Kharxanen cannot claim any bond at all when Chimele chooses Tejef for the *kataberihe* of *Ashanome*. Purifications will begin. One child will there be; and then this *nas* Tejef will have a ship and as many of the *okkitani-as* and kamethi as Chimele chooses to send with him."

"She is creating a *vra-nasul?*" asked Isande, amazed. "After all the grief he has caused?" Resentment flared in her, stifled by Daniel's gladness; and Aiela fended one from the other.

"They are *takkhe*," said Rakhi. "*M'metane,* I know your minds somewhat. You have long memories for anger. But we are not a spiteful folk; we fight no wars. Chimele has taken *vaikk*a, for his *sra* as a *vra-nasul* will serve *Ashanome* forever; but the *sra* she will take from him under her own name as her heir will forever be greater than the dynasty he will found. *Vra-nasul* in mating can put no bond on *orith-nasul*. So Tejef will make submission and both will keep their honor. It is a reasonable solution—one of your own working, *m'metanei*. So I advise you keep secret that small *vaikka* of yours lest Chimele be compelled to notice it. She is amused by your *chanokhia*: she has struggled greatly to attain that attitude—for if you know us, you know that we are frequently at a loss to determine any rationality for your behavior. We make an effort. We have acquired the wisdom to observe and wait upon what we do not understand: it is an antidote for the discord of impulses which govern our various species. I recommend the practice to you too, kamethi."

And with a nod of his head he went his way, mounted into the lift, and vanished from sight.

Aiela, came Isande's thought, *Chimele sent him*.

We have been honored, he replied, and expected argument from Daniel.

But Daniel's consciousness when it returned to them dismissed all thoughts but his own for the moment, for he had suddenly recognized across the concourse a human child and a red-haired woman.

He began, quickly, to thread his way through the traffic; his asuthi in this moment gave him his privacy.

Glossary of Foreign Terms

I

THE KALLIRAN LANGUAGE: like human speech in its division of noun and verb concepts. There is, however, a fossilized Ethical from the time of the Orithain Domination. Although the Ethical corresponds to the Verb of Orithain speech, it has been made an Adjective in the kalliran language.

arethme
(ah-RETH-may) city-deme of kalliran political structure: on the home world, equal to a city and all its land and trade rights; in the colonies, often equal to a hemisphere or an entire world, with its attendant rights.

ehs, pl. *ehsim*
(ACE) cubed measurement approximately 10 inches.

elethia
(el-eh-THEE-ya) honor, gentility, sensitivity to proper behavior; faithfulness to duty.

Esliph
(EHS-lif) the Seven Stars: a heavily planeted region lying between the *metrosi* and human space.

giyre
(GIU-rey) recognition of one's proper place in the cosmic Order of things; also, one's proper duty toward another. It is ideally mutual.

Halliran Idai
(hah-lee-HRAN ee-DYE) the Free Union, the political structure of the

	metrosi, the capital of which is Aus Qao, the fifth of Qao.
ikas	(EE-kas) disregarding of *giyre* and *kastien:* presumptuous.
kallia	(KAL-lee-ah) man, woman; men, women.
kamesule	(kah-MAY-soo-leh) to associate with the iduve; to be servile of manner.
kastien	(KAHS-tee-yen) being oneself; virtue, wisdom; observing harmony with others and the universe by perfect centering in one's *giyre* toward all persons and things.
marithe	(mah-REE-theh) a pale-pink wine.
men, pl. *meis*	(MEN, MACE) a linear measurement of approximately 10 inches.
metrosi	(MAY-tro-see) the Civilized Worlds, those within the original area of kalliran-amaut colonization.
Orithain	(o-rih-THAIN) mistakenly used as generic term for the iduve.
parome	(PAHR-ohm) governor of an *arethme*
Qao	(KHUA-o) the Sun; home star of the kalliran species.

II

THE IDUVE LANGUAGE: differs from both kalliran and human speech to such a degree that translation cannot be made literally if it is to be understandable. Paraphrase is the best that can be done.

First, there is no clear distinction between the concepts of noun and verb, between solid and action. Reality consists instead of the situational combination of Tangibles and Ethicals; but an Ethical may be converted to a Tangible and vice

versa. Most ideas are grammatically complete in two words:
an Ethical is affixed to the Tangible. Meanings may be altered
or augmented by Prefix, Infix, or Suffix upon either Ethical or
Tangible. The nature of these added particles may be: Negative, Intensitive, Honorific, Hypothetical, Interrogative, Im-
perative, Directional, Futuritive or Historical, Relational or
Descriptive.

Second: the language has only scant designation of gender.
It is impossible to distinguish sex save by adding the male
Honorific *-toj* or the female Honorific *-tak* to the word in
question. Concepts which would seem to make gender distinction inevitable (man, woman, mother, father, brother, sister,
husband, wife) exist only as artificial constructs in the iduve
language.

In the pronunciations given below, an asterisk (*) indicates
a guttural sibilant produced by -kk or -kh-: a throat-sounded
hiss resembling a soft *kh*.

akites, akitomei	(ah-kee-TEHS) a Voyaging Ship
akitomekkhe	(ah-kee-toh-MEK*-heh) worldbound; having bond to person or place outside the *nasul*.
akkhres-nasuli	(AK*-hress-NAH-su-lee) joining of two *akitomei* for the purpose of *kata-sakke* among the members of both clans.
anoikhte	(ah-noik*-TEH) bondless; not "free" (*akita*) but "loose," and therefore fair game for *m'melakhia, q.v.* Manlings (*m'metanei*) cannot enjoy *arrhei-akita;* by their very terrestrial natures they are *akitomekkhe* and therefore limited in their sensitivities.
arastiethe	(ah-rahs-tee-AY-theh) honor; the power and burden of being iduve, of being of a particular *nasul*, or simply of being oneself. Honor is the obliga-tion to use power, even against per-sonal preference, to maintain moral

and physical integrity. *M'metanei* naturally possess no *arastiethe,* but to describe admirable traits in *m'metanei,* the iduve have adopted the kalliran word *elethia.*

arrhei-akita   (AH-hrrey-ah-kee-TAH) being free; an ethical necessity for the happiness and *arastiethe* of the *nasul;* especially, the free range of their ship.

arrhei-nasul   (AH-hrrey-nah-SOOL) leaving clan, usually for *kataberihe* with another's Orithain. Doing so for any other reason is to invite violence from the receiving clan. Not the same as *arrhei-nasuli* (AH-hrrey-nah-su-LEE), which is exile from all the Kindred, equal to a death sentence.

Ashanome   (ah-SHAH-no-may)

asuthe, asuthi   (ah-SOOTH, ah-su-THEE) lit.: companion. A person linked to another by *chiabres.*

asuthithekkhe   (ah-su-thi-THEK*-heh) mental linkage.

Chaganokh   (cHag-ah-NOKH*)

chanokhia   (cHan-ok*-HEE-ah) artistry; (2) as an Ethical: the practice of virtue, the studied avoidance of crudity, and a searching after elegance and originality.

chiabres   (cHee-AH-bress) internal device for communication.

dhis   (d*eesss) lit.: nest. A communal embryonics laboratory and nursery for the *nasul.* Children leave at maturity.

dhisais, dhisaisei   (d*EE-sice) female driven to temporary madness by biological changes at childbirth; may last years.

e-   (ay) negative prefix: not, un-.

ghiaka, ghiakai   (zhee-AH-kah) curved sword, now ceremonial.

harachia   (ha-rak*-HEE-yah) lit.: presence, seeing. Visual impact of a person, thing, or situation which elicits an irrational emotional response.

idoikkhe, idoikkhei   (ih-DOYK*-heh) from *idois,* jewel. The bracelet of a nas kame, patterned with the heraldry of the *nasul,* and capable of transmitting sensory impulses.

iduve   (ih-DOOVh) man, woman, mankind.

Iqhanofre   (ik-HAH-no-fray)

izhkh   (izsk*) mountainous region of Kej IV famed for its geometric art.

kameth, kamethi   (KAH-met') Honorific of nas kame.

kataberihe   (kah-tah-beh-REE-heh) mating of an Orithain to produce *orithaikhti,* heir-children. Only children of such a mating may inherit the title; it goes to the eldest regardless of sex. The bond of *kataberihe* forbids the woman in the pair from *katasakke* for ten months after announcing her intention; the male suffers a ritual abstinence for twenty days. This is for the sake of establishing paternity, and for mental preparation, as *kataberihe-* mates are usually from another *nasul.*

katasathe   (kah-ta-SATH) pregnant

katasakke   (kah-ta-SAK*h) mating-for-children, requiring a three-month abstinence should the woman desire to change mates. It is also counted improper for the male to have more than one current mate. Each *katasakke* mating will almost certainly result in a child; such a high rate of conception was once advantageous to species survival. Extreme longevity and limited space on the *akitomei* have made it otherwise, giving rise to the custom of *katasukke*.

katasukke   (kah-ta-SOOK*h) mating-for-pleasure, done with *m'metanei*, and not (for aesthetic reasons) with amaut. This cannot result in offspring, and neither the purification period of *kataberihe* nor that of *katasakke* forbids *katasukke*.

Kej   (Kezh) the Sun; home star of the iduve.

-kkh-   relational infix, from *kame*, bond, bind. Binding or obligation: necessity.

kutikkase   (ku-tih-KAH-seh) lit.: things. Earthly necessities, food, bodily comforts, all arts save the pursuit or use of intangibles. Opposite of *chanokhia*.

lis, lioi   (lihss, LEE-oi) 1,000 paces, approximately ¾ mile.

Melakhis   (meh-lakh-HEESS) from *m'melakhia;* the Council of Acquisition, composed of the Orithain, his/her *sra,* and one member from each of the elder or major *sri* of the *nasul.* The *Melakhis* assists the Orithain in decisions of major importance and technical complexity.

Mijanothe (mee-jah-NOTHe)

m'melakhia (meh-meh-lak*-HEE-ya) desire of acquisition; sometimes used to approxi-
mate *m'metane* concept of "love";
sometimes translated "ferocity." A basic and constant activity of the iduve,
necessary for *arastiethe*. (2) *m.-tomes:*
the acquisition of prestige or spatial
lordship, needful as operating room
for the dignity and freedom of the
nasul. (3) *m.-likatis:* acquisition of
knowledge, most honorable of activities.

m'metane, m'metanei (meh-MEH-tah-nay) manling: a being which approximately conforms to
iduve appearance: kallia and humans.

nasithi (nah-sih-THEE) Honorific plural of
nas, a member of the *nasul*.

nas kame, noi kame (nahs KAH-may, noi KAH-may)
bondchild; a *m'metane* in service to
the *nasul*.

okkitan-as, okkitani-as (OK*-hee-tahn-AHSS) lit.: helper.
Amaut in service to the *nasul*.

Orithanhe (oh-rih-THAHN-heh) council of all
available *orithainei* of *orith-nasuli*, at
least twenty for a quorum. It meets
on the home world. Due to the iduve
predilection toward *arrhei-akita*, it is
almost never convoked.

paredre (pahr-ED-hre) ceremonial center of
authority of an *akites;* the hall of the
Orithain.

prha (prah) particle meaning "hypothesis"
or "one supposes."

serach

(SEH-rak*) funeral display; a destruction of *kutikkase* in proportion to the *arastiethe* of the dead.

sorithias

(so-rih-THEE-ahss) from *orithois,* mastery. The obligation of an Orithain to the *nasul.*

sra

(ssrah) bloodkin (ship) (2) *bhan-sra:* vertical (parent-child). (3) *iq-sra:* lateral (brother-sister; half-brother and half-sister).

-tak

female Honorific suffix.

takkhe

(tak*h) having *takkhenois* in agreement.

takkhenes

(TAKH*-he-nayss) group-consciousness of the *nasul,* by which decisions are made and justice determined.

Tashavodh

(tah-sha-VOD*h)

tekasuphre

(tek-ah-SU-frey) stupidity, irrationality, nonsense.

-toj

(tozh) male Honorific suffix.

vaikka

(VAI-k*hah!) or (vai-K*HAH!) a demonstration of *arastiethe;* could roughly be translated as "revenge" if not that *vaikka* is often taken in advance of actual injury, to offset *niseth* (disadvantage). *Vaikka* need not involve damage, for *arastiethe* can be demonstrated by help as well as harm. It is, however, a fighting or predatory instinct basic to the iduve psychology.

vaikka-chanokhia

an art form peculiarly iduve, practiced generally upon other iduve, as *m'metanei* have limited appreciation of *chanokhia.* True *vaikka-chanokhia* is such that the recipient cannot possibly reciprocate.

vra-nasul   (vrah-nah-SOOL) subject-clan; formed when an elder clan splits because of size or disunity.

III

THE AMAUT LANGUAGE: similar to kalliran speech in structure, with many kalliran words appropriated into the language, and showing much tendency to imitate the elaborate politeness styles of the iduve. The alphabet is native, but literature as such dates from first contact with the iduve.

amaut   (ah-MAUT) man, woman; people.

bnesych   (b'NAY-sikK) director; *karsh-* head at colony's foundation.

chaju   (CHAH-ju) a musky, potent liquor.

geshe   (GESSH-eh) a stringed instrument.

habish   (hah-BEESH) all-night bar and side-walk cafe, featuring music, singing, dancing, and *chaju*.

habishaap   (hah-beesh-APPPH) keeper of a *habish*.

karsh, karshatu   (kahrssh) basic family unit of the amaut, taking its name from the founder, either male or female, who acquired land and began the family line. Without land there is no *karsh* save the one of ancestry. Possessing land entitles one to found a *karsh* of a size commensurate with the productive capacity of the land.

Kesuat   (KEZ-wat) the Sun; home star of the amaut.

rekeb (REK-ebp) a sistrum-like musical instrument.

shakhshoph (sshak-SHOPPH) lit.: hiding-face. Politeness to hide true feelings from outsiders.

sushai (ssu-SHAI) from *sus*, Shade. A word of greeting.

- [ ] **THE BIRTHGRAVE by Tanith Lee.** "A big, rich, bloody swords-and-sorcery epic with a truly memorable heroine —as tough as Conan the Barbarian but more convincing."—**Publishers Weekly.**   (#UW1177—$1.50)

- [ ] **THE STORM LORD by Tanith Lee.** A panoramic novel of swordplay and a man seeking his true inheritance on an alien world comparable to DUNE.   (#UE1233—$1.75)

- [ ] **DON'T BITE THE SUN by Tanith Lee.** A far-flung novel of the distant future by the author of **The Birthgrave.** Definitely something different!   (#UY1221—$1.25)

- [ ] **DRINKING SAPPHIRE WINE by Tanith Lee.** How the hero/heroine of Four BEE city finally managed to outrage the system!   (#UY1277—$1.25)

- [ ] **GATE OF IVREL by C. J. Cherryh.** "Never since reading **The Lord of the Rings** have I been so caught up in any tale . . ."—Andre Norton.   (#UY1226—$1.25)

- [ ] **BROTHERS OF EARTH by C. J. Cherryh.** One of the most highly praised sf novels of the year. A Science Fiction Book Club selection.   (#UW1257—$1.50)

DAW BOOKS are represented by the publishers of Signet and Mentor Books, **THE NEW AMERICAN LIBRARY, INC.**

THE NEW AMERICAN LIBRARY, INC.,
P.O. Box 999, Bergenfield, New Jersey 07621

Please send me the DAW BOOKS I have checked above. I am enclosing
$_____(check or money order—no currency or C.O.D.'s).
Please include the list price plus 35¢ a copy to cover mailing costs.

Name_____

Address_____

City_____State_____Zip Code_____
Please allow at least 4 weeks for delivery

☐ **WALKERS ON THE SKY by David J. Lake.** Three worlds in one was the system there—until the breakthrough!
(#UY1273—$1.25)

☐ **THE RIGHT HAND OF DEXTRA by David J. Lake.** It's the green of Terra versus the purple of that alien world—with no holds barred. (#UW1290—$1.50)

☐ **THE GAMEPLAYERS OF ZAN by M. A. Foster.** It's a game of life and death for both humans and their own creation —the not-quite-super race. (#UJ1287—$1.95)

☐ **NAKED TO THE STARS by Gordon R. Dickson.** A classic of interstellar warfare as only the Dorsai author could write! (#UW1278—$1.50)

☐ **EARTHCHILD by Doris Piserchia.** Was this the only true human left on Earth . . . and who were the monsters that contended for this prize? (#UW1308—$1.50)

☐ **DIADEM FROM THE STARS by Jo Clayton.** She became the possessor of a cosmic treasure that enslaved her mind. (#UW1293—$1.50)

DAW BOOKS are represented by the publishers of Signet and Mentor Books, **THE NEW AMERICAN LIBRARY, INC.**

THE NEW AMERICAN LIBRARY, INC.,
P.O. Box 999, Bergenfield, New Jersey 07621

Please send me the DAW BOOKS I have checked above. I am enclosing
$_____(check or money order—no currency or C.O.D.'s).
Please include the list price plus 35¢ a copy to cover mailing costs.

Name_____

Address_____

City_____State_____Zip Code_____
Please allow at least 4 weeks for delivery